Lovers &
Players

Also by Jackie Collins

Deadly Embrace
Hollywood Wives – The New Generation
Lethal Seduction
Thrill!
L.A. Connections – Power, Obsession, Murder, Revenge
Hollywood Kids
American Star
Rock Star
Hollywood Husbands
Lovers & Gamblers
Hollywood Wives
The World Is Full Of Divorced Women
The Love Killers
Sinners
The Bitch
The Stud
The World Is Full Of Married Men
Hollywood Divorces

THE SANTANGELO NOVELS

Dangerous Kiss
Vendetta: Lucky's Revenge
Lady Boss
Lucky
Chances

Jackie Collins

Lovers & Players

SIMON & SCHUSTER

LONDON • NEW YORK • SYDNEY • TORONTO

First published in Great Britain by Simon & Schuster UK Ltd, 2005
A Viacom company

1 3 5 7 9 10 8 6 4 2

Simon & Schuster UK Ltd
Africa House
64–78 Kingsway
London WC2B 6AH

www.simonsays.co.uk

Simon & Schuster Australia
Sydney

A CIP catalogue record for this book is
available from the British Library

HB ISBN 0 7432 6802 4
TPB ISBN 0 7432 6803 2

Typeset by Rowland Phototypesetting Ltd
Bury St Edmunds, Suffolk
Printed and bound in Great Britain by
Mackays of Chatham plc

For all the Lovers & Players I have known.

Names not necessary!

Prologue

'Your father wants to see you immediately.'

'Huh?' Jett Diamond mumbled, rolling over in bed, almost dropping the phone as he groped in the dark for his watch.

It was four a.m. in Milan. Four a.m., cold and raining. He could hear the rain pounding down on the skylight in the bathroom.

The beautiful girl lying next to him stirred. 'Who is it, *carino*?' she murmured, flinging her arm across his chest.

'Go back to sleep,' he ordered, sitting up and automatically reaching for a cigarette.

Lady Jane Bentley was on the phone, his father's long-time girlfriend, and she sounded like she meant business.

'Do y'know what time it is here?' he said gruffly, lighting up and taking a long, deep drag.

'Yes, Jett,' Lady Jane replied evenly. 'And I repeat, your father needs to see you at once. There is a plane ticket for New York waiting for you at the concierge's desk at the Four Seasons Hotel. Be here at the house in New York at nine a.m. on Friday.' A long, meaningful pause. 'And, Jett, make absolutely sure you do *not* let him down. It is to your advantage.'

Before he could say anything, she hung up.

Man! He'd never liked her. Lady Jane Bentley with her phoney English accent and so-called impeccable manners. She'd been his father's constant companion for the last six years. The scandal was that she'd left her titled British husband, Lord James, for Red Diamond, the rambunctious, powerful,

1

controlling, four-times-married media billionaire. It had caused quite a few lurid headlines at the time.

Red Diamond. Jett's father.

Christ! What the *fuck* did he want?

* * *

Max Diamond, real-estate mogul, was in the middle of a dinner party when his cell vibrated. Max never went anywhere without his phone switched on. His team of trusted associates knew they could reach him at any time with any problem: that was the way he liked it. Besides, right now he was financially over-extended, and he needed to be available twenty-four-seven to deal with the crisis.

Discreetly he checked his cell to see who was calling him at eleven p.m.

Lady Jane Bentley. His father's paramour. What did *she* want? He hadn't spoken to either of them in months, even though they all lived in the same city. As a family they were not exactly close.

Intrigued, he excused himself and hurried into the library where he called her back.

One thing about Lady Jane, she was precise and to the point. 'Your father wishes to see you at the house. Nine a.m. on Friday,' she said. 'It's extremely important, Max.'

'Concerning what?' he asked curiously.

'Be here and you'll find out.'

Max nodded to himself. 'I suppose I can make it,' he said grudgingly.

'Both your brothers will be flying in.'

Now it sounded serious. Was the old man dying?

If he is, Max thought grimly, *it won't be a moment too soon.*

* * *

Chris Diamond was working out in his home gym when he got the call. Home gyms were a definite status symbol in L.A. If you didn't have a Cybex-equipped home gym, you actually had to mix with the sweaty masses at the L.A. Sports

Connection, and that meant you simply hadn't made it. Chris Diamond liked to think that, as one of the most sought-after entertainment lawyers in town, he had definitely made it. Hence, his state-of-the-art gym with a spectacular sound system, high definition TVs on three walls, while the fourth was a huge sheet of glass overlooking the glittering lights of L.A.

He'd purchased the house at the top of Coldwater Canyon, perched on the edge of a magnificent hillside, because of the incredible views. Then he'd proceeded to redo and rebuild until it was exactly the way he wanted it. Chris was a perfectionist: he liked things organized and in the right place. It gave him a feeling of security, something he'd never had while growing up.

'Nine a.m. on Friday,' Lady Jane said.

'Can't do it,' he replied, jumping off the Lifecycle and reaching for a pristine white hand-towel, which he threw round his neck.

'Why not?'

'I've got an important meeting in Vegas I can't break.'

'I strongly suggest you do,' she said calmly. 'Your brothers will be here, and your father expects you.' A long beat. 'I'm sure you wouldn't wish to disappoint him.'

Chris digested her words. 'Is he sick?' he asked at last.

'Be here. It is to your advantage,' she said mysteriously, and hung up.

* * *

Red Diamond reached for a dark-coloured cigarette with his gnarled right hand, and lit it with a gold Dunhill lighter.

He was seventy-nine years old and looked every year of it. His craggy face was lined and wrinkled, his sunken blue eyes faded and darkly shadowed. An aquiline nose and strong jaw-line gave hints of the imposing-looking man he had once been.

'Are they coming?' he demanded, his eyes raking over Lady Jane Bentley as the impeccably groomed woman entered his bedroom.

She nodded, wondering what he was up to this time, for

Red Diamond never did anything unless he had an agenda.

'You're sure?' he barked, blowing a stream of acrid smoke in her direction.

'Absolutely,' she said, waving away the smoke with a pained expression.

'All three of them?' he rasped.

'Yes,' she answered coolly. 'I contacted them as you requested, and they *will* be here.'

'Excellent.' A crafty smile spread across his weathered face. 'And so it begins . . .' he muttered, almost to himself.

Lady Jane nodded again. When Red Diamond wanted something, nobody dared argue, not even her.

What was he up to now? That was the question.

She was curious to know, but smart enough not to ask – Red never revealed anything until he was good and ready.

Like everyone else she would simply have to wait and see.

Chapter One

'What's your name, dear?' the bald man, with an abundance of hair sprouting from his ears, inquired.

'Liberty,' the young waitress replied.

'What's that?' he said, peering at her.

'Liberty,' she repeated. *It's written on my name-tag, asshole. Can't you see it?*

'What kind of name—'

Oh, puleeze! You got any idea how many times I've had to go through this conversation? Gwyneth Paltrow and Chris Martin named their baby Apple. Courteney Cox and David Arquette, Coco. What's so unusual about Liberty?

Ignoring him, she refilled the bald man's coffee cup and walked away. *Moron!* she thought. *Like, who does he think he is commenting on my name? It's none of his freakin' business. When I'm a famous singer-songwriter I won't question people's names. I'll be understanding and polite. I'll get it.*

She hurried behind the counter, still steaming. 'I'm *so* not down with this waitressin' crap,' she complained to her cousin, Cindi, who'd gotten her the job in the Madison Avenue coffee shop and, like her, was an aspiring singer.

'Never forget it pays the bills, girl,' said Cindi, a buxom twenty-three-year-old originally from Atlanta, with gleaming black skin, thick ankles, an ample ass, huge breasts, and a wide, inviting smile.

'*Singin'* should pay the bills,' Liberty said forcefully. 'That's what we do.'

'When we score a gig *that's* what we do,' Cindi pointed out. 'So while we're waitin' . . .'

'I know, I know,' Liberty said, frowning. 'Gotta make a living. Gotta pay the rent.'

The furrowing of her brow did not affect her startling beauty. Bi-racial, the product of a black mother and what she assumed was a mixed father – a man her mother refused to talk about, let alone reveal his identity – she was milk-chocolate-skinned with lustrous long black hair, elongated green eyes, thick brows, impossibly long lashes, cut-glass cheekbones, full lips, a pointed chin and a straight nose. Cindi was always carrying on about how she looked like Halle Berry, which kind of irritated Liberty because she considered herself an original and did not care to be compared to anyone – however gorgeous and successful they might be.

She was nineteen. She had plenty of time.

Or did she?

Sometimes she awoke in the middle of the night in a cold sweat, her heart thumping. What if she never got discovered? What if nobody listened to her songs or heard her sing? What if she ended up like her mom, a failed singer cleaning other people's mess all day?

Man, she was almost twenty, she'd been out of school four years, and *nothing* big had happened for her. Oh, sure, she'd made an amateur demo tape, scored a few gigs as a back-up singer, but not as many as she'd like. And no producer had stepped forward and said, 'Honey, you're *it*! I'm signing you to a contract here and now. You'll be the next Alicia Keys or Norah Jones, all you gotta do is name it.'

Where the *hell* were Clive Davis or P. Diddy when she needed them?

'Miss!' A sharp female voice brought her back to reality as an irate female customer attempted to attract her attention.

She sauntered over. At least she had attitude – nobody could take that away from her. 'Yes?' she said.

'Do you *know* how long I've been waiting?' the woman demanded in a high-pitched voice. 'Where are my eggs?' Sharp-featured, the woman was wearing a knock-off Armani suit and clutching a fake Vuitton bag on her lap.

No style, Liberty thought. *If you can't afford the real thing, then you may as well forget it.*

The man with her had nothing to say. Apparently his eggs were not such an urgent matter.

'I'm sorry,' Liberty said in an I-couldn't-give-a-rat's-ass voice. 'I'm not your table person.' She refused to say waitress, she found it to be demeaning, especially to this cow.

'Well, *get* me my "table person",' the woman, sneered. 'I've been sitting here for fifteen minutes.'

'Sure,' Liberty drawled.

For a moment their eyes met. The woman hated her because she was beautiful. It happened all the time. They wouldn't hate her if she was Beyoncé Knowles or Janet Jackson, they'd be fawning all over her the way people did with stars.

Once Mariah Carey had come into the coffee shop with full entourage in attendance and two massive black body-guards who'd never left her side. People had *freaked*. Paparazzi had gathered outside, and within ten minutes a huge crowd had formed – almost breaking the plate-glass window.

The owner of the shop, Manny Goldberg, had begun to panic, until his wife, Golda, decided it would be prudent to escort Miss Carey and her group into the kitchen where the star graciously sipped a cup of green tea, signed autographs and chatted amicably with the two Hispanic chefs.

Liberty had thought about approaching her, but in the end she'd chickened out. Cindi hadn't. Cindi had gotten the diva's signature on a paper napkin, which she'd stashed in her under-wear drawer along with various packets of condoms in all colours and sizes. Cindi was into being prepared.

'Rude little bitch!' Liberty heard the woman mutter to her male companion as she walked away from the table. 'Who does she think she is?'

Liberty was not bothered, she'd been called worse.

She was just about to go into the back when she spotted Mr Hip-Hop himself walking in.

She held her breath for a few seconds. This was the third time he'd been in this week. He always sat at one of her tables and left a massive tip, although he never spoke to her other than to give her his order.

Today he was with another man, a white man who seemed

to be all business. They were talking animatedly, with a lot of arm-waving going on.

She knew who he was. Damon P. Donnell, hip-hop mogul supreme, head of Donnell Records. His new offices were less than a block away, and he'd obviously picked the coffee shop as his breakfast stop-off.

She knew other things about him. He was thirty-six, dark-skinned with cropped hair and a killer smile. He usually wore tinted designer shades, a diamond stud earring, Nike running shoes and a cool suit with a silk T-shirt underneath. He was known for encouraging new talent – although almost all of his label consisted of male rap artists. He'd once been a performer himself, but had given it up except for the occasional charity event. He was married. *Damn!* No chance of getting him *that* way, because Liberty drew the line at playing with married men. His wife was an Indian princess from Bombay, and a consummate consumer. The two of them lived in a sixty-sixth-floor sprawling Westside penthouse with panoramic views of the city and, according to *Vibe*, his wife had converted three bedrooms into her own personal closet. They'd been married two years and had no children.

The first time Liberty had seen him she'd had no idea who he was. 'I think I'm in lust!' she'd muttered to Cindi. 'That dude is the *bomb*!'

Cindi, who was up on everything showbiz, soon filled her in. Cindi devoured *Essence, Rolling Stone, People, Us, The Star* and the *Enquirer*. She watched *Access, E.T., Extra* and *E!* every single day. 'That dude is famous, married, rich, an' *way* outta your reach,' Cindi had informed her. 'Forget it, girl, 'cause this big boy ain't lookin'.'

Sometimes Cindi got on her case a little too much. Her payback was an attempt never to mention him again, not an easy task.

Just as she was about to go over to his table, Cindi materialized and gave her a knowing nudge. 'Mr Wonderman's back – *again*. Mebbe I was kickin' it wrong, little cous', could be you *do* have a shot. If I was you, I'd go for it.'

'The knock-off queen at table four is screaming for her

eggs,' Liberty said, ignoring any mention of Damon. 'You'd better get over there before the cow throws a shit-fit.'

'I'm on it,' Cindi said, totally unconcerned. 'Think I forgot to order 'em. Ain't *that* a shame?'

Liberty approached Damon's table.

He didn't look up. 'Coffee,' he said, studying the menu as if he'd never seen it before. 'Large OJ. Egg-white omelette, bacon on the side.'

'I'll have the same,' said his friend or business associate or whoever the other man was.

She hesitated a moment, willing Damon at least to give her a quick glance. He didn't, but the other guy was sure giving her a thorough going-over with his beady little eyes.

'Certainly, Mr Donnell,' she said, making him aware that she knew who he was. 'Coffee and OJ on the way. Omelette and bacon to follow. Crispy, right?'

Finally he looked up, taking her in, his eyes – visible through his tinted shades – resting on the handwritten nametag above her right breast. But still he didn't say a word, merely gave her an almost imperceptible nod.

She moved off to get them both coffee. And maybe her demo CD?

No! Too soon. I've got to develop a relationship. Like a cool waitress–customer kind of thing.

Oh, yeah, now you can use the word waitress.

That's because he's not some whiny white woman who thinks she's better than me.

'Waitress!' screamed the woman in the knock-off Armani. 'I'm getting nowhere here. *Where* are my eggs?'

She was tempted to say, 'Stuffed up your dried-up old snatch where nobody's gonna find 'em.' But she didn't, because Manny and Golda wouldn't approve and, as bosses go, they were decent people, and she didn't want to get fired. Besides, she needed the job, and so did Cindi. As usual they were late on the rent, and bills were mounting. It was hard keeping up – they could never seem to get ahead.

Before working in the coffee shop she'd tried a variety of jobs. All horrible. Being a waitress was the best of the bunch, although it was murder on her feet. Usually she took the day shift, leaving her evenings free to write songs and hang with her musician friends, including her current boyfriend, Kev, a guitar player. She'd been seeing him for a few months, and he was a nice guy, but nothing serious. She didn't believe in serious, not before she'd forged a career.

'They're on their way,' she yelled across the room at the hateful woman.

'I should think so!' the woman huffed, raising her painted-on eyebrows to let everyone know how pissed off she was.

'Excuse me, Liberty,' said an older, regular customer, sitting by himself at a corner table. 'Might I get a refill?'

This one never gave her any trouble and always tipped well. She flashed him a smile and her most used words: 'Coming right up.'

She grabbled a pot of freshly brewed coffee from behind the counter, filled the man's cup and headed for Damon's table. Only before she could get there, a young boy play-ing with a toy car scooted it in front of her, and *bam* – she tripped over the toy, taking a fall, coffee pot smashing to the ground, hot liquid burning her arm, right ankle twisted beneath her.

Silence descended while everybody turned to stare at the crash site. After a few seconds, conversation resumed, and she was left sprawled on the floor, looking and feeling like a clumsy idiot.

For a few seconds she didn't know what to do, then she heard the horrible female customer laugh in a rude fashion. Quickly she got herself together, even though her arm was burning from the scalding liquid, but when she tried to stand, her ankle gave way under her.

Fortunately Cindi and Mr Regular Customer came to her aid. The older man helped her to a chair, while Cindi began clearing up the broken glass and spilled coffee.

'Are you all right?' Mr Regular Customer asked, genuinely concerned.

She nodded tearfully and shot a look across the shop to see if Damon was watching.

He wasn't. He was carrying on talking, gesticulating

wildly, his diamond stud earring flashing against the fluorescent lights.

She suppressed the urge to cry in earnest. Her arm was on fire, her ankle throbbed, and Damon P. Donnell hadn't even acknowledged her existence. Was *anything* ever going to go right for her?

Man, she needed a break and she needed it desperately.

Chapter Two

Jett Diamond had always experienced great success with women. They fell for his sexy Mediterranean blue eyes, sculpted cheekbones, the tousled lock of dirty blond hair that fell casually over his forehead, his athletic body and cocksure attitude.

Jett took full advantage of his appealing looks. Getting women had never been a problem. Getting *rid* of them was the hassle. They came. They stayed. They wanted more – when all *he* wanted was for them quietly to remove themselves from his apartment without turning into hysterical wrecks.

Gianna did not turn into a hysterical wreck when he informed her he had to leave for New York. Gianna was an Italian supermodel, edgy and assured: she was quite confident he'd be back before she even missed him.

Jett had arrived in Italy three years ago. At the time he was broke, a recovering alcoholic and a druggie. Within months he'd managed to clean up his act – thanks to an excellent rehab programme – signed with a modelling agency and soon after had made a name for himself, appearing in popular cigarette and liquor commercials on TV, and in print ads for everything from expensive cars to designer suits. The camera captured his particular brand of sexiness combined with a lazy insouciance that made him a big hit. Italian women responded to his badboy good looks with great enthusiasm.

Being a male model was hardly considered the most masculine career in the world, but it was one that enabled him to support himself in a decent fashion and not have to beg for handouts from his tight-fisted billionaire father or two half-brothers.

When Jett had moved to Italy he'd distanced himself from them, which was a good thing. Nobody connected him to the Diamond family – especially as he only used his first name. Jett. An American model in Milan. Anonymous was the way to go.

Gianna drove him to the airport in her latest acquisition – a gleaming yellow Lamborghini given to her by an ardent admirer. She and Jett enjoyed an open relationship, which suited them just fine. Neither of them wished to be tied down, they were both free spirits.

Before leaving the apartment, Gianna had given him a world-class blow-job. He'd sat back and enjoyed it. Who wouldn't? With her deliciously full lips and extraordinarily talented tongue, she certainly knew how to leave a man wanting more.

He didn't love her. But he sure loved what she did to him.

As he boarded the plane, he wondered what his father wanted. Three years. No contact. And now the call from Lady Jane.

You don't have to go, his inner voice informed him.

Really?

Yeah, really.

But, hey – I'm curious.

Of course you are. He's Red Diamond. And when he calls – everyone runs. Including you.

It had been that way all his life.

* * *

Five-year-old Jett was smart, but not smart enough for his father.

The family were gathered in the garden of the farmhouse in Tuscany. His stunning mother, Edie – an ex-model with exquisite bone structure, his thirteen-year-old half-brother – Chris, making a rare visit and Red – a man whom, even at that young age, Jett regarded as a frightening figure.

Jett had climbed up a tree and couldn't get down. Earlier in the day he'd been forbidden to climb it by a stern-faced nanny. But later he'd watched Chris snake up the huge oak tree like it was nothing, and he'd thought, Why can't I do that?

Now he was trapped up high, clinging tightly to a branch, and he was scared. So scared that tears coursed down his cheeks and his sturdy legs were shaking.

'Send up one of the guards,' Edie pleaded, clutching a martini glass.

'Hell, no,' growled Red. 'He got himself up there. Let the little bastard get himself down.'

'But he could fall,' protested Edie, nervously sipping her drink.

'Teach the disobedient little asshole a lesson.'

'He's only five,' Edie pointed out, her delicate hands trembling so hard that the ice in her drink clinked against the side of the glass.

'The kid's old enough to know better,' Red said, in a hard voice.

'I'll climb up and get him,' offered Chris. ''S easy.'

'Anybody ask you, moron?' Red shouted, glaring at his middle son.

Chris faded into the background. It was safer that way.

An hour passed. It was starting to get dark and rainclouds were gathering. Jett clung to the branch, almost losing his balance. By this time Red had sent everyone inside, and now he was walking towards the house himself.

'Daddy!' Jett screamed, his face contorted with fear. 'Don't leave me. Daddy! I'm scared. Daddy! Help me! Please!'

Red turned round, and looked up at the small boy whose eyes were wide with terror. 'Life lesson number one,' he roared. 'Never do anything you can't get yourself out of. Remember that, you stupid little piece of shit.'

Later that night, when he was sure everyone was asleep, Chris had snuck out of the house, climbed the tree and helped his sobbing brother down.

The next morning both of them received a fierce beating with Red's steel-tipped cane, and immediately after that, Chris was put on a plane back to America.

Jett wished his big brother was always around to save him. But it wasn't to be.

The tree incident was only the beginning.

*   *   *

Max Diamond was anxious to find out what the hell Red wanted. His best guess was that the old man had a terminal illness and wished to make amends for the way he'd treated everyone over the years. Especially his three sons whom he'd never given a shit about.

At forty-three, Max was one of the most successful real-estate tycoons in New York. He'd made it on his own with no help from his father. In fact, having Red Diamond as a dad was detrimental all the way. When he'd started out in business people had expected him to be rolling in money – but he'd never had a dime from his old man – he'd done it by himself. Hard work paid off, and Max had always been willing to work, asking no help from anyone, building his own empire. He'd certainly succeeded – until now: two banks had backed out of a major building project in Lower Manhattan that was already under construction. The multi-million-dollar commercial project needed an influx of funding immediately, or there was a chance he could lose everything.

Max was the oldest Diamond brother. Jett, at twenty-four, the youngest, and then there was thirty-two-year-old Chris. All three had different mothers. Max's mother, Rachel, had died shortly after giving birth to him. Chris's mother, Olivia, had perished in a plane crash. And Jett's mother – the once-beautiful Edie – lived out in Montauk nursing a steady supply of vodka and a series of decades-younger boyfriends.

Everyone knew about Edie Diamond and her bad habits. She was notorious. And who had made her that way? Red Diamond, of course. The old man had no respect for women and treated them badly. His pattern was to conquer, marry and destroy. He'd certainly done that to Edie.

Max had struck out in the marriage stakes once. He'd experienced a New York divorce with legs. His ex, Mariska – a Russian-born, steely-eyed blonde who lived to see her name mentioned in Suzy's column – had harboured no intention of going away quietly, in spite of an enormous financial settlement. They shared a child, Lulu, a very pretty, somewhat spoiled five-year-old. Mariska and Lulu resided in a luxurious penthouse in one of the Diamond buildings, the apartment was part of Mariska's more than generous settlement.

Max spent most weekends with his young daughter, whom he adored. They got along fine, enjoying all kinds of fun activities, such as riding on Max's Lear jet to Disneyworld in Florida, or a quick trip to the Bahamas for the water-slides at the Atlantis, Lulu's favourite hotel. Lulu loved spending time with her daddy, and the feeling was mutual.

Recently he'd gotten engaged. This had infuriated Mariska, who had always imagined that *she* would be the one to remarry first. 'Why you do this?' she'd demanded haughtily. 'You do not need another wife.'

Tough. He was getting married again, and this time he would make sure it lasted. He had no intention of ending up like his father with several ex-wives and three sons whom Red didn't give a damn about, and never had.

* * *

Junior prom and sixteen-year-old Max had a date with Rosemary, his steady girlfriend of one year, a pretty girl in a pink dress with roses in her hair and a toothy smile. Max had it all figured out – tonight was definitely the night. They'd been seeing each other for long enough, and although they'd done some pretty heavy necking, he was confident that later Rosemary would allow him to go all the way. They'd talked about it enough times, and he had condoms in his pocket so he was well prepared.

The prom was a blast. They danced all night, both got loaded, and on the way back to the house on 68th Street, she let him feel her up in the limo. Red and Max's step-mother, Olivia, were out of the country, leaving his five-year-old half-brother, Chris, with a nanny, so taking Rosemary to the house instead of some tacky hotel seemed like a no-brainer.

They began necking in the library with the Grease soundtrack playing on the stereo – Olivia Newton-John and John Travolta belting out 'You're The One That I Want'. Max was in full swing: he had the top of Rosemary's dress pulled down round her waist and her skirt hiked up. She had full, luscious breasts that he wanted to bury his head in, and a mound of curly black pubic hair that surprised him because there was so much of it. He knew that this was it: they were about to go all the way, the first time for both of them.

Just as Max was struggling to put on a condom, Red Diamond burst into the library, flicking on all the lights.

'Dad!' Max stammered, desperately trying to cram his hard-on back into his pants. 'I – I thought you were away.'

'Is that what you thought?' Red said, eyeing Rosemary, who was so embarrassed she didn't know what to do first – cover her breasts or pull down her skirt.

'Crap, Dad!' Max mumbled. 'We're on our way outta here. I – I didn't mean to—'

'Get your horny ass up to your room,' Red interrupted, still watching Rosemary. 'I'll see the young lady gets home safely.'

'But—'

'Get out, you horny little fuck!' Red snapped. 'Now!'

To his ongoing shame, Max had left his half-dressed girlfriend alone with his father and slunk up to his bedroom, limp dick hanging forlornly between his legs.

The next morning he called Rosemary. She refused to come to the phone. This went on for several days until her uptight-sounding mother informed him that Rosemary had left for an extended stay in Europe, and would he please stop bothering her.

It wasn't until four years later, when he was in college, that he'd run into Rosemary at a party. At first she'd tried to avoid him, but later he'd found out the real truth about what had taken place that fateful night. According to Rosemary, after he'd left the room, Red had forced himself upon her, raping her repeatedly until she'd fainted. When she'd recovered consciousness, Red had sent her home in a cab, threatening her with bodily harm if she told anyone what had taken place. Unable to stay quiet, she'd immediately told her parents and her father had stormed over to the house to confront Red.

After a long scene, Red had agreed to pay Rosemary's family a great deal of money in exchange for their silence.

'Why didn't you tell me?' Max demanded. 'Or go to the police?'

Rosemary shrugged as if it really didn't matter, although the pain behind her eyes revealed a different story. 'We both know there's nothing anyone could've done,' she said. 'Your father's got connections. Mine hasn't.'

It was as simple as that.

So, Red Diamond got away with raping a sixteen-year-old girl. And not just any girl: Max's first true love, his steady girlfriend.

When he'd confronted Red, his father had laughed at him. 'She was begging for it, son,' he'd sneered. 'Frothing at the bit. She needed a real man, not a useless specimen like you.'

'But she was my girlfriend, Dad. My girlfriend.'

'Let this teach you a lesson about women,' Red lectured. 'You can never trust 'em. Never. They're all whores one way or the other. You'll find out soon enough.'

And that was the only time they'd ever discussed it.

* * *

Chris's star client, Jonathan Goode, was setting off on a multi-city European tour to launch his latest movie, so Chris hitched a ride on the corporate jet the studio had thoughtfully provided to fly their star to New York, then onto Europe.

Jonathan Goode was an extremely famous worldwide movie star, but he was also a quietly pleasant man in his mid-thirties who did not appear to be driven by an out-of-control ego. In spite of being low-key, he was accompanied by the usual star entourage: his hawk-eyed manager, his female agent, an overbearing PR woman, a muscled fitness trainer, a lesbian stylist, his French personal chef, and two extremely efficient assistants. There was also his current girlfriend, a curly-haired Armenian actress who spoke very little English and smiled a lot, especially when there were cameras around.

Rumours about Jonathan's sexuality abounded. Was he gay? Bisexual? Or simply not interested?

18

Chris didn't know and he didn't care. Jonathan was a nice, unassuming guy, and what he did or didn't do in bed was nobody's business except his.

'How come this last-minute trip?' Jonathan asked, settling into a plush leather seat as two attractive flight attendants – a male and a female hand-picked by his manager – hovered over him.

'Family,' Chris replied, fastening his seatbelt.

'Ex-wife? Mother? Sisters?' Jonathan inquired, not really interested, but always polite.

'I don't have an ex-wife,' Chris said. 'My mom's deceased. And no sisters.'

'I have three older sisters,' Jonathan said with a self-deprecating grin. 'They taught me everything I *don't* know about women.'

Chris smiled, and understood why females across the world worshipped Jonathan Goode. He had that all-American boyish thing going for him. Like Kevin Costner and Tom Cruise, he had a hero aura, an aura that was extremely appealing to both women *and* men.

'Excuse me, Jonathan,' one of his assistants said, hurrying over and handing him a cellphone. 'It's Les Moonves, he'd like a word.'

Jonathan took the cell, while Chris picked up a magazine which happened to feature a buff-looking Jonathan on the cover practising some kind of martial arts.

It pleased him that the movie star seemed totally unaware that his father was Red Diamond. He'd never tried to hide it – on the other hand he'd never advertised it either. If people were curious, he steered them off the subject. Now that he'd managed to establish himself as one of the top entertainment lawyers in L.A., nobody asked or even cared.

It hadn't been easy. Olivia had divorced Red when Chris was ten, refusing to put up with his constant affairs. Olivia – a great beauty – had then moved to California where she'd met and married Peter Linden, a rich lawyer who'd wanted *her*, but not the baggage of a son. Reluctantly Olivia had chosen her new husband over Chris. Her choice resulted in him being sent to a tough military school, a brutal place that he barely managed to survive. After that it was college, and finally – at the suggestion of Peter – law school.

Yeah, anything to get rid of him. But he wasn't against attending law school, it was a profession he quite fancied, having observed his step-father's lavish lifestyle. Entertainment law interested him, especially as he planned on staying in L.A., a city he'd grown fond of. The weather was great, the women were very beautiful *and* available. What was there *not* to like?

He saw his real father, Red, twice a year. It was more than enough.

The day he passed the bar, Olivia was killed in a private plane crash on her way to celebrate with him. His stepfather, overcome with grief, blamed Chris and, shortly after Olivia's funeral, cut off all contact with his step-son. Apparently Peter Linden's grief did not last long, because six weeks later he married a larger-than-life, extremely famous blonde movie star.

A few weeks after his mother's funeral, Chris had called Red, whom he hadn't heard from since he'd informed his father of Olivia's death.

'What the *hell* do you want now?' Red had yelled over the phone. 'Money? Too bad, 'cause you're not getting it from me. I paid for every cent of your education – that's more than enough. Now, get your lazy ass out there an' *work* for a living like *I* had to. Nothin's gonna be handed to you on a silver platter. Go achieve something, *then* call me.'

Typical Red Diamond. Lose your mother – so what? Get your lazy ass back to work.

Disappointed, but hardly surprised by his father's unfeeling attitude, Chris had moved in with three friends from college. A couple of months later he managed to get a job at a Century City law firm, and began working his way up, determined to show *both* his fathers that he didn't need their money or their help. He would succeed without them.

His break came when he had a brief affair with one of the firm's clients. She was an older woman, an actress with no career. Since she had no future – Hollywood can be a cruel town for women to grow older in – Chris inherited her as a client. Forty-five and still extremely beautiful in a fragile way, she reminded him of his mother.

Resurrecting her career was definitely a challenge, but Chris got off on challenges. So, to everyone's surprise, including the actress's, he did the impossible: he brokered a gig for her on a new TV series, which went on to become *the* breakout hit of the season, and suddenly she was a very valuable client indeed. Even more important, she was *his* client.

After that, his days of sharing an apartment with three other guys, all of them struggling to make their share of the rent, were over.

A year later the law firm he worked at made him a junior partner, and from there it was a swift ride to the top. Chris had a knack of attracting all the right clients, and since the other partners were not stupid, they offered him a full partnership, which he happily accepted.

He was young, hot and in Hollywood. And when he called Red, there was a grudging acceptance in the old man's tone. 'Y' see?' Chris was tempted to say. 'I made it without you.'

But he didn't: he waited patiently for words of praise from his father's lips.

Those words never came. And while he pretended it didn't matter, it actually did.

Before leaving L.A., Chris had cancelled his trip to Vegas. Roth Giagante, the owner of the Magiriano Hotel, had not been happy. 'You're supposed to be here this weekend with my money,' Roth had informed him, sounding pissed-off. 'We had a fuckin' agreement, an' I don't get along with people who back out of agreements.'

'There's an emergency in New York I'm forced to deal with,' Chris had said. 'I'll make it to Vegas by Sunday. You have my word.'

'You'd *better* be here, otherwise you'll be using "emergency" in a different kind of sentence. Get it?'

Yes. He got it. Roth Giagante allowed him certain privileges because of his star clientele and showbiz connections. But over the past three months Chris had lost big, and Roth wanted his money. In cash. Six hundred thousand to be precise, and that was a huge amount of cash to come up with.

Roth would get paid. Eventually. Although the truth was he'd only managed to come up with two hundred and fifty thousand, which was stashed in his home safe back in L.A. He was banking on Roth giving him more time. Roth was cool, and if he promised him a visit from a couple of his star clients, it would take the edge off. Those Vegas big-shots were all the same – major star fucks.

Yes, Vegas was his downfall. He made great money, but for the last three months he'd blown it at the gaming tables. Things were serious, and yet he still couldn't seem to stop. It was an addiction that had him by the throat.

By the time Jonathan got off the phone, they were airborne, on their way to New York. Jonathan stood up, beckoned his girlfriend, and the two of them went into the bedroom and shut the door. Obviously further conversation was not on the movie star's agenda.

Chris didn't mind, in fact he was thankful. It had been a stressful week trying to get the money together to pay Roth, while still dealing with his roster of famous clients. They were a demanding group, calling him at all times of the day and night, which did not sit well with his latest girlfriend, Verona, an Asian Pilates teacher with exotic looks and incredible hands. Verona wanted to move in. So far Chris had resisted: he *liked* living alone. What was wrong with that?

The good news was that Verona was not an actress and, even better, she had no ambitions in that direction. This pleased Chris, who had recently broken off a destructive on-off affair with Holly Anton, a TV sit-com star who also happened to be a certifiable maniac. It was Holly who'd started him on his gambling kick. Holly *loved* Vegas, the city she'd been raised in, and soon they'd started spending every weekend there.

He didn't miss Holly, she'd driven him crazy with her insatiable sexual appetite, bouts of black depression, and paranoia concerning her career. Gambling had become his escape from her ever-changing moods.

Actresses. Never again. He felt lucky to have gotten out of that one alive.

One thing the Diamond brothers had in common was exceptional looks. They were all over six feet tall. Max was dark and brooding, Jett the quintessential bad boy with his dirty blond hair and intense blue eyes, while Chris had a look that was pure George Clooney in his *E.R.* days. Women fell for Chris's self-deprecating sense of humour and dazzling smile. And his being a successful lawyer in a town turned on by success was an added attraction.

Little did anyone know that, as successful as he was, his gambling debts were very worrisome.

Putting down the magazine, he closed his eyes and attempted to clear his mind. He was hoping this trip might solve all his problems. Being summoned to New York by his billionaire father could definitely be a sign that things were about to get better.

Before long he'd find out what Red wanted. The anticipation was a bitch.

* * *

'Your father doesn't mean it,' Olivia would say in a soothing tone.

Growing up, those were the words Chris heard his mother utter almost every day. Maybe she believed she was telling the truth, but from the moment he could understand what was going on, Chris knew that old Red Diamond meant everything he said and did. There were no second chances with Red.

The trick was to stay out of his way, which wasn't always possible, as Chris had discovered on more than one occasion.

His father was into corporal punishment. If any of his sons did anything that Red considered wrong, then in his opinion they deserved a good beating. And it seemed that Red took a great deal of pleasure in administering the punishment personally.

Once, when Chris was nine, he'd innocently scarfed down a box of chocolates he'd found next to Red's bed. How was he to know they were gourmet chocolates, hand-made especially for his father by a master chocolate-maker in Belgium and couriered to America by private jet?

Red was not happy when he discovered his chocolates were gone. His screams of fury could be heard throughout the house.

'Who the fuck *ate my chocolates?' he yelled, while Olivia*

attempted to calm him, and Chris hovered nervously outside the bedroom door.

Mae, the cook, came running out of the kitchen offering to make him some more.

'Are you mad?' Red yelled. 'I'm talking hand-made chocolates, woman, not that shit you come up with.'

Glaring at her boss, Mae retreated back to the kitchen, mumbling under her breath.

'Where's Chris?' Red shouted. 'Where's that dumbass useless boy?'

'I'm sure it wasn't him,' Olivia said, protecting her son as usual.

'Oh, you're sure it wasn't him,' Red said, mimicking her voice in a cruel fashion.

'I'll send for more chocolates,' Olivia said. 'I can—'

Whack! Chris heard Red strike his mother and, without a second thought, he raced into the room and began pummelling his father.

'Ha!' Red yelled, fending his son off. 'The kid's got balls after all. What a surprise!'

And for a split second Chris had felt a frisson of satisfaction. His father had actually praised him!

After that it was all downhill. A beating twice as long as usual on his bare backside, a beating so bad it had drawn blood.

He hadn't been able to sit down for a week, but at least Red thought he had balls. And, young as he was, he knew that was a good thing.

A year later his parents got divorced.

Chapter Three

Nancy Scott-Simon was a major control freak. Everything for her only daughter Amy's upcoming wedding had to be exactly right, and anyone who made a mistake better watch out.

Nancy was a thin, brittle-looking woman, with sharp cheekbones and jet black hair pulled back in a tight chignon. She favoured Oscar de la Renta suits, Ferragamo handbags, Gucci shoes and Valentino ballgowns. She also favoured fine antique jewellery handed down from her mother, Amy's grandmother, who was ninety years old and still as lively as a French poodle.

Nancy ruled from her impeccably decorated townhouse off Park Avenue. Five floors. Eight bedrooms. Five live-in staff.

Nancy's daughter, Amy, was a very pretty girl indeed. A New York princess with silky blonde hair (natural), a deceptively innocent face, dreamy turquoise eyes, soft lips, sun-burnished skin, and a slinky body suitable for the front cover of *Sports Illustrated* if she ever chose to pose – which of course she never would.

A rich girl, because Nancy Scott-Simon was a double heiress, and at the age of twenty-five Amy was due to inherit a large chunk of the family fortune.

Amy had grown up privileged, surrounded by nannies and drivers, butlers and bodyguards. She'd attended the finest private schools and vacationed in all the best places. Due to her family's enormous wealth there'd once been a kidnapping incident. Nancy referred to it as an incident, but Amy remembered the gruelling time she'd spent in captivity at the age of

25

fourteen with horror and dread. For forty-eight hours, after a nightmare trip stuffed into the filthy trunk of a car, she'd been locked, chained and blindfolded in a rat-infested cellar with no bathroom facilities and only a few chunks of dry bread and a bottle of water for sustenance. Not knowing what was about to happen to her next was terrifying. Every moment she spent in captivity was pure torture, especially when one or other of her captors – there were two men and a woman – entered the room and hurled verbal threats and insults her way.

Her mother had not called the police. Instead, she'd summoned the family lawyer, who'd paid the ransom. But nobody had paid for her humiliation and mental suffering.

After the ransom was paid, the kidnappers had bundled Amy back into the trunk of the car, and dropped her off in the middle of the night somewhere in Brooklyn. Sobbing hysterically, she'd managed to make a phone call, and the family lawyer's son had picked her up and delivered her home.

The trio of kidnappers were never caught. They got away with two million dollars in cash, while she escaped with her life.

Was it a fair exchange?

Absolutely not, although Nancy was happy because by not calling in the police or FBI she'd avoided all the nasty headline publicity. It never occured to Nancy that she'd put her daughter's life at risk, and it certainly never entered her head that Amy might need counselling after her horrifying ordeal.

'It's over,' she'd informed Amy in a let's-never-talk-about-it-again tone of voice. 'You must forget all about it.'

But it wasn't over for Amy, who'd suffered nightmares and flashbacks and a strong overall feeling that nowhere was safe.

Over the years she'd overcome her fears, and when she'd graduated from college she'd decided to take an independent step and move out of the family townhouse, get a job and live by herself. Nancy objected, but Amy had insisted, until eventually her mother had reluctantly relented.

After several weeks of looking, she'd scored a job at the high-profile fashion house of Courtenelli, run by the flamboyant, colourful Italian designer, Sofia Courtenelli.

Landing the job at Courtenelli was a coup. Amy was one of

three PR girls, who took care of promotions and publicity and, with her charm, education and appealing looks, she was an instant success.

Working was a revelation and she loved it. It was fun and exciting, and the big plus was that she got to meet all kinds of people she wouldn't normally encounter.

The only downside was the men. They hit on her relentlessly, driving her crazy. Everyone from the male models to the sales team, they all had one thing on their minds – nail little Amy Scott-Simon. After all, she was a major New York heiress, so why not?

Since Amy wasn't interested in casual sex, she found it no problem to turn them down. The truth was that she wasn't into sex, having made up her mind after many sweaty struggles from high school to college that she would save herself for marriage – or, if not marriage, the right man. Someone she could really trust. Plus there was the memory of her kidnapping and the sexual indignities she'd been forced to endure, which she'd confided to her best friend, Tina, but no one else, not even her mother, who would've thrown a hysterical fit if she'd known her teenage daughter had been sexually molested. It wasn't as if she'd been raped, although her kidnappers had forced her to do other things . . . things she didn't care to think about. She'd locked away the memories. It was better that way.

One memorable night at a fundraiser in Manhattan, she'd been introduced to Max Diamond, and even though he was much older than her, she'd been intrigued by his sophisticated style and courtly manners. Max struck her as someone who was safe. He also seemed to be a gentleman, unlike most other men she'd met. The other advantage was that, since he was so rich himself, he certainly wasn't after her inheritance, which was a big relief.

After several quiet dinners and long conversations, they'd begun dating seriously. She knew he was divorced and had a child, but that didn't seem to matter.

Right at the beginning of their relationship she'd been totally forthright and informed him there would be no sex. 'Never?' he'd said, perplexed and intrigued by her directness.

'Don't laugh at me,' she'd replied earnestly. 'I'm saving myself for the man I marry.'

'I can respect that,' he'd said.

'Really?' she'd said, delighted by his response.

'Yes,' he'd replied. 'I find your attitude most commendable.'

Hmm . . . a man who understood made a nice change. It was then that she'd decided he was definitely the man for her.

Three months later – much to Nancy's delight – Amy and Max had gotten engaged.

* * *

Every day after Amy finished work, Nancy expected her to come to the house and pore over the wedding plans along with Lynda Colefax, the wedding planner – a bossy, over-groomed woman of indeterminate age.

Amy was beginning to dread these little sessions. She couldn't stand listening to Nancy and Lynda go on about which guests were attending, where they'd sit, the flower arrangements, the table placements, the wedding cake, her dress, the music, the table linens. It was all so *trivial*. 'I don't care!' she was tempted to scream. 'It shouldn't be such a big deal. I *hate* being the centre of attention. I just want it to be over.'

Harold, her step-father, agreed with her. 'Too much fuss,' he grumbled. 'Too much money being spent.'

Naturally Nancy ignored him.

Amy's own father had drowned in a tragic boating accident on a weekend trip to Venice when she was three. A year later her only sibling – a brother – had passed away due to a rare bone disease. She had no memories of either of them, except a few family photos. She lived with an ongoing sense of sadness and loss, having convinced herself that if her father had been alive, her kidnapping might never have taken place.

Her step-father was a pleasant enough man, even though everyone knew he had no balls. Nancy had them firmly in her pocket. Nancy ruled. It was *her* money, *her* way of doing things. And Harold never dared get in her way.

As her wedding drew closer, Amy found herself unable to sleep at night, lying in her bed and wondering if perhaps she was making a huge mistake. Yes, her future husband was an important man, a business powerhouse. Handsome, in a dark, brooding way, he was also kind and thoughtful and genuinely cared about her. He'd accepted her no-sex-before-marriage rule and never tried to pressure her. He'd bought her a ten-carat diamond engagement ring and showered her with other expensive gifts.

Not that the gifts meant anything: they were merely surface signs of affection. Deep down she yearned for more than that. Deep down she yearned for her father and her brother, the missing men in her life.

Lately she had questioned her feelings for Max even more. Was she *really* in love with him? After all, he came with major baggage – an ex-wife, a child, *and* he was twenty-three years older than her, a fact that seemed to bother no one except her.

When she'd voiced doubts to her mother, Nancy had raised an elegant eyebrow and said, 'You couldn't make a better match, dear. At least we know he's not a fortune-hunter. He's an extremely eligible bachelor, and *you*'ve got him. Isn't *that* nice?' It would be so great if her mother was the kind of woman she could actually *talk* to. But no – Nancy wasn't that person. Nancy Scott-Simon was controlling and critical, and an expert at pressing all of Amy's buttons.

So that was that. One wedding coming up.

Chapter Four

Arriving back in New York, Jett was hit with a strong wave of nostalgia. New York, with all its frenetic activity and dirty sidewalks, was home: he'd grown up in the city, screwed up in the city, experienced many things – good and bad. Riding in a cab over the bridge, he realized how *much* he'd missed it, even though he'd left under a black cloud. Two arrests for drunk driving, an ex-girlfriend who'd called the cops on him because he'd given her a black eye – which she'd deserved, although he'd never have done it if he hadn't been stoned out of his head; a bad drug problem; a fight over money with his mom's then current boyfriend – an amateur boxer who'd beaten the crap out of him; and finally a vicious argument with Edie, his emotionally unbalanced mother.

Lady Jane Bentley had sent him a ticket but she hadn't mentioned where he was supposed to stay, so before he'd left Milan he'd called Sam Lucas, a black actor friend of his, and asked if he could sleep on his couch for a few days.

'You can have the whole place,' Sam had told him. 'I got a TV gig in L.A., so I need someone to bring in my mail an' water my plants. Make it yours, bro'.'

'That's great,' Jett had said, psyched that he didn't have to waste money on a hotel.

Although his modelling assignments paid quite well, he wasn't as flush as he'd have liked to be. Living with Gianna was expensive – she enjoyed hanging out at all the hottest restaurants and happening clubs, and there was no way he was letting *her* pay. As it was, she paid the rent and picked up all of their living expenses. He'd offered to contribute, but Gianna was having none of it. She was a highly paid supermodel and a bit of a control freak. Sexy too. What more could any guy ask?

Sam was a good friend who'd basically saved his life by staging an intervention and putting him on a plane to Italy, making sure that when he'd stepped off the plane there were people to meet him and get him into rehab. He owed Sam plenty, and one day, when the old man dropped, he hoped to be able to repay him big-time. Because who else did Red Diamond have to leave his billions to except his three sons? The old man was too tight to leave it to charity. And since Red Diamond considered all women inferior beings, Lady Jane stood *no* chance.

Not that Jett was desperate to inherit his part of the Diamond fortune. But he knew it was inevitable that one day he was destined to be very rich indeed. And who was he to fight it?

Hell, if he tried hard enough he might even learn to embrace it.

*   *   *

When it came to business, Max Diamond was obsessive. He arose every day at five a.m., worked out with his trainer until six-thirty, then read all the newspapers, checked out the stock market, and made numerous phone calls. He was at his desk by seven-thirty, alert and ready to handle anything.

Running a real-estate empire took time and smarts. There were always problems, crises to fix, things to be dealt with. He could've delegated more than he did, but he believed in being hands-on – it was imperative that he was available twenty-four hours a day. Especially now he was in the middle of a crisis with the banks. It was not a healthy situation, yet he felt quite confident that he could solve it. The Japanese were likely to jump in and save the day. Two important bankers were flying in from Tokyo especially to meet with him. At the suggestion of Clive Barnaby, his key executive, they had been invited to his bachelor party, which was one of the reasons he couldn't cancel it, much as he'd like to. Bachelor parties were hardly his style: he considered them a pathetic excuse for drunken married men to get their rocks off as they sat around hoping for a titty show – or, even better, a girl-on-girl sex scene.

Work was Max's passion. He'd always been determined to show his father he was no hapless loser – like Red had always told him he was.

During his marriage to Mariska she'd complained that he was never around when she needed him.

'To do what?' he'd asked. 'Escort you to the opera, the ballet, and every boring dinner party in town?'

'It is excellent business for you to be seen out with your stunning wife,' Mariska had responded. Modesty was not a quality she held in high regard.

'Mariska, I'm working,' he'd informed her. 'Working to keep *you* in the style you've so easily become accustomed to.'

'Donald Trump works too,' she'd argued, 'and he is seen everywhere.'

As usual he ignored the Trump comparisons, which Mariska was fond of making. Donald Trump lived life his way in a very public fashion, and that was his prerogative. Max had no desire to be part of the busy New York social scene, enduring endless mentions in the gossip columns and a successful TV show. Publicity did not interest him. In fact, he did everything he could to avoid it.

When he'd first encountered Mariska six years ago, she'd struck him as a simple girl who'd come to America from Moscow to pursue a dream. She already had her green card, thanks to what she assured him was a marriage of convenience to an accountant. She was divorced, working as a massage therapist and dating a business associate of his.

On their first meeting at a dinner party he'd sat next to her, and during the course of the evening complained of a pain in his right shoulder.

'I can fix that for you,' she'd said, slipping him her card. 'Call me, Max Diamond. I will make you feel like a new man.'

A few days later he picked up the phone and made an appointment.

Mariska's massage technique consisted of heady scented

oils and strong European fingers. She certainly did his shoulder a power of good, and it wasn't long before he invited her for lunch. Her Slavic features, straight white-blonde-hair and charming accent captivated him, not that he had much time for women – work always came first. But Mariska was intriguing, and he found himself making another lunch date with her. Later that week they met for dinner. Soon he was seeing her every night.

She treated him like a king, always putting him first, complimenting him, never asking for anything.

Max was not a very sexually adept man – until he began sleeping with Mariska, the missionary position suited him just fine. But Mariska was having none of it: in bed she took him places he'd never been before, and he didn't object.

Within months he'd asked her to marry him and she'd readily accepted.

It was only after the ring was on her finger that he'd realized what a conniving, devious, money-grabbing social-climber she really was.

Too late. He'd married her, and by the time he caught on to her real personality, she was pregnant.

He stayed in the marriage for the sake of Lulu, but when his little daughter reached the age of four he knew he couldn't take it anymore. It was imperative for his peace of mind that he escape.

Mariska did not want a divorce. She fought it every way she knew how, speaking to the press, his friends, business associates, hiring the best lawyers, which *he*'d ended up paying for, and generally making his life as difficult as possible.

Eventually he'd had to pay her a huge settlement. He considered it worth it just to be rid of her.

Now he'd met a wonderful girl, and soon he'd be married again.

This time he was sure it would work out.

*　　*　　*

'What're you doing tonight?' Chris asked Jonathan, as their plane landed.

'Going to bed as soon as I can,' Jonathan replied, yawning. 'I start off tomorrow with Matt Lauer on the *Today Show*. Then there's the press junket, followed by *Letterman*. I'll probably end up doing thirty interviews.'

'Thirty-five,' his P.R. woman murmured, *sotto voce*.

'That's heavy,' Chris said, not envying the life of a movie star.

'Gotta do *something* to cover your exorbitant bills,' Jonathan joked, flashing his boyish grin.

Chris let it slide. Yes, his bills were exorbitant but, damn, he was worth it: none of his clients had any complaints. He was on call twenty-four hours a day and they all took advantage.

'What are *your* plans?' Jonathan asked, still being polite.

Chris shrugged. He hadn't really thought about how he'd spend the night before meeting with his father. A man needed to be at the top of his game when he sat in a room with Red Diamond, so maybe the hotel and Room Service was the best idea.

On the other hand there were clients in town he should call, and since he was in New York, he might as well take care of business.

Before leaving L.A. he'd promised his youngest client, Birdy Marvel, that he'd try to attend her concert. Birdy Marvel was an eighteen-year-old singing superstar, who was steadily veering out of control. If she stayed on the path she was boozing and partying her way down, she could easily end up like Jett – who last time he'd seen his self-destructive half-brother, was a total wreck. So bad, that Chris had contacted Jett's friend, Sam, and begged him to do something. A few days later Sam had staged an intervention and put Jett on a plane to Italy. Unbeknownst to Jett, Chris had financed the trip, including Jett's eight-week stay in rehab.

'I might drop by to see my client, Birdy Marvel,' he said. 'She's got a show tonight.'

'How *delicious*!' exclaimed Jonathan's gay stylist, over-hearing. 'She's so . . . *bountiful*! I simply *adore* the way that little girl jiggles her pom-poms!'

'Fake tits,' said Jonathan's manager, joining in. 'I got a real hang-up about fake tits. Hate 'em.'

Chris nodded, although he'd never given it much thought. But he had to agree – there was nothing like the real thing.

Later, after checking into the Four Seasons, he decided against sitting through the concert. He'd seen Birdy perform a dozen times – he almost knew her moves better than she did. If he showed up at the after party full of compliments, she wouldn't know the difference.

Yes, that's what he'd do. Take a shower, make a few calls and go out later.

Chapter Five

'This *isn't* how it should be,' Liberty wailed, perched on the over-stuffed brown couch in the living room of her mom's small apartment, tucked away in the basement of Red Diamond's brownstone.

'You just gotta get down with it,' Cindi said, fussing around the place, arranging magazines in a pile next to her, and fluffing up the cushions. '*I* can't look after you 'cause of work, Kev's away, an' the doc wants the dressin' on your arm changed every day – you got burned, girl. It ain't no joke.'

'Tell me about it,' Liberty said gloomily.

'An',' Cindi added sternly, 'you gotta stay off that ankle. Now, I ask you, who better to watch you than your mom?'

'I can think of plenty of people,' Liberty muttered, furious with herself for no other reason than she'd had the bad luck to take such a disastrous fall.

'A coupla days,' Cindi said, 'An' you'll be *zoomin'* outta here.'

'Thanks a *lot*,' Liberty said ominously. 'That's if I survive that long.'

'Tell your mama to fix you those honey ribs you suck the crap outta,' Cindi suggested, licking her lips at the thought. 'You'll not only survive, it'll put some meat on your skinny self. How many times I gotta tell you? Guys get off on a handful.'

'Now you *sound* like Mama,' Liberty said grimly. 'And I'm *not* skinny.'

'You got no booty, girl,' Cindi teased. 'Men are into booty!'

'I'm down with it, cousin,' Liberty said tartly, ''cause *you've* got enough for both of us.'

'Ha ha!' Cindi said, grinning. 'An' don't that make *me* the popular one.'

Even though she weighed over two hundred pounds, Cindi was blessed with an abundance of confidence, especially when it came to her effect on the opposite sex.

'Okay, so I'll tough it out.' Liberty sighed.

'I'll come by every day,' Cindi promised, preparing to take off.

'No, you won't,' Liberty said, her face glum.

'Girl, I'm gonna try.'

'No, you *won't*,' Liberty repeated, knowing there was no way her cousin would give up her active sex life to babysit. To Cindi, making out was like scoring a home-run at baseball – she even kept her own personal score-card. And this weekend she had plans with Moose, a six-foot-four-inch-tall security guard, whose big claim to fame was that he'd once worked the security detail for a Britney Spears concert.

'Don't forget to leave out food for the Ragtags,' Liberty instructed. 'Just 'cause I'm not around doesn't mean they should go hungry.' The Ragtags was her name for a small band of homeless people who regularly came by the back of the coffee shop to pick up leftovers.

'I don't get why you encourage those stinky losers to hang out in the alley,' Cindi complained, turning up her nose.

'They don't hang out,' Liberty explained patiently. 'They come by at seven every morning to collect stuff that would normally get thrown in the garbage. And they only smell 'cause they got no place to shower.'

'Ha!' Cindi snorted. 'If you had *your* way, all those wackos would be crowdin' into *our* crib an' showerin' there.'

Liberty put on her pious face because she knew it irritated her cousin, and why should Cindi be having a good day? 'Just don't forget, that's all,' she said sternly. 'Those people depend on me.'

'Got it,' Cindi said, heading for the door. 'Now, don't go doin' nothin' crazy. Stay cool an' *no* fightin' with your ma.'

'Oh, right,' Liberty scoffed. 'Like *that*'s gonna happen.'

'Read magazines, watch TV an' don't give her no sass,' Cindi ordered, bossy as ever. 'You know how the two of you get when you're together.'

'Sure,' Liberty said, although they both understood that it wasn't going to happen. She and her mom, Diahann, shared an extremely acrimonious relationship, a classic love-hate deal.

Liberty loved Diahann because she was warm and beautiful and, well . . . just because she was her mama.

She hated her because for the past ten years her mom had worked as Mr Red Diamond's housekeeper and sometime cook, and it infuriated Liberty that the woman had given up on her career as a jazz singer to become some cranky old white man's freakin' *maid*. It was totally beyond her comprehension. Why? That was the question that screamed in her head every time she thought about it. Why? Why? WHY?

Diahann's explanation was simple: 'We needed the money, child, and a place to live where I didn't have to struggle to make the rent every month. Singin' was takin' me nowhere, so I did the smart thing an' quit.'

'What about my daddy?' Liberty had asked. 'Why can't *he* look after us?'

As usual, Diahann stonewalled her, refusing to talk about who or where her father was. After a while she'd given up asking, and accepted the fact that she obviously didn't *have* a daddy.

Liberty was nine when they moved into Mr Red Diamond's house. Tall for her age and gawky, she hated leaving all her friends behind in Harlem, where they'd lived in a crowded housing complex.

It might've been crowded, but at least it was home, and she'd cried when they left. She'd been especially sad to say goodbye to Tony, the twelve-year-old Puerto Rican boy in the apartment next to theirs. Tony had helped her with her homework, taught her to pick at a guitar, and sometimes he'd taken her roller-blading in Central Park. She was only nine, but she'd known a good man when she saw one.

Moving to the heart of Manhattan had thrown her into a totally diverse environment. Everything was different, and although they had their own space – cramped as it was – they were living in someone else's house. A big old miserable dark house inhabited by a big old miserable rich man who had her mom running around like a chicken on crack. It was a disturbing change of lifestyle, especially when she attended her new school – a school filled with rich snobby white kids from affluent families, who treated her like crap because she wasn't the same as them. They soon let her know she had three strikes against her. Strike one: her mom worked as a housekeeper. Strike two: she had no father. Strike three: even though she didn't look it, she was black.

The kids at school never let her forget who she was and where she came from.

She rarely saw Mr Diamond, and when she did it was from a distance. Mama had warned her that he didn't want children around, so she was always to use the basement entrance and never venture upstairs. Which – being a curious child – she did, but only when she knew everyone was out because, apart from Mama, there was a butler – Mae, the cook – Kirsti, the laundress – and three maids who took care of cleaning the floors and all the other heavy work. At least Mama didn't have to do *that*.

Over time she'd explored every inch of the big dark house, starting with the huge kitchen filled with copper pots and pans hanging above two enormous granite islands, and the walk-in cupboards crammed with several different sets of delicate china. There was a walk-in pantry stacked with dozens of jars, cans and packets of food – enough for an army.

Next she'd moved onto the dining room, a stately expanse of carved wood furniture, crystal chandeliers, and a sideboard containing a pirate's booty of silver. Candlesticks, dishes and cutlery abounded in the felt-lined cupboards.

After a while she'd headed upstairs and inspected Mr Diamond's bedroom, another big dark room with two fireplaces and cold, hardwood floors. A large four-poster bed dominated. It was covered with fine linens and cashmere blankets.

His closet – as large as a room – had suits lined up like a regiment of soldiers. Shirts, crisp and white – more than a hundred. Sweaters, shoes, belts, ties. It was all too overwhelming, like being in a fancy department store. His bathroom was filled with many different kinds of lotions and grooming products, plus numerous bottles of pills that she didn't dare touch.

As the years passed, she'd often roamed around the old house whenever she was sure it was safe to do so. Sometimes she'd sit in the oak-panelled library, flicking through his collection of leatherbound books. Other times she'd attempted to teach herself the piano. One of her favourite things to do was make up lyrics to the songs she planned on writing one day. Young as she was, music was her passion.

One day she'd decided to curl up in the middle of his bed just to see what it felt like. She'd stretched out and lain down. The bed was *very* comfortable and roomy, soft too. She had pulled a cashmere blanket round her and promptly fallen asleep, only to be discovered an hour later by Mr Diamond himself.

'What the *hell* do you think you're doing?' he'd screamed, prodding her in the back with his steel-tipped ebony cane. 'Get out!' he'd yelled, red in the face. 'Get out of my room, you nasty little intruder. How *dare* you invade my privacy? Get the *hell* out!'

She was twelve and feisty, and in the three years of living in his house this was their first encounter. She had jumped off the bed, stuck out her tongue at him, and yelled defiantly, 'You don't scare *me*, old man.' Then she'd raced from the room.

That night a very distressed Mama said things were difficult with Mr Diamond and it was best if she went to live with her aunt Aretha and cousin Cindi for a short while. 'You'll be happier there,' Mama had said, staring at the floor. 'An' it'll only be until I can talk Mr Diamond into having you back.'

As if she had a choice.

'Cool with me,' Liberty had answered, holding back tears, because it really wasn't cool at all: she had no desire to be sent away. 'I hate it here, anyway,' she'd added defiantly. 'It stinks. An' I hate that horrible man you work for. *He* stinks. *I hate everything!*'

'Maybe in a few months you'll come back,' Mama had said, holding back tears of her own. 'Mr Diamond's not such a bad man, you'll see.'

'No, thanks!' she'd said fiercely. And she'd meant it.

Moving back to Harlem to live with her aunt and cousin turned out to be a pleasant surprise. They'd recently relocated to New York from their home in Atlanta after the death of Cindi's father. Aunt Aretha – her mother's sister – was the total opposite of Mama. Overweight, cheerful and full of laughter, Aretha worked in a cake factory and obviously enjoyed her job, especially the perks. Nobody was crazy enough to turn down free cakes and cookies, not in Aretha's world.

Cindi, who was three years older than Liberty, welcomed her like a sister. The two of them connected immediately, and for the first time since moving to Mr Diamond's house, Liberty felt like she had a family.

The really good news was that she got to go back to her old school and there was Tony, fifteen and more handsome than ever. The bad news was that he had a girlfriend, a skinny white girl with lank yellow hair and a gap between her front teeth.

Liberty confided her crush to Cindi, who immediately decided that the girlfriend presented no problem, and that they could easily do something about it. So, on Liberty's thirteenth birthday, Cindi helped fix her makeup and straighten her hair so that it wasn't a mass of unruly frizz. Next, Liberty put on her tightest T-shirt and skinniest jeans, adding a pair of high-heeled sandals, borrowed from Cindi, which were too big, but who cared? Then the two of them made their way to the bowling alley where Tony had a night-time job.

At thirteen Liberty was already a knock-out, and with the makeup, tight jeans and new 'do', she looked at least sixteen. Tony couldn't help but notice and, with a little coaching from Cindi on how to behave, Liberty got herself a boyfriend.

Cindi's coaching had included a lesson on how to give a boy oral sex. 'You don't have to screw 'em,' Cindi had informed her matter-of-factly. 'All you gotta do is give 'em a little of this,' she'd added, demonstrating with her generous mouth on a banana. 'Do it right, girl, an' the dude'll be yours for as long as you wanna keep him.'

I want to keep him forever, Liberty had thought, so she did as Cindi suggested, and Tony put up no objections.

Unfortunately, a year later Tony graduated from high school and moved to Miami with his mom, which was a big blow because having a boyfriend was a whole new deal: it had made Liberty feel important, like she mattered to someone.

After Tony left there was no stopping her. Getting boys was easy. Cindi was right: give 'em a few minutes of what they liked best, and they hung around until you were done with them. She soon became an expert at pleasing whichever boy she fancied. Oral sex was no big deal and, as President Clinton had informed the nation, it wasn't really sex.

She didn't get into the real deal until she was sixteen and fell madly in love with the lead singer in an amateur rock group. He was a white rapper from England who emulated Eminem. Skeleton thin, with piercing eyes and a tough demeanour, he soon had her totally hooked – not only sexually, but sometimes he let her sing with his group, a real high. He also encouraged her to keep writing her songs, which she did with great enthusiasm.

Once again she thought she'd found the perfect boy.

'Watch it, girl,' Cindi had warned her. 'Stud's a player – I'm on it every time.'

Liberty didn't care whether he was a player or not. He had her juices flowing – creative and otherwise – and that was enough.

But, of course, Cindi was right. He turned out to be just another bad boy, who gave her a dose of the crabs and left her for a skanky teenage stripper with huge fake boobs.

She never did move back to the Diamond mansion, although Mama asked her to on many occasions. It was more real hanging with her aunt and cousin, both of whom enjoyed having her around.

Mama visited once a week on Sunday, her day off. Sometimes Liberty felt that Aretha was her mom, and her real mom was just a distant relative, someone she didn't know that well. Aretha was nurturing and caring, showering both girls with equal amounts of love.

Now, seven years after leaving, she found herself stuck in her mama's cramped apartment with a sprained ankle and a burned arm.

Great! She could just imagine the lectures she would have to endure for the next few days.

It simply wasn't fair.

Surely it was time she scored a break?

Chapter Six

After settling into Sam's apartment, Jett started making calls. After a three-year absence he wasn't planning on spending his first night back in New York hanging out by himself, especially with the thought of seeing Red early in the morning looming over him. Dear old Dad. What a trip *he* was.

In a way Jett was wary of a face-to-face. On the other hand, what the fuck? He was no longer a snivelling little kid lurking in the background, waiting for his father to beat the shit out of him. Screw Red Diamond. He could handle anything the old man dished out.

Checking out his Palm, he avoided calling any of his former pals who, at the time he'd left, had been heavily into the drug scene. This didn't leave him with many options, but after a couple of calls he connected with Beverly, a striking make-up artist originally from Guiana. Beverly was an ex-girlfriend of Sam's, and she'd been in on his intervention.

'How're you *doin'*?' she asked, sounding as if she might really care.

'Not too bad,' he replied. 'Thanks to you and Sam and a few others who gave a fast crap whether I lived or died.'

'Hey, you were *such* a screw-up we *needed* to get you outta here.'

'Don't remind me.' He groaned, not anxious to revisit old memories. There were too many, and they were too embarrassing.

'Okay, okay,' Beverly said, laughing. 'I won't go there.'

'Thanks.'

'Anyway, word is you're doin' fine in Italy, so it all worked out.'

'Yeah, mainly 'cause of you,' he said gratefully, for it was Beverly who had arranged the introduction to the Italian modelling agency who'd signed him.

'It was your time to catch a break, an' I'm psyched it happened for you,' Beverly said warmly.

'I guess this means I owe you, so I was thinking that maybe I can buy you dinner tonight. Like an old-friends kinda deal.'

'Me and my new guy?'

'There's a new guy?'

'Honey, there's *always* a guy. An' you'll like him.'

'I will?'

'Would I stick us with a dud?' she said playfully.

'It's happened,' he countered.

'How would *you* know?' she said, laughing again. 'You were always so outta it . . .'

'Hey, Bev, I might've been stoned, but there's certain things a person never forgets.'

'Okay, okay,' she admitted, 'there could've bin a couple of short-term losers.'

'A *couple*?' he exclaimed, snorting with laughter.

'Thanks, Jett,' she said, mock-serious. 'But I gotta tell you – this one's a keeper.'

'Bring him. Where d'you wanna go?'

'How about Il Cantinori, eight thirty?' she suggested. 'Remember Il Cantinori?'

'Sure,' he said ruefully. 'I only hope they don't remember me. I gotta sneaking suspicion I wrecked the place one night.'

'You did. But Frank, the owner, is a cool guy, so don't sweat it. Besides, you're with me,' Beverly said confidently, adding casually, 'Anyway, that was then, this is now – an' you're a changed person. Right, baby?'

'You'd better believe it.'

He clicked off his cell and thought about calling Max or Chris. Then he decided, why do that? He'd barely heard from either of them since their father's seventy-fifth birthday cele-bration four years ago when he'd *really* been out of his mind and embarrassed everyone with his behaviour. Shit! Falling into a three-tier cake with an under-age Puerto Rican hooker he'd picked up on the street was truly not the way to go. Especially with his pants off.

Thinking back, he considered it quite funny, although he would bet money his family didn't. They were probably *still* talking about his bad behaviour.

Well, they'd be shocked tomorrow when the new, sober, semi-successful-in-a-career-they-wouldn't-approve-of Jett showed up.

Yeah. He was certainly going to surprise everyone.

* * *

Max wondered if being summoned to his father's house had anything to do with his upcoming wedding. Probably not. He'd done the proper thing and sent Red and Lady Jane Bentley an invitation. So far he had received no response. He wasn't surprised: it was just like Red to be rude – the old man had no manners. Of course Red *would* come, but because of who he was he didn't feel it necessary to reply.

Red Diamond was a much-married lecherous snake who'd managed to get rid of each of his wives as soon as he was ready to move on. Max often wondered about the demise of his own mother, Rachel. She'd given birth to him, and apparently died of heart failure six months later in her sleep. A perfectly healthy woman, twenty-six years of age. Max wasn't sure he believed it. A vibrant young woman with no health problems. How had something like that happened?

Sometimes, late at night, the thought crossed Max's mind that maybe Red was in some way responsible. But then he always dismissed it as impossible. Red couldn't possibly be *that* bad.

Or could he?

After Rachel's death, Red had married another beauty, Olivia, and she'd given birth to Chris. The new marriage hadn't stopped him screwing around, for when it came to sex, Red was insatiable, preying on any woman he could. Eventually he'd divorced Olivia and married Jett's mother,

Edie, whom he'd managed to turn into a raging alcoholic.

Quite frankly, Max didn't give a damn if Red showed up at his wedding or not. Why should he allow Amy to be contaminated? His bride-to-be had yet to meet the snake – what a treat *she* had waiting for her.

Nancy Scott-Simon was outraged at Red Diamond's lack of manners. 'How am I supposed to seat your father and Lady Jane?' she'd demanded, glaring at her soon-to-be son-in-law. 'And what about the rehearsal dinner? Will your father be giving one since *I* am handling the wedding?'

'No rehearsal dinner,' Max had said at first. But Nancy was having none of it, so to keep the peace he'd arranged to give it himself. He was taking over a room at the Waldorf Astoria, and a hundred and fifty people were attending on Sunday night. He had *not* invited Red or Lady Jane, deeming it unnecessary.

Tomorrow night was his bachelor party. There was nothing he looked forward to less.

* * *

Birdy Marvel was pretty in a trashy, vacuous way. Petite and stacked, she was only just eighteen, and an idol to the entire teenage female population. Her records sold in the millions, and her fans faithfully followed everything she did. There was an elite group of young girl singers – Britney, Hilary, Lindsay, and the Olsen twins, but right now Birdy Marvel was top of the heap.

When Birdy was sixteen, Chris had guided her through the process of becoming emancipated from her parents. Young as she was, Birdy could be a sharp number: she'd been singing and dancing since she was eight, and felt – quite rightly – that her parents were frittering away her millions on themselves.

Chris had won her the freedom she desired, and along the way he'd negotiated ten per cent of her future earnings.

Birdy had helped make him rich, and he'd helped her career soar.

Problem was, rich didn't last when he blew most of his money at the gaming tables in Vegas.

Birdy had her own problems. She was a little coke freak who loved to party and get down and dirty. She coupled those dangerous habits with a knack for always picking the wrong men. Birdy had an eye for bad boys who treated her like crap. Her current companion was Rocky, a biker she'd picked up on the beach in Santa Monica. Recently she'd given him the title of tour executive, and insisted that he was paid a generous salary.

Coke supplier might have been a better title.

Rocky went everywhere she did. With his shaved head, black leather outfits, chains, and muscled arms, tattooed from his fingers to his massive shoulders, he was quite a menacing figure. The tabloids were having a blast with this one: there were new outrageous headlines every week. Birdy didn't seem to mind the headlines calling her everything from a white-trash princess to a teenage tramp. 'Any publicity is good publicity,' she warbled, quoting her brain-dead PR, who also happened to be her second cousin.

Birdy greeted Chris at the party in a stoned state. For an eighteen-year-old she sure looked rough, in spite of a dressed-to-thrill outfit of micro-mini, red leather bustier that concealed little, major midriff action with a diamond navel piercing, and short white go-go boots. Her hair was in its usual tousled state, lips sticky with pink gloss, eyes rimmed with jet black kohl, and she was chewing gum – another of her addictions. He noticed that she'd added a couple of new tattoos. A small dove on her left shoulder, and a skull and crossbones on her exposed hip-bone.

Chris always had to remind himself that she was only eighteen, and would grow out of this rebellious stage. He tried to protect her as best he could, but as her lawyer he could only do so much.

'Chris!' she yelled, running over and hugging him. 'I'm totally psyched you made it! Wasn't the show, like, *amazing*?'

'Amazing,' he agreed.

'Like, what a wild audience, huh? Totally out there.'

'Dynamite.'

'I'm *so* happy you're here,' she cooed, grabbing his hand and squeezing it hard. 'There's something we gotta talk about.'

'Now?'

'Yeah, but it's personal stuff,' she said, edging closer. 'Which means we gotta hang somewhere private.'

No chance of that since, as usual, Birdy Marvel was the centre of attention. Several photographers were busy catching her every move, while Rocky hovered nearby, eyeing Chris suspiciously. He didn't like Chris. The feeling was mutual.

'Where are you staying?' Chris asked his young client.

'Trump International. Oh, yeah, an' I'm thinking of buying a condo in the Time Warner building. Wouldn't *that* be like the *coolest*? The views are to *die* for!'

Yeah, Chris thought. *I'm sure Rocky would love it.* 'I'll try to come by sometime tomorrow afternoon,' he said. 'That way you can tell me what's going on without an audience.'

'That'd be totally awesome.' Then, lowering her voice, she added, 'Not a word to Rocky. Like, call me on my cell an' we'll fix a time.'

'Trouble in Bikerland?' he asked, hoping she was about to dump the overgrown biker.

'No, silly!' She giggled, rubbing the tip of her snub nose with a stubby finger. 'Rocky is like *totally* the most awesome dude on the planet.'

'*I* believe you,' Chris said drily. 'Thousands wouldn't.'

'Don't be so mean,' she said, giggling again. 'He's a real hottie.'

'We'll catch up tomorrow,' Chris said, not wishing to get into a discussion about how hot Rocky was.

'Promise?' she said, fidgeting like an anxious little kid.

'Absolutely.'

He already had his day planned. The meeting with Red in the morning. Lunch with a client. A couple more meetings. Dinner with another client. Then on Saturday morning he'd catch an early flight back to L.A. And on Sunday, Vegas.

It was all work. He could handle it.

Chapter Seven

With her wedding only a week away, Amy's co-workers at Courtenelli had decided she needed one wild night out on the town. She'd tried to put them off, but they were having none of it. 'You're getting *married*,' Yolanda, a big-bosomed Latina brunette, informed her. 'We have to *celebrate*.'

'Yes,' agreed Dana, a curvaceous redhead with a sexy overbite. 'You can't get hitched without a bachelorette night. It's tradition.'

'And don't think,' Yolanda interrupted, 'that your intended is not going to have himself a bachelor night. An' those things get *wild*. Strippers, hookers, all *kinda* slutlings.'

'Slutlings?' Amy said, frowning. 'What are *they*?'

'Girls from hell!' Dana joked. 'An engaged woman's worst nightmare!'

'You guys are so cynical,' Amy said, shaking her head. 'Believe me, Max is not like that.'

'Oh, *sure*,' Yolanda and Dana chorused together, both rolling their eyes. 'He's a *man*, isn't he? He's got a *dick*, hasn't he?'

At that moment Sofia Courtenelli appeared. In the over-crowded field of fashion, Sofia Courtenelli was a star. Chic and no-nonsense, she was in her early fifties, well preserved, with pale copper hair worn in a severe bob, skilfully applied dramatic eye make-up and a permanent St. Tropez tan. Although Sofia was a hard worker, she still managed to spend most weekends either in the South of France or the Hamptons, depending on the season. Sofia was a party animal.

'Amy!' she said imperiously, snapping her fingers, showing

off silver nail polish and an assortment of diamond rings. 'Follow me.'

'Yes, Miz Courtenelli,' Amy said, trailing her boss into Sofia's luxuriously appointed office.

'Sit down,' Sofia commanded, waving her towards an over-stuffed gold-lacquered chair with leopard-print upholstery and ornate carved legs.

Amy sat, wondering what was on the agenda. She didn't usually get a one-on-one with her glamorous and somewhat intimidating boss.

'Is true you getting married?' Sofia said, in her low-down, slightly accented voice. Amy nodded. 'To Max Diamond?'

'That's right,' Amy agreed, wondering what was coming next.

'Hmm . . .' Sofia murmured, picking up a silver Cartier pen and tapping it impatiently on her Roman marble desk-top. 'He is quite the catch, no?'

Amy wasn't sure what she was supposed to say, so she mumbled a quick 'Thank you.'

'Is good,' Sofia said, nodding to herself.

'Uh . . . yes.'

'Maybe I come to the wedding,' Sofia added casually, as if it had only just occurred to her.

Oh, crap, they hadn't sent her an invitation, even though Nancy had wanted to. Amy had thought having her boss there would be too nerve-racking. Now she had no choice. 'Uh . . . we'd love you to come,' she lied, quick as a flash.

'*Bene*,' Sofia said, twirling a trio of thin diamond bracelets on her tanned and slightly scrawny wrist. 'I bring Carlo.'

Everyone knew about Sofia's toy-boys. She had a line-up she paraded to various events, and Carlo was currently her number-one pick. Lean and lizard-like, twenty-two-year-old Carlo was a raging bisexual. Apparently this didn't bother Sofia, as it was rumoured she was into girls as well as toy-boys, so why *would* it matter?

'That's great,' Amy said, trying to sound enthusiastic.

Oh, God, her mother was going to kill her: this would definitely screw up Nancy's extremely well-thought-out seating arrangements.

51

'And who make your dress?' Sofia inquired, her mild tone hiding a sudden flash of annoyance as she realized it obviously wasn't the House of Courtenelli.

'Uh . . . Valentino,' Amy muttered. 'My mother—'

'No need to explain,' Sofia said, holding up an authoritative diamond beringed hand. 'Although – how you say? – press-wise, is bad thing you not ask *me*.'

'My mother—' Amy began.

Sofia cut her off again. '*Prego*, dear,' she said dismissively, indicating the door. 'We speak enough.'

Amy slunk out. Of course, Sofia Courtenelli was right. She *should*'ve invited her to the wedding, *and* asked her to design the dress, instead of listening to her mother, who'd *insisted* on Valentino, a close personal friend.

Too late now.

Amy hoped this little breach of etiquette hadn't put her job in jeopardy. Even though she was getting married, she planned on continuing to work. She and Max had not discussed it, but she saw no reason for him to object.

Later that day she had lunch with Tina, her best friend from college. Tina, a petite brunette, was happily pregnant with the enviable glow that many pregnant women project. Married for two years to Brad, a commodities dealer, Tina was excited about her baby, due in a couple of weeks.

The two of them went to downtown Cipriani, where Amy told Tina about her uncomfortable meeting with Sofia Courtenelli, before seguing onto the offer she'd received of a bachelorette party from her co-workers, and how she really didn't want one.

'Yes!' Tina said, thumping the table with her fist. 'It's a *fabulous* idea. You *need* to cut loose – you're way too uptight.'

'Me?'

'Yes, you.'

Amy wrinkled her nose. '*Thanks.*'

'Come *on*, Amy, get real, you're marrying a man you haven't even *slept* with. How weird is *that*?'

'Shout a little louder,' Amy said, glancing around the restaurant. 'The person at the corner table didn't hear you.'

'Listen to me,' Tina said, lowering her voice. 'What if Max is a dud in bed? You wouldn't even *know*.'

'Yes, I would,' Amy answered stubbornly. 'I *certainly* would.'

'How?' Tina persisted, leaning her elbows on the table and staring at her best friend.

'I might be the last virgin in Manhattan, but I've had my experiences.'

'Neckin' ain't fuckin',' Tina said succinctly, putting on a loud Brooklyn accent.

'You are *so* crass,' Amy said, once more darting her eyes around the restaurant to see who'd overheard *that* little gem.

'You have *no* idea how crass I can be,' Tina said, breaking into laughter.

'Oh, yes, I do,' Amy retorted, nibbling on a breadstick. 'We were college room-mates, remember?'

'How could I ever forget? That first year you were a total pain.'

'So were you.'

'No, I wasn't,' Tina objected, shaking her head. 'I was merely trying to figure you out. You were *so* introverted. It wasn't until you told me about the kidnapping thing—'

'Don't!' Amy interrupted. 'I confided that in strict confidence, and I never want to talk about it again.'

'You should've seen a therapist,' Tina said. 'I don't understand your mother . . .'

'That's okay' Amy said dryly. 'Nobody does, including me.'

'Look, here's the deal,' Tina said, tapping her fingers on the table. 'I adore my husband – Brad's the best. But I have to tell you, there are times I kind of wish I'd experimented more before getting married. Y' know, put myself out there and gone wild.'

'Really?' Amy said, surprised. 'But you and Brad are such a fantastic couple. You never fight, you're always in sync, you—'

'Yeah, yeah,' Tina interrupted, feigning a yawn. 'We're perfect, and I would *never* cheat on Brad. However,' she added pointedly, '*you*'ve still got a window of opportunity, and in view of your sexual history – or non-history – it's kind of important you don't rush into marriage with absolutely *no* experience. So . . . my advice is that you should put yourself out there and have a quick fling. As long as you're careful, you've got nothing to lose.'

'You can't be serious,' Amy said, frowning. 'It would be—'

'It's not as if I'm suggesting a relationship,' Tina said, interrupting again. 'More like, y' know, a sexy one-nighter.'

'Tina! You're out of control!'

'C'mon, sweetie,' Tina cajoled. 'If you don't do something wild now, you'll *never* know, and that would be sad.'

'What if I don't *want* to know?' Amy said, trying to convince herself how wrong Tina was. 'What if I'm perfectly happy with the way things are?'

'The least you can do is think about it,' Tina said, teasingly adding, 'Who knows? You might even enjoy it.'

On her way back to the office Amy couldn't help thinking over Tina's outlandish suggestions. A quick fling. A sexy one-nighter. It *so* wasn't her. And yet . . .

The next day her friends at work were all over her about the bachelorette party. Finally she'd agreed, just to shut them up.

Tonight was the night.

In a way she was dreading it.

On the other hand – why *not* have some fun? Like Tina said, she might even enjoy it.

Chapter Eight

'Lookin' *good*, my man,' Beverly exclaimed, hands on hips. '*Real* good.'

Jett grinned at his old friend. 'And you – what can I say? You're *still* the hottest babe in New York.'

'Yeah, not bad for an old bag,' she said wryly. 'I'm gonna be thirty any minute. Freakin' *thirty*! How is that possible?'

'I heard tell thirty is the new thirteen,' he said, winking at her.

'Stoned or sober, you always *did* know the right thing to say,' she replied, indicating her companion, a thin white dude with a scraggly beard and long hair pulled back in a ponytail, very nineteen-seventies. 'Meet my man, Chet, he's a musician.'

'Hey!' Jett said, holding out his hand.

Chet responded with a hostile nod.

Beverly gave an amused laugh. 'He thinks we fucked,' she said, quite unperturbed. 'Keep on telling him we didn't.'

'Hey, man, I can *promise* you we didn't,' Jett assured Chet, whose sour expression remained the same.

Dinner was all about catching up. Beverly wanted to hear everything about his stay in Italy, so over a good old American steak and a side of fries, he filled her in.

Chet did not appear to be the talkative type. He sat at the table totally silent, until Jett got him discussing his music. Then, finally, he warmed up. It turned out he was a session musician who'd jammed with Springsteen and the Stones. He was also in AA, so they bonded over that, and by the time Beverly suggested they drop by Gatsby's – *the* hot new club –

55

they were not exactly close but at least they were having a conversation.

In the cab on the way to Gatsby's, Jett changed his mind. 'Y' know, I'm feeling kinda jet-lagged,' he said, stretching his arms and yawning. 'You two go have a blast. I'm gonna bail.'

'No way!' Beverly insisted, giving him a playful punch in the chest. 'You're comin', I insist.'

'Gimme a break,' he said weakly. 'It's five a.m. Milan time. And my girlfriend gave me *some* sweet send-off.'

'Too bad,' Beverly responded, refusing to take no for an answer. 'Consider this your welcome-back party. You are *not* bailing!'

'I'm not, huh?'

'Like I said – no way.'

He grinned and reached for a cigarette. 'Guess I'm coming.'

She grinned back. 'Guess you are.'

Beverly knew the doorman at Gatsby's. She sashayed over to the menacing-looking man, gave him a big hug, a kiss on the cheek, and he ushered them into the club past a milling crowd of wannabes. The scene reminded Jett of the old days when he'd been on familiar terms with every doorman and bouncer in town. They'd all known him. They hadn't all welcomed him.

Man, he'd been thrown out of more places . . .

But things were different now. He was in control and he had to admit it was a pretty nice feeling.

* * *

Any excuse and Mariska was on the phone. 'Lulu has a temperature and she wishes to see you,' his ex-wife informed him.

Max stifled his aggravation. It was late and he did not relish going out again. 'I'll come by in the morning,' he said stiffly.

'That is not good enough.' Mariska sniffed. 'Your daughter wants to see you *now*.'

He knew that Mariska was hoping he was lying in bed next to his fiancée. Anything she could do to disrupt his relationship with Amy was okay with her.

Well, too bad, he wasn't. He and Amy did not live together. They had not even had sex. Amy wanted to wait until they were married, and he respected her for that. A girl with morals. It made a refreshing change from the usual social piranhas who chased after him for his money, hot to score a rich husband.

'Okay,' he muttered.

'Okay *what?*'

'I'll be there in fifteen minutes.'

'I would think so,' Mariska said, in the superior tone he hated.

Mariska was extremely fond of getting the last word. It didn't bother him because he was used to it, although after he and Amy were married, things would have to change. No more phone calls in the middle of the night unless it was an absolute emergency. His ex-wife would soon learn that he was no longer available.

He buzzed down to the garage to have his car brought up, not pleased to have to go out, but concerned about Lulu. After calling for his car, he wondered if he should speak to his personal physician or wait until he saw his little daughter, then decided it was best to wait. Damnit, this was so inconvenient.

Mariska greeted him at the door to her apartment clad in a diaphanous negligee and high-heeled mules trimmed with fur. She was perfectly made up as usual, her shoulder-length flaxen hair straight and shiny.

It occurred to Max that she was still a very attractive woman, so why couldn't she find a man to take her off his hands? It shouldn't be *that* hard.

Unfortunately he knew the reason only too well. She had no desire to become involved with anyone because she would never relinquish the title of Mrs Maxwell Diamond. It gave her the cachet she required. Social acceptance was of utmost importance to Mariska, and even though she was the *ex*-Mrs Diamond, in her world it still counted.

'How's Lulu?' he asked, stepping inside the marble foyer.

'Asleep,' Mariska replied, unfazed. 'You cannot disturb her.'

'What do you mean, I can't disturb her?' he said brusquely. 'You told me she *had* to see me.'

'Unfortunately you took too long,' Mariska replied, steely-eyed as usual. 'It is good she is sleeping.'

He wanted to slap her face. He wanted to put his hand-print on that creamy white skin and make his mark.

But he didn't. He kept his temper in check. This move was typical of Mariska, so he wasn't surprised. 'I'll go take a look at her,' he said, attempting to move past his ex-wife.

'No,' Mariska said, blocking his way. 'You'll wake her. You know what a light sleeper she is.'

'Of course I know,' he said shortly. 'She's my daughter, isn't she.'

It was a statement, not a question. So when Mariska murmured a sly 'Maybe,' Max was shocked. 'What did you say?' he demanded.

'I said maybe you should go home now,' Mariska said, turning away from him.

But the damage had been done.

Max left her apartment in a fury, the seeds of doubt firmly planted.

*　*　*

As soon as he could get away with it, Chris ducked out of Birdy's party and headed over to Elaine's, where he joined up with his one writer client, Gregory Dark – a grizzled bear of a man who specialized in writing gritty crime stories based loosely on fact. Three of Gregory's books had been made into successful movies, and Chris was currently negotiating a major new deal for him at Universal.

Gregory was English, overweight and pushing sixty. He had rheumy eyes that had experienced a thousand hang-overs and a shock of startlingly thick white hair. He spent half his time in Hollywood, where he kept a Malibu beach house and the requisite blonde girlfriend, and the other half in Manhattan, where he inhabited a book-filled apartment with his crabby, lesbian-inclined wife.

Gregory was an old-school type guy. He was into drinking

Jack Daniel's, smoking strong Cuban cigars and showing off his extensive gun collection.

'Have a drink,' Gregory said, in a deep whisky-soaked voice. He was sitting with a couple of cronies – one of them a former police captain. 'How's the shifting shit in California?'

Gregory always made out that he was not a fan of L.A. However, he seemed very happy when he was lounging on the deck of his six-million-dollar house in the Malibu Colony with his blonde babe by his side, and movie stars as his neighbours.

'We're making progress on the new deal,' Chris said, pulling up a chair. 'Should have contracts for you to look over in the next couple of weeks.'

'Cannot wait, dear boy,' Gregory drawled sarcastically. 'This time I want *everything*.'

'You'll get it,' Chris said, ordering Scotch in a tall glass with a lot of ice. He'd learned how to keep up with Gregory's drinking habits and still look as if he was imbibing. Ice was the secret. Plenty of it.

'Excellent,' boomed Gregory, and, turning to his friends, 'This boy is the best.'

Chris did not appreciate being called 'boy', but he knew it was just Gregory's way, and since the old guy was such a big-bucks client, what did he care?

After two drinks he made his exit and took a cab back to the Four Seasons. On the way he called one of his assistants in L.A., and listened while Andy filled him in on the day's business. Nothing he couldn't deal with on his return to L.A. No major problems, although there was always *something* going on.

Tomorrow morning he'd see his father, and maybe by the time he left New York, he'd be a hell of a lot richer.

Chapter Nine

In a way Diahann Dozier dreaded spending the weekend with her daughter. Whenever they got together there was always a fight involved. Liberty had never really forgiven her for abandoning a going-nowhere singing career and settling for a steady income with a permanent home.

Diahann was well aware that her daughter considered her job as Mr Diamond's housekeeper demeaning and beneath her. But Liberty was only nineteen and had no idea of what life was all about or how hard it could be. She'd learn soon enough the difficulties of being out there on your own, especially for a woman with a baby to support.

Diahann sighed. Liberty was a beautiful girl, stunning in fact, so if she was smart she'd find herself a decent man and settle down. Enough of this I-want-a-career nonsense. Diahann knew well enough how hopeless it was chasing dreams that never materialized.

Over the years she'd made it her business to discourage her daughter as much as she could, which wasn't easy, because Liberty was a stubborn girl and there was no getting through to her. Plus she *was* talented, but Diahann knew that talent wasn't enough to get you where you wanted to go. There were too many pretty girls with talent who were prepared to do anything to make it. Unfortunately doing anything didn't guarantee a thing. Luck and timing was what it was all about. Finding the right mentor who believed in you and worked steadily to build your career.

Diahann sighed again. Mariah Carey was a shining example of luck and timing. If the famous singer hadn't met Tommy

Mottola, and if the powerful record mogul hadn't decided to create a star . . .

Diahann made her way downstairs to her basement apartment in Mr Diamond's brownstone, thinking that she was happy to have her daughter home – if only for a few days. On the other hand, Liberty would probably be full of criticisms and snippy remarks – unless she'd changed, which was highly unlikely.

It would be so nice if they could get along for once. But Liberty harboured too many issues, and Diahann was wise enough to realize that she was asking the impossible to expect her daughter not to get on her case.

* * *

The afternoon dragged by. Unused to doing nothing, Liberty found herself severely bored. She thought about working on one of her songs – there were several unfinished lyrics she was desperate to complete. Then she decided it wouldn't fly. She had to be in the mood to write: it was impossible to just pick up a pen and create magic.

Too bad. She wished she could. She wished many things – number one being she wished she had a father.

Fact of life: according to Mama, she didn't. For Mama refused to discuss who her father was, and no amount of questioning had ever produced results. Even Aretha had no clue who that man might be. 'Your mama never told no one nothin',' Aretha had informed Liberty, when she'd first moved in. 'Lil' sis left home when she was sixteen to chase some kinda singin' deal in New York, an' a few years later, when she got herself knocked up, she never told no one back in Atlanta. She must've bin doin' okay, 'cause she had you all by herself, raised you till she sent you t' me, never got married, an' we never heard nothin' regardin' no steady man. 'Course, your mama's always bin private 'bout things, that's her way. We're sisters, only we ain't that close.'

Liberty had listened carefully, for this was more information than Diahann had ever confided. 'Why do you think she gave it all up and started working as a maid?' she'd asked.

'Gave up *what*, sweet thing?' Aretha had answered, exasperated. 'From everythin' *I* heard she was strugglin' from week to week tryin't' make a livin' singin' in all kinda dives. A steady job along with some place to live must've seemed pretty damn nice. No rent. No worries. An' let me set you straight, she be that man's *housekeeper*, not his maid.'

'Same thing,' Liberty had muttered.

'No, it ain't,' Aretha had argued. 'It's not like she's down on her hands an' knees scrubbin' the old dude's crapper.'

Liberty often thought about the possibilities of who her father was. Before they'd moved into Mr Diamond's house Mama had entertained plenty of boyfriends. She remembered one man in particular: his name was Leon and he was tall (she was tall), he had artistic hands (so did she) and, like Mama, he was a singer. As far as she could recall he'd moved in for a while when she was five, and treated her as if she was *his* kid. He'd taken her on long walks through Central Park, visits to the zoo and, best of all, every Saturday afternoon he'd sat her down and let her listen to all his favourite recording artists. Marvin Gaye, Smokey Robinson, the Temptations, Gladys Knight. She'd *loved* it. By the time she was seven she was familiar with all the soul greats and, to the amusement of the grown-ups, she could manage a fair imitation of Diana Ross or Patti LaBelle.

Sometimes, as a special treat, Leon and Mama would sing a duet, and she'd sit watching them, totally enthralled, thinking that they sure made a handsome couple, and they sounded wonderful.

Leon had lived with them for a couple of years, until one night Liberty had woken up to a fierce amount of screaming and yelling, and in the morning Leon was packed up and gone.

Looking back, she'd realized that his skin was very black, and so was her mama's. *Her* skin was light, a creamy milk chocolate, so she'd finally reached the regretful conclusion that Leon couldn't possibly be her dad. This saddened her, but there was nothing she could do about it.

One memorable day, shortly before she was banished from Mr Diamond's house, Mama had stood her in front of the bathroom mirror and lectured her about the colour of her skin. 'See that face starin' back at you?' Mama had said sternly. 'That's a black face, girl. Black. You hear me?'

'Yes, Mama,' she'd said, frightened by the intensity in her mother's tone.

'There's a lot of prejudice in this discriminating world we live in, an' society will see you as black, so you'd better know it now.'

'I do, Mama,' she'd whispered.

'Then tell me.'

'I'm black.'

'That's right, an' don't you *ever* forget it. 'Cause even though you're light-skinned an' could pass if you wanted, the truth will always come out.'

'Yes, Mama.'

'You're a smart girl, you can do anything you set your heart on. Don't *ever* let being black hold you back.'

'I won't.'

She'd felt bold that day – after all, it was her *right* to know. 'Was my daddy a white man, Mama?' she'd asked, holding her breath. It was not the first time she'd asked that question, but this time she'd hoped for an answer.

Diahann had frowned, rolled her eyes, and muttered something about it didn't matter, her daddy wasn't around, never had been, and Liberty should stop asking about him.

Great! Going through life without knowing. It wasn't fair. She was entitled to the information, and today, trapped in her mama's apartment, she was determined to find out.

After all, it wasn't as if she was twelve anymore. She was nineteen, and her mother better respect the fact that she needed to know the truth.

Chapter Ten

A my was happily doing all the things she never usually
got to do, such as smoking weed, getting drunk on
double lychee martinis, screaming at the trio of male
strippers her best friends had thoughtfully provided, and
generally letting loose.

Usually she was such a 'good girl', a dedicated worker,
a credit to her well-connected family. Tonight she was a 'wild
girl', egged on by her hard-living friends. Tonight she'd
decided to forget about the past experiences that had always
held her back, and go for it.

The strippers were a trip – three brawny Australian lads
with bulging thigh muscles, lusty smiles and six-pack abs.
Much to the girls' delight, they were not shy about taking
everything off. While one of them gave Amy a dangerously
intimate lap-dance, Tina snapped pictures with her digital
camera. The girls were screaming with laughter.

Amy was screaming along with them. She was having a
great time, the best time she'd had in months, what with all
the wedding preparations wearing her down.

After a couple of hours in a private room at Gatsby's,
Yolanda suggested they move into the main club where Usher
was rapping on the sound system about women and sex and
betrayal, and the place was jammed with a writhing, sweating
crowd intent on chilling out to the loud music.

'Order another drink,' encouraged Yolanda, as they all
squeezed onto the leather banquette in a corner booth.

'Yeah,' agreed Carolee, a frighteningly thin Courtenelli
house model. 'You gotta get wrecked, like, *really*.'

'I *am* wrecked,' Amy protested, with a small drunken giggle. 'Anymore lychee martinis and I'm throwing up all over some lucky person.'

'Maybe *him*,' Dana said, with a sly glance at the ridiculously handsome man lounging in the adjoining booth. He was accompanied by a stunning six-foot-tall black woman, and a skinny white man with a ponytail.

'Wow!' whispered Tina, leaning forward and checking out the good-looking one. 'Now he's *hot*!'

'Stop!' Amy admonished. 'You're married *and* pregnant, so cool down.'

'I can look, can't I?' Tina asked innocently. 'And may I remind you that *you* can do *more* than look.'

'Shut up!' Amy giggled, thinking that it was about time she downed a cup of strong black coffee before she slid under the table.

And yet why would she do that when she was having so much fun?

* * *

Lounging in a booth at Gatsby's, Jett was feeling relaxed, even though he was not drinking or doing drugs. Both activities were strictly off his agenda, but he felt mellow and chilled out all the same. Sometimes you just had to suck it up and realize there were things you couldn't do. He'd learned his lessons the hard way, and now he didn't miss it. No alcohol. No drugs. He understood he was an addict, therefore he had to resist. Pretty simple, really.

Sipping Diet Coke, he checked out the action. There was plenty going on. The dance-floor was alive with beautiful, sexy women. He glanced over at Chet, who was chain-smoking French cigarettes, while Beverly was busy chatting to a group of girls in the next booth. Before long he found himself joining in the conversation.

It was a kick talking to a bunch of females who actually spoke his language. Three years in Italy was a long time to be away, and the truth was he'd missed America and all it had to offer.

After a while he realized that one girl in particular kept catching his attention. She was a real knock-out in a Reese Witherspoon, Gwyneth Paltrow kind of way. She had that silky blonde hair, shy-smile thing going. And the most appealing eyes. So all-American. So pretty. So nice.

As the evening progressed, he found himself becoming more and more attracted to her, and even though she was drinking along with the others, he sensed there was something different about her. Not only was she insanely pretty, but he couldn't help noticing that she had a great body – and great bodies were his speciality.

It didn't take long for his jet-lag to vanish. Leaning over he asked her if she wanted to hit the dance-floor.

She was about to say no, but a drunken shove from one of her friends persuaded her to get up.

Grabbing her hand, he led her onto the crowded floor and they started to dance.

As if on cue, the disc jockey switched from Outkast to a slow Marc Anthony salsa beat. Not about to miss the opportunity, Jett pulled her close. 'So . . . uh . . . what're you girls doing out by yourselves?' he asked, inhaling her perfume, a mixture of fresh soap and seductive Angel. 'Is this a no-boyfriend night?'

'Somebody's getting married,' Amy murmured, feeling surprisingly comfortable in his arms.

'Not you, I hope,' he joked, pulling her even closer.

And she smiled.

They stayed on the dance-floor a long time before he managed to steer her over to the other side, away from her friends. Out of sight, he edged her into a corner and began kissing her.

'You'd better stop that,' she murmured, attempting to push him away.

'Why?' he said teasingly. 'You're not into kissing?'

'I . . . uh . . .'

He pulled her close again and kissed her some more. This time she didn't push him away. She had soft lips, so soft and inviting that he felt the beginning of a hard-on just kissing her.

Amy was as into it as he was. Earlier she'd smoked a joint,

drunk too much, and now her inhibitions were at a dangerously low level. Besides, this guy was *so* good-looking, with
his tousled dirty blond hair and mesmerizing blue eyes. Maybe
Tina was right. One last fling . . .

'Let's get out of here,' he whispered in her ear, after
twenty minutes of serious tongue action.

'I . . . I don't know you,' she responded, feeling confused
and excited but becoming more turned on by the minute.

'Hey – I don't know you either,' he said, caressing her silky
blonde hair. 'But, believe me, I'd like to.'

'Yes?' she asked tentatively, shivering slightly.

'You bet,' he said, kissing her again.

She felt dizzy. Soon she'd be a married woman. Forever
faithful. No more opportunities to explore.

Only right now she was single, free, she didn't have
to answer to anyone, and this might be her last chance to
do something totally out of character. Something completely
and utterly crazy.

Tina *was* right. One wild fling before the doors of
matrimony closed and she became the good, faithful wife.

'Where are you taking me?' she whispered, feeling light-
headed and suddenly quite bold as he steered her towards the
exit.

'I'll think of somewhere,' he answered, a strong possessive
arm firmly round her narrow waist.

Outside on the street he waved down a cab and bundled
her inside.

'And we're going where?' she asked breathlessly.

'Now, now, don't get paranoid, I'm not kidnapping you,'
he joked.

'That's not funny,' she said, sinking back against the
cracked leather seat, quickly shutting out the bad memories
that threatened to flood back.

He didn't get it. Of course he didn't. He had no idea who
she was. Poor little rich girl. Poor little *engaged* rich girl. Why
would he know?

He kissed her all the way to Sam's loft in Soho.

They didn't speak. Not a word.

She was well aware that she'd had too much to drink: her

head was spinning, but somehow it didn't bother her. She *wanted* this. It was her choice, nobody was forcing her to do anything.

Once they arrived, he paid off the cab driver, then pushed her up against the wall outside Sam's building and started once more with the kissing.

She could barely breathe. It was as if they couldn't keep their mouths off each other, and he was such a *great* kisser.

Are you out of your mind? a stern inner voice suddenly yelled inside her head.

Yes! she fired back. *And I don't intend to stop.*

You'd better!

Says who?

He unlocked the downstairs street door, urgently pulling her inside. She came with him willingly. He led her straight to a tiny elevator where he crowded her into a corner. Within seconds his hands were everywhere.

She knew that this was the moment she should tell him to stop, reveal the truth about her situation and beat a hasty retreat. Because if she didn't do it now there was no turning back.

'You're so freakin' beautiful,' he whispered, leading her out of the elevator and into the apartment. 'You do know that, don't you?'

No, she didn't know it. Max never told her. Max was polite and proper, always the perfect gentleman. Max plied her with expensive presents that she didn't need and didn't want. Max was safe. This guy wasn't.

Inside the small apartment their kissing marathon continued, both of them totally into it.

After a while Jett began undressing her, slowly at first, then becoming frantic.

She responded by ripping at his shirt, pulling down the zipper on his pants.

They were kissing and fumbling with their clothes, laughing, until suddenly he picked her up as if she was weightless, and carried her into Sam's bedroom where he placed her gently on the bed.

This is it! she thought. *This is it. It's time to stay or run.*

Before she could make up her mind, he began to kiss her again, sucking her bottom lip, moving down to her breasts, positioning himself over her, stroking her skin, which was so soft and smooth – like fine cashmere. His lips found her nipples and she threw back her head with abandon and thought she might melt with pleasure. She didn't want him to stop. Ever.

And when he moved on top of her, she gave a long, deep sigh, opening herself up to him.

He started to push inside her, when he suddenly realized she was a virgin. It was a shock. 'Damn!' he muttered, abruptly pulling away.

'Don't stop,' she said, reaching out to guide him back. 'Please don't stop.'

'Hey . . .' he mumbled, wondering why he was suddenly turning into Mr Nice Guy. 'You've had a few drinks and, uh . . . I'm not about to do something you might regret in the morning.'

'Who says I'll regret anything?'

'This *is* your first time, right?'

'Of course not,' she lied, wishing he'd just continue what he'd been doing, because even though the room was doing a slow spin she was beyond caring: she needed this tonight, and nothing was going to stop her now. 'Keep making love to me,' she said softly. 'I want to feel you inside me.'

Oh, Jesus, she was so gorgeous and he was totally hooked, why *would* he stop?

Resuming his position, he made love to her for what seemed like hours, until finally she fell asleep wrapped in his arms, warm and soft and so very lovely.

He'd never felt so totally at peace and satisfied. Within minutes he, too, was asleep, breathing in her sweet, sweet smell, totally content.

When he woke in the morning there were drops of blood on the sheets and the girl he'd spent the night with was gone.

It was then that he realized he didn't even know her name.

Chapter Eleven

Unable to sleep, Max considered it Mariska's fault. She'd purposely summoned him to her apartment, pretending Lulu was sick just so that she could ruin his night. He was sure she'd assumed he was with Amy.

Wrong. As usual.

And what exactly had that muttered 'maybe' been about when he'd said, 'She's my daughter, isn't she'.

Surely Mariska wouldn't stoop *that* low, intimating that Lulu might not be his child.

Yes. Mariska was a prize bitch, capable of anything. The woman would stoop as low as she had to if it meant getting his attention.

He truly loathed her, and he had good reason to. Several weeks ago a man had turned up at his office, a scruffy man with obviously dyed black hair and a sparse moustache. Clad in an ill-fitting suit and scuffed fake alligator shoes, the man had reeked of cheap cologne as he'd waylaid Mrs Barley, Max's executive assistant, and informed her that he had personal and sensitive information regarding the ex-Mrs Diamond, and that Max could either see him or read about what he had to say in the *National Enquirer*.

After Mrs Barley had appraised him of the situation, Max had opted to see him. And what a tale he had listened to regarding his dear ex-wife.

The man, Vladimir Bushkin, claimed that Mariska – whose real name he informed Max was Paulina Mari Kuchinova – had entered America with a false identity and a false passport. And how did Vladimir know this? Well, apparently he was her legal husband. And her marriage to the poor hapless American accountant, *and* to Max, were both acts of bigamy.

At first Max hadn't believed him: the man's story was beyond preposterous. However, when Vladimir produced photos and documents, including a marriage licence, Max had realized that it was more than likely he was telling the truth. The woman in the wedding photos was certainly a younger, not at all polished Mariska, and the name on the wedding licence was indeed Paulina Mari Kuchinova.

'She was prostitute,' Vladimir announced casually, as if this was not particularly interesting news. 'I was her pimp.'

'Christ!' Max exploded, already imagining the headlines if this ever got out.

'She double-crossed me,' Vladimir continued. 'Picked up stupid American at hotel bar in Moscow. Gave him good sucking and got him to marry her. She already had false papers in place. The scheming sow had been planning to get out of Moscow for a while. One day I woke up, she was gone. I vowed to track her down. It wasn't easy task, but here I am.'

'What do you want?' Max had asked, his stomach churning.

'Plenty,' Vladimir had replied, with an evil laugh. 'Whatever I deserve to keep mouth tightly shut.'

And Max had realized he was caught in a devastating trap.

* * *

After a good night's sleep Chris was up early, ready to rock 'n roll and face his father. He was pleased, because usually he didn't sleep well in hotels. He had an ongoing fear of being trapped in a burning building, and a high-rise hotel in Manhattan seemed just the right venue for that to happen, especially after 9/11. He still couldn't shake the images of those poor souls jumping from the windows of the towering buildings. It was his recurring nightmare.

After watching Jonathan do his I'm-just-a-regular-guy act with Matt Lauer on the *Today Show*, he had breakfast downstairs while reading the newspapers, which was quite relaxing until he came across an item about one of his clients on Page Six in the *New York Post*. Lola Sanchez, Latina diva supreme, had supposedly been spotted making out at Gatsby's with her latest co-star, a young blond hunk.

This was not a good thing because Lola was currently engaged to Oscar-winning film director Russell Savage, and Russell would not take kindly to his so-called fiancée hanging out with another man, especially a sexy macho actor.

Chris sighed. Knowing Lola, she'd deny everything and insist that he sue the newspaper, which he would not advise because it was probably all true. Lola Sanchez was a man-eater – she simply couldn't help herself – show her an attractive co-star and she would gobble the man up for lunch, dinner and morning coffee.

It was too early to phone his office in L.A. and alert them to expect her call, so he decided not to worry about it for now.

Further down in the column there was a blind item, which he was sure referred to Birdy Marvel.

> *Which singing teen with all the right attributes recently got a piercing in a very private place indeed? And which singing teen's biker boyfriend filmed the entire event in graphic detail?*

Nice. How long before *that* particular movie turned up on the Internet?

Didn't these girls ever learn? Although he knew exactly what Birdy would say: 'It didn't do Paris Hilton or Pamela Anderson any harm, did it?'

He tried calling Birdy on his cell, just to warn her that if there *was* a video she should make sure it was kept under lock and key and that nobody could get their hands on it – especially Rocky.

Her road manager informed him she was asleep, and couldn't be disturbed.

He finished his egg-white omelette, signed the check and left the hotel. It wouldn't do to keep Big Daddy waiting.

*   *   *

As Jett strode along Park Avenue heading for his father's house, his mind was elsewhere. He couldn't stop thinking about last night and the girl with the silky blonde hair. When he'd worken up she was gone, vanished. And he hadn't even asked her for her name. She was amazing, and he was in love or lust or something along those lines.

The truth was that he couldn't wipe the stupid grin off his face, and that indicated she wasn't just another one-night stand. God knew, he'd had enough of those.

He had a strong suspicion that this could turn out to be the real thing, so if he was serious and *really* wanted her, there was no way he should crowd her. That meant that even though he was hot to hook up with her again, experience told him it was probably better to wait a day or two, give her space, let her think about him and wonder.

It occurred to him that he might have taken advantage of her because, even though she'd denied it, she *had* been a virgin, he had no doubt about that.

Then he thought, hell, no. She'd wanted him as much as he'd wanted her. Besides, he'd acted like a gentleman, offering to stop, only *she* hadn't wanted him to.

Now what? She shouldn't be too hard to track – someone from the club would know who she was. And if they didn't, Beverly would soon find out for him, because Beverly knew everyone. He called her on his cell and left a message. After that, he thought about contacting his mother, then decided to put it off until after he'd met with Red. Who knew what the old man would have to say? And Edie – if she was sober enough – would want to know every detail. Besides, Edie had no idea he was back in town, so there was no hurry to reach her. It wasn't as if they shared a traditional mother-son relationship, and last time he'd seen her they'd parted on really bad terms.

Thinking about his mom was a real downer. She had been so vibrant and beautiful, but Red had made her into a neurotic, needy drunk. Not that he could criticize: in his own way he'd been worse than her, but at least he'd allowed his friends to save him. Edie didn't care. Once her life with Red was over she'd moved to an ocean-front house in Montauk where, over the years, she'd entertained a series of younger boyfriends and existed on a steady diet of cigarettes and vodka, which had soon killed her exquisite looks.

Jett had been thirteen when his parents split. Like his brothers before him, he'd been packed off to a strict military school, which he'd hated. He'd run away a couple of times, been caught and severely punished by Red, who'd sent him off to a tough-love camp in Arizona for difficult boys. Two years of that and he was ready to explode. College was never even an option: he'd wanted his freedom and, since Edie didn't relish the thought of him living at home, she gave it to him. On his seventeenth birthday she granted him an allowance and told him to go do his thing. Which was exactly what he did. New York was waiting, and he was ready.

Sex, drugs and rock 'n roll. Until his rescue, Jett had been the master.

Right now he didn't want to think about Edie – he'd do that later. He preferred to dwell on the girl from last night.

Things had a way of happening fast. Here he was, back in America for only a few hours, and he'd met someone very special. How out there was *that*?

Then he got to thinking that maybe this was the way it was supposed to be. Fate. Yeah, fate. He was *meant* to be in the club last night, just like he was meant to go to Italy and clean up his drug and booze-addicted ways.

Not that he was religious, but maybe this was God's way of saying, 'You did good, so here's your prize. Handle her with care.'

Now all he had to do was find her.

Chapter Twelve

Opening her eyes, Amy was overcome with a hangover from hell and, even worse, she was filled with an overwhelming feeling of guilt. What had she done? What totally *insane* thing had she done?

Lying in bed, the covers pulled tightly to her chin, she began to go over the chain of events that had led her to cheat on her fiancé. First there was the bachelorette party, then the drinking and taking a few hits on a joint. Followed by more drinking and slow-dancing with a guy who was *so* enticing and attractive that she'd ended up going to his apartment and having sex. Great sex. Mind-blowing sex. The kind of sex she was supposed to have with Max on their wedding night.

Oh, God, she'd *slept* with a total stranger. Given up her virginity to a man she'd just met. And as far as she could remember, she'd actually *enjoyed* it!

Why had she allowed herself to do it? How could she have betrayed Max in such a way? It was so *wrong*.

Suffused with even more guilt, she got up and made her way into the shower, thinking about how she'd woken at four a.m., grabbed her clothes and hurried from his apartment. Downstairs in his building she'd taken a quick peek at the mailbox. Apartment 10A. S. Lucas.

What did the S stand for? Steven? Sonny? Scott? It would have been nice to know his name.

Out on the street she'd hailed a passing cab and huddled on the back seat until it delivered her home. Safely in her own apartment, she'd thrown off her clothes and crawled into bed.

Now it was four hours later and she was experiencing a throbbing headache.

I'll never drink again, she vowed. *Never! This is it for me.*

But she was well aware that it was too late to take back what had already happened.

As soon as she emerged from the shower, Tina was on the phone, demanding to know exactly what had taken place.

'Nothing,' she responded weakly, clutching the phone with one hand and a towel in the other.

'Liar!' Tina said, sounding excited. 'You *left* with that hot guy.'

'I did not!' she protested.

'Oh, please.' Tina snorted disbelievingly. 'I *saw* you sneak out. I was worried.'

'Then why didn't you stop me?'

''Cause you're a big girl, and we had that talk. Remember?'

'Yes, I remember,' she said miserably.

'So?' Tina said, still pushing for information. 'What's the deal?'

'He dropped me home, that's all.'

'I'm pregnant, not stupid,' Tina said crisply. 'I'll pick you up at one, we'll go to Serendipity for lunch and you'll tell me everything.'

'I don't feel like eating, let alone talking.'

'Why not?'

'I'm suffering from a massive hangover, thanks to all my so-called friends.'

'Too bad,' Tina said cheerily. 'We're having lunch anyway.'

'Do we *have* to?' Amy said, wishing she could crawl back into bed and forget about everything.

'Yes, we have to. I'll see you later.'

Since Tina was about to give birth there was no arguing with her. It wasn't worth the effort.

Dressing slowly, Amy kept on going over the ramifications of what she'd done. It wasn't a good thing. Oh, no, it wasn't good at all. She'd been a bad, bad girl, and she deserved to be punished.

So why was there a smile on her face? Damnit! Why the *hell* was she smiling?

The second she walked into work, Yolanda was all over her pushing for details.

'Details of *what*?' Amy said weakly, heading for her desk, wishing everyone would leave her alone. '*Nothing* happened.'

'Sure,' Yolanda drawled, pulling a disbelieving face as she followed her. 'You're glowing. *Something* must've happened.'

'No, it didn't,' she said, switching on her computer, willing Yolanda to vanish conveniently.

'Oh, yes, it did!' Yolanda said, refusing to go away. 'We *all* saw you leave with that hot guy.'

'I don't even know his name,' she said, hoping Yolanda might give her a clue.

But Yolanda's cell rang, putting an end to the conversation.

Hmm . . . not that she cared *what* his name was. After all, it wasn't like she would ever see him again.

The sexy stranger was her secret wild card – a lustful night of pre-wedding insanity she would never share with anyone, not even Tina.

Max Diamond was the man for her.

Everyone thought so.

* * *

Jett was the first to arrive at the Diamond brownstone on 68th Street. The butler who answered the door was a new one. Not that Jett was familiar with his father's staff, but there'd been an English butler who'd stayed around for a few years. This one was German and quite stoic as he ushered Jett into the panelled library, leaving him to contemplate the many shelves of ceiling-high leatherbound books.

Wandering around the room, Jett noticed that, just as he remembered from his childhood, there was nothing personal. No photographs of family, no trophies or knick-knacks, no magazines, just a pristine copy of the *Wall Street Journal* folded on a side table next to a dark brown stiff leather couch.

Nothing had changed. Red Diamond did not believe in personal mementoes. The room was a mirror-image of Red. Cold, musty and unwelcoming.

After a few minutes, he sat down on the couch and picked

up the newspaper. As he stared at the print, images of the girl from last night flashed through his head again. She was a peach. A beautiful, perfect peach. The kind of girl he'd always dreamed of.

And he would see her again soon . . . very soon.

* * *

'How was it?' Max asked.

Amy hung onto the phone, her palms slick with sweat. Had her fiancé found out? How was that possible? Oh, God, what was she going to say? How could she explain her one night of insanity? This was unbelievable!

'It can't have been *that* bad, sweetie,' Max said affectionately. 'Just you and the girls. Surely you had an enjoyable time?'

Relief swept over her. Of course, he was asking about her bachelorette party. 'I drank too much,' she blurted.

'That figures,' he said understandingly. 'They must have been pouring it down your throat, and there was nothing you could do.'

'That's about it,' she managed.

'It's exactly what I'll have to put up with tonight,' he grumbled. 'Bachelor parties are so goddamn dumb, I wish I didn't have to go. So help me – if they haul in strippers, I'm out of there, and that's a promise.'

'You don't have to promise me anything,' she said, feeling more guilty than ever.

'Why?' he said, sounding amused. 'You *want* me cavorting with strippers?'

'No, no, of course not,' she said, almost stammering. 'It's just that . . . well . . . on a bachelor night you can do anything and it doesn't count. Anyway,' she added lamely, 'that's what I've heard.'

'Sweetheart, I *do* love you,' he said, laughing.

'You too, Max,' she said, on automatic pilot.

'You're the sweetest girl I ever met.'

NO! I'M NOT. I CHEATED ON YOU WITH

ANOTHER MAN AND THERE'S NO WAY I CAN TAKE IT BACK.

'Thank you.' She gulped.

'I'm right outside my father's house,' Max said. 'I'll call you later.'

She clicked off her phone. If he ever found out what she had done . . .

Oh, God, it didn't bear thinking about.

Chapter Thirteen

Jett wasn't alone for long – within minutes Max had arrived. Jett stood up, and they exchanged a somewhat stilted greeting.

'You're looking well,' Max said. 'Better than the last time I saw you.'

Oh, yeah, Jett thought, *he has to get a dig in, doesn't he?* 'Last time you saw me I was sick,' he pointed out.

'No,' Max contradicted. 'If I remember correctly, you were drunk on your ass.'

'Alcoholism is a sickness,' Jett explained, wondering why his brother had to get on his case the moment he saw him. 'I've been clean for three years.'

'Is that right?' Max said as if he didn't believe him.

'Yeah, that's right,' Jett retaliated, ready to defend himself.

Before they became involved in a pissy little fight, Chris burst in. Chris. Mr L.A. with his deep tan and George Clooney smile. Wearing a lightweight Armani suit he looked fit and well. 'Guys!' he said. 'Long time. You both look great. Good looks run in the family, huh?'

Jett felt a lot closer to Chris than he did to Max. There was something intimidating about Max, something he didn't care to tangle with. Chris was warmer, nicer, although his two older brothers were somewhat alike with their dark good looks. Two traditionally handsome men, while Jett was the odd one out with his dirty blond hair and piercing blue eyes. When they were kids, Chris had always called him 'surfer kid' and 'little runt'. Not that they'd seen much of each other, but when they *had* got together, Chris had always looked out for him.

80

'Hey,' Jett said, 'anyone know why we're here?'

'Beats me,' Chris said, shrugging. 'I'm thinking the old guy might be sick and finally remembered he has three sons.'

'I doubt it,' Max said grimly.

'You doubt what?' Chris asked. 'That he's sick, or that he remembers us?'

'We'll soon find out,' Max said.

A maid entered the room and asked if they required any refreshments. Chris requested coffee, as did Max. Jett asked for a bottle of water.

After the maid left the room, Chris turned to his younger brother. 'Where're you staying? I would've called you last night, but I had no idea where to find you.'

'A friend lent me his apartment.'

'Lucky you,' Chris said, sitting down on the couch, and stretching out his long legs. 'When did you fly in?'

'Yesterday.'

'I hear things are going okay for you in Italy,' Chris remarked, checking out messages on his BlackBerry.

Jett nodded. 'I'm clean and sober if that's what you mean.'

'That's great, but I'm talking about the modelling. Saw your photo in one of my girlfriend's Italian fashion magazines. She was way impressed when I told her you were my kid brother.'

'Modelling?' Max interrupted disapprovingly. 'You're doing modelling?'

'S' right,' Jett said. 'Magazine stuff and some TV commercials.'

'I thought all models were gay.'

'Now you *sound* like our old man,' Chris said, laughing. 'You gotta haul yourself into the present, Max. Haven't you heard of Tyson?'

'Mike Tyson?'

Chris rolled his eyes, 'I give up!'

The maid returned with two cups of coffee and a bottle of Evian.

Chris pocketed his BlackBerry and took a gulp of coffee.

Max consulted his watch. 'It's nine-fifteen,' he said irritably. 'I was asked to be here at nine.'

'We were all told to be here at nine,' Chris said.

'Christ!' Max said, tapping his fingers on the coffee-table. 'When does it stop?'

'When does what stop?' Jett asked.

'This manipulative crap,' Max said harshly. 'This controlling shit. He still seems to think he can treat us like we're twelve.'

'You think he's gonna change now?' Chris asked.

'At least he can't beat us,' Jett remarked. 'Man, he was quick with his freakin' stick. I've *still* got the marks on my ass.'

'I'll find out what's going on,' Max said, getting up and walking towards the door. 'I have appointments, a business crisis to deal with. I can't afford to waste anymore time.'

'And I have to get back to L.A. There's a phone backup of demanding clients waiting for me,' Chris said, winking at Jett. 'How about you, surfer kid?'

'Hey, you're the one who lives in California,' Jett answered, grinning.

'And very nice it is too. Come visit sometime. I've got a great house you can stay at.'

'Thanks, but I was thinking of hanging around New York for a couple of weeks,' Jett said, dying to tell someone about last night. 'Y' see, I met a girl—'

Before he could finish, the door opened and there stood Lady Jane Bentley, an elegant woman in a Chanel-suit-and-pearls kind of way. Auburn hair worn in an upswept style, minimum make-up, frosty eyes and a fixed smile.

'Good morning, boys,' she said, obviously going for the mother-figure posture. 'Your father and I are so glad you could make it.'

Jett barely remembered her. His only encounters with Lady Jane were blanks on account of his having been drunk or stoned out of his mind.

Chris had met her a few times, most memorably when she'd visited L.A. with her two English step-nieces. They'd stayed at the Peninsula Hotel and she'd expected them all to be treated like visiting royalty.

Fat chance. The only people treated like royalty in Hollywood were the stars and moguls who made over thirty mill a year. Other than that it was everyone for themselves.

Since they lived in the same city, Max knew her best. He considered her a cold fish, the type of woman his father deserved.

Lady Jane surveyed Red's three sons and wished that they didn't exist. Even though Red rarely spoke about them, she was well aware that they represented the continuation of his bloodline, and therefore they were a threat. Eventually she expected Red to marry her, in spite of the fact that whenever she brought up the subject he laughed in her face, which did not please her: she was a determined woman used to getting her own way, exactly like him. However, she persevered, for she knew that as he got older he would weaken, and she *would* become the fifth Mrs Diamond. Then they could all go to hell.

'I do hope everyone had a pleasant experience getting here,' Lady Jane continued. 'Travelling today is quite appalling. There's no such thing as first class anymore. Everyone is treated as if they're cattle. Unless you travel by private plane it's quite hopeless.'

Not only is she an icy bitch, she's a snob too, Chris thought. Which made it difficult for him to understand why she was with old Red, who'd belched, farted and sworn his way to the top of the heap with no apologies to anyone.

Oh, yeah, money, money, money. What else?

'I flew in on Jonathan Goode's plane,' Chris offered. 'Guess you're right. Private is the only way to go.'

Lady Jane was unimpressed. She was probably one of the few women in America who had no idea who Jonathan Goode was.

'Where's Red?' Max asked, getting right to the reason they were all there.

'I'm so sorry to disappoint you,' Lady Jane said, coolly distant. 'Your father is not feeling very well today, so unfortunately he cannot see you.'

'What?' Max said, furious.

'However,' she continued, 'he expects all three of you to be here on Monday morning at the same time. I do hope that's not an inconvenience.'

'Are you *serious?*' Chris said. 'There's no way I can sit around New York for the weekend. I flew in specially for this meeting.' He favoured her with a long, hard glare, the kind of look he usually reserved for the business affairs suits at the studios. 'This is bullshit!'

'Is that how lawyers speak in L.A.?' Lady Jane said, lip curling. 'Little wonder it's a town full of barbarians.'

Jett began to laugh – he couldn't help himself. This was such a ridiculous situation. The only reason the three of them were there was to see if the old man was leaving them money. *He* needed a handout, but Max and Chris were rolling in it, so why were *they* jumping hoops? It didn't make sense.

'What's the matter with Red?' Max demanded. 'How sick is he?'

'I strongly suggest you meet here at nine a.m. on Monday and allow your father to tell you himself,' Lady Jane said, adding succinctly 'I can assure you it is to your advantage to do so.'

'Jesus Christ!' Chris muttered.

'I'll be here,' Jett said, kind of pleased to have an excuse to stay in New York. Not that he'd been planning on leaving any time soon. After all, he had a girl to find.

'Looks like you're giving me no choice,' Chris said, not willing to take off while Max and Jett stayed for the meeting. That would *not* be a smart move.

'We'll see you on Monday then,' Lady Jane said, exiting the room.

'What do you think's the matter with him?' Jett asked, as soon as she'd left.

'No idea,' Max said. 'I saw him a few months ago when he was as objectionable and loud as usual.'

'How did he look?' Jett asked, swigging water.

'Old. But strong as the proverbial horse.'

'So . . .' Chris said. 'Looks like I'm stuck here for the weekend. Either of you want to meet up later for dinner?'

'You can always count on me if it's a free meal,' Jett said quickly. 'Now that I don't drink, I'm the cheapest date in town.'

'Can't do dinner,' Max said brusquely. 'I'm sure you both

84

know I'm getting married, and tonight some friends – well, business acquaintances really – are throwing me a bachelor party.'

'A bachelor party,' Chris said. 'Are we invited?'

'*I* didn't know you were getting married,' Jett said. 'I thought you already had a wife. *And* a kid, who I'd love to meet sometime – considering I'm her uncle.'

Max felt threatened on both sides. As if he didn't have enough problems, now he was about to get stuck with his brothers for the weekend. This did not factor into his plans.

On the other hand, even though they were not close, they *were* family and, God knew, he didn't have anyone else except Lulu. 'Of course you're invited,' he said stiffly. 'It's not something I'm looking forward to, but you're more than welcome to come.'

'Wouldn't miss it,' Chris said, winking at Jett.

'Me neither,' Jett said. 'Haven't had a proper lap-dance since I left the good ole US.'

'I'm hoping there'll be no strippers,' Max said. 'It's not that kind of party.'

'You gotta know there *will* be strippers,' Jett said, grinning. 'If it's a bachelor party that's something you can bet on.'

The brothers walked outside the house and stood talking on the sidewalk for a few minutes, unaware that Red was watching them from an upstairs window.

The old man cackled gleefully as he spied on his three sons. How he enjoyed manipulating people. Here he was, almost eighty years old, and when he said 'Jump', everyone did. It was amusing, especially as he didn't even have to leave his house to get a good laugh.

*   *   *

Red Diamond was a mogul in the true sense of the word. He was a self-made man who had come from an impoverished Polish immigrant family. Born in America and named Jana Polanska in 1926, he'd been a school drop-out by the time he was fifteen. His father, a butcher, who was prone to beating him to a pulp at the slightest provocation, kicked him out of the house in the middle of the night. His mother, a pale, frightened woman, allowed it to happen without a word of protest.

Bitter and filled with anger – his psyche forever damaged by the emotional and physical abuse he'd endured, young Jana was a survivor. He lived on the streets for a few months, then moved in with a sex-crazed older woman who expected him to service her twice a day. Eventually he got tired of her, lied about his age and landed a job selling advertising at an established, but not particularly successful, magazine.

By the time he was twenty, he'd legally changed his name to Red Diamond, and married his boss's spinster daughter, Miriam, a plain woman ten years older than him. After his early experiences he was an expert at pleasing older women. He knew exactly what they required – hard dick and plenty of it.

Soon he was virtually running the magazine, which, after a few years, he had turned into quite a profitable venture. With the magazine doing so well, it spawned several others, all of which Red was in charge of. He was making good money and quickly learned everything he could about investing. Before long he had found his forte as an investment whiz, who somehow made all the right moves.

By the time he was thirty, he'd amassed a small fortune with which he bought a chain of TV and radio stations. He kept them for a few months, then sold them for a huge profit.

When Miriam's father died, Red was in line to take over. He was already running things, so it was no surprise to anyone. Red Diamond changed the way the magazines were run. He brought in advertisers ready to spend more than ever before. He touched on subjects that were once considered taboo. He hired the best photographers, writers and models.

As time went on he got bored with the magazine business, and began buying and then selling for a large profit a series of small companies. If anyone got in his way, too bad.

Soon he had built himself a media empire, and by the time he was thirty-five, he was well on his way to becoming a billionaire.

Red was a notorious womanizer. Miriam put up with his indiscretions for many years, but two weeks after her second miscarriage she took her own life.

This did not affect Red's rise to the top. A year after Miriam's demise, he met and married Max's mother, Rachel, a beautiful woman from a good family.

The day Rachel married Red, her family disowned her. Red immediately made it his business to bankrupt Rachel's father, and when she begged him not to, he took much pleasure in laughing in her face.

Nobody fucked with Red Diamond and got away with it. Nobody.

*   *   *

The New York brownstone was Red Diamond's favourite residence. He'd long ago given up the elegant apartment in Monte Carlo overlooking the bay, the magnificent villa in Marbella, with two swimming-pools and a sunken tennis court, the luxurious London penthouse located near Buckingham Palace and the rambling farmhouse in Tuscany Edie had persuaded him to buy.

Red no longer travelled, since 9/11 he'd rarely left New York. It wasn't necessary – there was nowhere he wanted to go, no one he wanted to see. He'd done and seen it all. There was nothing left for him to discover.

Lady Jane often tried to talk him into going places. A ball in Venice. A political dinner in Washington. '*You* go,' he instructed her. 'I'm not moving.'

And he didn't have to. He oversaw his various businesses by e-mail, video conferences and phone. He had hand-picked people in place who took care of everything, and if anyone screwed up, he knew about it immediately. Red Diamond had highly paid spies everywhere.

He imagined what his three boys were thinking. They were probably under the impression that he was at death's door, ready to embrace them and leave them a shitload of money.

No such luck. They were damn fortunate he'd been such a hard task-master during their formative years. It had made them the men they were today, and that wasn't such a bad thing.

Red believed in challenges, roadblocks and, as successful as his two eldest sons were, he was interested in seeing how they handled themselves when faced with adversity.

He thought about Max first. Very successful in real estate, Max had needed a jolt to take it to another level. So Red, for his own amusement, had arranged that jolt. The two banks pulling out of Max's billion-dollar building complex was no random act.

Next there was Chris who'd got into trouble in Vegas. Pure stupidity. Gambling was for morons. Red had far-reaching connections, and he was determined to make sure his middle son learned a good lesson.

As for Jett . . . well, he wasn't surprised the boy was a fuckup. With a drunken whore like Edie for a mother, he'd never had any expectations that his youngest son would achieve anything. Still . . . the boy appeared to have given up his bad habits, but that didn't mean he shouldn't be tested.

One thing Red knew for sure, he couldn't wait to see the look on all three of their faces when he told them the *real* reason he'd summoned them to his house. They'd shit themselves, and he would have one big smile on his face.

Too bad for them. Red Diamond always got the last word.

Chapter Fourteen

On Friday morning, Liberty was still asleep when Diahann quietly left the apartment to fix Mr Diamond's breakfast. Recently he'd announced that he didn't want anyone preparing his food except her. This had not gone down well with Mae, his full-time cook. Mae, a large, elderly black woman, had been in his employ longer than anyone. 'What *that* shit be about?' Mae had demanded, stamping her foot. 'My food ain't good 'nuff for the old fool? That be the way things goin' down here?'

Diahann had managed to calm her, although it hadn't been easy. They both knew what a difficult and tyrannical man Red Diamond was: he treated everyone with the same rudeness and lack of respect.

Diahann often felt that she understood him better than most people. She certainly understood him more than the skinny-assed white woman who'd planted herself in his life several years ago. Lady Jane Bentley, indeed. The only reason the witch had a title was because she'd married some doddering old Englishman who happened to be a lord. None of the staff liked her, she treated them as if they were only there to do her bidding, and her Madonna-style British accent fooled no one. The woman was not their boss, yet she acted as if they all worked exclusively for her.

The staff in the kitchen loved nothing better than a good gossip, and usually Diahann ignored the incessant bitching and back-stabbing, but today the talk was about Red Diamond's three sons, sequestered in the library, and she couldn't help listening. Red Diamond's business was common knowledge among his staff, so they all knew it was unusual for him to have any contact with his sons, and everyone was curious as to why they were at the house.

'They're surely handsome,' sighed Letty, the young Irish maid who'd taken them refreshments. 'They look nothing like the Master.'

'That's 'cause Mr D. always hitched himself to fine-lookin' wimmin,' Mae said knowingly, busily chopping fruit with a sharp knife. 'I bin through every one of his poor wives. Seen 'em come, seen 'em go an', believe me, he *always* picked 'em pretty.'

'How long *have* you worked here, Mae?' asked Letty, stealing a slice of apple.

'Mosta me damn life,' Mae replied, slapping the young girl's hand away. 'Cooked for all them boys since they was little. They sure was cute then. Mebbe I should take a stroll into the library, see how they turned out.'

'Lady Bentley's with them,' Letty said.

'An' what's *she* talkin' to them about?' Mae demanded, as if it was her right to know.

'I wasn't in there long enough to hear.'

Listening to their conversation, Diahann couldn't help wondering about Red Diamond's three sons. She was well aware that none of them had had it easy. Red was hard on everyone, especially his boys.

After she'd fixed the eggs exactly the way the old man liked them, she put them onto a tray and asked Letty to take them up to his bedroom, explaining that she had to get back downstairs.

'Why's that?' Mae asked, always eager to know everybody's business. 'You feelin' poorly?'

'No, Mae,' Diahann replied patiently. 'My daughter's staying with me over the weekend.'

'Little Liberty!' exclaimed Mae, expertly slicing a pineapple. 'How's that pretty missy doin'?'

'She hurt her ankle at work,' Diahann said. 'Other than that, she's well.'

''Bout time you two spent more time together,' Mae said. 'Wasn't right when you bundled her outta here.'

'I didn't *bundle* her out of here,' Diahann replied, immediately on the defensive. 'You *know* I didn't have a choice.'

'I wanna see that girl,' Mae continued, wiping her hands on her apron. 'Liberty was always sumpin' special, singin' an' dancin' round the place. I *miss* havin' that little beauty around.'

Diahann remained silent. Keeping things private was her way. She certainly didn't need to hear what Mae had to say, especially about her daughter.

*   *   *

Liberty had not had a chance to talk to her mom. The night before, Diahann had rushed in, changed the dressing on her arm, fixed her a cup of vegetable broth and hurried back upstairs to prepare Mr Diamond's dinner. By the time she came back downstairs, Liberty was already asleep.

Typical, Liberty thought sourly. *As usual, Mr Diamond comes first*. It had been that way ever since they'd moved into the house.

Now, checking out *The View* on TV, she almost fell off the couch when they announced that one of their upcoming guests was Princess Tashmir Donnell, wife of hip-hop mogul, Damon P. Donnell.

Damn! What in crap's name was Damon's *wife* doing on TV? *He* was the star of the family.

She sat up straight, eyes fixed firmly on the screen. Man, this was not her week. If Tashmir turned out to be a singer, that would *really* put her over the edge.

However, when Tashmir Donnell sashayed onto the screen, quite exotic in an Indian princess kind of way, it turned out that the woman was peddling a line of jewellery.

Ha! Liberty thought. *Damon's wife selling jewellery. How low down is* that?

Lined up on a table in front of the four hosts of *The View* was an outrageous array of necklaces, rings and earrings, all studded with rubies, diamonds and emeralds.

Like anybody can afford that shit, Liberty thought, still glued to the screen.

After a few moments of idle chat, Joy Behar got right down to it. 'How much does *this* little bauble run?' she inquired, picking up a magnificent necklace and dangling it in front of the camera.

'Oh, that,' Tashmir answered vaguely. 'Eight or nine.'

'Hundred?' questioned Meredith Viera, leaning forward in her chair.

'Thousand,' said Tashmir, smugly.

After gasps from the audience and more jewellery questions, Star Jones got down to the real nitty-gritty and asked what it was like being the wife of Damon P. Donnell.

Tashmir, who was clad in a gold and purple sari and projected a gracious if somewhat phoney manner, said, 'My husband keeps me *very* busy. Damon is Mr Energy. I merely trail along behind him trying to keep up.'

I bet, Liberty thought. *You trail along behind him after you skip out of your three-room closet in your multi-million-dollar apartment and jump into your customized royal blue Bentley.*

She hated her. But that wasn't right, was it? How could she hate someone she didn't even know just because Tashmir was married to the man who could do something for her career? Hmm . . . that was if he ever cared to notice her existence.

Then she thought, *What* career? Here she was, stuck in Mama's apartment. How pathetic was *that*?

Anyway, all she did was serve the man eggs and pour him coffee. It wasn't as if he'd ever heard her sing, so why *should* he notice her? As far as he was concerned she was a waitress. A server. He probably didn't even realize she was missing.

Abruptly she picked up the remote and switched off the TV. Why go through the torture? Watching Princess Phoney wasn't making her feel any better about herself.

A few minutes later Diahann walked in. 'How're you feeling?' she asked, picking up a blanket from the floor.

'Crappy,' Liberty answered irritably, staring at her mother, who could have been quite beautiful if she would only take the time to fix herself up and lose a few pounds. 'My arm's still throbbing a bit, although my ankle's stronger. At least I can walk on it.' She shot Diahann a wary glance. 'Don't worry, Mama, I'll be out of here by Monday for sure.'

'No rush,' Diahann said, plumping up a cushion. 'I *like* having you here.'

'Sure you do. Littering up your couch, screwing up your weekend. Bet you're thrilled.'

'Cindi said that if you're feeling okay, she'll pick you up before work on Monday,' Diahann said, removing a couple of empty glasses from the small coffee-table in front of the couch. 'Isn't your boyfriend due back then?'

'Yeah, Kev'll be back late that night.'

'Maybe I can meet him.'

'Why?' Liberty shot back, her green eyes narrowing. 'It's not as if I'm *marrying* the dude.'

'You've been seeing him a while, haven't you?'

'Hey,' Liberty said belligerently, not about to get into a discussion about her boyfriend, 'if this is question time, maybe *I* can get a few in.'

Here we go, Diahann thought, taking a long, deep breath to prepare herself. 'Of course,' she said, remaining calm. 'I was hoping we could talk.'

'You were?' Liberty said disbelievingly.

'Yes. It feels as if I hardly see you anymore.'

'Not *my* fault.'

'Well,' Diahann said, treading carefully, for she didn't want to upset her daughter, 'you *did* cancel the last two times we were supposed to get together.'

'I've been busy.'

'I understand, but—'

'Mama,' Liberty interrupted, determined that today she was going to find out the truth. 'Don't you think it's time you told me who my father is? I can't go on pretending it doesn't matter, and that we're never gonna talk about it. Surely you understand – I *need* to know.'

There. She'd said it. Now it was up to her mom.

Diahann sat down on the edge of the couch and gave a deep sigh. 'There's a reason I've never told you, Libby,' she said, biting down on her bottom lip. 'It's . . . difficult.'

'How *difficult* can it be, Mama? I have a *right* to know.'

Diahann nodded quietly.

'For the longest time I thought it might be Leon,' Liberty continued. 'Then I got it – how could it be? His skin's too dark, like yours. So then I got to thinking – what am I? Black, like you've always told me? Half white? What *am* I, Mama? You can't go on hiding things from me. I'm nineteen. You *know* it's time.'

'I was even younger than you when I left home.'

'I've heard that story a thousand times,' Liberty said impatiently.

'There I was – getting off the bus in New York with two hundred dollars in my pocket and a ton of ambition,' Diahann said, sighing ruefully. 'Seventeen, an' imagining I'd be the next Anita Baker.'

'You could've been if you'd kept at it.'

'No, I couldn't.'

'Yes, you *could*,' Liberty insisted. 'You're a *real* good singer. That's a talent nobody can take away.'

'But I wasn't good *enough*.'

'Why you *always* gotta put yourself down?' Liberty said, exasperated. 'I can remember you sneaking me into that jazz club you used to sing at, and you sounded amazing.'

'What did *you* know? You were a baby – seven, eight years old.'

'Hey, where do you think I got *my* talent?'

'It never happened for me, Libby,' Diahann said flatly.

'That's 'cause you gave it up.'

'No. It gave *me* up. After many years of slogging away in nightclubs an' recording studios I was forced to realize that I wasn't gonna make it. Besides, I had *you* to think of.'

'Sorry,' Liberty said sharply. 'I didn't *ask* to be born.'

'You know that's not what I meant. I always loved you, Libby, but after a while things got too hard. You were coming up to your ninth birthday, an' one morning I woke up an' *knew* we needed to get us some kind of real security, not a month-to-month struggle where I wasn't even sure I could make the rent.'

'Then how come you didn't marry one of your boyfriends? As far as I remember you had plenty.'

'Yes, there were plenty, an' every damn one of them turned out to be a loser. The offer of a steady job was too good to pass up, so I took it, and the *only* time I've regretted it was when I was forced to send you to live at my sister's place.'

''Cause of Mr Diamond,' Liberty said flatly. ''Cause the mean old bastard wanted me gone.'

'Mr Diamond warned me when he hired me that he wouldn't tolerate having a child around. I promised to keep you out of sight.'

'Great! The invisible kid.'

'You were a wild thing, Libby. I couldn't watch you every second. Any chance you got you roamed all over the house.'

'Hey, Mama, that's about *all* I had to do,' Liberty said heatedly. 'We were living in the wrong neighbourhood. You dragged me away from all my friends, sent me to some fancy new school where they never accepted me.'

'The day Mr Diamond discovered you sleeping on his bed he was furious. There was nothing I could do.'

'Yes, there *was*,' Liberty said, eyes blazing. 'You could've quit your job.'

'Aren't you listening to me? We *needed* the money. How would *you* have managed if you'd had a child to support and a career going nowhere?'

'I wouldn't have taken a job as a maid,' Liberty shot back accusingly.

'Housekeeper.'

'Housekeeper, maid, what's the difference? I would've made it . . . somehow.'

'I did what I could,' Diahann said softly. 'I sent Aretha money every week for your upkeep, and since you seemed happy there with your cousin, I didn't insist on you coming back, 'cause after a while I got Mr Diamond to agree that you could.'

'Aretha never told me you sent money.'

'Surely you didn't imagine I'd abandoned you altogether? Who do you think paid for your singing and dancing lessons?'

'I . . . I didn't think. Aretha never mentioned it.'

'She wouldn't. Aretha liked being your mama instead of

me.' A long pause. 'You got any idea how I *felt* all those Sundays when I came to visit and you all treated me as if I was an intruder?'

'I suppose it must've been hard,' Liberty said, reluctant to give her mom any credit.

'Believe me, it was.'

'So,' Liberty ventured, 'about my dad . . . was *he* one of your losers? Is *that* why you've never told me about him?'

'No,' Diahann said. 'He wasn't a loser.'

'Then *who* was he?' Liberty asked, her voice rising. 'Why won't you tell me?'

'The truth is I hardly knew him.'

'What does *that* mean?'

'I was eighteen, touring in Europe, singing back-up for Isaac Hayes.'

'You never told me you were in Europe,' Liberty said accusingly.

'I can remember thinkin', this is it – my career is finally takin' off,' Diahann said. She hesitated a moment, then continued: 'One night in Berlin I met a drummer at a studio session. He was a handsome guy – German mother, black father. He was funny an' nice, an' we ended up spending the night together.'

'Yes?' Liberty asked, hanging on every word.

'The next day the tour left Berlin,' Diahann said, turning away. 'A few weeks later I discovered I was pregnant.'

'With me,' Liberty stated.

'Yes, with you.' Another long, deep sigh. 'I was so scared. I tried to contact him, but it was too late.'

'Too late for what?'

'There's a reason I never wanted to tell you, Libby.'

'Tell me *what*?'

'I . . . I found out he was killed in a car crash the day after I left Germany.'

'You – you mean he's dead?' Liberty stammered, her head spinning. 'My father's *dead*? Is that what you've been hiding from me all these years? He's *dead*!'

'I'm so sorry, baby,' Diahann said, attempting to take her daughter's hand.

'Oh, my *God*, Mama!' Liberty said, snatching her hand away. 'How come you kept it from me all these years?'

'Do you think it's easy telling you you're the result of a one-night stand? I wanted more for you, baby. I honestly believed it was better if you *didn't* know.'

Liberty's green eyes blazed with anger. 'That was *my* choice, not yours,' she cried.

'You're right,' Diahann said quietly, bowing her head.

'What was his name?'

'It's not important.'

'Maybe not to you,' Liberty fired back.

Another long pause. 'Mervyn.'

'Mervyn *what*?'

'Brown.'

Mervyn Brown. At least she now knew the name of the man who'd fathered her. And Mama had kept it a secret all this time. It wasn't fair, she should have been told years ago.

'What did he look like?' she asked, forcing herself not to cry.

'I told you, he was a good-lookin' man.'

Liberty was silent for a while, trying to digest all this unexpected information. Yes, she had a father. A *dead* father.

'I want to see a photo of him,' she said at last.

'I'm sorry . . .'

'C'*mon*,' Liberty said, suddenly more angry than anything else. 'No photo, *nothing*.'

'Sorry.'

'Stop *saying* that.'

Diahann shrugged helplessly.

'He must've had a family,' Liberty said, stomach churning. 'Did you even *tell* them about me?'

'No.'

'Why not?'

'The man was married, Libby. *Married*.'

'Oh, this is just getting better and better.'

'I felt his family had enough grief to deal with. How could I add to it?'

'Jesus, Mama, they're *my* family too,' Liberty cried, holding back tears of frustration and longing. 'This means I have *grandparents*. I should try to reach them.'

'Don't even think about it.'

'Why not?' she asked angrily. 'Why the *hell* not?'

''Cause if you want to know the whole story I *did* phone them.'

'And?'

'They called me a black American whore and warned me never to contact them again.'

'Oh, God!'

'So now you know. There's nothing more I can tell you.'

Liberty shook her head in disbelief. She felt empty inside. Somehow she'd always believed in the fairy-tale that somewhere out there was a man who would claim her as his, a man who would love her and nurture her and be proud to call her his daughter.

Now that dream was truly shattered.

Damnit, she was *not* going to let it get her down. One way or another, she would make a success of her life. Nothing and nobody was going to stop her.

Chapter Fifteen

They stood on the sidewalk outside Red Diamond's house, three brothers wondering what kind of game their father was playing now.

'I have to go,' Max said impatiently, cracking his knuckles. 'Call my assistant, she'll give you the details for tonight.'

'Wanna do lunch?' Jett asked Chris, as soon as Max had taken off.

'I got calls to make, people to see,' Chris said, worrying about what he was going to tell Roth Giagante, who was waiting – not so patiently – in Vegas. Then, seeing the disappointed look on his brother's face, he decided it wouldn't kill him to spend time with the kid because the truth of the matter was that, as far as family was concerned, Max and Jett were about it. That's if he didn't count Red, and why would he? Red had never given a damn about anyone but himself. 'Tell you what,' he said, 'meet me at The Four Seasons around one. We'll grab a bite in the restaurant. Then I have to drop by Birdy Marvel's.'

'*The* Birdy Marvel?' Jett said, impressed.

'She's a client.'

'Man, she's hot.'

'I can tell *you* haven't changed,' Chris said, laughing. 'It's all about pussy.'

'As a matter of fact I *have* changed,' Jett said, suddenly serious. 'Last night I met a girl—'

'You can tell me about it later,' Chris said, sprinting to the kerb and waving down a passing cab. 'Right now I gotta go make some calls.'

Jett watched as Chris jumped into the cab and took off. It was good to see him again, Chris had always been the brother he was closest to, and now that he was back in New York maybe they could spend more time together. Yeah, two brothers hanging out. Why not?

As he started walking down the street his cell rang. He checked out the caller ID. It was Gianna.

Hmm . . . he'd all but forgotten about his Italian super-model and her magnificent blow-jobs.

'*Ciao, bello*!' Gianna cooed, sounding her usual upbeat self. 'Why you no phone yesterday when you arrive?'

Already he was in trouble, yet it hadn't even crossed his mind that she expected him to check in.

'How you doin', baby?' he said, reminding himself that she *was* kind of his steady girlfriend, although it was totally out of character for Gianna to act clingy.

'*Perfectto*!' Gianna purred.

'Glad you're having fun without me.'

'Listen, *carino*,' Gianna continued, in her low-down throaty voice, 'I tell you something good.'

'Hey,' he said cheerfully. 'I'm always into hearing something good.'

'A big job. You and me. Together. My agent, he – how you say? – negotiate *bene*. I fly New York Sunday. Monday we do fittings. Tuesday we do print ads for the new Courtenelli collection. Sofia Courtenelli request *me*, and *I* suggest *you*. They ask for Mark Vanderloo or Brad Kroenig, but I say no, *you*.' She paused triumphantly. 'So you see, is *molto bene. Capische?*

Oh, he understood all right. Gianna was coming to New York. And what was he supposed to do about *that*?

* * *

Max headed straight for his office where he was shocked and angry to discover Vladimir Bushkin lurking in the reception area. Didn't he have enough problems? Now this low-life was there – for *what*? More money? He'd paid him *plenty* to keep his blackmailing mouth shut.

Ignoring the man, he stalked into his private domain, slamming the door behind him.

Mrs Barley buzzed him immediately. 'There's a Mr Bushkin waiting out here,' she said, sounding flustered. 'He doesn't have an appointment, but he's most insistent.'

'I'm sure he is.'

'Will you see him, Mr Diamond?'

Did he have a choice? 'Send him in,' he said gruffly.

A few seconds later Vladimir slunk into the room, like the slimy rat he was. Unshaven, with shifty eyes, the Russian man sat down uninvited.

Max was in no mood to put up with more greedy demands. 'What do you want?' he asked.

'New York very expensive place to live,' Vladimir announced, picking at a hangnail.

'So move,' Max said roughly.

'Not nice attitude,' Vladimir responded. 'You and me, we have agreement, yes?'

'The agreement was, *I* pay, *you* vanish. So what the hell are you doing sitting in my office?'

'Not friendly, Mr Diamond.'

'Listen to me, Vladimir, tell me what you want and get out.'

'I want only what I am entitled to,' Vladimir answered grandly.

Christ! The little shit wasn't going away any time soon. 'Entitled, my ass,' Max snapped.

'Silence expensive. But you rich man, you afford to buy. Yes?'

Immediately Max realized he'd handled the situation all wrong. Right from the start he should've got his lawyer involved, made the Russian prick sign an unbreakable legal agreement. Instead of which he'd been so panicked at the thought of anyone finding out the truth about his non-marriage and obviously illegitimate daughter that he'd paid Vladimir a goodly amount of money in cash. In return he'd expected the Russian to keep silent and vanish.

It seemed this was not to be.

'How much this time?' he asked harshly.

'I am not greedy man—' Vladimir started to say.

'Cut the shit,' Max interrupted. 'How much?'

'I need five hundred thousand for business venture I—'

'Five hundred thousand!' Max exploded. 'That's twice as much as I paid you last time. There's no way I can—'

'Problem none,' Vladimir interrupted, unexpectedly standing. 'I make discreet inquiries. Tabloid papers, they pay much for good story. *Juicy* story.'

'You blackmailing son-of-a-*bitch!*'

Vladimir shuffled towards the door. 'I read interview in magazine about you. You say business come first. I say same thing. This just . . . business.'

*   *   *

Chris called Roth Giagante in Vegas. Roth's assistant informed him that Mr Giagante never rose before noon. Chris felt enormous relief that he didn't have to speak to the man. Instead he left a message saying that due to a sickness in his family he had to stay in New York and would be unable to get to Vegas before the following weekend.

After making the call he felt a lot calmer. He'd given himself time to somehow come up with the balance of the money he owed, and maybe on Monday, when he finally met with Red, he'd receive a welcome surprise. He wasn't thinking he'd inherit a lot, maybe a few million, but right now he'd settle for anything.

After he'd paid his debt to Roth Giagante, there would be no more gambling. He'd worked hard to make a lot of money, so where was the sense in pissing it all away chasing a lucky streak that never seemed to happen? Although Atlantic City was less than an hour away, and while he had time to kill, a whole weekend in fact . . .

No! he told himself sternly. *No more gambling.*

After a few more phone calls back and forth to his office in L.A. he met Chris for lunch at his hotel.

As his brother walked into the restaurant, women's heads turned. Jett had the look, the sexy bad-boy look that women always seemed to go for. Colin Farrell, Owen Wilson, Brad

Pitt – Jett was better-looking than any of those guys. And the most endearing quality he possessed was that he didn't seem to know it.

'You shoulda been an actor,' Chris remarked, only half joking. 'Maybe I should hook you up with a Hollywood agent.'

'Hey,' Jett said, pulling up a chair, 'anything that makes me money.'

'You broke?'

'Not exactly, but who doesn't want big bucks?'

'Yeah, tell me about it,' Chris said, studying the menu.

'My girlfriend drives a Lamborghini, and *I* didn't buy it for her,' Jett said, reaching for a bread roll.

'You have a steady girlfriend?'

'Not exactly. We kinda live together in her apartment.'

'*Her* apartment?'

'Gianna's a big model in Italy. We, uh . . . have an arrangement.'

'And that means?'

'She gets to screw guys who buy her Lamborghinis, and I get to live rent free.'

'Sounds like a deal.'

'Yeah. Only that's not what it's all about, right?'

'Whatever works for you, little bro',' Chris said, summoning the waiter and ordering a steak.

'It did,' Jett said, going for the salmon. 'Up until last night.'

'What happened last night?'

'I met a girl. A very special girl.'

'Listen to you!' Chris said, laughing. 'You've been in town all of twenty-four hours.'

'Yeah, but shit happens, doesn't it?'

'To you, yes.'

'My first night here I got together with this girl, and she's so freakin' special I gotta hunch everything changed for me.'

'A one-night stand and everything changed,' Chris said, raising a cynical eyebrow. 'Sure it did.'

'I'm not kidding, Chris,' Jett said earnestly.

'In that case, I have questions.'

'Like what?'

'Like, who is she? And does she drive a Lamborghini, 'cause the Lamborghini girl sure sounds like a keeper.'

'Now you'll *really* think I've lost it.'

'Go ahead, I'm a lawyer, I can take it.'

'Uh . . . here's the thing. I don't even know her name.'

'Uh-huh.'

'I met her in a club, we looked at each other and that was it. She came home with me.'

'Difficult to nail, huh?' Chris drawled sarcastically. 'She must be from L.A.'

'It wasn't like that.'

'Of course it wasn't. Did you fuck her?'

'That's cold, man. It was more like making love. And . . . here's the kicker. Turns out she's a virgin.'

'You mean *was* a virgin.'

'Well . . . she wanted it as much as me. I even offered to stop, but she—'

'Spare me the details,' Chris said drily. 'One roll with a virgin and you're in love with a girl who kind of forgot to give you her name. Obviously a class act.'

'I'm telling you, she's special, Chris,' Jett insisted. 'Besides, I can easily track her down.'

'Then how come you're not onto it? Why are you sitting here with me talking about her instead of finding her?'

'She needs time . . .'

'Jesus, little bro', are you *listening* to yourself?' Chris said, shaking his head. 'High school is *over*. Stick with the Lamborghini – she sounds more your style.'

'You don't get it.'

'Oh yes, I do. Been there, done that.'

'Not with this girl.'

'Hey, if she's so important to you, you'd better go find her.'

'I will.'

'Only do me one big favour.'

'What?'

'Do not propose until you've recovered your senses.'

'Like, I'm crazy, but not *that* crazy,' Jett said, cracking a grin. 'I'll see how it goes.'

'You might not be drinking, but you're *still* a nut,' Chris said, shaking his head again.

'And how's *your* love life?' Jett asked, switching the subject because, much as he wanted to continue talking about the girl, he figured he'd said enough, and the annoying thing was that Chris wasn't taking him seriously.

'I have two rules,' Chris replied. 'Work first. Pleasure second.'

'That's harsh, man.'

'No, little bro'. That's *smart*.'

Chapter Sixteen

'Spill,' Tina said, linking her arm companionably through Amy's as they headed down the street on their way to Serendipity.

'What?' Amy answered, filled with guilt, yet still strangely elated.

'Spill,' Tina repeated. 'Take pity on this poor pregnant, *fat* woman and tell me everything.'

'You do know that you're a very bad influence?' Amy grumbled.

'Me?' Tina said innocently.

'Yes, you.' Amy sighed.

'Which means you did the deed!'

'I did not!'

'Oh, yes, you did,' Tina exclaimed triumphantly. 'It's written all over your face.'

'Don't *say* that.' Amy groaned, fervently wishing last night had never happened.

'Why? It's not a *bad* thing,' Tina said matter-of-factly. 'It's your last chance and you grabbed it. Therefore, as your best friend and adviser, I'm proud of you.'

'You are?' Amy said unsurely, as they entered Serendipity and were ushered to a table upstairs.

'Yes,' Tina said firmly, accepting a menu from a friendly waiter, who then took their drinks order. As soon as he left, she leaned across the table, obviously determined to find out everything. 'Intimate details, please,' she said. 'I have to live vicariously now.'

Amy glanced around the half-filled restaurant. 'I don't

know what you're carrying on about,' she said vaguely.

'Oh, please!' Tina said, adding in her best persuasive voice, 'You have to talk about it, otherwise you'll bottle everything up and that won't do you any good at all.'

'You think?' Amy said, refusing to meet Tina's penetrating stare.

'Yes, I think,' Tina said insistently. 'Which means you'd better tell me everything.'

Amy began to weaken. Even though it was her big secret, she had this insane urge to talk about him – the stranger, Mr S. Lucas, apartment 10A. His image kept running through her head. His face – so handsome – the lock of blondish hair that fell across his forehead, his mouth, his blue eyes, his hands, his . . . everything.

'I – I really don't understand how it happened,' she said hesitantly. 'I guess I must've had too much to drink. I . . . I was thinking about what you said and—'

'And he was *sooo* hot that you couldn't help yourself,' Tina offered, finishing Amy's sentence for her. 'You reached that intoxicating moment of no return and went for it. Would I be on the right path here?'

'That's *exactly* what happened,' Amy said breathlessly. 'It was almost like an out-of-body experience. I couldn't seem to say no.'

'And you didn't want to.'

'No,' she admitted. 'I didn't.'

'Was it great?' Tina asked, eyes gleaming.

'Huh?' Amy said, nibbling on a breadstick, although she wasn't hungry. In fact, the thought of food made her stomach turn.

'Oh, nice!' Tina exclaimed, watching her. 'Stuff your face and leave me hanging.'

'What?'

'I repeat,' Tina said, 'and I'm speaking very slowly, was it great?'

'I can't talk about it anymore. I mean, what if Max finds out?' Amy muttered, swallowing hard, and almost choking on the breadstick.

'There's no way he'll find out,' Tina assured her.

'He might,' Amy said, thinking of the consequences if he did.

'Not unless you're foolish enough to tell him,' Tina said, handing her a glass of water.

'I would *never* do that.'

'Well,' Tina said, 'I hope you used a condom.'

Now panic joined her feelings of guilt. Who the hell was thinking condoms when they were so caught up in the passion of the moment? *He* certainly wasn't, and neither was she.

'Of course,' she lied, ashamed of her behaviour, and yet, in spite of everything, *still* suffused with the warm glow that refused to go away.

'Smart girl,' Tina said, followed by a loud 'Ouch!'

'What's the matter?'

'This baby boy has some kick!' Tina grumbled, clutching her stomach. 'I'm telling you, this little tyke is destined to be the greatest football-player in the world, or some kind of insane wife-beater!'

* * *

Later in the day Max called again. Amy was instantly on guard. Had he found out somehow? It wasn't like Max to call her more than once a day.

'I'm taking Lulu for tea at the Peninsula,' he said. 'I'd like you to meet us.'

'Today?' she said hesitantly.

'Yes, today.'

'Well . . .' she said, stalling for time, 'I *am* working.'

'For now you're working. Soon you'll be giving it all up, so what does it matter if you leave early?'

Was Max under the mistaken impression that as soon as they were married she was quitting her job? No way.

'Look,' he continued, 'I've had a lousy day, and I need to be surrounded by the women I love.'

Major guilt trip. He wouldn't love her so much if he knew what she'd done last night.

'I . . . um . . . I'm supposed to be going over to my mother's. Big meeting with the wedding planner.'

'That's later, isn't it?'

'Uh, yes.'

'Four o'clock. The Peninsula. Oh, and see if you can pick up some of that Hello Kitty stuff for Lulu.'

Just what she needed – Max and his precocious five-year-old. Lulu had a habit of regarding her with baby pursed lips and accusing eyes. Obviously Mariska had taught her daughter exactly how to behave when faced with the enemy – and there was no doubt about it: in Lulu's mind she *was* the enemy, the nasty lady who'd stolen daddy away from her mommy.

Staring blankly at her computer screen, Amy thought about googling S. Lucas. What *was* her mystery man's first name? Steven? Simon? Was *he* thinking about *her*?

Damn! There was absolutely no way she could get him off her mind.

And yet she had to. It was imperative that she stop thinking about him. After all, she would never see him again.

She was marrying Max Diamond, and that was that. Case closed.

Chapter Seventeen

I n spite of the fact that his brother was so dismissive of his big new love, Jett still decided to tag along and meet Birdy Marvel. After all, she was famous – so why not?

The pop princess greeted them in her penthouse suite wearing frayed Daisy Dukes, silver roller-blades, and a skimpy T-shirt emblazoned with the slogan KISS MY ASSETS. She was surrounded by her entourage, a colourful group of twenty-somethings who attended to her hair, make-up and outfits, and laughed at her jokes. *Baby sycophants*, Chris thought, as he introduced her to Jett.

Birdy took one look and liked what she saw. 'Where you bin hidin' *him?*' she demanded, sucking a purple frozen popsicle.

'Italy. I live in Milan,' Jett said, noticing that she had a bad case of acne on her pointed chin, but she was cute, all the same.

'Cool,' Birdy said, suggestively licking her popsicle. 'One of these days I wanna take a trip to Venice. Hear it's dope.'

'Jett just stopped by to say hello,' Chris said. 'So now that he has, he's leaving. That'll give you a chance to tell me what's on your mind.'

'He can stay if he wants,' Birdy offered, casually flopping into a chair and throwing her legs over the side. ''S long as he doesn't report to the tabloids.'

'Thanks for the offer, but I gotta split,' Jett said. 'It was great meeting you.'

'Likewise,' Birdy said, suddenly all coy and proper as Jett headed for the door. 'He's *hot*,' she announced, to his retreating back.

'Superhot,' agreed her stylist, a short plump girl dressed from head to toe in red leather, with matching red hair and thick black eyebrows, one of which was pierced with a tiny silver dove.

'Okay, get lost,' Birdy said, waving her entourage out of the room. 'I gotta talk private stuff with my sexy lawyer.'

Obediently they trooped out.

'Where's Rocky?' Chris asked.

'With his grandma,' she answered, purple ice dripping onto her fingers.

'Rocky has a grandma?' Chris said, raising his eyebrows.

'She's eighty an' still rides a hog,' Birdy replied, licking her sticky fingers one by one.

'That must be quite a sight,' Chris said drily.

'You're not into Rocky, are you?' Birdy said, squinting at Chris through ever so slightly bloodshot blue eyes.

'As long as *you* like him, that's all that matters, isn't it?'

'Yup.'

'And you *do* still like him?'

' 'Course,' she said, sucking her popsicle down to the stick, then tossing the stick onto the floor.

'So what is it you want to talk privately about?'

'Stuff,' she said vaguely.

'Go ahead.'

'I'm pregnant, an' I wanna marry Rocky,' she blurted excitedly.

'Whaaaat?'

'Like, I wanna do it this weekend so, Chris, you'd better arrange it.'

'Me?' he said, shocked.

'You're my lawyer, you take care of *everything*.'

'I'm a lawyer, not a Justice of the Peace.'

'Whatever,' she said, waving her hands in the air. 'I pay you to get things done, so do it.'

Age had not improved Ms Birdy Marvel's manners, and if he wasn't getting a fat percentage of her income he would tell her exactly where she could stuff her imperious orders. But right now he could not afford to lose any clients, so he nodded, as if he was considering her options.

'You'll need a pre-nuptial,' he said, taking out his Palm to make some notes. 'And Rocky's lawyer will have to check it out before he signs, so we're definitely not talking this weekend.'

'Why not?' she whined.

'I just told you why not.'

'Who cares about a stupid pre-nup thingummy?' she said, getting up and extracting a can of Red Bull from the mini-bar.

'*You* do.'

'Rocky warned me you'd be all pissy about it,' she said, pulling a face. 'So we worked something out.'

'What did you work out?' Chris asked, keeping his temper in check.

'Well . . . since *I*'m the one with all the loot, we thought it only fair that Rocky gets something if our marriage doesn't last, which of course it, like, *will*, 'cause we're, like, *full on* in love. So you gotta draw up some kinda paper that pays him a million bucks a year if I don't stay married to him for five years.'

Bingo! Birdy never disappointed. 'You're kidding, right?' He sighed.

'No,' she said, swigging Red Bull from the can.

'You must be. Either that or you're certifiable.'

'S'cuse me?' she said, widening her eyes.

'You're talking like a crazy girl. Surely you remember *why* you wanted the emancipation? We worked hard to see that you gained control of your money, and that's the way it should stay.'

'I get it, Chris,' she said earnestly. 'Only here's the thing, Rocky's so totally *awesome*.'

'*How* long have you known him?'

'A coupla months,' she said, smiling dreamily.

'It's all fun now, but when you're in a relationship, things change.'

'Not with me an' Rocky.'

'I'm not saying you shouldn't promise him *anything*. I can draw you up a document that'll serve *both* of you and if Rocky doesn't accept it, then you shouldn't marry him.'

'Oh, Chris,' she responded, pouting, 'you can be such a downer.'

'I'm merely protecting you, Birdy,' he said sternly. 'Do you understand that if you guaranteed him a million per year for five years, and he left you after four and a half, the guy would walk away with five million of your hard-earned money? Do you *really* understand that?'

'Don't sweat it, Chris. Rocky and I will be together for, like, *fifty* years.'

'Then there's no problem, is there?'

'I guess not,' she said unsurely. 'So can I get married this weekend?'

'It's not going to fly,' he said, his mind racing. 'New York marriage laws are different from California.'

'Why?'

'They just are.'

'Man, I really wanna do this,' she said, starting to sulk.

'Have you considered Vegas?' he said, formulating a plan.

'I *looove* Vegas,' she cooed, her face lighting up. 'Vegas is hot!'

'Good. Because if you do it in Vegas,' he said, still thinking fast, 'I can get you the presidential suite at the Magiriano, a big reception, and numerous other perks. Also, I'll make a deal to sell exclusive wedding pictures to *People* or *Us*, or one of the tabloids, then you can give half of that money to Rocky, and if *that* doesn't keep him happy—'

'Oh, wow!' she said, clapping her hands. 'Can we do it *next* weekend?'

'It might be possible,' he said, thinking this would definitely get him off the hook with Roth Giagante, and that was a major plus, because if Birdy got married at Roth's hotel it would mean millions of dollars' worth of free publicity for the Magiriano, and there was no way Roth would object to *that*.

'You're the man, Chris,' Birdy squealed, jumping up and throwing her arms round him. 'We're such an awesome team. I'm totally psyched you're my lawyer.'

'So am I. But remember, I'm the one who thinks for you and all *you* have to do is perform.' She nodded enthusiastically. 'Now, about this pregnancy thing,' he continued. 'Are you *sure?*'

'Not exactly,' she answered vaguely. 'I'm late but, y' know, whenever I'm on the road I'm always late.'

'You are?'

'Rocky says it would be like totally *amazing* if we had a baby.'

Of course Rocky would say that: Rocky was out to secure his position with one of the biggest earners in show business.

'Has he got kids with anyone else?' Chris asked, deciding he'd better do some heavy detective work before this joke of a relationship went any further.

'Man!' Birdy yelled excitedly. 'I *swear* you're a freakin' psychic! How'dja *know*?'

'A wild guess,' he answered calmly. 'How many?'

'One little boy. But, y' know, I totally get off on kids, so I'll take care of it too.'

'You will, huh?'

'Course.'

'Pay all its bills? Pay for Rocky's ex-girlfriend?'

'Wife,' she corrected, draining the can of Red Bull and tossing the empty can onto the floor.

'Wife?' Chris said, raising his eyebrows.

'*Ex*-wife,' she said casually, like it was a minor detail.

'You've seen the divorce papers?'

'No, but—'

'Get them, Birdy. I can't arrange anything before I see them.'

'Oh, Chris,' she pouted like a little girl, 'now you're spoiling everything.'

'No, Birdy,' he answered sternly. 'I'm simply making sure nobody hurts you, and don't you forget it.'

And that's why they pay me the big bucks, he thought, with a certain amount of satisfaction. *For saving their asses, not to mention their money.*

* * *

What could he do to shut Vladimir Bushkin up once and for all? Max knew he had a major problem on his hands, and money wasn't about to solve it. Of course, he could hand over more cash, but it was a given that Vladimir would soon be back for more.

Or he could threaten deportation, and in return Vladimir would sell his dirty little story to the tabloids.

Or he could *what*? What the fuck *could* he do? This wasn't some Hollywood movie where he could take a hit out on the blackmailing Russian low-life. Those things didn't happen in real life.

Or did they?

Of course they did. It was naïve to think otherwise.

What would Red Diamond do? Big Red, as he'd been called by his cronies and hangers-on. Big Red, would think nothing of crushing Vladimir like a bug.

Max remembered fragments of conversations he'd heard while he was growing up about how Red had dealt with anyone who got in his way. Apparently he'd left a trail of shattered lives and broken men in his wake, and never given it a second thought.

Yes, Red Diamond would know how to deal with a roach like Vladimir Bushkin, no doubt about that.

But Max was at a loss. Even if he considered putting a hit out on the blackmailing Russian, how would he go about it?

Listen to yourself, he thought. *Thinking about arranging for someone to be killed. This is pure insanity.*

It was all Mariska's fault, the duplicitous, scheming *bitch*! Mariska. Mother of his child. And shouldn't he be getting a DNA test to make sure he *was* Lulu's father, although he loved the little girl. If it turned out she wasn't his, he would be devastated.

And yet he had his future to think about, and his future was Amy, the lovely Amy. If she knew about this sordid mess with Vladimir and Mariska she would be disgusted. He hadn't even told her about his problems with the banks, and he should, because at any moment the news was going to break and it would be all over the financial pages. He had his enemies too, and they would like nothing better than to see him fail. He was, after all, Red Diamond's son.

He glanced at his watch and realized it was almost time to collect Lulu and take her for tea.

The thought of seeing Mariska filled him with a deep-seated loathing. He wanted to shake the truth out of her, which wouldn't do any good because even if he confronted her with Vladimir's story she was bound to lie. It was her way.

Then it occurred to him that perhaps *she* was the one who should deal with Vladimir. After all, she had just as much to lose if the story came out. She would be exposed and humiliated: her social life in New York would be over, and that was all Mariska had ever cared about – her damn social position.

Yes, this might be the answer.

He'd told the Russian to come back next week. 'I'll have the cash for you,' he'd promised. 'Do *not* do anything foolish.'

Which left him a short time to think about how he was going to handle the situation.

It would have been a lot easier if he hadn't had a bachelor party to attend, a crucial meeting with the Japanese bankers who were flying in to see him, and an upcoming wedding.

But things were never easy. That was one of the few lessons he'd learned from Red.

* * *

Jett left Birdy Marvel's hotel and immediately got on his cell, trying Beverly's number again. This time she picked up. 'Where have you been?' he said accusingly. 'I left messages this morning.'

'*You* disappeared last night, and where have *I* been?' Beverly said. 'You're somethin', Jett.'

'Hey, listen, Bev, I need a favour.'

'Then quit with the pissy attitude.'

'The girl I left with last night, who is she?'

'I didn't see you with a girl.'

'Yes, you did, you saw me talking to her, then we were dancing and I left with her. Now I need to know who she is.'

'Uh . . . excuse me,' Beverly said. '*You* left with a girl, and *I*'m supposed to find out who she is? Ever heard of exchanging names? It helps, y' know.'

'Hey, just be happy that I'm back, sober, an' *maybe* – just maybe – in love.'

'Mr Romance strikes again! One thing about you, Jett, you're an original, but then you always were. Sober, *not* sober, fucked-up, straight.'

'Thanks. I think.'

'By the way, shouldn't you be attending a meeting while you're in town?'

'Gimme a break, Bev' he groaned. 'I only just got here.'

'I can direct you to meetings *crammed* with gorgeous girls – all the hot models are in cocaine rehab. You'll feel *right* at home.'

'Sure,' he said, with a dry laugh. 'That's exactly what I need, a dysfunctional hook-up with an ex-stoner model. Can't wait!'

'I can think of worse things.'

'Not interested. Just find me the girl's name and call me back.'

'For you I'll try.'

'Try hard, it's important.'

He took a cab back to Sam's apartment. The maid had not been in, and the bed was as he'd left it, in the same tangled mess. He sat down on the edge, noticing that the sheets smelt of sex and his mystery girl's scent. It was a heady combination.

Jeez! He hadn't felt this way since he was a teenager and got laid for the first time by one of his mother's friends. Talk about excited!

There was no doubt in his mind that he had to find her, and he needed to do so before Gianna arrived in town, because that would only complicate matters.

It was definitely decision time. Should he stay with the Italian supermodel and all she had to offer? Or should he start taking chances, allow himself to fall in love and go for a new start?

It would be so much easier if he had financial security. And maybe . . . on Monday . . . the old man would finally come through.

Goodbye, Gianna.

Hello . . . who?

With Beverly's help he'd soon find out.

Chapter Eighteen

C indi turned up unexpectedly in the early afternoon, and announced that she'd taken the rest of the day off work. Clad in an orange velour tracksuit that emphasized her large curves, she was grinning as if she'd just discovered she'd won the lottery.

'How come you're taking time off?' Liberty asked, still shaken by her earlier conversation with her mom and the shockingly sad revelations about her father.

'Told Manny I had a fearful pain in my gut, an' he didn't argue 'cause biz was kinda slow, an', girl – I am one *fine* actress,' Cindi boasted, grabbing a handful of nuts from a dish on the table and stuffing them in to her mouth.

'But with me out an' all—'

'Chill, we still got jobs – that's if we wanna keep 'em.'

'Why *wouldn't* we?' Liberty said, frowning. 'You know we need the money. We're way late on all our bills.'

''Cause,' Cindi announced triumphantly, 'I have scored me a two-day gig dancin' in a music video.'

'No shit?'

'Yup, an' I'm gettin' paid three hundred a day, an' we start shootin' tomorrow.'

'*What?*'

'It's an all-weekend shoot, so now I gotta go get me a costume fittin'. But first I had to stop by an' give you the news. It's something', huh?'

'It sure is. How did it happen?'

'These two guys came in an' I served 'em coffee. Before I can flip a coin, they're eyeballin' me big-time. Then they're

118

tellin' me I'm 'xactly the kind of girl they're lookin' for to be in Slick Jimmy's music video.'

'*What* two guys? And who's Slick Jimmy?'

'One's the producer, not sure 'bout the other dude. Slick Jimmy's a rapper. Word is, he's droppin' a hot CD single. This is his first music video, an', girl, *I* am in it!'

'Did you happen to mention you're a singer, not a professional dancer?'

'Hey, little cous', I got my moves,' Cindi boasted, smoothing down her orange top, her enormous boobs straining the material. 'An' they're not lookin' for pros, so quit with the questions an' be down with it. I'm gonna be on *Tee Vee*. People'll *see* me. It'll run on MTV, VH1, everywhere!'

Liberty tried her best to look enthusiastic even though she didn't quite get it. Although Cindi was pretty, she was also extremely large. Big, bountiful breasts, solid rolls of flesh around her middle, and an ass that made J-Lo look positively skinny. Think Queen Latifah and Carnie Wilson before their major weight loss.

'What kind of outfit you get to wear?' she asked, trying not to be envious.

'These dudes told me the video's set in 1920s Chicago, so it's a nightclubby kinda deal. Hmm . . . I'm seein' somethin' slinky an' way sexy, 'cause this girl's got *plenty* to show off.'

'It's – it's great. I'm so happy for you.'

'You bet your ass it's *great* – for *both* of us, 'cause if you feel okay, I'm takin' you with me. Mebbe when they see you they'll put you in the video too.'

'Oh, sure!' Liberty said drily. 'A limpin' gimp with a burned-up arm. That'll *really* get 'em goin'!'

'How *are* you feelin'?' Cindi asked. 'Here I am, carryin' on 'bout myself, an' you're sittin' here all down an' low.'

'Believe me,' Liberty said fervently, 'I am *so* ready to get outta here.'

'Your mama bin in your bizness?' Cindi asked, helping herself to another handful of nuts.

'No, I've been into hers and now I can't wait to leave.'

'You're *supposed* t' be restin' up.'

'No way. I'm coming with to your costume thing, and

then back to our place. I can't stay here. This house is makin'
me crazy. I hate everything about it.'

'Shouldn't you tell your mom you're leavin'?'

'I don't have to tell her anything.'

'Where *is* she anyway?' Cindi asked.

'Where do you *think*? Runnin' around after Mr D, probably wiping his wrinkled old ass. You know what, Cindi? She's
that old dude's freakin' *slave*. I can't take the way she caters to
him like he's some kind of *king*. It stinks.'

'Oh, Lordy,' Cindi sighed, waving her hands in the air,
'nothin' ever changes around here. You two ain't *never* gonna
get along.'

'Let's not get into it now,' Liberty said, gathering together
her things. 'We should split before she comes back.'

'How about leavin' her a note?'

'*No*, Cindi.'

'You sure you can walk?'

'Don't worry about it. I'll manage.'

'If you say so.'

'I say so,' Liberty said, hobbling to the door.

If there was one thing she was sure of, she needed to get
away from her mother and she needed to get away fast.

* * *

The costume-fitting place was on the fifth floor of an old
building in the middle of the garment district. The elevator
was so small they barely both squeezed into it.

'This is a *trip*!' Cindi said enthusiastically. 'Better than
fillin' coffee cups all day an' shovin' yesterday's pie at a buncha
ungrateful customers.'

'They're not *all* bad,' Liberty said, thinking of Damon P.
Donnell.

Cindi took a small hand mirror out of her purse and
studied her face. 'How you feelin' now?' she asked, licking her
generous lips. 'Anythin' hurtin'?'

'I'm good,' Liberty said. Later, when they got home, she'd
tell Cindi everything. Right now was not the time. Besides, she
needed to fully absorb it herself.

'You *sure* you're walkin' okay?' Cindi asked, still en-amoured with her reflection.

'Who's walking? I'm standing in an elevator getting crushed to death by your tits.'

Cindi giggled. 'It's my fine tits *got* me this gig.'

'You think?'

'I ain't dumb, girl. I've seen plenty of rap videos. They're gonna want me to kinda, uh . . . jiggle 'em. Like you said, it's not as if I'm a professional dancer.'

'And you're okay with that?'

'Honey, if they're stupid enough to pay me, I'll stand on my head an' whistle "The Star Spangled Banner"!'

At the costume place they were greeted by Fantasia, a tall, ultra-thin black woman with an extreme Afro and a chiselled face. 'You girls here for the video?' Fantasia asked, checking them over.

'Ｓ right,' Cindi said. 'I'm the one who's in it, an' this here is my cousin.'

'Follow me, ladies.'

Cindi shot Liberty an excited look as they moved through the crowded space, squeezing past racks of hanging clothes.

Standing around in various stages of undress were several other large black girls. *Oh, now I get it*, Liberty thought. *This is a big girls' video, the bigger the better*. No surprise they'd chosen Cindi.

The outfit Fantasia handed to Cindi was not slinky and sexy, it consisted of a bejewelled bra and a brief pair of matching hot pants.

'You *gotta* be shittin' me!' Cindi exclaimed, holding up the hot pants with an incredulous look. 'There's no freakin' way I can squeeze *my* booty into *this* itty-bitty thing. My stuff's gonna be in your face an' *then* some.'

'That's what they're lookin' for, hon,' said Fantasia, usher-ing her towards a curtained cubicle. 'Put it on an' let's see how it fits.'

'I can't show *everything*,' Cindi protested, hesitating before getting undressed.

'Everybody else does.'

121

'How many everyone elses *are* there?' Cindi asked, a touch belligerent.

'Eight of you. You'll all be shakin' and shimmyin' in the background while Slick Jimmy raps his down-an'-dirty heart out. So you'll be showin' some skin – you flaunt more than that on the beach.'

'Not me,' Cindi said sourly. 'I wear a one-piece.'

'You in or out?' Fantasia inquired, suddenly impatient. 'Make up your mind, 'cause I got other girls to fit.'

'Crap!' Cindi grumbled. 'I thought I was gonna be wearin' somethin', y' know, all kinda sexy.' She glanced at Liberty. 'What do *you* think?'

'It's not exactly dignified, but it *is* a paid job, and we could use the extra money . . .'

'Hmm . . . It's plenty more than I get workin' in the coffee shop,' Cindi mused. 'An' it's not like I'm *shy*.'

'Do it,' Liberty encouraged. 'It's a trip.'

Cindi put on the skimpy outfit. It failed to contain all of her ample curves. Her breasts were barely covered, while her ass hung cheekily out of the hot pants.

'We're gonna have to do alterations,' Fantasia said, all business. 'I'll bring it to the set tomorrow.'

'Does that mean you're finished with me?'

'For now. We'll see you at the shoot.'

'Let's go get coffee,' Liberty suggested.

'You mean have someone serve *us*?' Cindi giggled, quite excited.

'Why not? We're paying.'

'*And* we'll leave 'em a big fat tip,' Cindi said, ''Cause I am makin' *money*! An' *you* are comin' with me, girl. I am *not* doin' it alone. No freakin' way.'

They linked arms and walked down the street, heading into an unfamiliar coffee shop.

'I hope you remembered to feed my Ragtags,' Liberty said, sliding onto a counter stool.

'Yeah, yeah,' Cindi said, immediately reaching for a menu.

'Was Damon in today?' Liberty asked, trying to make it casual.

'He was,' Cindi replied, studying the menu.

'Um . . . did he ask why I wasn't around?'

'Oh, yeah,' Cindi said sarcastically. 'The first thing the dude does when he comes in is say, "Where's that hot bitch who always serves me my coffee an' eggs? I notice her every day, but I ain't bin talkin' to her 'cause I'm a *married* man." '

'Very funny, Cindi.'

'*I* served him today, an' if it's any consolation he didn't talk to me either.'

'That's 'cause you were too busy scoring yourself a gig with those other two guys.'

They both laughed.

'At least the video'll be somethin' different,' Cindi said.

'It's all good,' Liberty agreed. 'We gotta make the most of every single moment.'

'Right *on*, sister.'

And they high-fived each other, grinned, and suddenly Liberty didn't feel so bad.

Chapter Nineteen

'You look tired,' Max remarked as Amy joined him and Lulu in the tea room of the Peninsula'.

'Yes, Daddy, Amy's tired! Tired! *Tired*,' Lulu sing-songed happily, grabbing for the Hello Kitty bag Amy carried.

Amy resisted handing it over. Lulu immediately began to whine: 'It's mine! Mine! *Mine!* My present. Gimme my present. I want it!'

'I want never gets,' Amy said sternly. 'Try saying "please", Lulu. Then you can have it.'

Lulu promptly burst into tears. 'Amy's being mean,' she cried. 'Mean! Mean! *Mean!* I hate Amy!'

'Stop it!' Max said sternly. With everything else that was going on, he was hardly in the mood to deal with a crying child. 'And *never* use the word "hate" – it's a bad, bad word.'

'Mommy says it about you,' Lulu answered slyly. 'I've heard her.'

'Give Lulu the bag,' Max said, turning to Amy. 'I can't handle a meltdown.'

'When she says "please",' Amy countered, determined not to stand down. It was important that Lulu got used to some ground rules. Obviously her mother allowed her to get away with anything.

'What?' Max said irritably.

'She's five, Max. She can say "please".'

'No, Lulu *can't*,' Lulu said, a malevolent gleam in her eyes. 'Can't! Can't! *Can't!*'

Max snatched the bag out of Amy's hand and handed it to

Lulu. This made Amy furious. She was marrying this man, which meant that she was inheriting his daughter, and if he was going to condone this child's rude behaviour, she was not happy. 'You shouldn't have done that,' she said to Max.

'What's the matter with you?' he said, attempting to steer the conversation away from Lulu. 'You're tired and irritable.'

'No,' Amy countered. '*You*'re the one who's tired and irritable.'

'I have a lot on my mind, Amy. A *lot* on my mind. More than you know.'

'Then why don't you tell me about it? Maybe I can help.'

'I can't now,' he said curtly. 'I've got to take Lulu home and then I have to get ready for this thing tonight, which I am *not* looking forward to.'

'Can you please tell me why you're doing something you don't want to?' she said, wishing he would be more open with her.

'Because I have to,' he said shortly. 'It's business.'

'Since when did a bachelor party become business?' she persisted.

Lulu was busy opening the bag, taking out a Hello Kitty purse, a colouring book and a box of crayons. '*I want more*,' she demanded shrilly.

'Sorry, that's it,' Amy said shortly. 'And a thank-you might be nice.'

'Want more! More! *More!*' Lulu shouted at the top of her voice.

People at other tables turned to stare.

'Someone's got to teach this child some manners,' Amy said.

'That's not *your* job,' Max replied.

'When we're married, will it be my job?'

'When we're married, your job is to make *me* happy.'

'Really?' she said, quite startled at his chauvinistic attitude. 'And what will *your* job be?'

'To make *you* happy, of course,' he answered, realizing that Amy was not herself, and perhaps tea with Lulu hadn't been such a good plan. The two of them needed more time to get to know each other. 'Darling,' he said, trying to sound understanding, 'what *is* the matter with you?'

'Nothing's the matter with me. It's you and Lulu. She's behaving like a spoiled brat.'

'Brat! Brat! *Brat!*' Lulu shrieked. 'Don't *like* stupid present. Don't *like* Amy. Gimme something else, Daddy. Lulu wants something else.'

Amy shook her head and turned to Max. 'Please don't ask me to buy her anything again.'

'I think she had a difficult day at school,' Max said, making excuses.

'*I* had a difficult day at work,' Amy retorted. 'But I'm not chanting about hating people.'

'Maybe this wasn't such a good idea,' Max said, desperately trying to avoid a confrontation.

'Do you want me to go?' Amy asked, jutting out her chin.

'No, of course not.'

'It seems like you do.'

'Sweetheart,' he said, leaning over and taking her hand in his. 'Let's not get into a fight, please. I've had a lousy week, so why don't we have a quiet dinner tomorrow night, just the two of us?'

'I'm sure you'll want to be quiet after your wild bachelor party,' she said.

'Do you have any idea how much I'm not looking forward to it?' He groaned. 'You *know* how bad they are. After all, you had to suffer through yours last night, didn't you?'

'It wasn't any fun,' she said, immediately feeling guilty.

'They never are,' he retaliated.

'No, really,' she said, almost panicking. 'I couldn't wait to get out of there.'

'What kind of a show did the girls put on for you?' he inquired. 'Naked firemen? A cop with a boom-box? Not male strippers, I hope.'

'Oh, no,' she said quickly. 'Nothing like that. We just sat around talking and had a few drinks.'

'You don't drink,' he pointed out.

'I do sometimes. I drink champagne.'

'That's what I like about you, Amy. You're different from

other girls. You haven't run around this city jumping into bed with every rich guy you see. You're a beautiful, pure girl and that's why I love you.'

'Pure! Pure! *Pure!*' Lulu chanted loudly, sneaking a sly, vindictive look at Amy.

'I think I'll go, Max,' Amy said, deciding she couldn't take a moment more of Lulu. 'I've got a headache and you know my mother's expecting me at the house for yet *another* meeting with the wedding planner. You don't mind, do you?'

'How about some tea before you run off?'

'No, it's better for you to enjoy your time with Lulu by yourself.'

'If you're sure.'

'I am.'

'Then I'll call you tonight, the moment I get home.'

'I'll probably be asleep.'

'I'll call anyway. I'm sure you'll be anxious to hear all about my evening from hell.'

'It can wait until morning, Max,' she said, rising.

'Okay.' He stood up and kissed her cheek. 'I love you, Amy.'

'You too,' she found herself replying.

And she couldn't help it, but her mind was filled with doubt.

*   *   *

Chris was in his hotel room about to take a shower when Birdy Marvel called. 'Rocky totally *gets* the whole Vegas thing,' she said. 'We both do. Is it all arranged?'

'I'm one phone call away from finalizing everything.'

'Awesome! Rocky's finding his divorce papers. We're like *so* organized, you should be proud of me. We're havin' a celebration at Gatsby's later – drop by.'

'I'll be at a bachelor night for my brother.'

'The hot one?'

'My other brother.'

'You mean there's three of you? All cute?'

'You're engaged, Birdy,' he reminded her.

'Can *I* come to the bachelor party?'

'*That*'d cause a riot.'

'I could give your brother a lap-dance,' she teased. ''Specially if he looks like Jett.'

'Y' know, for an eighteen-year-old you sure are growing up fast.'

Birdy giggled. 'Just f–ing with you, Chris. Come for a drink later, an' *don't* bring strippers. Oh, yeah, maybe do, 'cause I kinda get off on watching girls strut their goodies. Who knows?' she added cheekily. 'Maybe I could get *me* a lap dance.'

'Birdy, Birdy,' Chris sighed, 'you're incorrigible.'

'Me?' she said innocently.

'Yes, you, and try to stay away from the paparazzi.'

'Like I can do *that*,' she snorted.

As soon as he hung up, the phone rang again. This time it was his L.A. girlfriend. 'You're not going to be happy, Chris,' Verona said, in one of those voices that spelled doom.

'Why not?' he answered carefully.

'It's raining in L.A., and there's dozens of leaks all over your house.'

'Can't the maid fix them?'

'She can't climb up on the roof and fix leaks.'

'Then call the roofer. He can put tarps around everything until it stops.'

'I'm not in charge of your house, Chris. I don't live with you, remember? You left me the key, so I came over to check. If I lived here I could deal with it.'

'Stop being pissy, Verona. You can deal with it if you want to.'

'I can't,' she said stubbornly. 'It's not my responsibility.'

'You can,' he argued.

'I suggest you have someone from your office take care of it,' she said, copping an attitude.

He shook his head. This was unbelievable: sweet, gentle Verona was turning the screws so that he would invite her to move in, but he had no intention of doing so. Living with Holly Anton on and off for eighteen months had been an experience he never planned to repeat. He *liked* living alone.

Was that such a terrible thing? Why did women always feel they had to chase after a commitment?

'How bad *is* the rain?' he asked.

'It's been pouring since you left. They're sayin' it won't stop for at least another few days. Apparently it's the biggest rainfall we've had in years.'

'Can you at least call one of my assistants and tell them to deal with it?'

'No, Chris, *you* call them, it's not up to me.'

'Thanks, Verona,' he said shortly. 'You're a big help.'

'No problem,' she answered sweetly.

He took out his Palm and left himself a message. *As soon as I get back to L.A. dump Verona.*

* * *

Jett called Beverly's answering-machine three times before she finally got back to him.

'I told you – when I know something you'll hear from me,' she said, sounding pissed off.

'Are you tellin' me the whole day has gone past and you *still* haven't found out who she is?'

'I'm not a detective, Jett. The barman at Gatsby's will know. He'll be in after ten.'

'You can reach me at my brother's bachelor party. Call me if you find out anything.'

'You're really hung up on her, aren't you?'

'I am,' he confessed. 'She's different, Bev, really different.'

'When you *do* find her, I hope she's worth the wait.'

'That's a given,' he said confidently.

'Gotta go,' Beverly said. 'I'm preparing my stuff for tomorrow.'

'What's happening tomorrow?'

'Making up a bunch of fat girls for a hot new rap video. It'll be fun. You should come by, visit the set.'

'Maybe I will. But, Bev, do me a big favour and get me that number.'

* * *

After Amy had left, Max felt bad about the way he'd treated her. Naturally Lulu came first, but Amy was a close second. Yes, Lulu *was* spoiled, but she was only five, so her bad behaviour should be excusable.

He watched as his cute little daughter pushed a half-eaten cucumber sandwich around her plate and almost spilled a glass of milk. She was so pretty, and she had *his* eyes – he was *sure* she had his eyes.

'Wanna go home, Daddy,' she said, after a few minutes. 'Lulu's bored.'

'Okay, sweetheart,' he said. 'Daddy'll get the check.'

'Wanna go *now*,' she said, lower lip quivering. 'I'm bored! Bored! *Bored!*'

'Okay, Lulu, keep it down, we're leaving.'

His car and driver were waiting outside. It was a short ride back to the penthouse where Lulu resided with her mother. He escorted his daughter upstairs. Mariska's elderly personal maid, Russian-born Irena, answered the door. Max couldn't stand her. The feeling was mutual.

'Mrs Diamond around?' he asked, entering the apartment.

'She is,' said Irena, glaring at him. 'You wish see her?'

'If she's available. I'll wait in the living room.'

''Bye, Daddy,' Lulu said, with an angelic little smile, as her British nanny appeared to claim her. 'See you soon! Soon! *Soon!*' And she skipped off.

Max walked into the living room. Since their separation Mariska had made many decorating changes. Her style was certainly not his. She favoured ornate silver frames, old paintings of ancestors she'd never had, and an abundance of heavily embroidered cushions sitting on overstuffed couches. When they'd first moved into the apartment he'd had it decorated by a professional. Now it was a mish-mash of different styles, very unappealing.

He made his way over to the liquor cabinet and poured himself a Scotch on the rocks.

Five minutes later Mariska came in. Obviously she had not been expecting him because her hair wasn't in its usual groomed state and she was not fully dressed. 'What do you want, Max?' she asked, tightening the belt on her Chinese silk robe.

'I need to talk to you,' he said belligerently. 'Is that all right?'

'You should let me know in advance when you want to talk,' she said bad-temperedly. 'Most times you cannot wait to get out of here.'

'Yes, well, today there's something we must discuss,' he said, taking a hefty swig of Scotch. 'Incidentally, Lulu is behaving like a brat.'

'She's *your* brat as well as mine,' Mariska said sharply. 'So, if she's behaving badly, it's *your* fault.'

'Why is it *my* fault?' he asked, ready for an argument. 'She doesn't live with *me*.'

'Are you accusing me of being a bad mother?' Mariska demanded, challenging him to do battle.

'No,' he said, backing down. 'I'm merely saying someone should teach her better manners.'

'Oh, *please*,' Mariska said dismissively. 'She's five.'

'Anyway,' Max said, 'close the door. This is private. I don't want your nosy maid listening in.'

'I hope it's about money,' Mariska said, sitting down on the couch and crossing her legs. 'I've been speaking with friends, and everyone tells me my settlement is not fair, *especially* as you're about to marry that silly rich girl who's far too young for you.'

'Amy's not too young for me,' he said curtly. 'And your settlement was plenty fair.'

Mariska threw him a condescending look. 'I hear that tonight you're having a *bachelor* party.'

'How do *you* know?'

'Not much goes on in this city that I *don't* know about,' she said smugly.

'If that's the case, Mariska, then you probably know about your ex – or should I say *current* husband, Vladimir Bushkin.'

The colour drained from Mariska's face. 'I – I don't know what you're talking about,' she stammered.

'Yes, you do,' he said. 'And we should discuss what we're going to do about Vladimir.'

'Who is this Vladimir?' she muttered, refusing to look at him.

'Oh, for God's sake, stop it,' he snapped, tired of her games. 'I *know* who he is. I've seen the official papers. He's your legal *husband*, which means that you and I were never married.' There was a long, stony silence. 'Do you have any idea what this means?' he said, glaring at her.

She glared back. 'I still don't know what you're talking about.'

'Then I suggest you think about it,' he said coldly. 'We will meet tomorrow, and in the meantime you can exercise your memory and come up with some answers, because the son-of-a-bitch is blackmailing me, and I'm sure *you* don't want him running to the tabloids anymore than I do. Tomorrow we'll come up with a solution together.'

And with those words he got up and slammed his way out of her apartment.

* * *

'You *dumb* fuckhead.'

'Huh?' Chris said, fresh out of the shower as he picked up the bathroom phone.

'Dumb *motherfucker*,' the harsh voice repeated.

'Roth?'

'Yeah, it's Roth, you Hollywood asshole.'

'Didn't you get my message?' Chris asked, reaching for a towel.

'I got it all right. What kind of a shit-assed game d'you think you're playin'?'

'No games, Roth, I swear,' Chris said, knotting the towel round his waist. 'It's a legitimate family thing keeping me in New York. It's my father . . . He's, uh . . . very sick.'

'Fuck your father an' fuck you,' Roth growled. 'I *want* my fuckin' money.'

This was not the Roth Giagante he knew, the affable, laid-back owner of the Magiriano Hotel.

'I want you to listen to me, Roth. You've been bitching about your hotel losing money – that the Palms and the Hard

132

Rock are getting all the young action. Well, I have an answer for you—'

'Fuck *you*. This is about your fuckin' debt. Nothin' else.'

'I understand, and you'll get your money. But right now I'm about to offer you something that'll assure the Magiriano a worldwide publicity bonanza.'

'I'm sendin' someone to see you in New York,' Roth said ominously. 'You can expect a visitor.'

'So can you,' Chris said quickly. 'Birdy Marvel wants to get married at your hotel.'

'You're pissin' on the wrong guy,' Roth said, and the line went dead.

Chris wasn't sure if Roth had hung up on him or if they'd been cut off. Whatever it was, it wasn't good. And mentioning Birdy Marvel had not exactly sent Roth singing to the rafters. Obviously the Vegas bigshot didn't get the enormous publicity bonanza Birdy Marvel would bring to his hotel.

Chris wondered if it was worthwhile flying home for the day.

No, he decided, it wasn't. He'd explain everything to Roth when he got back to L.A. late on Monday.

Then he started thinking. What the hell was that visitor threat? Christ! Surely Roth wasn't serious?

Just in case, he decided to take out some protection. He called down to the front desk and requested a driver-body-guard for the evening.

'Certainly, Mr Diamond,' said the concierge, used to such requests.

'Eight o'clock.'

'He'll be waiting for you. We'll call your suite.'

After that he felt better. 'Jesus Christ,' he muttered, wondering why his life had suddenly turned to shit. His immaculate house had major leaks, Verona was turning into a bitch, and now Roth had become an impossible gangster-style pain in the ass. If he hadn't promised to go with Jett to Max's bachelor party, he would've cancelled and stayed safely in the hotel.

I need a drink, he thought, and went to the mini-bar,

where he selected a miniature of Jack Daniel's and drank it straight from the bottle.

Ever since Red's request to see him, nothing had been going right. It was the curse of his old man. Why didn't the old bastard drop dead and leave them all alone?

Was that too harsh?

No.

* * *

An hour later Jett arrived at the hotel. 'Nice suite,' he said, wandering around. 'You believe in treating yourself good, huh?'

'I'm not married, got nobody else to spend it on except me,' Chris said.

'Be nice if I could say the same.'

'You can.'

'No,' Jett answered, walking to the window and staring out at the New York skyline. 'I wish I could say I've got nobody to spend it on except me. Problem is, I haven't got much to spend.'

'You gotta be making money modelling?'

'Horse crap compared to what *you* guys pull in. You and Max are rolling in it.'

'If only that was so,' Chris said. 'Unfortunately, little bro', I've got myself into something kinda dumb.'

'You?' Jett said, sounding surprised. 'C'mon, Chris, you're a sharp lawyer. Dumb is *my* bag.'

Chris shrugged. 'I started gambling.'

'Gambling?'

'I had this girlfriend, Holly Anton, a complete maniac, sex and anything else you can think of. Every weekend we flew to Vegas, and before I knew it I was hooked on poker and blackjack. It wasn't long before I'd lost a *lot* of money. Now I owe big and they're chasing me for it.'

'Who's chasing you?' Jett asked, lighting a cigarette.

'Some Vegas bigshot. You can't give those guys a cheque, they want cash, and right now I don't have it.'

'How much are we talking?'

'Plenty. I flew here to see if Red's about to kick it and leave us something.'

'Same reason I'm here,' Jett said, inhaling deeply. 'Our old man treated us like trash, and our mothers the same way, but he's still our father. I was thinking this could be how he's gonna make it up to us.'

'We'll see,' Chris said guardedly. 'Do you have to smoke in here?'

'Is it bothering you?'

'Frankly, yes.'

'Then you'd better not go to Europe,' Jett said, stubbing out his cigarette. 'Everyone smokes there.'

'Did you ever get into gambling?' Chris asked curiously.

'No, just booze, women and drugs. That was enough. Smoking's my only addiction now.'

'It must be a satisfying feeling to put all the crap behind you.'

'Trust me,' Jett said, with a rueful grin. 'It's *never* behind you. I'm twenty-four and I'm an alcoholic. Oh, sure, a *recovering* alcoholic, but you never know what tomorrow brings. When I was drinking I was a wild man, the kind of person you didn't wanna be around.'

'You're telling *me*?' Chris said. 'I remember Red's seventy-fifth birthday party when you walked in with the Puerto Rican hooker. You were wearing no pants *and* feeling no pain. That was *some* sight!'

They both started laughing.

'I expect that particular scene went down well with the family, huh?' Jett said wryly. 'Especially Red.'

'Oh, yeah, it was a laugh riot!'

'Here's the good news. I'm not the same person today.'

'That's nice to know.'

'I'm the new, improved, sober and boring Jett. And I couldn't care less if I ever have another drink.'

'Okay, little bro',' Chris said. 'I believe you. Now it's time to hit the road and see what Max's bachelor party has in store for us.'

'I had no clue he was even divorced until I got here. Who's he marrying now?'

'Dunno. Guess we should ask him.'

'Yeah,' Jett said, grinning. 'Guess we should.'

Chapter Twenty

'Are we going somewhere?' Lady Jane Bentley asked, entering Red Diamond's pristine dressing room where he was busy picking out clothes.

'No, *we*'re not,' Red replied, choosing a white shirt from a hanging row of immaculate others. '*I* am going to Max's bachelor party.'

'Excuse me?' she replied. 'You're going where?'

'I'm *going* to my son's bachelor party,' Red repeated, his voice rising. 'What are you, woman – *deaf*?'

'I wasn't aware you were invited.'

Red threw her a withering look. He was fast becoming bored with Lady Jane Bentley. Six years was long enough to be with one woman. Besides, getting old was not for the weak. Now, when he required a hard-on, he had to take Viagra, and that infuriated him. A hard-on was a hard-on, not something manufactured by a little blue pill.

'Red Diamond doesn't need an invitation,' he said off-handedly, her very presence irritating him.

'I don't understand,' she said, well aware that he was not in a mood to be pushed, but pushing anyway.

'Yes, I can imagine it must be difficult for you to under-stand something so simple,' he replied. 'You're not exactly a brain.'

'I told your sons you couldn't meet them this morning because you were feeling unwell,' she said, refusing to go away.

'So?' Red cackled. 'As you can see, I've made a rapid recovery.'

'Surely it will seem odd if you turn up uninvited.'

'Why are you so interested in my business?'

'You *are* my business, Red. I've lived with you for six years, and even though we don't share a bedroom, everything you do concerns me.'

'What does not sharing a bedroom have to do with anything?'

'Sharing a bedroom is true intimacy.'

'To you it is,' he said disdainfully. 'To me it's shit. If I want to fart all night I don't care to listen to your complaints.'

'Is it necessary to be so crude?'

'What's crude about farting? Too rough for your delicate ears?'

'Sometimes I fail to understand you,' she said, her mouth tightening.

'You don't understand much today, do you?' he said, attempting to ignore her.

She decided to stay silent. It was no good arguing with Red when he was in one of his cantankerous moods. However, going to a bachelor party, especially for one of his sons, was so out of character. She didn't like it.

Lately she'd felt that what little control she had over him was slipping away. Red never listened to her anyway. The only reason she stayed was because he was almost eighty, and how much longer did he have? She presumed that since she'd invested six good years she would be well taken care of. Red Diamond was one of the richest men in the world, and *she* was the person closest to him. He hated everyone else, as he never tired of telling her, so she was quite confident that she would inherit the bulk of his fortune, and that was why she stayed and put up with his uncouth behaviour and rudeness.

'Very well.' She sighed. 'If you're going out, I might go out also and have dinner with a friend.'

'You have friends?' Red said, a sarcastic tinge to his voice.

'Is that such a surprise?' she answered, determined not to allow him to get the better of her. 'I realize you never make the effort to meet them, but I have many friends in New York.'

'After you divorced your husband, do you think he was

sorry to see you go?' Red inquired, selecting a four-hundred-dollar silk tie, and holding it up to the mirror.

'Why do you ask?'

''Cause you're not the greatest cocksucker in the world,' Red said, with a crude chuckle, knowing she'd be offended by his language and not caring.

'How *dare* you speak to me like that?' Lady Jane said, her face flushing a dull red. 'I've told you before, I will not put up with your crass vulgarities.'

'If you don't like it, you know what you can do,' Red muttered, hoping she might take the hint. 'And right now you can get out while I finish dressing.'

She stared at him for a moment, prepared to do battle if she had to. Then she realized that letting go was the smart move for now.

He would pay for his lack of civility. Oh, yes, he would definitely pay.

*   *   *

After leaving Mariska's apartment, Max went home, took a shower, had another couple of drinks, tried to call Amy – who did not answer her phone – dressed, and finally set off.

'Make sure I'm out of here by eleven,' he ordered his driver tersely as they pulled up outside the private gentlemen's club where his bachelor party was to take place.

'Yes, sir, Mr Diamond.'

'Christ!' Max muttered, under his breath. 'I wish I didn't have to do this.'

His driver said nothing.

Max made his way into the club, a venue chosen by two of his younger executives, both married, both new fathers, both out to have a raucous good time.

The club was closed for the night so the private party could take place without any gawkers. In the main room three tables were set out in front of a circular stage, each table seated ten people.

Max looked around and groaned inwardly, suspecting what he was about to endure.

He was greeted by Clive Barnaby, his chief executive, a tall, thin man with pointed features and caterpillar eyebrows. 'Max!' Clive said, clapping him on the shoulders. 'This is going to be *some* night.'

A young topless waitress sidled over, seeming completely oblivious that her breasts were on show. 'What would the bachelor boy like to drink?' she asked, with a wide and somewhat phoney smile.

'Give me a Scotch on the rocks,' he said, trying to avert his eyes from her perky nipples, randomly scattered with silver glitter.

'Yes, *sir*,' she said, with another fake smile.

'You're absolutely sure there are no photographers here?' Max said, turning back to Clive.

'Would I let anyone do that to you?' Clive said. 'The only camera on the premises is my digital. We'll print out a few photos just for our own amusement.'

'No pictures,' Max said sternly. 'Not with your camera or anyone else's.'

'You don't want any souvenirs of tonight?' Clive asked, disappointed.

'I don't even want to *be* here tonight.'

'Your brothers are over there,' Clive said, gesturing toward the centre table. 'I didn't even know you *had* brothers, Max. It's quite a surprise they're here.'

'No surprise to me,' Max said evenly. 'I invited them.'

'You forgot to mention it.'

'I didn't realize tonight was so formal.'

'There's a list of guests at the door. We wouldn't want anyone from the gossip columns sneaking in.'

'I'm hardly Donald Trump. Why would they be interested in anything *I* do?'

'Mariska's often in the columns. And now that you're getting married to Amy Scott-Simon, it's quite a story.'

'For fuck's sake!' Max snapped. 'I hate this!'

'Calm down,' Clive said quickly. 'You're not going to see anything tonight that you haven't seen before.'

'That's comforting,' Max said sarcastically.

'The Japanese contingent are by the bar. Believe me,

they're *very* happy to be here. I'll make sure they get a front-row view of all the action. If this doesn't seal the deal I don't know what will. Come over and say hello.'

Max followed Clive to the bar, where he made sure Mr Zagawaski and Mr Yamamoto felt suitably honoured.

After dealing with the two Japanese bankers, he strolled over to his brothers and sat down. 'What's going on?' he said.

'Well,' Chris replied, downing a vodka on the rocks, 'if you *really* want to know, my house in California is springing leaks, I'm breaking up with my girlfriend, I'm being chased by a guy to whom I owe money in Vegas, but, hey, apart from that I'm doing fine.'

'You owe money?' Max said disapprovingly.

'A gambling debt.'

'I've never gambled,' Max said, drumming his fingers on the table. 'It's throwing money away.'

'You got *any* vices?' Jett asked curiously.

'Mariska,' Max answered drily. 'She was vice enough. And, as you know, I dumped her.'

'How's Lulu?' Jett asked.

'Lulu's a fantastic little girl, you *should* meet her.'

'When?'

'I suppose I could arrange a brunch tomorrow,' Max said thoughtfully. 'We usually spend Saturdays together.'

'That'd be great.'

'How about you?' Max asked, turning to Chris. 'Can you make it?'

'Sorry, I have to see Birdy Marvel. She wants to get married, so it's pre-nup time.'

'The singer?' Max said. 'She's Lulu's favourite. Perhaps you can arrange to get her an autographed picture.'

'How old is Lulu now?'

'Five.'

'Isn't she a little young to be a fan of Birdy Marvel?'

'Let me know when you meet her,' Max said. 'Five is yesterday's ten. Lulu's very grown-up.'

After drinks and mingling, everyone sat down. Dinner was served by six topless waitresses assisted by a dozen waiters. The waitresses wore nothing but high heels, sheer black stockings with lacy suspenders, and the mere whisper of a skirt. The waiters were fully dressed.

Caesar salad was the first course, followed by large portions of Kobe steak, with creamed horseradish potatoes and an assortment of steamed vegetables.

As Max chewed his steak, Red Diamond walked in. The shock was intense as the entire room fell into silence. Everyone knew who Red Diamond was.

Almost choking on his steak, Max stood up. 'What're *you* doing here?'

'Surprising you,' Red said, clicking his fingers at a waiter to pull up a chair for him next to Max.

'Jesus, I – I thought you weren't feeling well this morning. We came to the house for the meeting, and Jane told us—'

'I recovered,' Red interrupted, 'so I thought I'd come visit my boys.' He glanced over at Chris and Jett. 'Hello, boys,' he said sarcastically.

Jett froze. Red frightened the shit out of him. He never knew what to say in the presence of his father, even now, when there wasn't a chance in hell the old man could take a stick to him.

Chris nodded, angry and resentful – the way Red always made him feel. And wasn't the old man supposed to be on his deathbed? Why was he all dressed up in a suit and tie looking healthy as a fucking horse? 'Hey, Dad,' he managed.

'Do *not* call me Dad,' Red answered gruffly. 'Sounds *old*. Call me Red. I've told you that since you were dumb little kids. Don't any of you *ever* listen?'

'Sure, Red,' Chris mumbled, still in shock, and not too happy that he'd been forced to stay over – for *what*? Red Diamond did not look as if he was going anywhere soon.

'Where's the girlies?' Red inquired, sitting down. 'Where's the cooze-fest?'

Red was the last person Max had expected to appear at his bachelor party. How the hell had the old man known about it anyway? Christ! As if the evening wasn't uncomfortable enough.

Somehow or other he got through dinner, keeping a sharp eye on Red, who kept groping the half-naked waitresses. Chris and Jett weren't any help: they spoke to each other in low voices, trying to pretend that the man who'd beaten the crap out of them when they were growing up wasn't sitting a couple of feet away.

After dinner there was a series of ribald speeches, then finally the moment Max had been dreading – on came the strippers. Twelve nearly naked girls who couldn't wait to get in everyone's face, much to the delight of his other guests, especially Red.

The girls started off in clever little outfits, everything from school uniform to black-leather dominatrix gear, each girl more voluptuous than the next. The strippers were all shapes and sizes. The only thing they had in common was perfect bodies, and they sure knew how to use them. After a while a slippery pole sprang up in the middle of the stage, and each girl proceeded to caress and slide around it as if it were their greatest lover. They licked it, they rode up and down, they wrapped their long legs round it and simulated sex.

Max glanced around. The Japanese bankers seemed extremely happy. Chris was drinking too much. Jett was sitting back with a noncommittal expression, while Red was producing hundred-dollar bills and crudely sticking them into the girls' crotches, his gnarly fingers copping a feel. Finally all twelve lined up, removed their G-strings, then proceeded to do a Rockettes-style high-kicking dance, giving every man in the place a bird's eye view of their most private parts.

After that came the obligatory girl-on-girl show. Two spectacular women appeared on stage: a flame-haired beauty and a brunette, both with amazing bodies and plenty of enthusiasm.

Red was really into it. At one point he was almost on the stage with them, throwing money onto their undulating bodies, wheezing his appreciation.

The flame-haired woman was going down on the dark-haired one when Max decided he'd had enough. 'Gotta get out of here,' he mumbled to Chris, who was no help at all. 'Can't take another minute of this.'

'Hey,' Jett said. 'I'll come with you.' He was anxious to distance himself from his father and get over to Gatsby's. Besides, there was nothing more difficult than being in the company of drinkers when he couldn't indulge, didn't *want* to indulge. Even the girl-on-girl show was failing to turn him on: it was all so mechanical – 'You touch my left tit,' 'I'll stick my tongue in your pussy,' and so on.

'Max, you can't leave,' Chris said, suddenly coming to life. 'This is your damn party. There's no way you can walk out on it.'

'Yes, Mr *Diamond*, it's *your* party,' cooed one of the strippers, tossing a purple feather boa round his neck. 'We have lots more fun coming up.'

She stationed herself next to him until the two girls finished their show. Then, with the help of two other strippers, she pulled a reluctant Max up onto the stage. Once they'd got him there, they sat him on a chair, tied his hands behind him, and one by one they each proceeded to give him an extremely intimate, totally naked lap-dance.

The men began whooping and cheering, while Max suffered through every minute of his ordeal. He'd never felt more humiliated. Why the *fuck* was he allowing it to happen? What would Amy think?

He saw Red watching him, and immediately felt like a kid again, the callow teenager whose father had walked into the room when he was just about to make out with his steady girl-friend. Red had screamed at him to get out, and he'd run to his room like a lamb, while his lech of a father had proceeded to rape his girlfriend. Red had fucking *raped* her. Max felt waves of anger envelop him.

Christ! That had been a living nightmare, and so was this.

By the time he finally got out of there it was past one. He couldn't wait to get home and shower the smell of the girls off him. Their cheap cloying perfume clung to his clothes, making him nauseous. Even worse had been the sight of old Red Diamond drooling over the strippers, offering crude comments, jotting down phone numbers. It was all too much.

When he'd left, Red was still there, surrounded by the stars of the girl-on-girl show, and several of the strippers. They were all grabbing at the hundred-dollar bills he was handing out.

At least the Japanese had enjoyed themselves.

Fuck 'em. Fuck everyone. They either wanted to invest in

his project or they didn't. Why did he have to prostitute himself to make sure it happened?

Too late now. He'd done it, and it had better produce the expected results.

* * *

Gatsby's was an out-of-control zoo. Lurking outside the club were bands of paparazzi, several cops, and an unruly crowd of wannabes pushing to get in.

'What's goin' on?' Jett asked a cop, as he made his way to the front of the line.

'Birdy Marvel's inside,' the cop replied with an I-wish-I-was-in-there-with-her grin.

Beverly had left his name at the door, so Jett was able to cruise right through. After looking around for a few minutes he tracked her down. She was sitting with Chet, sipping a cosmopolitan.

'Now, don't get mad,' she warned him, before he could say a word. 'I'm still on it.'

'You mean you haven't found out who she is?' he asked, frustrated beyond belief.

'Not yet,' she said. 'The group of girls from last night aren't regulars. They were here for a bachelorette party. I got the number of the one who booked their table.'

'And?'

'Tried it, no answer.'

'Did you leave a message?'

'What kinda message would I leave, Jett?' Beverly asked. 'Oh, yeah, *I* know – *my* friend screwed *your* friend last night. I got no idea what she looks like, an' *he* didn't *quite* get her name, so, uh, who is she?'

'Give me the number, Bev.'

'Does that mean I'm off the hook?'

'It means I'll take it from here.'

She handed him the scribbled number on a piece of paper. He pocketed it and immediately felt better. Now he could relax. His mystery girl was only a phone call away.

* * *

Chris ended the night with one of the performers from the girl-on-girl show, the statuesque flame-haired beauty with large breasts and very long legs. Her name was Sonja and she was originally from Slovakia. She informed him she usually charged three thousand dollars a night, but for him her sexual favours were free.

Hookers. They were all the same whether they charged three dollars or three thousand. It was sex for sale, however much it cost. That didn't mean he wasn't vaguely flattered that she was giving it up for free.

Living in L.A., Chris often used the services of high-class call-girls. First of all, they were usually more beautiful than the actresses and models. Even more important, all they wanted from a man was his money. They didn't want to accompany him to the Oscars and the Golden Globes. They had no desire to be photographed with him. No dinner in a fancy restaurant. No sulks when you forgot their birthday and failed to send flowers on Valentine's Day. And . . . sexually it was anything *he* wanted and, best of all, no demanding equal orgasm.

He took Sonja back to his hotel, where she danced for him privately. Her toned body with large breasts and hard, extended nipples was a real turn-on.

He was half drunk and not happy about seeing Red, but he managed to lose himself in the arms of a very accomplished woman whom he *wasn't* paying.

She pumped him dry and then some. Sonja knew her business.

There was something about getting laid by a stranger that was extremely soothing.

In the morning Sonja was gone. So was his gold Rolex.

When he went into the bathroom a note was scrawled on the mirror above the sink:

MR GIAGANTE EXPECTS
PAYMENT. I TOOK MINE.
NEXT TIME YOU WON'T BE
SO LUCKY.
P.S. YOUR COCK NEEDS A
SERVICE.

Chapter Twenty-One

While heavy rains pounded California, New York was experiencing mild January weather. It was cold and crisp, with intermittent sunshine.

Waking up on Saturday morning, Amy decided to take a bike ride in the park. One of her fellow workers – Nigel, who was English, gay and on the design team – always enjoyed hitting the park, so she phoned him and asked if he cared to accompany her.

'Absolutely,' Nigel said, never one to miss out on anything. 'I'll grab my cycling shorts and meet you in half an hour.'

Being with Nigel was almost like spending time with a close girlfriend. He was fun, chatty and a good listener.

'Did you hear they're flying a model in from Milan to be photographed for the new ad spots?' he asked, as they rode their bikes vigorously through the park.

'What model?' Amy asked, taking long, deep breaths.

'The Italian supermodel, Gianna. She's *très* famous. Always in Italian *Vogue*.'

'Why didn't they book any of the girls here?'

'Because *our* supermodels take it off for Victoria's Secret, and Sofia considers that tacky,' Nigel said, narrowly avoiding a running dog. 'Sofia Courtenelli is not interested in promoting a bunch of semi-*strippers*. Madam is going for class, so she's flying in the Italian. The ad campaign will also feature a male model, I'm hoping it's Mark Vanderloo – he's my absolute fave. Those abs! Oh, my *God*!'

'Is he gay?'

'How would *I* know?' Nigel replied archly. 'I'm not the arbiter of who's gay and who's not.'

'Somebody should've told me about this,' Amy grumbled. 'It's a good column item. I could've placed it in Liz Smith. When is this model arriving?'

'Sunday or Monday,' Nigel said. 'I'm not quite sure.'

'Great! How can I get column space if she's arriving tomorrow? Sofia is really annoying.'

'Why's that?'

'Because all she's really interested in is personal publicity. And it's not so easy getting her name in the columns.'

'Donatella Versace seems to have no problem,' Nigel remarked.

'Do *not* mention Donatella Versace around Sofia,' Amy said.

'Why not?'

'Because I have a strong suspicion Sofia is jealous.'

'And why would that be?'

'Donatella has the advantage of the celebrity aura. Y' know, the shocking murder of her brother in Miami, *and* she's friends with Madonna and Naomi Campbell.'

'Even Naomi's showing too much skin,' Nigel mused, swivelling his head to check out a passing jogger with muscles to spare. 'Personally,' he added, 'I'm *thrilled* we're flying in someone new.'

Amy's cell rang. She clicked on, balancing the phone under her chin.

'Good morning,' Max said.

'Hi.'

'Are you ready to hear about last night?' he said, sounding remarkably cheerful for someone who was supposed to have a hangover.

'I'm bike-riding in Central Park with Nigel.'

'Sounds most energetic.'

'You should try it one day,' she said, zooming down an incline, Nigel in hot pursuit.

'Personally I prefer the stationary bike.'

'How *was* last night? Did you get wild and crazy?' she asked hopefully.

'Actually it was quite an experience, considering Red showed up.'

'Your *father* came to your *bachelor* party?' Amy exclaimed. 'How did *that* happen?'

'He ruined the entire night. Not that I was enjoying myself, but his arrival put a damper on everything.'

'I'm sure it did.'

'Anyway, that's not why I'm calling. My brothers are in town, I'm taking them to brunch with Lulu at the Pierre. I thought you might like to join us.'

'I can't.'

'Look,' he said persuasively, 'I realize how difficult Lulu was yesterday, but you've got to remember she's only a kid, and she's extremely fond of you.'

'It's not Lulu, Max, it's Grams. You know I always visit her on Saturdays. She looks forward to seeing me.'

'Oh, yes, I forgot.'

'But I have a terrific idea,' she said brightly. 'How about inviting your brothers to the rehearsal dinner tomorrow night?'

'Your mother will throw a fit. You know how she is when it comes to seating.'

'Too bad. After all, *you*'re paying for it.'

'So I should do it?'

'Yes, I'll deal with Nancy.'

'That's bold of you.'

'I can be bold when it matters.'

'Then I'll invite them.'

'Absolutely,' she said. Then, weakening, she added, 'If I get out of Grams's early, I'll try to stop by for coffee.'

Clicking off her cell, she concentrated on the bumpy path ahead.

'Was that the bridegroom-to-be checking up on you?' Nigel inquired, pedalling furiously to keep up with her.

'Max doesn't check up on me.'

'Maybe he should,' Nigel said slyly.

Amy's cheeks flushed. 'Excuse me?' she said, wondering if Nigel had heard anything about her big night out.

'Nothing,' he murmured.

'Where's *your* boyfriend today?' she asked, hurriedly switching subjects.

'Asleep. Marcello *craves* his beauty sleep. He would sooner *die* than indulge in any physical activity.'

'That's rather dramatic.'

'So is Marcello. That boy lives for drama.'

'You've been together a while, haven't you?'

'A year and a half. I've never stayed with *anyone* longer than two years. Another six months and it's onto the new and shiny.'

'Uh . . . are you two . . . um . . . faithful?'

'Miss Amy!' Nigel said, in a mock-shock tone. 'What kind of a question is that coming from one so young and pure?'

'Oh, fall off your bike!'

'You'd like that, wouldn't you?'

'Not if I have to pick you up and carry you to the emergency room.'

'Feisty little madam today, aren't we?'

'Takes one to know one!'

*   *   *

Amy's grandmother resided in a private apartment at the top of the Waldorf Towers Hotel. Her Vietnamese houseman, Hueng, who'd been in her employ for almost fifty years, lived in a room downstairs.

Grandma Poppy was quite a character. Lively and sharp of tongue, at ninety years of age she still had a hairdresser come to the hotel every morning to style her silvery white hair. She wore couture clothes, smoked a pack of cigarettes a day, and was quite fond of a couple of glasses of wine with lunch *and* dinner.

She had two dogs, a cocker spaniel and a miniature poodle. They sat at her feet all day while she read biographies, smoked, sipped wine and watched CNN. She was an avid Larry King fan. In fact, she'd named her dogs after him: Larry and King, her two obsessions.

Grandma Poppy adored her granddaughter. Every time

Amy visited, she gave her an exquisite piece of jewellery from her vast collection.

'Hi, Grams,' Amy said, kissing her on both cheeks. 'Sorry I'm all sweaty. I was bike-riding in the park.'

'You *always* look pretty, doesn't she, Hueng?' Grandma Poppy said, tossing the question to her faithful manservant, who was well into his seventies.

'Yes, ma'am,' Hueng replied.

'Now, dear,' Grandma Poppy said, fiddling in the jewellery box she kept on a table next to her. 'Let's see what I have for you today.'

'Grams, you don't *always* have to give me presents,' Amy objected. 'There's nothing I need.'

'You might not need it, dear,' Grandma Poppy said, coming up with a thin diamond tennis bracelet, 'but one day you will learn that *needing* is not what counts. Accept these little trinkets I give you and store them away like a squirrel.'

'Yes, Grams,' Amy said obediently.

'One never knows what the future will bring. You're marrying a much older man. Men – you can never trust them, dear. They all have a wandering eye.'

'Grams, that's really not true,' Amy said, fastening the bracelet round her wrist.

'Yes, dear, it is. Men don't care about being faithful. If I can teach you anything, I can teach you that.'

'I'm sure my father was faithful.'

'Of course he wasn't,' Grandma Poppy scoffed.

The thought of someone being unfaithful to Nancy Scott-Simon made Amy smile. 'I shouldn't think Harold screws around on Mom,' she said, knowing full well that Harold would *never* cheat – he wouldn't dare.

'A lady never uses vulgar words, dear,' Grandma Poppy scolded. 'Pour me a glass of wine, Hueng. It's lunchtime, and this child must be hungry.'

'I'm not really,' Amy said, even though she'd learned long ago never to argue with Grandma Poppy, the woman was a force of nature.

'Yes, you are,' Grandma Poppy said. 'Hueng, call downstairs and order two Caesar salads.'

Amy bent down to pet the dogs. Both of them growled and backed away, the only human contact they put up with was from Grandma Poppy.

'Don't bother them, dear. They're feeling blue today.'

Hueng appeared with two glasses of wine.

'How're the wedding plans progressing, Amy?' Grandma Poppy inquired, taking a hearty sip of wine. 'Is your dear mother driving you completely mad as usual?'

'You guessed!'

'Ah, yes. Nancy is a classic anal retentive. I was older when I had her and she was raised by a series of nannies. Perhaps it was a mistake.'

'Why would it be a mistake?' Amy asked curiously.

'I never saw her, I was too busy following my dear husband across the world. She resents me for that.'

'I'm sure she doesn't.'

'Nothing I can do now. Your handsome grandfather was a world traveller,' Grandma Poppy said, a gleam in her eyes. 'We'd go on safaris in Africa, adventures in Peru, vacations in strange and wonderful places. We travelled the world together. He was quite a man.'

'Was *he* faithful, Grams?' Amy asked, wondering about the grandfather who'd died before she was born.

'Of course not,' Grandma Poppy answered crisply, as if it didn't matter. 'No man is. Don't you listen to *anything* I try to teach you?'

After lunch, Amy got on the phone to Tina and asked if she could drop by.

'Sure,' Tina said agreeably. 'All I'm doing is sitting around feeling fat. Brad's deserted me for some stupid ball game. Men!'

'Can I bring you anything?'

'Oooh, let me see – chocolate. *Tons* of milk chocolate. Brad refuses to buy it for me, but *he*'s not carrying around this big balloon of a stomach all day. Selfish shit!.'

'Chocolate,' Amy repeated. 'Plenty of it. I'll be there in about twenty minutes.'

Hmm . . . theme for the day, Amy thought. *Men are unfaithful, selfish bastards! So why am I marrying one?*

Good question.

Tina was waiting anxiously for her when she arrived. 'Oh, God, I'm *craving* this stuff,' she said, grabbing the bag of chocolate out of Amy's hands. 'Brad said the doctor told him I shouldn't put on anymore weight. What does he think I am – an idiot? I *know* I shouldn't, but if you can't pig out when you're pregnant, when the hell *can* you?'

'That's true.'

'Thank God *somebody* understands,' Tina said, tearing off wrappers and stuffing chocolate into her mouth. 'Come into the kitchen – I'm making coffee.'

'Sorry to drop by so unexpectedly,' Amy said, following Tina into her messy kitchen.

'You're my best friend *and* you brought chocolate – believe me, you're more than welcome,' Tina said, pouring her a mug of coffee.

'I've been thinking about the other night.'

'Good memories, I hope.'

'Not so good, I'm afraid.'

'Okay, spill.'

'I guess I kind of feel *guilty*.'

'You do?' Tina said, chocolate dribbling down her chin as it mixed with a mouthful of the hot coffee.

'Yes, I do. And I'm thinking that shouldn't I try to find out who he is?'

'The man you had unbelievably horny sex with?' Tina asked, walking back into the living room.

'I never *said* that,' Amy objected, following her.

'Are you *nuts*? Why would you want to know who he is? That would spoil everything.'

'I don't know . . .'

'You don't, huh?' Tina said, lowering herself into a comfortable armchair.

'Here's the thing,' Amy said. 'I . . . uh . . . I'm not sure I can marry Max.'

'*What?*' Tina yelled, almost spilling coffee on her distended stomach. 'Now I *know* you're nuts.'

'Listen' Amy said. 'If Max did the same to me, I wouldn't want to marry *him*.'

'Oh, Jesus!,' Tina said, wagging her finger in Amy's face. 'Don't even *think* about telling him.'

'Why?'

'It was a one-nighter, and believe me, it's *not* being unfaithful when you're *not* even married.'

'But I feel too guilty to go through with it. Honestly, Tina, I think I *should* tell Max.'

'You're being *ridiculous*,' Tina scoffed. 'The rehearsal dinner is tomorrow night. You're getting married any minute. Max is *perfect* for you. He's handsome, rich, a caring daddy to his kid and, most of all, he loves you. Do *not* ruin a good thing, Amy.'

'I know, but—'

'Enough of this nonsense!' Tina said firmly. 'You'd better pull yourself together *pronto*. You'll have a *great* marriage.'

'I will?'

'Yes, you will. Everyone gets freaked out when the big day gets closer. It's only natural. So start thinking clearly – Max is *it*! He's your Brad. This time next year you too can have a belly swollen out to kingdom come!'

'Thanks, I can't wait!'

'Now that we've settled your nerves,' Tina said, patting her stomach, 'pass me more chocolate. This fat woman is *desperate*!'

Chapter Twenty-Two

Saturday morning Cindi and Liberty were up early. Beyond excited, Cindi insisted that they splurge and take a cab to the video shoot. The night before she'd cancelled her date with Moose, the security guard. This had given Liberty a chance to fill her cousin in on everything that had taken place in the short time she'd spent with her mom.

'Wow!' Cindi had exclaimed, after listening carefully. 'She finally came out with info on your dad an' he's *dead*? That's bad shit. How come she never told you before?'

'She never told anyone, did she?'

'Aretha always kinda suspected it was the manager at one of those clubs she sang at.'

'Now we know – it wasn't.'

'I'm callin' my mom,' Cindi had said. 'See what she has t' say about it.'

'You can't tell her,' Liberty had answered quickly. 'Diahann doesn't want anybody knowing.'

'Why's that? 'Cause he was *married*?'

'Don't ask me, I'm *still* in shock.'

'But you must wanna find him?'

'Aren't you listening to me? He's *dead*, Cindi, *dead*.'

'Are you *sure* she's handin' you the truth? Germany's a long way away, an' if she *was* singin' back-up for Isaac Hayes, you can bet my mom would've known it.' Before Liberty could stop her, she'd picked up the phone, put it on speaker, and called Aretha. 'Hey, Mom,' she'd said, 'did Diahann ever go to Germany singin' back-up for Isaac Hayes?'

'If Diahann went to Germany, *I*'d sure as hell *know*,'

155

Aretha had said. 'An' if she did one damn thing with Isaac Hayes, I'd *certainly* know. *Hallelujah!* That man is a god! Saw him in concert once – there he was, all naked, covered in gold chains, his manly body glistenin' with sweat. Oh, Lordy, *Lordy*! That man is one *sexy* hunka beef! I wouldn't mind—'

'Mom! Please don't be talkin' to me 'bout *sex*, that's nasty!'

'Why you askin' anyway?'

''Cause Diahann told Libby she was on tour with Isaac Hayes.'

'Believe me, baby, it never happened.'

'But you don't know *everything* she did. *You* were in Atlanta, an' *she* was in New York.'

'Honey,' Aretha had said firmly, 'if *my* sister took that fine ass of hers abroad, the whole family woulda known. She *always* told us 'bout the *good* things goin' on.'

'You're *sure*?' Cindi had said, exchanging a look with Liberty.

'Yes, baby, I'm sure.'

'Thanks, Mom. Oh, an' listen to *this* – *I* am gonna be in a music video. You'll be able to watch me on TV. How about *that*?'

'*What*?' Aretha had yelled. 'This means we're celebratin'. You an' Libby get your asses over here Sunday. I'm cookin' us a fried-chicken feast!'

'I'm workin' on the video Sunday.'

'Now, don't you go givin' me no sass, Cindi. You be here soon as you're through, you hear me, child?'

After Cindi hung up, she and Liberty had sat around mulling over everything. They'd decided that either Diahann was making up stories, or Aretha hadn't known what the hell was going on.

Now they were in a cab on their way to the video shoot.

* * *

There were quite a few pretty, sexy and overweight girls milling around the studio. The choreographer, Benny Cassola, a young Hispanic man with shiny black hair pulled back into a ponytail, was attempting to shepherd them into a line-up. 'You,' he said, gesturing to Cindi, 'you part of this group?'

'I sure am,' she said, hurrying over.

'I'll be teachin' you some key moves. You gotta be natural, listen to the music an' stay loose. I'm lookin' for sexy an' juicy – the juicier the better. All you gotta do is shake it like Jell-O.'

'Shake *what*?' Cindi asked, as if she didn't understand what he was getting at, although she totally did.

'Everythin' you got.'

Cindi took a look round the studio. There were men everywhere – musicians, publicists, engineers, cameramen. She'd never been shy about taking her clothes off in front of men, but this group presented quite a challenge.

'Don't sweat it,' Liberty whispered soothingly, giving her a little shove towards the line-up of girls. 'You'll be amazing.'

'Sure.' Cindi snorted. 'With my ass hangin' out while all these horny gorillas arc eyeballin' me like I'm *meat*!'

'At least we're on a sound stage. That's something to celebrate.'

'*You* ain't takin' your clothes off,' Cindi pointed out. '*I* am.'

Slick Jimmy's song began booming over the speakers.

> *Fat girls got it goin'.*
> *Fat girls in the hood,*
> *Fat girls got the booty,*
> *Does a man real good.*
> *Fat girls fuckin' in the park.*
> *Fat girls blowin' for a lark.*
> *Fat girls got it goin'.*
> *Fat girls in the hood.*

'Crap!' Cindi whispered, outraged. 'It's a *fat* girls' song. I ain't *fat*, I'm *womanly*. I know I got booty t' spare, but that don't make me *fat*! *Damn!*'

'Get into it, have fun,' Liberty encouraged. 'It's experience.'

'Experience, my ass!' Cindi snapped.

As soon as Benny got all the girls together, he started

teaching them a series of basic moves – bend, shake and jiggle. Cindi fell into the routine immediately.

Standing on the sidelines, Liberty was fascinated, watching Benny as he circled the girls like a panther, style and grace personified.

'You'll all get individual marks to hit,' Benny informed his line-up of large, bootilicious females. 'I want you to keep it *movin'*, keep it *sexy*, an' most of all, keep it *smooth*. You can do it, ladies.'

Cindi was busy checking out the other girls. At over two hundred pounds she realized she was the skinny one of the group, which immediately boosted her confidence.

When Benny felt they had it down, he sent them off to get their hair and make-up done.

'Come on,' Cindi said, dragging Liberty into the large make-up room where several make-up artists and hair-stylists buzzed around, looking professional and busy.

'Hey – you,' said a tall, striking woman, beckoning Cindi. 'Come sit over here.'

'Me?' Cindi said, not sure it was her being summoned.

'Yes, *you*. I'm Beverly. Welcome to my chair.'

'Hi, I'm Cindi.'

'Okay, Cindi,' Beverly said, preparing her make-up brushes. 'You got a real pretty face. My job is to make it even prettier.' She glanced at Liberty, who was standing by the chair. 'And who're you?'

'Cindi's cousin.'

'Watchin' out for her, huh?' Beverly said, concealing a yawn.

'Late night?' Liberty countered.

'Gatsby's. Best club in town.'

'Wow!' Cindi said excitedly. 'I read about that place in *US* magazine. Wasn't that where P. Diddy threw a big party?'

Beverly nodded. 'I was there,' she said casually, like it was no big deal.

'*Shit!*' Cindi exclaimed. 'You get to hang at fancy places 'cause you make up stars? How fine is *that*?'

'I work for whoever's payin' me,' Beverly answered, soaking a cotton ball in astringent. 'Today I'm doin' make-up on you girls. Next week I'm workin' on a photo shoot for *Glamour* with Vivica A. Fox.'

'You're making up Vivica A. Fox?' Cindi said, duly impressed as Beverly dabbed her face with the cotton ball. 'That girl is *somethin'*!'

Beverly took another quick glance at Liberty. 'You need your eyebrows plucked,' she remarked.

'What's wrong with my eyebrows?'

'Too thick. They're dominatin' that *beautiful* face. You gotta do somethin' about 'em. It'll make all the difference.'

'I thought thick eyebrows were in,' Liberty said defensively.

'Honey – you're wrong,' Beverly said, proceeding to smooth a Peter Thomas Roth expensive moisturizer over Cindi's face.

'Umm . . . feels real nice,' Cindi said, loving the experience of being pampered.

'Now your make-up'll glide on,' Beverly explained. 'Always remember to moisturize. Black skin needs special care.'

'I will.'

'So,' Beverly said to Liberty, 'if I get a moment, I'll pluck 'em for you later.'

'I'm not sure I want to do that.'

'You gotta treat your eyebrows like your snatch,' Beverly said matter-of-factly. ''S all about groomin', baby.'

Liberty and Cindi exchanged startled glances in the mirror. Had this tall, striking woman actually *said* that?

By the time Cindi was fully made-up, she looked as if she'd experienced one of those make-overs so popular on morning TV shows. And when Fantasia appeared with her skimpy costume, and she wriggled into it, it actually flattered her bountiful curves.

'Dead-on sexy,' Liberty said encouragingly, as they headed back to the set. 'I'm telling you, you're looking *way* better than any of the other girls.'

'You sure?'

'Course I'm sure.'

''Cause I'm kinda jittery.'

'You? Come *on*. Nothing gets *you* nervous – unless it's the thought of not getting laid on a Saturday night!'

Cindi grinned, hoisting her massive bosom. 'You're right! Not me! I'm a winner, girl. I got *championship* booty!'

After more rehearsals, Slick Jimmy put in an appearance, surrounded by his posse. Slick Jimmy looked like a cross between Snoop Dogg at his pimping best, and Johnny Depp in *Pirates of the Caribbean*. He was no Usher, but he had his own look with his low-slung baggy pants, a big sweatshirt that hung below his knees, pirate headgear, and oversized dark shades.

The girls stood around staring at him while his song continued booming over the speakers. He began lip-synching, while the director, Maleek – a young African-American man with thick black dreadlocks and very white teeth – began telling Benny where he wanted the girls placed.

Liberty hovered on the sidelines, watching. There was no doubt about it, Cindi had big brass balls. There was no way *she* could have stood up there in front of all these men in such a tiny outfit, shaking her ass at the camera. But Cindi was acting like she'd done it a hundred times before.

Then, out of nowhere, *he* walked in. Damon P. Donnell. The Man himself.

Liberty jumped to attention. Damon P. Donnell was in the same place she was, and she *wasn't* serving him coffee. This was a first.

People were fussing all over him, seeing he got a director's chair to sit in, high-fiving him, generally kissing his butt.

'Is Damon Donnell something to do with this record?' she asked one of the assistants, who'd been hanging around her trying to score a date.

'Mr Big Time. Yeah, Slick Jimmy's on his label.'

'No kidding?'

'Wanna meet him?' the assistant asked, sidling closer.

'Sure.'

'If you hook up with me later I'll arrange it.'

'I'm engaged,' she said, backing away.

'Don't see a ring.'

'That's 'cause it's through my husband-to-be's nose.'

The assistant scowled. 'You're one of those smart-ass girls, aren't you?'

'I try to be,' she answered coolly, watching Damon across the set. He seemed so laid-back and in control, with a look that screamed success.

After a while he got up and strolled over to the Craft Service table. Realizing this was her opportunity, she almost flew across the set. 'Mr Donnell,' she said, approaching him boldly, trying not to limp, wishing she'd fixed herself up more instead of just jeans and a T-shirt.

'Huh?' he said, turning round. 'Do I know you?'

'I'm Liberty. I serve you breakfast every day in the coffee shop across the street from your office,' she said, her words spilling over each other. 'But in the *real* world I'm a singer and I'm good. All I need is a chance, and I was, uh . . . hoping you could find the time to listen to my demo.'

He looked her over very slowly with his dark smoky eyes. It was the first time she'd seen him without his shades, she decided he had the most soulful eyes she'd ever seen.

'Yeah, I know you,' he said at last, tapping the diamond stud embedded in his left ear. 'You're the girl took a fall. You doin' okay?'

She was shocked that he actually *did* remember her. 'Uh . . . that's why my arm's bandaged,' she stammered. 'It's only a surface burn. I'm feeling better already, my—'

'What you doin' here?' he interrupted, reaching for a carrot stick.

'My cousin's one of the, uh . . . dancers.'

'You like the song?' he asked, taking a casual bite of carrot, dark smoky eyes still checking her out.

'The truth, or should I lie?'

'Go ahead,' he said, faintly amused. 'It's a hit whatever you gotta say.'

'Then why ask me?' she countered, recovering her composure.

''Cause I wanna know.'

'Love the beat, hate the lyrics,' she said quickly.

'You do, huh?' he said, pinning her with his eyes. 'An' why would that be?'

'They're sexist.'

'I don't think so.'

'You're wrong.'

'*I*'m wrong?' he said, surprised she would dare to argue with him.

'Yes.'

'Then you gotta think the whole rap world is sexist.'

'Most of it is. I mean, it's all about violence an' putting women down.'

'It's about freedom, baby.'

'No. It's about dissing women.'

'You ever heard of female rappers?'

'I like Missy Elliott and Queen Latifah's early work. I'm more into singer-songwriters – y'know, Norah Jones and Alicia Keys. I write my own songs, too.'

'Who doesn't?'

'I told you – I'm good.'

'Confident too,' he said, locking eyes with her. It was a moment.

'Guess you'd better come see me,' he said, breaking the look.

'You mean that?' she asked breathlessly.

'It ain't my nature to say things I don't mean,' he said, reaching into his jacket pocket and flicking her his engraved card.

'Do I just come by your office?' she asked, studying it.

'Pick up the phone, call my assistant, Fay, tell her I said you should come in. She'll make an appointment for you. Don't forget to bring your demo.'

This was like some kind of dream. And it was happening because Cindi had been picked to appear in a music video. How lucky was *that*?

'When should I call?'

His eyes were all over her. *Finally* he was aware of her existence. 'Soon,' he said.

Maleek, the director, came over, gave her a perfunctory glance, realized she wasn't anyone important, and began talking to Damon.

Damon turned away from her. Apparently their conversation was over.

Wow! So much had gone on in the last two days. Her

mother's confessions about her father, and now this. She had been *talking* to Damon P. Donnell, and he'd actually suggested she come up to his office and play him her demo. He'd given her his card!

Stay cool, she warned herself. *This could all turn out to be nothing.*

But how could she stay cool when things were turning around at such a rapid pace? It simply wasn't possible.

Chapter Twenty-Three

Chris was more disturbed by *your cock needs a service* than by his missing gold Rolex. What was *that* all about? He'd never had any complaints before.

The fact that he'd had a woman in bed who was obviously employed by Roth Giagante was not a comforting thought either. How had she gotten into Max's bachelor party? Didn't coincidences like that only happen in movies?

Apparently not.

He thought about placing a call to Roth in Vegas, then he realized it was way too early, so he decided it was okay to wait until later.

The previous night he'd had no chance to discuss Red's surprise appearance with his brothers, although he and Jett had muttered a few things to each other, like, 'What's the son-of-a-bitch doing here?' and 'Why is he looking so fucking healthy?' Max was not in on their exchanges, he was too busy having a lousy time.

Jett came by his hotel at eleven. Chris was getting kind of used to hanging with his kid brother. He had friends in L.A., but nobody to whom he was really close. He was a workaholic, and lately a degenerate gambler. Between the two, it had kept him pretty busy.

Oh, sure, he had girlfriends. Verona, who was on her way out. Holly Anton, who'd driven him totally crazy. The truth was that male friends were hard to come by in L.A. Most so-called friends were rooting for your failure, not your success.

'How come he cancelled the meeting with us yesterday

morning?' Jett asked, helping himself to a glass of orange juice from the room-service trolley.

'He did it to piss us off,' Chris replied, pushing an egg-white omelette around his plate. 'That's his way, always has been. But I'm not jumping rope anymore. If the goddamn meeting doesn't take place on Monday, I'm outta here.'

'I agree with you,' Jett said, 'not that I'm leaving New York, but I'm not jumping either.'

'What *are* your plans?' Chris asked.

'I told you about the girl. I'm still looking for her.'

'You haven't tracked her yet?' Chris said, looking surprised.

'It's in the bag,' Jett said confidently, reaching for a croissant. 'I have a number but nobody's answering. It's probably an office. I can wait until Monday.'

'So . . . do you want to hear what happened to *me* last night?' Chris said, pouring himself more coffee.

'Go ahead, surprise me.'

'I brought one of the strippers back here. She stole my gold Rolex and left me a nasty note.'

Jett started to laugh. 'That's the kinda deal used to happen to me.'

'Great! Now it's happening to me,' Chris said dourly. 'And *I* don't like it.'

'What did the note say?'

'Try this on for size – "your cock needs a service".'

Jett burst out laughing. 'That's cold, man.'

'You're telling me.'

'You callin' the cops?'

'No way.'

'It was a gold Rolex.'

'It was also a message from my guy in Vegas.'

'No shit?'

'Yes,' Chris said, nodding. 'It was. This is something I gotta take care of.'

'How you gonna do that?'

'I'm considering asking Max for a short-term loan.'

'That means you don't think Red's coming through.'

'You saw him last night, sniffing pussy like it was his first time. Did he *look* like a guy on the way out?'

'Guess you're right. The old dude ain't goin' nowhere soon.'

'Which means I'm screwed.'

'Wait until after the meeting on Monday before you say that.'

'Nothing's going to change between now and then, that's for sure.'

'You think?' Jett said, picking up the paper. 'Hey – how about the rain in L.A.? I talked to Sam this morning, he said it's brutal.'

'We have sunshine all year long,' Chris said. 'A few days of rain won't kill anyone.'

'Sam told me there was a mudslide and people *were* killed.'

'Fuck!' Chris said. 'I hope my house is okay.'

'People are dying, and you're worried about your house?'

'Shallow, isn't it?' Chris said, with a hollow laugh. 'Guess I've been living in L.A. too long.'

'Why wouldn't your house be okay?'

'It's sitting on the side of a freakin' giant hillside, and Verona informed me there are leaks all over it.'

'Tell her to call someone.'

'She won't do anything about it unless I invite her to move in. And, believe me, I am *not* going there.'

'No housekeeper?'

'Not on weekends.'

'It'll be okay,' Jett said, throwing down the paper.

'Like I don't have enough problems,' Chris grumbled.

'Saw Birdy at Gatsby's last night,' Jett remarked, pouring himself more juice.

'And?'

'She was with this big biker freak. Looked like they were in a fight, so I stayed away.'

'Great!'

'Do you know him?'

'That's the guy she's planning to marry.'

'Nice.'

'Right. I should call her, then we'll take off.'

'Maybe you should stop and pick up another Rolex, just in case,' Jett said, grinning.

'Fuck *you*!' Chris responded, but he couldn't help grinning too.

* * *

Early Saturday Max received a full report from Clive Barnaby regarding the Japanese bankers. According to Clive they had enjoyed the bachelor party immensely and were now eagerly anticipating the big meeting on Monday.

'Looks to me like it's in the bag,' an enthusiastic Clive told him over the phone. 'After the party I had to take them out for drinks. Believe me, they *like* the ladies.'

'Did they end up with girls?' Max asked.

'Who knows? I finally left them at four a.m.'

'So, we'll see,' Max said.

'How about you? Did *you* have a good time?'

'How could I when my father appeared out of nowhere?'

'I must say, that was a surprise to everyone. I had no idea you were so tight with your old man.'

'We're not exactly tight. As you know, when it comes to business I've always separated myself from him.'

'I understand,' Clive said. 'That's why I was taken aback when he came walking in.'

'You and everyone else.'

Later, Max picked up Lulu and took her to the Pierre. His little daughter was on her best behaviour. He'd promised her that if she didn't do any whining and ate all her lunch, he'd buy her a big present.

'I wanna get a white rabbit with yellow fur ears and a red cape,' Lulu announced matter-of-factly. 'And furry boots. My rabbit should have furry boots, Daddy. Pink ones, or green. No orange ones.'

'If we can find one, that's what you'll get,' Max agreed. 'But *only* if you behave yourself when you meet your two uncles.'

'Uncles,' she said, smiling cheekily. 'Will *they* bring me presents?'

'I don't know. Maybe if you sit here like a little lady.'

'Yes, Daddy, I will. I promise, Daddy. Lulu's a *good* girl,' she said, flashing him an angelic smile. 'A *very* good girl.'

'We'll see.'

'Is Amy coming, Daddy?'

'She might drop by later, and if she does you'd better be nice to her.'

'Yes, Daddy, me be *very* nice,' Lulu said, widening her eyes. 'Lulu's a good, *good* girl.'

Both Chris and Jett were totally charmed by their niece, who was at her most adorable. Her table manners were impeccable, she never interrupted anyone and, as a bonus, she ate all her lunch without threatening to throw up.

'My daddy's buying me a present,' she announced, scarfing a dish of chocolate ice-cream. 'A *big* present.'

'Lucky you,' said Jett. 'What're you getting? A spaceship?'

'*No*, silly!' She giggled hysterically. 'Only *boys* like space-ships.'

'Then *what?* A great big castle full of soldiers?'

'You're *so* silly,' she said, giggling even more. 'Soldiers are for *boys*. I'm a *girl*.'

'Oh, you're a girl, are you?' Jett said, grinning. 'I didn't know that.'

'Yes, you *did*.'

'No, I *didn't*.'

'Will *you* buy me a present?' she asked coyly, tilting her head on one side.

'Maybe, if I get to see you again.'

'Promise?'

'I promise, 'cause you're very cute, and I missed all your birthdays, but now that we're friends—'

'Friends!' she chanted, grabbing Jett's hand. 'Friends! Friends! *Friends!*'

'She likes you,' Max said.

'Happens with all the girls,' Jett replied, winking at his little niece.

After lunch Jett announced he planned to drop by a video shoot. 'My friend Beverly's doing make-up for a new rap artist. Why don't you all come?'

'I wouldn't go *near* a video shoot unless it involved one of my clients,' Chris said. 'Been there, done that.'

'Maybe you could score a new client,' Jett said. 'This rapper is supposed to be the next Jay-Z. Name's Slick Jimmy, he probably needs representation.'

'Slick Jimmy, huh? Think I'll pass. I've got enough crazy clients. Besides, I should see if Birdy's surfaced.'

Before he could phone his youngest client, she was on his cell, insisting that he come over to her hotel immediately.

'What's up?' he asked, knowing it wouldn't be anything he wanted to hear.

'Just get here,' she said, her voice quavering, as if she was about to burst into tears.

'How about you and the kid coming to the video shoot?' Jett asked Max. 'Lulu might enjoy it.'

'Some other time,' Max said. 'Lulu's nanny is taking her to the park, and I'm about to embark on a sit-down with my ex.'

'Sounds deep.'

'I expect it will be,' Max said, his expression grim. He was not looking forward to meeting with Mariska, but then again, Vladimir was *her* problem as much as his, so why should *he* be the one stuck with it?

Lulu gave everyone hugs, while Max remembered to invite them to the rehearsal dinner the following night.

Outside on the sidewalk Max glanced up and down the street to see if he could spot Amy. He was anxious for her to meet his brothers: this was the most time they'd spent together, and it was turning out to be quite a worthwhile experience.

Maybe family wasn't such a bad thing after all.

Chapter Twenty-Four

'**O**ut!' Red Diamond screeched, his face turning puce with anger. 'I want you *out*.'

Lady Jane Bentley, who was sitting at her dressing-table brushing her hair, paled and said nothing.

'Pack up your bony ass and go,' Red snarled. 'Get the fuck out of my house. I've had enough of you.'

It was Saturday morning and he'd marched into her bedroom full of piss and vinegar. She had no idea what had caused this sudden confrontation, she just knew it was upon her with no warning.

'Why are you acting like this?' she demanded, standing up and facing him. 'We haven't had a fight. Nothing's is different.'

'*Everything*'s different,' he replied. 'Last night I spent in the company of younger women, *vital* women, women who were able to make me hard again. It finally dawned on me that I've been wasting the years I have left with a dried-up old *snob*.'

'You're disgusting,' she said, turning away from him.

'I found the life force I've been missing for the last six years,' he roared. '*You* can't stand sex. Every time I'm on top of you, you lie there like a wooden board giving me *nothing*.'

'I've done everything you've ever asked me to,' she said, making a supreme effort to remain calm.

'Yes,' he sneered. 'Even sucked my cock when I've had to *beg*.'

'How dare you speak to me in such a fashion?'

'I'll speak to you how I want.'

'You can't possibly mean what you're saying.'

'Every goddamn word,' he replied impatiently, cracking his knuckles.

'And where do you expect me to go?' she asked coldly. 'Let us not forget that I left my husband and gave up everything to look after you for the last six years.'

'Look after me?' he roared. 'You make me sound like a decrepit old invalid, and that's something Red Diamond will *never* be.'

'I did *not* call you an invalid.'

'Who gives a fuck what you said? You're boring. All you do is nag me about travelling abroad, and spend my money at an alarming rate. It's enough. I want you out. In the future I plan on enjoying my freedom.'

'Do you now?' she said, a slow fury building within her. 'Well, plan away, because *I* am not going anywhere.'

'What?' he said, his leathery face twisted with anger.

'You heard.'

'Do you *understand* who I am?' he yelled. 'Once I bring in my lawyers, they'll force you out *immediately.*'

'Call them,' she said, refusing to back down. 'I have a right to be here. This is my home too.'

'I advise you,' Red said, his rheumy eyes glittering with malice, 'do *not* get into a pissing match with me, because I can assure you that no woman has *ever* gotten the better of Red Diamond.'

She regarded him for a long, silent moment. It was probably true – no woman ever had. He'd managed to kill off three wives, and the fourth was a broken-down drunk who lived a pathetic life. But she, Lady Jane Bentley, was different. She was made of stronger stuff, and she refused to be intimidated by this churlish old man. She was smarter than he thought. She knew plenty about Red Diamond, things he would never want anyone to know.

'When we have negotiated a suitable settlement, and *only* then, I will consider leaving,' she said evenly. 'You can deal directly with me, or you can speak to my lawyers. Whichever you prefer.'

'A settlement.' He cackled. 'We'll *see* about that.'

'Yes, we will,' she answered calmly, refusing to be treated

like one of his whores. 'Tell me, Red,' she added, 'exactly what surprise do you have in store for your three sons on Monday? How *else* are you planning on ruining their lives?'

'Ruining their lives?' he bellowed. 'Those boys would be *nothing* without me. Look at what they've achieved.'

'Yes,' she said succinctly, 'and, I might add, *without* an ounce of help from you.'

'*Bitch!*' he muttered. 'You know nothing.'

'I *know* how you forced those two banks to withdraw from Max's project. I also know you've been in touch with Roth Giagante in Las Vegas, insisting that he pressure Chris for the money he owes. Not very fatherly acts, are they, Red?'

'I'm teaching them a lesson,' he growled.

'They're grown men, Red. Why do you keep punishing them? What have they done to deserve this kind of treatment?'

'Have you been spying on me?' he shouted, his craggy face darkening. 'How do you know all this?'

'I don't *spy*, I protect. And I might remind you that you will never find anyone who'll protect you the way I do.'

'Bullshit!'

'And I should also warn you that if you think *I* spend money, start seeing other women and you'll find out how much *they* spend. I have made your home a place of calm and beauty. I entertain when you request me to. I even put up with the call-girls you meet at your secret apartment on 59th Street – the apartment you think I don't know about. Well, I *do* know about your whores, Red. And I know plenty of other things that I'm sure you wouldn't want to become public knowledge.'

'Last night I got more action from a bunch of strippers than I've had from you in six years,' he growled, 'so you can get your blackmailing ass out of my house, 'cause I've no use for it anymore. Do you *understand* what I'm saying? I'm finished with you. Finished. Done.'

'You really are a vile man,' she said, controlling the icy fury that helped her to stay strong.

'Then get the *fuck out*,' he screamed.

'Not until I'm ready, Red. And that you can depend on.'

* * *

On the way over to Birdy's hotel, Chris received another call. This time it was from Jonathan Goode, who should have been on his way to Europe, but apparently was not.

'I need to see you, Chris,' said Jonathan, not sounding like his usual in-control self. 'It's urgent.'

'Where are you?'

'My apartment,' Jonathan said, and gave him the address.

'I'm on my way to a client now. Soon as I'm through, I'll make it over to you.'

Christ! Who the hell invented cellphones? People could reach you wherever you were – it was ridiculous. First Birdy, now Jonathan. All he needed was a call from Lola Sanchez and his day would be complete.

*   *   *

'Vladimir is not good man,' Mariska said, in a highly agitated state as she paced round her living room, her high heels clicking on the marble floor.

'You're not telling me anything new,' Max said evenly.

'Vladimir is dangerous. You do not understand *how* dangerous.'

'Maybe not, Mariska. But I do understand that he's *your* problem, not mine.'

'No, Vladimir is *our* problem,' she said vehemently. 'I was *never* married to this man – the so-called papers he showed you are forgeries.'

'I'm relieved to hear that.'

'He can do bad things to us, Max. Very bad things.'

'I doubt it.'

'In California,' she said thoughtfully, 'they kill people who get in your way.'

'*What?*'

'In California Robert Blake doesn't like his wife so the newspapers say he kills her, or perhaps arranges to have it done. Phil Spector doesn't like the girl who comes back to his house, so *poof* – maybe he shoots her. We should do this to Vladimir.'

Jesus Christ! It was the same scenario that had crossed

his mind. Coming from Mariska, it seemed surreal. 'How can you even *think* something like that?' he said harshly.

'You want your daughter to be called illegitimate in the newspapers?' Mariska said. 'Lulu. *Our* Lulu.'

'That won't happen.'

'If Vladimir is not silenced, it will.'

'Has he contacted you?' Max demanded.

'No,' she said, looking away from him.

Immediately he knew she was lying. Mariska had never been a convincing liar.

'You *have* seen him,' he said accusingly. 'You might as well tell me the truth, Mariska, because it will come out eventually.'

'All right,' she admitted. 'He came to my door last night. There was nothing I could do.'

'And you let him in?' Max said, shocked that she would be that stupid.

'What was I *supposed* to do? He informed the desk clerk he was my *brother*.'

'Christ! What did he want from you?'

'Money.'

'And?'

'I told him I would talk to you.'

'He's already getting money from me.' A long beat. 'Mariska, if you swear to me that you have no connection with him, that the papers he has are indeed forged, then I can arrange to have him arrested.'

'No,' she said quickly. 'Think of the headlines—'

'*What* headlines? If he's a fraud, whatever they write doesn't matter. I'll sue their asses.'

'But you see, I – I *did* know him once, long time ago,' she said, once again refusing to make eye-contact. 'Vladimir was a – a business acquaintance of one of my cousins.'

'Jesus *Christ*!' Max exploded. 'Why didn't you tell me this before? You're *unbelievable*.'

'I'm sorry, Max. I—'

'*Were* you married to him, Mariska?' he interrupted. 'You'd better tell me, because we're not playing games here.'

'Absolutely *not*.'

'Why should I believe you?'

'Because I tell you truth,' she said defiantly.

'I hope so.'

Mariska began pacing again. 'We must get rid of him, Max,' she said. 'If we don't, there will be trouble.'

'What trouble?'

'I know people who can handle this situation for us. It will cost fifty thousand dollars.'

'Are you *insane?*'

'In Russia we understand how to deal with the enemy.'

Had he really been *married* to this woman at one time?

'I will find out where he's staying,' Mariska continued. 'I have friends in Moscow. They'll know.'

'Oh, I see. You can just call Moscow and say, "Where is Vladimir Bushkin staying?" and they'll tell you. It's that easy?'

'I have connections,' she said, in a low voice. 'Get me the money and our *problem* will vanish.'

'I refuse to *pay* to have someone killed,' he said angrily. 'This conversation is *over.*'

'No, Max, it's not. You must think about it overnight. We'll talk tomorrow.'

'I can't tomorrow. It's my rehearsal dinner with Amy.'

'In the morning when your mind is clear.'

'Didn't you hear me?' he said, exasperated. 'I just told you I'm *busy* tomorrow.'

'You bring me cash,' Mariska said, not listening to a word he uttered, 'and I will take care of everything. There is no need for you to be involved.'

'*No*, Mariska. *Listen* to me. *No!*'

'Max, I understand men like Vladimir. This is the only way.'

'We'll *see* about that.'

* * *

Two clients, both demanding to see him, both claiming it was urgent. Ladies first, so Chris hurried over to Birdy's hotel.

He was let in to her suite by the cousin who doubled as her useless assistant. Clad in baggy dungarees and a skimpy T-shirt emblazoned with the words B. MARVEL ROCKS, this cousin

175

was a less attractive version of Birdy with stringy hair and a blank expression.

'Where is she?' Chris asked, striding into the suite and looking around. 'She told me it was urgent.'

'In the bedroom,' Birdy's cousin said, chewing gum. 'Y' can go on through.'

The bedroom was in darkness, drapes firmly closed.

'Can somebody put a light on?' Chris said, groping his way into the room. 'I can't see a thing.'

Birdy flicked on the bedside light. She was propped in the middle of the bed surrounded by the tabloids, several entertainment magazines and a slew of discarded candy wrappers.

Chris immediately saw why she was so anxious to remain in the dark. The pretty young singer was featuring a lethal black eye and a badly swollen split lip.

'Who did this to you?' he demanded, a redundant question because he already knew the answer.

'He didn't mean it,' Birdy mumbled, in a little-girl voice. 'We were, like, *fighting*, and he kinda hit me by accident.'

'Some accident,' Chris said, scratching his head.

'I told you,' she said, distressed that Chris didn't believe her, 'it was a *mistake*. Rocky wouldn't hit me on purpose.'

'We should call the police,' Chris decided.

'No!' Birdy shrieked, sitting up straight. 'If I'd wanted to call the cops I would've done it last night. Rocky was, like, *upset* 'cause of the whole pre-nup thing. I should've given him what he wanted, I know I should.'

'Birdy, do you still want me to be your lawyer?' Chris asked sternly. 'Because if you do, you'd better start listening to me.'

'I *did* listen to you,' she answered sulkily. 'Look where it got me.'

'Where's Rocky now?'

'He was here earlier all kinda *sorry*,' she sighed, reaching for a tissue, 'but I'm, like, *so* not speaking to him.'

'I take it the marriage is off?'

'No way!' Birdy exclaimed, shocked at the thought. 'I'm punishing him 'cause I'm, like, *mad* he messed up my face. We're still getting married, though.'

'Birdy,' Chris said, as patiently as he could, because getting through to his youngest client when she imagined herself in love was not the easiest of tasks, 'you can't be in love with a man who beats you up.'

'It was a one-time thing, Chris,' she explained, rubbing the tip of her nose. 'He made me, like, a *solemn* promise that he'd never do it again.'

'You'd better tell me how it happened,' Chris said, resigning himself to the fact that Rocky was going nowhere fast.

'Well,' Birdy said tremulously, 'we were, like, coming out of Gatsby's last night, an' there were paparazzi everywhere – they were, like, pushing and shoving, trying to goad us into stuff. This made Rocky even madder, 'cause we'd already bin fightin' in the club.'

'Where were your bodyguards?'

'My fault, 'cause we kinda ran out without them,' she admitted sheepishly.

'Smart move.'

'Sorry,' she said, her voice getting smaller and smaller.

'And then?'

'Rocky was like *kickin*' one of the photographers out the way, so *I* tried to stop him. That's when he turned around and like accidentally punched *me*.'

'Great!' Chris said, considering the ramifications.

'It's possible they might've, y' know, got some of it on camera,' Birdy admitted.

'Got some of *what*?' Chris asked, frowning. 'Not Rocky beating you up in public, I hope?'

'I suppose so,' she said, shamefaced.

'Then I guess I should prepare for a lawsuit from the photographer?'

'*He* didn't get hurt,' she whined. 'Only me.'

'Even better.'

'I was wondering, Chris, if there's anything you can do to keep it out of the rags.'

'Too late now, you should've called me last night. The photographers have already sold their shots.'

'Can't we release a statement saying that, y' know, it was all, like, an *accident*?'

'Let's see what they've got first. Then we'll talk about statements.' He took a beat. 'Have you seen a doctor?'

'Room Service sent up a raw steak last night,' she said, pulling a disgusted face. 'I put it on my eye. It stank up the whole room.'

'How about your lip? Does that need attention?'

'Hurts,' she said, in her little-girl voice.

'We should get you a doctor. You might need stitches.'

'Don't *wanna* see a doctor,' she mumbled, holding back tears.

'I'm sure the hotel doctor is very discreet. I'll call the concierge and see what he can arrange.'

'Sorry, Chris,' she said, even more tearful now. 'I didn't *mean* for this to happen.'

'It happened, Birdy,' he said. 'And you should think very seriously about marrying a man who treats you this way.'

'I'm still marrying him,' she said defiantly, 'so you go ahead and arrange the wedding in Vegas. I told Rocky you'd give him the money from whoever buys exclusive rights to our wedding photos.'

'And that didn't please him?'

'He was pissed when I said I couldn't do the million-dollars-a-year thing if our marriage didn't last.'

'I think *I* should talk to him, straighten out a few things.'

'No,' she said quickly. 'He'll just get mad at you, then take it out on me – that's his way of dealing.'

'Nice guy.'

'He is, *really* he is,' Birdy said, as if she believed it. 'You've just gotta *know* him the way *I* do.'

Women and abusive men, they never learned. Chris wished he could make her see the error of her ways, but Birdy was in love or lust, so right now she was seeing nothing.

He made a call, and soon after that a doctor arrived. Chris showed the portly man into the bedroom, then paced around the living room waiting for him to leave so he could get over to Jonathan and sort out *his* drama, whatever it might be.

As the doctor emerged ready for a conversation, Chris's cell rang. He checked caller ID, saw it was Verona, and decided she could wait.

Once he'd finished conferring with the doctor and made sure Birdy was all right, he took off to see Jonathan. On the way he called Verona back.

'What's up?' he asked brusquely. 'I'm in the middle of meetings.'

'I'm calling as a friend,' Verona said.

Hmm . . . sounded ominous. Maybe *she* was breaking up with *him*. Not such a bad deal – it would save him the trouble.

'That's nice, Verona,' he said, stifling a yawn. 'I'm thrilled to hear it.'

'I'm afraid I have bad news.'

More bad news? What now?

'There's been a mudslide,' she continued. 'Your house is more or less wrecked.'

'My *house*?' he said, alarmed. 'What are you *talking* about?'

'I was driving by to make sure everything was okay because of the rain, and it must have just happened. There were fire trucks and paramedics – everyone was wondering if there was anyone inside. I told them no.'

'My house?' he repeated. 'This is fucking impossible!'

'It's not my fault, Chris,' she said, in an annoyingly sanctimonious tone. 'Blame it on the weather. It's *still* raining here.'

'Jesus *Christ*!' he exploded. 'How bad *is* it?'

'It's bad, Chris. Your house is virtually buried under a complete landslide of mud. We're lucky we weren't in it – we could've been buried alive.'

'My house is buried with everything in it?' he said incredulously. 'My *house*?'

'I'm afraid so.'

'Call both my assistants. Get them over there immediately.'

'I would, Chris, but I don't have their home numbers. It's best if you do it.'

'You really are a big help, aren't you?'

'If we lived together, I could be.'

He clicked off his phone, contacted his main L.A. assistant and told him to get over to his house and see what he could salvage. 'There's a safe in there somewhere,' he said. 'Find it! And when you do, don't let it out of your sight.'

Chapter Twenty-Five

'Come with me,' Beverly said, beckoning Liberty to follow her. 'I got a few minutes so I'll take care of your eyebrows.'

'I'm not sure if I—' Liberty began, scared that Beverly was going to ruin her. She *liked* her thick eyebrows: they gave her face character.

'You *need* it, sister,' Beverly interrupted. 'An' I'm doin' it for free, so let's go.'

'Okay,' Liberty said, getting up. Why not? She had nothing to lose except her eyebrows. Besides, Damon P. Donnell had taken off an hour ago so there would be no more brief encounters.

They went to the make-up room, where Beverly sat her down in a chair, threw a towel round her shoulders and said, 'Bet you've been told this many times, but I'm addin' myself to the list. Your face is incredible, major bone structure. Ever considered modelling?'

'Not really,' Liberty replied, staring at herself in the long row of mirrors. 'Modelling doesn't interest me. I'm a singer.'

'A *working* singer?' Beverly inquired.

'Yeah,' Liberty answered, with a rueful laugh. 'Workin' as a waitress.'

'Do you realize that with a face like yours you could be makin' a shitload of money modelling?'

'I could?'

'You bet, babe,' Beverly said, taking a step back to study Liberty's face. 'Want me to set you up with an agent?'

Could this day *get* any better? First Damon, now this offer.

180

Things were definitely looking up. 'Why are you being so nice?' she couldn't help asking.

''Cause I've been there, done the whole waitressin' gig,' Beverly explained. 'Oh, yeah, an' I know *all* about people treatin' you as if you don't exist.'

'You've got that right,' Liberty said, thinking of the woman in the knock-off Armani.

'The reason I got into make-up was 'cause somebody helped *me*,' Beverly explained. 'So . . . whenever I can, I try to give back.'

'But you're so beautiful,' Liberty said. 'How come *you*'re not a model?'

'I like what I do. It suits me,' Beverly said, shrugging. 'Besides, I'm too old to be a model now. I'm gonna be thirty soon.'

'That's *old*?'

'In the modelling world it is,' Beverly said, nodding to herself. 'They call 'em dinosaurs.'

'Who's a dinosaur?'

'Oh, Cindy Crawford, Linda E,' Beverly said casually. 'Any girl over the big three-O.'

'Wow!'

'So, whaddaya think? Wanna give it a shot? Make yourself some *real* money. It worked for Whitney Houston. She was a successful model until she got into singing.'

'Maybe I'll take you up on it,' Liberty said tentatively.

'You *should*,' Beverly said, producing a lethal pair of tweezers. 'Now, don't go gettin' all panicky on me, 'cause I'm goin' *way* drastic on the eyebrow thing.'

'You are?' Liberty said, wondering if it was too late to chicken out.

'Lean your head back an' relax,' Beverly said encouragingly.

'Is this going to be painful?'

'Maybe,' Beverly said, starting to pluck.

'Ouch!' Liberty yelled, almost leaping out of the chair. 'That *hurt*.'

''Course it hurts,' Beverly said matter-of-factly. 'Gotta *suffer* for beauty. You've never plucked 'em, have you?'

'No,' Liberty said, making a face.

'I can tell. You got a *forest* growing there, girl.'

'Oh, *great*!'

'I *could* wax 'em, less painful, but I don't have my equipment with me.'

'I can put up with the pain,' Liberty said, gritting her teeth. 'As long as it'll look good.'

'Suffer, hon. Believe me, it's a lot more fun than a Brazilian!'

'What's a Brazilian?'

'Man!' Beverly said, her hands moving swiftly. 'You really are green.'

Liberty closed her eyes and thought about the end result. Cindi was always perusing the fashion magazines and pointing out *before* photos of people like Madonna and Jennifer Lopez. They'd both featured extremely thick eyebrows: now they looked sensational. Maybe their raging success was all to do with their eyebrows.

Yeah, right!

'How do you think the shoot's going?' she asked, attempting to take her mind off the little stabs of agony as Beverly plucked away.

'It's rollin'. You gotta *love* that raunchy beat.'

'Do you *know* Slick Jimmy?'

'I know 'em all,' Beverly replied. 'We hang at the same clubs.'

'That must be fun.'

'Yeah, Jimmy's a cool dude. This is his big break – that's if he doesn't blow it.'

'I'm into his music, not his lyrics,' Liberty said, getting used to the pain. 'I told Damon P. Donnell that.'

Beverly stopped what she was doing. 'You told *Damon* you didn't like the lyrics?' she said, raising an eyebrow.

'Why?' Liberty asked innocently. 'Isn't that okay?'

Beverly laughed as if she didn't quite believe what she was hearing. 'Nobody tells Damon *anything*. That man is *king*.'

'Well,' Liberty said casually, 'he asked my opinion, so I gave it.'

'He did, huh?'

'I told him I liked the beat, and that the lyrics were way too sexist. So's the video, with all those girls stickin' their boobs and butts in the camera. What kind of a message is *that* sending out?'

'It's what the industry wants,' Beverly pointed out. 'Those in-your-face, sexy kinda videos sell mucho records.'

'Too bad.'

Beverly resumed plucking. 'What's *your* deal, music wise?'

'I'm a singer-songwriter, more like, you know—'

'Who? Diana Krall?'

'No, she's jazz and, anyway, I hate comparisons. My mom was a singer,' she added wistfully, remembering the times Diahann was actually singing. 'Growing up, we always had music around. I was totally crazy about Sade.'

'Ah . . . "*Smooth Operator*", now *there* we have a classic,' Beverly said. 'Is that your kind of sound?'

'Yes and no. I hope I'm an original. I told Damon – I can call him Damon, can't I?'

'Dunno,' Beverly said, with an amused expression. '*Can* you?'

'I don't see why not.'

'Exactly *how* long were you talkin' with him?'

'Long enough that he gave me his card, suggested I bring him my demo.'

'You'd better watch out,' Beverly warned. 'They all want one thing, an' us girls know *exactly* what that is. Damon might be king, but underneath the bling, he's no different from all the other horn-dogs out there.'

'I know that,' Liberty said. 'He's married, right?'

'Only 'bout as married as a dude can get. And his old lady – in the biz we call her Spenderella – girl, you do *not* want to mess with that woman. No way.'

'I'm not planning on doing so.'

'Tashmir's a piranha,' Beverly warned. 'If she catches you with her man, she'll beat your ass raw with her eight-hundred-dollar Manolos! And, hon, I am *not* kiddin'.'

* * *

As soon as Cindi got a break, she grabbed Liberty by the arm and hurried her over to the Craft Service table.

'I'm starvin',' Cindi complained, grabbing a handful of potato chips and a can of Coke. 'All this damn dancin' is sappin' my God-given energy.'

'You're doing great,' Liberty said encouragingly. 'You look better than any of them. You're the sexiest one out there.'

'How big does my butt look?' Cindi demanded, stuffing potato chips in her mouth. 'Too big? Or just right?'

'I'm telling you, it's hot. The guys on the set are drooling big-time.'

'I bet they are,' Cindi said, reaching for a sticky Danish. 'Girl, what *happened* to you?' she suddenly exclaimed. 'You're lookin' *way* different.'

'Beverly plucked my eyebrows. You like?'

'Damn! *Big* improvement,' Cindi said, biting into the Danish. 'D'you think she'd do mine?'

'Forget about my eyebrows, I have big news,' Liberty said, and proceeded to tell Cindi about her encounter with Damon.

'*Oh . . . my . . . God!*' Cindi exclaimed, mouth dropping open, sugar decorating her chin. 'I *knew* this was gonna be a righteous day!'

'Yes,' Liberty said dreamily. 'He didn't have his shades on and, Cindi, he has these great eyes. Kind of penetrating and sexy.'

'Huh?'

'You heard.'

'Oh, man!' Cindi said, taking another bite of Danish. 'I don't dig the way you're soundin'. Face it, girl, the dude is *married*, an' you know we got a rule – married men are a *way* no-go zone.'

'I'm not thinking of him in *that* way. I'm just saying he has very soulful eyes. They kind of look right through you. Y' know what I mean – intense.'

'*Sheeit!*' Cindi groaned. 'You're fallin' in love.'

'No, I'm not,' Liberty protested.

'Hmm . . .' Cindi said, taking a swig of Coke. 'Wait till Kev finds out you met Mr Big.'

'I'm not telling Kev.'

'How come?'

''Cause I'll take Damon my demo, see if anything works out and if it does—'

'Oh, it's *Damon* now, is it?' Cindi teased. 'Whatever happened to *Mr* Donnell.'

'Don't screw with me, Cindi, this is serious stuff.'

'Poor Kev.' Cindi sighed.

'Why poor Kev?'

''Cause you got it bad an' that ain't good,' Cindi sing-songed.

'Damon P. Donnell is business,' Liberty said earnestly. 'He can help me.'

'Oh, *sure* he can, with his *big* soulful eyes and his *big* soulful dick.'

'You're *such* a bitch. It's *not* like that.'

'It's *always* bin like that, little cous' – from the first day you set your baby greens on him you were wham-bam hooked.'

'That's only because I admire his talent. He's special—'

'They're *all* special when they're standin' there with a hard-on.'

'Get *off* it, Cindi.'

'I will if you will.'

In the afternoon, Vanessa, the current hot girl in several hit videos – including one with Usher, which she made sure everyone knew about, arrived on set.

Vanessa was Puerto Rican, a sexy dark temptress, with waist-length hair, a curvy body and major attitude. She thought she was a star, and acted appropriately. Her job was to slink all over Slick Jimmy, while the so-called fat girls, in various stages of undress, undulated around him.

'That 'ho's a bitch on wheels,' Beverly confided. 'I won't touch her. She travels with her own make-up crew, let *them* have the pleasure.'

Clad in a scarlet slash of a dress, Vanessa was all over Slick Jimmy, who put up no objections.

After a couple of takes, Vanessa *really* started playing the diva. Stepping forward to confront Maleek, she began to spew a litany of complaints in a harsh Brooklyn accent. 'Dude, I ain't down with the way things are goin' here. I *hate* how you shootin' me – the mothafuckin' lightin' is shit. We gotta start again.'

Maleek was not pleased. He stood for her complaints for a while. Then, when Slick Jimmy started getting into it, he blew, and informed Vanessa that if she didn't like it, she could walk.

She walked.

Maleek immediately called a break, went off in a corner and got on the phone.

A few minutes later he came straight over to Liberty. 'You were the girl talking to Damon earlier, right?' She nodded. 'Liberty, that's your name?' She nodded again. 'Okay, Liberty, seems you got yourself a gig.'

''Scuse me?'

'Damon wants you in the video.'

'Me?'

'Yes, you.'

'Doing *what*?' she asked blankly.

'Replacing Vanessa.'

'I – I'm a singer, not a dancer.'

'You're callin' *Vanessa* a dancer?' he said, with an amused expression. 'I don't think so.'

'But—'

'Listen to me,' he said impatiently, 'all you gotta do is the same as her – drape yourself around Slick Jimmy an' look smokin' hot. You can do that, huh?'

'In case you haven't noticed, I've got a sprained ankle and a burned arm.'

'We'll cover your arm, an' no movin', just drapin'.'

'Look, I—'

'Bev, Fantasia,' Maleek yelled, cutting her off. 'Get over here. Damon wants this girl to look *hot*. She needs make-up, hair extensions – the works. Fantasia, see if she'll fit into Vanessa's dress, an' I wanna see some kinda fur wrap coverin' her arm. *Work* it, ladies, we're way behind.'

Liberty shook her head. Now her day was totally surreal. What exactly had she done right?

And yet – why not? Hadn't she been wishing for a break?

Beverly whisked her back into the make-up room and sat her down in the chair again. 'See what happens when you get your eyebrows plucked,' she quipped. 'Girl, I am gonna make you look *fine*.'

'This is crazy,' Liberty said, shaking her head. 'How did it happen?'

'Damon says jump, everyone jumps,' Beverly replied, stepping back for a minute and studying Liberty's face with a critical eye. 'Guess you made *some* impression. Did they tell you how much they're payin' you?'

'We didn't get into that. Should I ask for the same as Cindi?'

'Forget it,' Beverly said, beginning to apply a creamy make-up base to Liberty's face with a damp sponge. 'Tell 'em you want a thousand bucks 'cause you're a feature player.'

'A thousand?' Liberty gasped. 'They'll never pay that! It's a fortune.'

'You want *me* to tell 'em?' Beverly said, working away. 'I'm tight with those guys.'

'Could you do that?'

'Sure, an' when you're a big singin' star you can hire me as your personal make-up artist. Oh, an' if anyone asks – you're a member of the union.'

'Is that okay to say?'

'Man,' Beverly said, shaking her head, 'somebody's gotta teach you how to deal. How old *are* you?'

'Nineteen. I can deal. I've been around.'

'Nineteen, huh? You're still a baby. An' big bad Damon's shinin' his light on you, so watch out – you gotta be *real* careful.'

'Of what?'

'I told you once, I'll tell you again. Damon is a major player,' Beverly said, applying pale copper eye shadow to Liberty's eyelids with her finger. 'A big fat *major* player.'

'As long as he likes my demo.'

'An' if he does, what you gonna do?' Beverly asked, standing back to survey her work. 'You gonna fuck him an' hope that lands you a recording contract? 'Cause if *that*'s your game, you'd better remember to make him wait until *after* you sign a contract.'

Liberty shrugged. 'I have no plans in that direction.'

'Maybe *you* don't, but you can bet your ass Damon does.'

'Like you said, he's married.'

'In the hip-hop world being married means nothing,' Beverly announced, producing a soft beige lip gloss. 'Those guys are like athletes – screwin' around is their national pastime. Man,' she added, rolling her eyes, 'I could tell you stories.'

'You sound so jaded.' Liberty sighed. 'I'm sure they're not *all* like that.'

'Sure, babe, believe what you like, but I'm givin' you the *real* truth.'

'If that's the truth, then it's sad.'

'Allow me to tell you what those guys do,' Beverly said. 'They nail a beautiful girl, use her for as long as it amuses them, then the fuckers move on. Oh, yeah – an' if the wife finds out, they zip down to the jewellery store an' buy wifey-pie another ten-carat diamond ring. What the fuck? It's only money.'

'Why are you telling me this?'

''Cause you're new, *and* you're a genuine beauty – especially now I've dealt with your damn eyebrows!'

'Oh, thanks, this is all happening because of my eyebrows, right?'

'Listen t'me an' learn. Damon *always* goes for the beauties. Like Prince, his bag is to score the prize. An' right now you're it.'

'Y' know, Bev, in spite of what you think, I *have* been around. Working as a waitress you get to know *exactly* what most guys want. Besides, I have a boyfriend. I promise you – I *can* look after myself.'

'I'm sure you can, hon, only you're movin' into a whole different league now, so all I'm sayin' is, watch it.'

'I will.'

'Do *not* believe the hype an' the promises, an' make *sure*, whatever they promise, see your own lawyer an' get it in writing.'

'Thanks, that's good advice. I think.'

'Free, too,' Beverly said, applying a dark contouring blush to Liberty's cheekbones.

'Trouble is, I don't *have* a lawyer,' Liberty said ruefully.

'Hmm . . .' Beverly responded, with the hint of a smile. 'Now *why* am I so not surprised?'

Chapter Twenty-Six

When Jett arrived at the video shoot, Beverly was still busy working on Liberty's face. 'Hang around if you want,' Beverly said, stopping to give him a quick peck on the cheek. 'I'll be through soon.'

'No,' he said. 'Rap's not my thing. I gotta get moving.'

'At least say hello to Liberty while you're here.'

'Who's Liberty?'

'The new girl on the block,' Beverly said, winking at Liberty. 'An' she's sittin' right here, babe.'

'Hey,' he said, giving Liberty a quick look through the mirror.

'Hey,' Liberty responded, equally casual.

The fact that they barely exchanged glances surprised Beverly, because she'd thought Jett would be all over the exotically beautiful girl. Hmm . . . perhaps he *was* in love.

'Did you call that number?' she asked, still working on Liberty's face.

'Tried it a few times, no answer,' he said, cracking his knuckles. 'Guess I'll havta wait until Monday.'

Then it occurred to him that on Monday Gianna would be in New York. Man! Nothing was ever easy.

'You want a coffee, anything?' Beverly offered.

'No, thanks, Bev. You're busy, so I'm takin' off. I'll call you later.'

He left the studio, and on the way to Sam's apartment he started to feel guilty that he hadn't contacted his mother. As soon as he got to Sam's, he picked up the phone before he changed his mind. 'Mom?' he said, when Edie answered.

'Now *that*'s a word I haven't heard in a long time,' Edie responded, sounding relatively sober.

'It's Jett,' he said, immediately groping for a cigarette.

'I guessed it was, since you're the only person who calls me *Mom* and you *are* my son. Not that I've heard from you in a long time,' she added reproachfully.

'I've been living in Italy,' he said, wishing she could sound a little happier to hear from him. 'You knew that.'

'Where are you now?'

'Back in New York. I, uh . . . flew in for a few days.'

'What for?'

'To meet with Red,' he said, knowing *that* piece of information would not go down well.

'That *bastard*,' she said bitterly. 'Why would you want to meet with *him*?'

'He kind of summoned me. Sent me a ticket.'

'Oh,' she said, pouncing. '*He* summons and *you* jump.'

'Yeah, Mom,' he admitted. 'I guess I jumped. But he *is* my dad, and Lady Jane insisted it was important.'

'You spoke to *her*? That phoney witch.'

'She's the one who called,' he explained. 'And when they arranged for the ticket, I thought I'd take advantage of a free trip. Y' know, get to see you an' all.'

'No such thing as a free trip, Jett,' Edie said ominously. 'You'll end up paying, one way or the other.'

'Maybe,' he said, inhaling poisonous smoke.

'Your father's never going to change,' Edie said flatly.

'I know that.'

'When do *I* get to see you?'

'Do you want to?' he replied, remembering that the last time he'd seen her they'd had a huge fight. He couldn't even remember what it had been about.

'You could drive out to the house tomorrow,' she suggested. 'I'm here. I never go anywhere.'

'I dunno, Mom,' he said. 'I gotta meet someone at the airport, then I promised Max I'd drop by his rehearsal dinner tomorrow night.'

'Max?' she said. 'Since when are you close to *him*?'

'He invited me, I thought I'd go.'

191

'Why?'

'Hey,' Jett said, getting off the subject of family, 'any chance of you coming into the city?'

'For what?' she snapped. 'I *hate* the city. I *hate* being any place where I'm forced to breathe the same air as Red Diamond.'

'Then we should try to get together next week.'

There was a long silence, finally broken by Edie. 'Have you seen him yet?' she asked.

'Who?' he said, playing dumb, although he knew exactly whom she meant.

'Who do you *think*?' she said, sounding peeved. 'That *son-of-a-bitch* I was married to.'

'Uh, yeah, I saw him,' Jett replied, trying to keep it light. 'He turned up at Max's bachelor party.'

'What is this – family-reunion time?' she said, a familiar slur creeping into her voice. 'All of a sudden it's Max this and Max that. *I'm* your family, not those half-brothers.'

'I know, Mom.'

'Is Chris there too?' she asked, taking off on a fact-finding mission.

'Yeah, he's around.'

'I'm sure you're aware it was *him* who paid for you to go to Italy, get into rehab and straighten yourself out.'

'Who'd you hear *that* from?'

'I have my sources. You should thank him. I'm positive Max didn't put a hand in *his* pocket. Tight bastard,' she added disdainfully, 'exactly like his father.'

He heard the clinking of ice in a tumbler – another familiar sound from his childhood. Edie had always started the day drink in hand – it was among his earliest memories. 'You doing okay, Mom?' he asked, treading carefully. 'You're not drinking, are you?'

'I had a glass of water,' she said belligerently. 'Is that all right with you, Mr *Reformed* Alcoholic?'

To avoid a fight he hurriedly dropped the subject. 'So . . . are you with anybody now?' he asked, keeping it casual. 'Some handsome young stud?'

'None of your damn business,' she told him, her words

definitely tripping. 'And *you*'d better behave yourself around my gentleman friends 'cause, if I recall correctly, last time you got the bejesus beaten out of you.'

Oh, great. Fond memories. Stoned as he'd been, there was no forgetting the low-life she'd been supporting at the time.

Big fucking deal, so he'd thrown a few insults the loser's way. How was *he* supposed to know the creep was a professional boxer?

'I'll call you tomorrow, Mom,' he said, suddenly overcome with a desperate urge to get off the phone.

'Do that,' she said sourly. 'If you can find the time.'

He put down the phone and stubbed out his cigarette. One thing for sure, she'd certainly managed to wipe the smile off *his* face.

Unfortunately, there was nothing new about *that*.

* * *

Max was seething. What kind of game was Mariska playing, and how could he find out?

It was all too suspicious. First Vladimir turning up at his office, then Mariska claiming she was *not* married to the Russian, when she knew perfectly well he'd seen the marriage papers.

Were they forged? Should he call in an expert?

No, he couldn't do that because it meant bringing in people who would then know his business.

Goddamn it! He was trapped in an impossible situation.

He called Amy. 'You never made it to brunch,' he said accusingly, ready to vent his bad mood on someone.

'I'm so sorry,' she said apologetically. 'It wasn't my fault. Grams was in one of her talkative moods and it was impossible to get away.'

'How's Grams doing?' he asked, softening, because none of this was Amy's fault and he shouldn't be taking it out on her. The truth was that she and Lulu were the only two worthwhile people in his life.

'Brilliant for ninety,' Amy answered cheerfully. 'She looks better than either of us.'

He didn't laugh. He wasn't in the mood for laughing. 'So tonight we'll have that quiet dinner, just the two of us.'

'I was hoping to get an early night,' Amy responded.

'I'll make sure you get home in good time,' he promised.

There was a long silence. Amy broke it: 'Is everything okay, Max?' she asked.

'I told you, I have a lot on my mind business-wise. We'll talk later.'

'Very well,' she said reluctantly, because she still felt unbelievably guilty and she wasn't looking forward to spending time alone with Max.

'I'll pick you up at eight,' he said, still thinking about Mariska and the devious plan she was plotting. Fifty thousand to kill someone, and she was under the impression *he'd* come up with the money.

Oh, no, he was much too smart for that.

* * *

By the time Chris reached Jonathan's Goode's apartment, he'd made a decision. He was going to hop a plane to L.A., stay a few hours and fly right back for the Monday morning meeting with Red. Not only was he worried about his house but there was the matter of his safe, currently stuffed with two hundred and fifty thousand dollars in cash ready to be transported to Vegas and Roth Giagante. He could not afford to lose track of that money.

Jonathan's New York apartment, once featured on the cover of *Architectural Digest* with an eight-page spread inside, was a salute to sleek modern style. Jonathan was an avid student of architecture: he enjoyed clean lines, structural simplicity and stark furniture.

A barefoot Jonathan answered the door himself. Wearing rumpled chinos and a loose shirt, he looked worried. There was no sign of any entourage.

'What's up?' Chris asked, walking in.

'What's up is extremely embarrassing,' Jonathan replied, leading Chris through to the pristine kitchen.

'Whenever I'm summoned to anyone's apartment it's

always about something embarrassing,' Chris replied, perching on a chrome stool. 'Not to worry, Jon, I've heard it all and then some.'

'Can I fix you a health drink?' Jonathan inquired, busying himself chopping mangoes, bananas and papayas, then tossing them into a blender with some rice milk.

'Not really,' Chris said. 'I kind of indulged myself last night and, now I'm suffering the consequences. I'll have coffee – that's if you're making it.'

'Coffee's no good for you,' Jonathan said. 'I refuse to keep it in the apartment.'

'Then I repeat,' Chris said, 'what's up?'

Jonathan switched on the blender, and was silent for a long moment as the fruit tossed and turned. Then he switched it off, poured his drink into a tall glass and gave a long-drawn-out sigh. 'Uh . . . I guess we all do things we prefer to keep quiet, especially when you're an actor in the public eye.'

'What're you trying to tell me?'

'It's not that I'm ashamed,' Jonathan said hesitantly, 'but I realize that if this got out it could ruin my career.'

'Keep going,' Chris encouraged.

'Well,' Jonathan said, gulping down his health drink, 'there are times I walk a dangerous street.'

'And what street would that be?' Chris asked, although he already suspected what the movie star was about to reveal.

'Look, I'm not trying to hide anything from you, Chris,' Jonathan said, speaking fast, 'but, please, this is between you and me. Lawyer privileges, right?'

'Of course.'

Jonathan set his glass on the counter. 'I'm gay,' he said, in a barely audible voice.

'I gather there's a problem?'

'A *big* problem,' Jonathan said. 'Last night I met a man.'

'Yes?' Chris said, anticipating what he was about to hear.

'He was nice-looking, clean-cut,' Jonathan continued. 'Rough trade isn't my style. I invited him back here, and we, uh . . . had a good time—'

'Can I interrupt?' Chris asked, flexing his fingers.

'Go ahead.'

'Where was your girlfriend?'

'We have an arrangement. She's, uh . . . kinda into women, career-wise it suits both of us. So far we've managed to fool the media.'

'This is getting more complicated by the minute,' Chris commented.

Jonathan pushed a hand through his thick hair. 'I realize you're shocked,' he said, his boy-next-door face serious.

'Who, *me*?' Chris replied. 'I'm a liberal, Jonathan. Whatever you do is your business. I couldn't care less.'

'I always knew I liked you,' Jonathan said, relieved that he wasn't being judged.

'Fill me in on what happened next.'

'Well . . . the guy and I had our fun and, um, when he was leaving, I offered him money.'

'Was he a professional?'

'No, he wasn't, and as soon as I tried to hand him the money, I realized I'd made a big mistake.'

'How did he react?' Chris asked, mentally picturing the scene.

'He became extremely insulted and angry. "Who the fuck do you think you are?" he began screaming at me. "Big fuckin' movie star hiding in the closet. You think you can buy everything and everyone. Well, I've got a news flash for you – you can't. I can blow your image apart in a heartbeat."'

'What happened then?'

'He asked me if I knew what he did. I told him I had no idea.'

'Give me the clincher.'

'Turns out he's a journalist for a prominent gay magazine and, believe me, I might've got fucked last night, but now I'm *really* fucked. What are we going to do, Chris? What the *hell* are we going to do?'

Chapter Twenty-Seven

Why did crises always happen on weekends? Lady Jane Bentley was unable to reach her lawyer, who happened to be on a three-day fishing trip to the Bahamas. She needed to speak to him but, in the meantime, she decided it was best to carry on as if nothing had happened. It was not unusual for Red to experience fits of unreasonable rage, but this time his rage was directed at her, and she did not appreciate it. The fact that he'd demanded she 'get out' was shocking. Oh, yes, over the years they'd been together they'd had fights over inconsequential things, but never anything like this.

She soon realized it would be prudent to put her time to good use. Since their initial morning blow-out she had not seen Red. According to his precious housekeeper, Diahann – and what kind of a name was *that* for a housekeeper? – he had left the house saying he would not be back until late.

Lady Jane suspected he'd gone to his so-called secret apartment – the one he hadn't realized she knew about – where he was probably entertaining the whores he'd come into contact with at Max's bachelor party.

She had a good mind to call Max, confront him. But then she thought, why do that? Max wasn't responsible for his father's vile behaviour.

Instead she began a systematic search of Red's private office, going through his desk drawers, opening every file, checking out his e-mails, inspecting every letter and document. There was a copying machine in his assistant's room, and since his assistant was never there on weekends, she made a copy of anything she thought might be useful. At one point Diahann entered the room and had the audacity to ask what she was doing.

'Excuse me?' Lady Jane said, giving the woman an imperious look. She'd always hated Red's housekeeper, the sleazy black woman who didn't even *look* like a housekeeper, more like a gone-to-seed showgirl. 'Are you actually asking *me* what I'm doing in here?'

'You're at Mr Diamond's private computer,' Diahann pointed out, crossing her arms. 'Mr Diamond does not allow anyone to use it.'

'Do you *realize* who you're talking to?' Lady Jane said, amazed at the woman's nerve.

'Yes, I realize, Lady Bentley,' Diahann replied, holding her ground. 'But Mr Diamond has told me many times that nobody is to come in here.'

'I am working under *his* instructions,' Lady Jane said, furious at this interruption. 'Therefore I suggest you take it up with him if you have any problems. And if you *dare* to question me again, I will make *sure* you are fired.'

Diahann gave her an insolent stare and left the room.

Lady Jane decided that if she remained in residence, she would definitely make sure Red got rid of the woman, although she'd tried in the past and had no luck.

Red Diamond liked to hang onto his servants. He actually imagined that by keeping people in his employ a long time it ensured their loyalty.

Lady Jane knew it to be exactly the opposite.

* * *

As soon as Chris had finished with Jonathan Goode, he took a cab to the airport, not bothering to check out of his hotel because he'd be back the next day.

On the way to Kennedy he spoke to Andy, his young African-American assistant, who was usually very reliable. 'I'm flying in,' he said curtly. 'On my way to the airport now.'

'There's no point in you coming to L.A.,' Andy argued.

'I'm sorry to be the one to tell you, but your house is a no-go area.'

'What're you *talking* about?'

'The city has it red-tagged as a possible slide down the hill.'

'*Son-of-a-bitch!*' Chris said tersely. 'Did you find my safe?'

'They won't let anyone near the house.'

'Andy,' he said, in a voice that meant he would accept no argument, 'I want you to go back there, *break* in and get my goddamn safe. That's if you value your job.'

'You don't understand what's going on here,' Andy said, attempting to explain. 'It's non-stop torrential rain, huge storms, and people are being swept away. In Conchita houses were buried under the mudslide. Many people lost their lives.'

'*C'mon*,' Chris said, refusing to believe it was as bad as Andy was making out. 'This is L.A. we're talking about.'

'I know,' Andy said miserably, 'and it's a disaster.'

'I'm flying in anyway. Have a car and driver at the airport, and meet me at my house.'

'You're not listening to me, Chris. There's no house to meet you at.'

'Get in your fucking car, go to my fucking house and stay there,' Chris said, losing it.

He managed to get a United flight out. Unfortunately there were no seats left in first class, so he had to make do. He complained bitterly to anyone who cared to listen.

Jeez! he thought, *I'm turning into my father's son. Screaming at my assistant to break into a house that's been red-tagged. Bitching about not being in first class. What happened to me?*

Then he remembered Jonathan and his problem. It was a whole lot bigger than his. Jonathan's entire career was at stake, and what was he going to do about *that*?

He'd told Jonathan not to worry, that it was taken care of. 'I *am* worried,' Jonathan had replied, throwing him an I-trust-you-implicitly look. 'Nobody knows about this except you, Chris. I'm depending on you.'

What was he supposed to do? Pay the guy off?

Yes, that was usually the answer. Jonathan had said he

would pay as much as he had to – anything to shut the journalist up.

Chris nodded. In his experience most people could be bought. It all depended on the price.

* * *

Toying with her meal, Amy couldn't help noticing that Max definitely had something on his mind. This was no big deal, because she did too. Valiantly she tried to make conversation, but Max kept on staring off into space as if his thoughts were elsewhere. She hoped and prayed he hadn't found out about her one wild night.

The waiter cleared their dishes and asked if they wanted coffee and the dessert menu.

Amy shook her head. Max requested the check.

'Are you *sure* you're ready for the rehearsal dinner tomorrow night?' Amy asked, determined to get him talking before they left.

'I'm ready,' he said curtly. 'Why wouldn't I be?'

She sighed and picked up her glass of wine. 'You saw Mariska today, didn't you?'

He nodded. 'How did you know?'

'She always puts you in a bad mood.'

'You think so?'

'It's true, Max. You're much happier when you deliver Lulu to her nanny and you don't have to see your ex.'

'Problem is, Mariska's always there,' he said, grimacing. 'There's no avoiding her. She gets her kicks torturing me.'

'Something else is bothering you,' Amy said, leaning across the table. 'I wish you'd tell me what it is.'

'Business problems,' he answered gruffly. 'Nothing I can't solve.'

'It's *helpful* to share, Max. After all, we *are* getting married soon.'

'Yes, sweetheart, and I for one can't wait,' he said, as the waiter brought the check. 'You do know how much I love you, don't you?' he said, throwing down his black American Express card.

No, she didn't. It would be nice if he told her more often. And why had he so readily accepted her no-sex-before-marriage rule?

Then there was the biggest question of all – what had made her sleep with a total stranger? How could she *ever* explain that?

Max signed the bill and stood up.

Dinner was apparently over.

* * *

The plane ride to L.A. was non-stop bumpy all the way. By the time Chris arrived he realized he might have made a mistake. He'd told Andy to have a car and driver at the airport. The car was waiting, and so was the rain: it was still pouring down in windswept torrents. Andy was right – L.A. was one big mess.

The driver insisted on telling him bad-weather stories all the way down the freeway.

Chris sat in the back wishing the goddamn driver would shut the fuck up: he needed to concentrate on everything he had to take care of. First there was Jonathan – a big priority. Then Birdy and *her* problems. His house – exactly how damaged was it? And, of course, Roth Giagante and the money he owed.

When he reached his home, he had to give Andy credit, because even though it was pitch black and late, the young man was sitting in his SUV waiting patiently for him. Now *that* was loyalty.

Chris got out of the car, ran over and tapped on Andy's window. 'Did you get my safe out?' he yelled, over the pounding rain.

Andy rolled down his window and handed him a flashlight. 'Take a look, Chris,' he shouted. 'Your house is buried under a ton of mud. I can't get anywhere near the front door, can't even *see* it.'

Chris took the flashlight and walked over. Things were far worse than he'd imagined. There *was* no house, just a giant mountain of mud, and large signs red-tagging his property.

'What arrangements have you made about getting it cleaned up?' he yelled, thinking that once they got rid of the mud, his house would emerge pristine and undamaged.

Yeah, sure.

'Can't do anything until the rain stops,' Andy replied, trying to shelter them with an umbrella. 'Then they'll be able to bring in heavy dredging equipment and get to work.'

'Fuck!' Chris said, getting thoroughly wet, his shoes sinking into the soggy ground. 'I came home to *this.*'

'I *did* warn you,' Andy pointed out. Then, anxious to please, he added, 'I'll deal with it, Chris. I'll do everything I can.'

'Fuck!' Chris repeated, shaking his head as rain soaked through his clothes. 'This is a fucking *joke.*'

*   *   *

After dinner, Max took Amy home, pecked her on the cheek and that was that. Another unsatisfying evening with a man she wasn't sure she still loved.

Upstairs in her apartment she wandered from room to room, restless and confused. Was she doing the right thing? Could she go through with it? *Was* Max the perfect man for her?

Oh, sure, it was easy for Tina to tell her he was – but Tina wasn't marrying him, *she* was, and she couldn't get her night with S. Lucas out of her head. His handsome face kept floating in front of her, his mesmerizing blue eyes, his muscular body and the way he'd held her in his arms . . .

She wondered if *he* was thinking about *her.*

Probably not. It was likely he was one of those guys who slept with lots of women, and never gave them a second thought. How sad was *that*?.

And yet, even if it was true, she *still* couldn't stop thinking about him.

And, even worse, she didn't want to.

*   *   *

By the time Chris checked into the Four Seasons it was past midnight. He'd instructed Andy to book him out on an early-morning flight to New York, so after a good night's sleep he'd be on his way back.

After ordering a bowl of hot soup and a medium rare steak from Room Service, he picked up the phone and finally reached Roth Giagante in Vegas.

'Where are you?' Roth asked gruffly.

'Back in L.A.' he said, not about to take any shit. 'My house has been destroyed.'

'Didn't do it,' Roth dead-panned.

'That's not funny,' Chris snapped.

'You get what you ask for,' Roth said, adding a casual, 'How'd you like your New York gift?'

'She was very accommodating,' Chris replied, thinking how much he couldn't stand this man. '*Especially* when she took off with my gold Rolex. Was that part of the plan, or are you too cheap to pay her the going rate?'

Roth laughed. It wasn't a friendly sound. 'I'm expecting you here tomorrow with my money.'

'Your money happens to be in my safe, and right now my safe is buried under a mudslide somewhere in my house. So, I'm afraid you'll have to wait.'

'You *shitting* me?' Roth growled.

'Send one of your goons to check my story. Go ahead – maybe *they* can dig it out.'

'Does this mean you're not coming tomorrow?'

'No, Roth,' Chris said, clenching his jaw. 'You'll get your goddamn money next week. Right now I'm involved with more pressing problems – like nowhere to live, everything I own is destroyed, and I gotta fly back to New York for a meeting. As I said, you'll have to wait. And, oh, yeah, don't bother sending me anymore visitors.'

'Quit givin' me orders, you dumb prick.'

'*You*'re the dumb prick,' Chris answered, beyond caring. 'I'm offering you a chance to host Birdy Marvel's wedding at your hotel, which would mean millions of dollars worth of free world-wide publicity, and you're not even entertaining the idea. If you were *smart* you'd speak to your PR people and listen to what *they* have to say. I'm giving you twenty-four hours to get back to me. Then I'm calling Peter Morton at the Hard Rock. He's a smart guy, *he'll* get it. And don't worry, you'll get your fucking money!' He slammed the phone down. Man, it felt good!

Naturally he couldn't sleep. How could he? His house was wrecked with everything he owned in it, and how could he stop himself thinking about all the things he'd lost? It was making him feel sick. His house was a symbol of everything he'd achieved. Now it was gone, and there was nothing he could do about it.

Outside, the rain continued to pour down.

Talk about losing control – it was not a pleasant feeling.

Chapter Twenty-Eight

Acting as Liberty's spokesperson, Beverly went to Maleek, the director, and informed him that Liberty required a thousand dollars a day for the two days she'd be working on the video.

'It's already set,' Maleek said. 'She's getting *two* thousand a day, Damon's instructions. The dude is into her.'

'We need it in writing,' Beverly replied, trying not to look too surprised that this was all so easy.

'In writing? Or how about she gets paid cash?' Maleek suggested. 'That way she puts it into her pocket an' walks away.'

'Cash'll do nicely,' Beverly said, thinking that she should've asked Liberty for commission. Not seriously, though – Beverly's latest philosophy was all about giving back, and it was working. She'd met Chet, and he was the first decent man she'd hooked up with in a long time.

When Beverly told Liberty about the money, there was a stunned silence. 'Two thousand dollars a *day?*' Liberty said at last. 'A *day?* Are you *sure?*'

'Don't sweat it. They were probably paying Vanessa *plenty* more. Besides,' Beverly added, teasing her, 'Damon *likes* you, he really *likes* you.'

'He does?' Liberty said, remaining cool.

'So says Mr Director.'

Liberty didn't even want to ask what *that* meant. She took off to find Cindi, who was in a complaining mood. 'Ha!' Cindi bitched, when she told her. 'I gotta shimmy around with my *ass* hanging out, shovin' it in the freakin' camera, an' all *you* gotta do is stand there glammed up like some kinda *diva*.'

Cindi stared at her reflection in a full-length mirror. '*Sheeit!* This ain't fair.'

'You'll think it's even less fair when you hear what they're paying me,' Liberty said excitedly.

'More than I'm gettin'?' Cindi said, narrowing her eyes.

'Try two thousand a day,' Liberty said, still in shock that she was about to make such an unbelievable amount of money for basically doing nothing.

'Man!' Cindi yelled, jumping up and down. 'We're freakin' richer than freakin' *shit*! We can get ourselves that flat screen TV we bin talkin' 'bout *forever*. I ain't even *mindin'* that you're gettin' more than me.'

'*First* we pay our bills,' Liberty said, thinking about what a relief *that* would be. 'Do you *know* how many bills we've got piled up that *I* keep on juggling 'cause *you* refuse to deal with them?'

'That's 'cause you're better at it than me,' Cindi said, adjusting her costume. 'You're the smart cookie, *I'*m the booty queen!'

'That's *right*,' Liberty agreed, laughing.

'You'd better call your mama,' Cindi said.

'Why would I do that?'

''Cause you should tell her to drop by *my* mom's tomorrow night. We'll all celebrate together.'

'I'm not sure I want to see her,' Liberty said uncertainly. 'I *still* don't get why she couldn't've told me about my dad before. It's not *fair* she waited all these years.'

'She probably figured you wouldn't wanna know you had a *dead* daddy, that it was better for you to grow up with, y' know, some kinda hope.'

'Yeah,' Liberty said bitterly, '*false* hope.'

'Let's not get into it now,' Cindi said. 'There's too much slammin' shit goin' on.'

'When *am* I supposed to get into it?' Liberty muttered, almost to herself.

'What time's our call tomorrow?' Cindi asked, quickly changing the subject.

'Ten. According to Bev, they're not into starting early in the rap world.'

'Man, Bev is the coolest,' Cindi said enthusiastically. 'She's gonna fix *my* eyebrows tomorrow. I'm tellin' you, for sure it's the eyebrows got you the gig. Just you wait till Damon sees you *now*. He's gonna dump his old lady an' the two of you'll hook up *permanent*. Mrs Damon P. Donnell. Try *that* on for a tight fit. It's all good, girl.'

'Zip it, Cindi,' Liberty said, looking around to make sure no one had heard. 'Don't even rag on it. It's not like I'm thrilled about being The Girl in some dumb rap video. I'm only doing it for the money. All I want is for Damon to get off on my voice.'

'Sure,' Cindi drawled sarcastically. '*I* believe you.'

By the time Liberty was dressed and ready, it was late. Slick Jimmy was pleased to see her hit the set but, as Beverly was quick to point out, Slick Jimmy was pleased to see anything female. His group of overweight, sexy mamas were feeling the heat: they'd been at it all day, there was only so much booty to be jiggled and they were dragging. They lounged around in various stages of exhaustion, while Jimmy's CD blared over the loudspeakers.

Lousy lyrics, great beat, Liberty thought, for the second time, as she stepped in front of Maleek for his approval.

Maleek was not happy with her look, which immediately made her feel insecure. He requested further hair extensions, a more exotic makeup, and he wanted her dress to cling. Instead of shooting her piece, they rehearsed instead.

'You'll do your thing tomorrow,' Maleek decided. 'Damon wants you perfect an' so do I.'

Hmm . . . Damon wanted her perfect. *That* was interesting, especially coming from a man who until today had basically ignored her.

She'd been thinking about Beverly and her offer to set her up with a modelling agent. It sure beat the hell out of pouring coffee, so she thought she might ask her if she was serious, because if it *was* a serious offer, she would *definitely* pursue it.

The time had come to take chances, and she was more than ready.

Chapter Twenty-Nine

Gianna had left a message on Jett's voicemail that she
expected him to meet her at the airport.

Of course she expected him to meet her, Gianna was
used to getting everything her way.

He went all out and hired a limo. Might as well pick her up
in style.

When Gianna got off the plane, cleared Customs and began
striding through Kennedy, clad in thigh-high leopard-print
boots and a short, chocolate brown belted Prada raincoat, a
couple of random photographers appeared out of nowhere and
snapped her picture. They weren't certain who she was, but
they quickly realized she was someone.

As soon as she saw Jett walking towards her, she threw out
her arms and shouted '*Ciao, carino*. It is so *molto bene* to see
my boyfriend.'

All of a sudden he was her boyfriend? Well, yes, of course
he was, they lived together, didn't they?

'Hey, baby,' he said, hugging her. 'You smell great.'

'No, no, I smell of aeroplane,' she said, wrinkling her nose.
'Is *disgustoso*, I need a shower.'

'What hotel am I taking you to?' he asked, grabbing her
Louis Vuitton carry-on bag, which weighed a ton.

'No hotel, *carino*, I stay with you,' she said, tossing back
her long hair.

This was a surprise, and not a welcome one. How could he
pursue a new relationship while Gianna was sharing his bed?
'Well,' he said slowly. 'I kinda didn't ask Sam if it—'

'*Prego!*' she exclaimed. 'Of *course* Sam invite me.'

'Sam doesn't know you,' Jett pointed out.

'Ah . . . but if he did,' she said, smiling knowingly, 'you *certain* he invite me.'

She was right, there wasn't a man in the world who would turn Gianna down.

He had to admit she looked spectacular. Tall and slender, with a mane of auburn hair, cat-like eyes and full, luscious lips. Men were stopping to stare as she sashayed past, like they couldn't quite believe such a magnificent creature existed, for Gianna's looks were extremely feral.

'I'm not sure Sam's apartment is fancy enough for you,' he said, taking her arm. 'There's hardly any space in the bathroom for your make-up and stuff. Plus there's no magnifying mirror, and you *know* how you *love* your mirrors.'

'What I need, *carino*, when I have you?' she said affectionately. 'I've missed my Yankee boyfriend *molto molto*.'

Yankee boyfriend? It was her new favourite expression. She'd learned it from her grandfather, a Second World War veteran, and Jett hated it.

'Hey, I've missed you too,' he said, not really meaning it, because the girl whose name he didn't know was on his mind big-time.

'Have you been a bad boy?' Gianna teased.

'Only as bad as *you*,' he retaliated.

'Ha! *Incredibile!* I see only one other guy. Mr Lamborghini. And we like him, *sì?*'

'How *is* my favourite car?' he asked, as they made their way through the airport.

'I put in garage. Is *bene*, huh?'

'How long you staying?'

'We shoot photographs. We go home.'

'Not *we, you*,' he said quickly. '*I* have to stay around for a couple of weeks.'

'*Perchè?*' she asked, disappointed.

''Cause there's a few things I gotta take care of before I can leave.'

'*Che cosa* things?'

'Family stuff.'

'You make Gianna *triste*.'

'Sorry, baby. It can't be helped.'

In the limo she hugged him again, her tongue snaking its way into his ear. 'Gianna cannot *wait* to be alone with you,' she whispered. 'We make *delizioso amore* all night.'

'*Later* tonight,' he corrected. 'Earlier we're invited to my brother's rehearsal dinner.'

'*Che cosa* rehearsal dinner?'

'Something people do before they get married.'

'I thought that was sex,' she said, her hand descending on – to his thigh.

'*You* think everything's sex.'

'Is *bene*, no?' she said, with a husky laugh.

'Not always.'

'*You* like, you *know* you do,' she cooed, her hand moving further up. 'How they say in American? You insatiable – *sì?*'

'Maybe we should wait until we get to the apartment,' he said, deftly removing her hand. 'There's a driver up front getting his rocks off watching our every move.'

'So? That is bad?' she said, snuggling against his shoulder, her tongue once again flicking towards his ear.

And he realized there was no escaping Gianna.

* * *

Sunday noon, Nancy Scott-Simon had arranged a major sit-down with Lynda Colefax, the wedding planner. She wished to make sure that all final details were in place since mishaps were not on her agenda.

Wandering around her mother's dining room, fervently wishing she was somewhere else, Amy listened while the two women droned on about the usual subjects – flowers, seating, guests. It seemed their appetite for wedding trivia was never-ending.

'Amy, will you kindly concentrate?' Nancy scolded. 'Who do you wish to sit at the head table?'

'Family, Mother.' She sighed. 'We've been over it a hundred times. Family, Tina and Brad.'

'What about Sofia Courtenelli and her escort?' Nancy said. 'Shouldn't *they* be at the head table?'

'I don't want *them* at the head table, Mother.'

'Sofia Courtenelli *is* your boss,' Lynda pointed out, determined to be involved in every single decision. 'Etiquette dictates—'

'I still don't want her at the head table,' Amy interrupted, wishing Lynda would butt out of stuff that was none of her business.

'Max has *still* not told me if his father will be attending,' Nancy said irritably. 'It's appallingly bad manners.'

'Absolutely,' agreed Lynda.

'I think he *will* be coming,' Amy offered. 'He was at Max's bachelor party. That's a good sign, isn't it?'

'It's not that I *care* whether he comes or not,' Nancy said snippily. 'It's simply so *rude* not to reply. I should call Lady Bentley and ask her myself.'

'Allow me to take care of it,' said Lynda, jotting a reminder onto a large Gucci writing pad.

'No,' Nancy responded. 'It's something *I* should deal with personally.'

An hour later, Amy was thrilled to get out of there. The wedding plans were making her dizzy. What a ridiculous fuss about one day.

She hailed a cab, and was just about to give the driver her address, when she made a spur-of-the-moment decision and instead gave him the address of her mystery man – an address that was, somehow or other, embedded in her brain.

Not that she planned on ringing his bell: she just thought she might take another look at the building where she'd spent the night and lost her virginity.

Why not? She had nothing else to do.

*   *   *

Lady Jane continued putting her time alone to good use. If Red Diamond wished to treat her as if she was dispensable, she would do whatever it took to protect herself.

On Saturday night he did not come home, so on Sunday she resumed her investigation of his private domain, printing out several e-mails from Red to Roth Giagante at the

Magiriano Hotel in Las Vegas requesting that he pressure Chris to pay his debt, and other e-mails from the two banks Red had forced to withdraw from Max's building project.

She discovered nothing new about Jett, except a detailed report from the rehab clinic in Italy.

For a fleeting moment she felt sorry for the three young men. Having Red as a father must have been a hideous experience. And yet they'd all managed to survive and do well. At least, two of them had – who knew how Jett had turned out?

She had no idea why Red had summoned them to a meeting on Monday morning. He was probably going to inform them they were inheriting nothing, and because he was Red Diamond, he wanted to tell them personally. That way he could watch them cringe.

Red Diamond was exactly what everyone said he was. A true bastard.

*　*　*

Max decided there was no way in hell he was giving Mariska blood money to get rid of Vladimir Bushkin. If she swore to him that the marriage papers were fake, then he *would* take it up with the authorities and have Vladimir deported. Yes, that was what he'd do and, by God, she'd better not be lying.

He went over to her apartment on Sunday morning. Irena, her personal maid, opened the door and let him in. 'Is she around?' he asked.

'I get her,' Irena muttered.

A few minutes later Mariska came into the living room. She seemed unusually pleasant, and since this was not a happy occasion, he knew she must be up to something. 'Do you have the money?' was the first thing she asked.

'I never agreed to bring money,' he answered.

'Yes, you *did*,' she said, the good mood fast slipping away.

'No, I *didn't*,' he said sharply. 'Where's Lulu?' he added. He didn't want his little daughter overhearing their conversation.

'Out with her nanny.'

'Let me explain why I'm here,' he said, trying to keep his

temper under control. 'The next time Vladimir comes to my office, I'm calling in detectives and having him arrested for extortion.'

'You *cannot* do that,' Mariska argued, her demeanour turning positively icy.

'I *can* and I *will*,' Max said. 'So, Mariska, understand that if you have anything to tell me, you should do it now.'

'I can't believe you did not bring the money,' she said, her face sulky. 'You are so *stupid*. Things are already in motion.'

'What *things* are in motion?' he asked, alarmed that she might have done something foolish.

'I need that cash. I have people to pay.'

'For *what*?'

'Stop acting so innocent, Max. You *know* what.'

'No, Mariska,' he said harshly. 'Whatever you've arranged, you must put a stop to it immediately.'

'It's too late.'

'It had better not be.'

They stared at each other for a long moment, both busy with their own thoughts.

Finally Max broke the silence. 'For God's sake, Mariska, *were* you married to Vladimir or not? I need to know the truth.'

'You want the truth – I tell the truth,' she said, practically spitting at him.

'Go ahead,' he said, dreading what he was about to hear.

'Yes,' she said, her voice rising. 'I *was* married to Vladimir. Does that make you happy?'

Max felt his heart sink, furious that she'd just confirmed his worst fears. How could he have been married to this lying, conniving *bitch*?

'I came from poor family,' Mariska continued. 'Moscow was hell-hole, I had to get out somehow.'

'While we're on a truth kick, Mariska, were you working as a prostitute too?'

'No!' she said, glaring at him. 'How dare you *think* that?'

'Why shouldn't I? You've lied about everything else.'

'You must understand, Max, there was no *choice* for a beautiful woman other than to prostitute herself, but I *never did that*. When Vladimir tried to force me to do certain things, I managed to escape, and came to America.'

'So you and Vladimir were never divorced?'

'If he'd suspected I was leaving—'

'This means that when you married the accountant, then *me*, both marriages were false? You committed bigamy?'

'Surely you now realize why we *must* get rid of him,' she said bitterly.

'Jesus *Christ*, Mariska, why couldn't you have been truthful with me before?'

'You left me, Max,' she said accusingly. 'You left me alone.'

'I did *not* leave you alone, I left you with a large financial settlement *and* the pleasure of our child.'

'I will *never* forgive you for leaving me,' she said, eyes glittering dangerously. 'Now you're marrying this stupid girl. Everyone is laughing at you.'

'You really *are* a piece of work,' he said, still trying to control his temper, because all he wanted to do was slap her until she cried out for mercy. He would *never* forgive her for what she'd done to Lulu. *Never*.

'Everywhere there are rumours,' she continued. 'I hear you are in financial trouble. How you think that makes *me* look?'

'That's all you're interested in, isn't it?' he said wearily. 'The way *you* look.'

'Appearances are important.'

'*You* want to talk about appearances. Did you ever think about me and Lulu? Our marriage was a sham, and you *know* what that makes Lulu.'

'With Vladimir gone, nobody will ever know.'

'You're fucking crazy.'

'You will see – disposing of Vladimir is our only answer.'

'*No*, Mariska, I'm having him arrested, and I don't give a damn *what* the newspapers say.'

'You should, Max, because it affects *your* daughter.'

'Leave Lulu out of this. I've already spoken to my lawyers about gaining full custody.'

'That will *never* happen.'

'You want to bet?'

'You're a smart man, Max, so listen carefully. Vladimir will *not* be coming to your office again. I have taken care of the situation. And bring me cash, or there will be more problems to deal with. People perform services, they expect to get paid.'

He stared at her in shock, realizing what she was implying.

She met his gaze, cool and composed.

And he knew, filled with dread, that maybe this time she was speaking the truth.

*　*　*

Huddled in the back of the cab across from the apartment where she'd spent her one wild night, Amy began to feel like a stalker. *What* was she doing? Was she planning on getting out of the cab, going up to his apartment, knocking on his door, and saying, 'Hi, I'm the girl from the other night. Do you remember me?'

No, she wasn't doing that.

Then why *was* she here? It was stupid.

The cab driver had his radio on – Kid Rock was mumbling about kicking someone's ass.

'How long we gonna sit here, Miss?' the cab driver asked, turning his head and throwing her a squinty look.

'I'm, uh, waiting for somebody,' she answered vaguely. 'Five minutes or so. Is that okay?'

'*You*'re paying,' he said, picking up a copy of the *New York Post* and proceeding to read the sports pages.

Now what? She was here on a whim and it was a total waste of time.

Just as she was about to tell the driver they could leave, a limo pulled into sight and stopped in front of the building.

She leaned forward, and sure enough there he was, S. Lucas, getting out of the limo looking even more handsome than she remembered. He had on jeans, tennis shoes, and a denim workshirt, his dirty blond hair flopping on his forehead.

Should she get out of the cab and pretend she was just passing? Should she run over to him and say, 'Hi – I thought we should talk about what happened between us.' Or would a simple 'What's your name?' suffice?

215

Before she could decide what to do, he leaned down and began to help someone out of the limo. It turned out to be possibly one of the most beautiful women Amy had ever seen.

She cringed against the back seat of the cab, holding her breath as she watched the beautiful woman throw her arms round his neck, and kiss him – long, lingering kisses.

He started laughing, while attempting to push her away in a don't-stop-I-really-like-it fashion.

Was the woman his wife, girlfriend, *what?*

The driver of the limo opened the trunk and unloaded several Louis Vuitton suitcases, which he then lugged into the building.

And all the while the beautiful woman kept hugging S. Lucas, and touching him in places Amy didn't want to think about.

After a few minutes the two of them vanished inside, and she could finally breathe again.

'We can go now,' she managed.

'Okay, where to?' asked the cab driver, throwing down his newspaper.

'Home,' she said, in a small voice. 'Where I belong.'

Chapter Thirty

As soon as he saw his home in daylight, Chris realized exactly what a disaster area it was. His white house was buried under a huge amount of mud. Even worse, the structure looked like it was half collapsed, and a good part of it seemed about to teeter down the hillside.

The unexpected L.A. weather had demolished his home, and what could he do about it?

Exactly nothing.

There were certain things he could control, like his feelings about his father, the way he dealt with his clients, his love life – but not the weather.

He stood there in the driving rain staring at his once immaculate home for a long time, thinking about all the work he'd put into it, and everything he'd lost. His Cybex-equipped gym, his specially crafted pool table, his collection of rare movies on DVD, his multiple plasma TVs, everything he possessed.

This was an act of nature, and he wasn't sure if insurance covered natural disasters. Only this wasn't about the money, this was about losing his home.

Andy met him there, then drove with him to LAX.

'You've *got* to get my safe out,' Chris instructed him. 'It's imperative that you do. And be sure to stay around when they dig it out. It's on your head if anything gets stolen.'

'I won't leave the site,' Andy assured him. 'I'll set up camp in my car. No leaving until you tell me to.'

'You're a good kid,' Chris said, and decided that Andy definitely deserved a raise.

Once he was settled in the airport lounge waiting to board his plane back to New York, he called the journalist Jonathan had entertained at his apartment. The man's name was Wes Duncan, and Chris had checked him out on the Internet. He was indeed a legitimate journalist working for *Stud* magazine, one of the better gay publications.

Chris introduced himself and told him how much he admired his work, especially the piece he'd written on homophobia in Hollywood.

Wes seemed to enjoy the compliments, until Chris revealed he was Jonathan Goode's lawyer. When Wes heard that, he became verbally abusive, carrying on about movie stars who thought they owned the world.

Chris let him rant for a while, then hit him with the words every writer longs to hear. 'You're very talented, Mr Duncan. Have you ever thought about writing a screenplay?'

Silence. Then, 'Well, I *do* have some ideas . . .'

'Excellent. Because I'm ready to *pay* for those ideas.'

Another, shorter silence. Then, 'How much?'

Bingo! Everyone was for sale. All you had to do was establish a price.

*   *   *

It seemed to Jett that Gianna was being overly affectionate. He couldn't remember her ever being *this* clinging – she was all over him. Maybe America had this effect on her, because the moment they entered Sam's apartment she was intent on making love. He demurred, he simply wasn't feeling like it.

'I take a shower, *then* we do it,' Gianna announced, flouncing into the bathroom, shedding a trail of expensive clothes along the way.

When she emerged ten minutes later there was no escape. She strode toward him like a magnificent panther – sleek, naked and ready for action.

Even though he wasn't in the mood, he *was* a man, and automatically his dick jumped to attention.

She threw her arms around his neck and licked his face.

'Ah, *carino*, I miss you,' she whispered seductively. 'You have everything Gianna likes.'

Her hands were all over him, caressing his balls, stroking his cock, making him rock hard.

He couldn't resist her. They fell on top of the bed and began indulging in sexual acrobats, because that was what Gianna was into. She refused to lie there and allow a man to do what he had to do, she got her kicks taking control and giving him intense pleasure.

By the end of their lovemaking session he felt more as if he'd experienced a vigorous workout. There was only one word to describe Gianna, and that was 'predatory'. She was like an animal – she wanted to fuck, eat and sleep, in that order.

She flopped on the bed, arms thrown above her head, long legs spread wide. 'Gianna sleep now,' she said, with a satisfied smile. 'You wake me one hour before we go.'

Once she was asleep, he started thinking about what his mom had told him. That Chris had paid for him to go to Italy and covered his treatment in rehab. How come his brother had never mentioned it? He'd always thought Sam had paid for everything.

He called the Four Seasons. There was no answer from Chris's suite, so he tried Max.

'Is Chris coming tonight?' he asked.

'He's on a plane back,' Max replied.

'Back from where?'

'He flew to L.A. There was an emergency, something to do with his house.'

'You're kidding me?'

'No. There's devastating storms and rain hitting the coast. Seems his house was one of the casualties. He'll try to make it in time for dinner.'

Even though he was somewhat in awe of Max, this bonding between the three of them was kind of nice. Jett felt like he was part of a family, something he'd never experienced before. When he was growing up, Edie had always been so busy with her drinking, and her steady stream of younger boyfriends, that she'd never had time for him. As for Red – well, the idea of Red as a father figure was one huge joke.

The moment Gianna awoke, she wanted to make love again. At twenty-four, Jett had plenty of stamina, so once more they went a few rounds. As far as he was concerned it was purely a physical thing. In his mind he was still thinking about the mystery girl and how he couldn't wait to see her again.

After their second vigorous lovemaking session, Gianna insisted on finishing him off with one of her spectacular blow-jobs.

Man, she knew how to send a man flying and *then* some. Which was quite rare, because beautiful women were usually not into giving head. Jett had always found they felt it was their right to receive, not give. Although with him they usually changed their minds.

Finished with sex, Gianna began to unpack, flinging expensive clothes all over the bedroom, piling bottles and jars of make-up into the small bathroom, plugging her iPod speakers into the wall outlet so that her favourite Brazilian and Spanish music blared throughout the apartment. She was a big Marc Anthony and Carlos Santana fan, and sang along at full volume. One talent Gianna did *not* have was singing.

'What I wear, *carino?*' she fretted, producing many elaborate designer outfits and holding them up against her naked body.

'Dunno. Never been to one of these events,' he said. 'You'll look fantastic whatever you decide.'

'And you – what *you* wear?'

'I guess Levi's won't cut it, huh?' he said, pushing his hands through his hair and grinning.

'*Prego*,' she said mischievously, fishing out a maroon plastic garment bag from her suitcase and handing it to him. 'For you.'

'What's this?' he asked, unzipping it.

'A gift from Mr Armani,' she replied, with a jaunty wink as he extracted a sleek black Armani suit. 'For my *molto* handsome Yankee boyfriend,' she said, with a seductive smile. ''Cause he make me *veree* happy.'

* * *

After a long, hot shower, Amy felt she'd washed away all memories of her one night of craziness. She'd seen her mystery man in the light of day with another woman, the two of them affectionate and loving. That was enough for her. As far as she was concerned, it was over, a closed chapter, a memory she would try not to think about again.

She didn't regret it, because it had made her realize that passion was a good thing, and she would find that same passion with Max when they consummated their marriage. Actually, it was a relief, because now she could concentrate on the rehearsal dinner and her husband-to-be. And she *did* love Max. Tina was right, he'd be a perfect husband.

Impulsively, she picked up the phone and called him. 'Just wanted to tell you how excited I am about tonight,' she said softly.

'Hi, sweetie, how are you?' Max responded, pleased to hear from her.

'Great, actually. The wedding meeting went well and Mother was pleased.'

'I'm glad for you. I know how difficult your mom can be.'

'She's still wondering about your father. Have you any idea if he's coming or not?'

'I'll find out in the morning. That's a promise.'

'Uh . . . Max,' Amy said tentatively. 'I'm sorry if I've seemed a bit edgy these last few days but, you know, what with the wedding coming up so soon, and my mother driving me crazy, not to mention that bossy wedding planner, it's all been a bit of a strain.'

'That's okay,' he assured her. 'I haven't been exactly calm myself.'

'I know you didn't want to go through the ordeal of a rehearsal dinner,' she continued, 'but it *is* traditional, and it's for my mother, so having the dinner tonight really helps *me* out.'

'I have *no* objections. Your mother organized everything, all *I* have to do is pay.'

'Max?'

'What now?'

'I love you,' she said impulsively.

'You, too, sweetheart. See you soon.'

She dressed slowly, taking her time. Vera Wang had designed a simple lilac silk dress for her. She added matching shoes, a discreet diamond pendant, the tennis bracelet Grandma Poppy had given her, and a pair of diamond stud earrings – an earlier gift from Grandma Poppy.

When she was ready she stood and stared at her reflection in the mirror.

Amy Scott-Simon, soon to be Mrs Maxwell Diamond. It would all work out.

*   *   *

On the plane back to New York, Chris was seated next to a young actress he vaguely knew. Her name was Inez Fallon, and she was overly talkative, which was exactly what he *didn't* need. They'd met once or twice when he was with Holly, and it was obvious she liked him, or maybe she liked what he represented – a powerful L.A. entertainment lawyer. He could almost hear her mind ticking. *If I sleep with him, will he advise me for free?*

She informed him she was flying to New York to appear on *Letterman*. Her latest movie, a horror flick, was about to open, and she planned on doing a lot of promotion.

'Have you been on *Letterman* before?' he asked, attempting to be polite.

'No, but I heard he *hates* women,' she confided. 'Then I heard he either hates them or flirts with them, so I'm gonna flirt. I'll wear something so low-cut and sexy that he won't have a chance to be rude. And I'm told his studio is *freezing*, so my nipples will be *very* happy!'

'Shouldn't think you can outdo Drew Barrymore,' Chris remarked.

'Why? What did *she* do?'

'Jumped on his desk and flashed her breasts in his face.'

'I can do that,' Inez said, quite seriously.

'Do you *want* to?' he asked curiously.

'If it sells tickets I'll do whatever it takes.'

Actresses. They were all the same. Anything for attention.

Verona was different. But Verona wanted commitment, so now she was out. He hadn't bothered calling her in the short time he'd spent in L.A. Why even go there?

'Can I pick your brain?' Inez asked, leaning close.

Sure, free advice, and she hasn't even fucked me. 'Go ahead,' he said.

'I've been offered two movies and I can't decide which to choose. One's with Leonardo DiCaprio, and the other's with Johnny Depp. Who do *you* think is the hottest?'

So that's what it came down to. Who's the hottest? Not, who's the most talented? Or, who's got the best script? Just, who's the hottest? Pretty dumb. 'I'd toss a coin,' he said, feigning a yawn, hoping she might get the hint that he wanted to catch a nap. 'Either way you can't go wrong.'

'Brilliant!' she said, a smile lighting up her ambitious face. 'I never thought of that.'

Earlier he'd called Max and told him he didn't think he could make it in time for the rehearsal dinner.

'I'd really appreciate you being here,' Max had said. 'I want you to meet my fiancée. And who knows? Red might turn up again, which means I'll definitely need your support.'

'Okay, I'll come straight from the airport,' he'd promised, 'although I'll probably be late.'

'As long as you get here.'

The flight attendant leaned down and whispered in Inez's ear that Colin Farrell was on board. 'He's travelling incognito,' she said conspiratorially. 'Sitting in the back of first class. I thought you'd be interested.'

'Oooh,' Inez said, giggling at the thought of the adventure this might lead to. 'Is anyone in the seat next to him?'

'No,' the flight attendant assured her.

'Uh, excuse me,' Inez said to Chris. 'Colin's an old friend. I'll be back in five minutes.'

That was the last he saw of her, which didn't bother him at all. At least now he could get a few hours' sleep.

* * *

Mariska was nowhere in sight when Max arrived to collect Lulu to take her to the rehearsal dinner. Once more Irena answered the door. He nodded at the overweight, frumpy woman, and asked her to fetch Lulu.

Seconds later Lulu appeared, dressed up in a pink party dress, and happy as could be.

'Me goin' party, Daddy,' she announced proudly. 'Gonna see my uncles, *and* Amy, *and* all your friends.'

'Yes, you are, sweetie,' he said, bending down to give her a hug. 'And you look so pretty.'

'Mommy fixed my hair,' she said, posing. 'Nice, Daddy?'

'Yes, Lulu, very nice.'

'Can Mommy come too?'

'No, sweetie. Mommy's busy.'

He managed to escape from the apartment without running into Mariska. He'd already convinced himself that she was bluffing: there was nothing she could do about Vladimir Bushkin. She'd like to, but she wasn't capable of it.

'Lulu wants a present,' Lulu announced in the elevator on their way down to the car.

'No, sweetie-pie, not tonight.'

'Me *want* present,' she said, pouting. 'Daddy *promised*.'

'I said not tonight, sweetie. You're coming to a very grown-up dinner, and you're a lucky girl to be invited.'

'Lulu wants a present,' she repeated, her face suddenly crumbling, tears forming in her big blue eyes.

'No, Lulu,' he said sternly.

'Lulu's tired.' She sighed, lower lip trembling. 'And hungry.'

It suddenly occurred to him that Nanny Reece should be accompanying them. Why hadn't he thought of it before? Especially as Lulu was supposed to sleep overnight at his apartment.

As soon as they got out of the elevator, he hurried to the front desk and called upstairs. Nanny Reece answered the house phone. He informed her that she was to come with them, then reminded her that Lulu would be staying the night, and that she should be with her.

'Mrs Diamond told me I could have the night off,' Nanny Reece said, sounding irritated.

'Sorry, Nanny, you can't. I need you to be with Lulu. Mrs Diamond should've told you.'

'Very well, Mr Diamond,' Nanny Reece said. 'I'll be down in five minutes.'

Yes, he definitely should've thought about it before. In fact, *Mariska* should've thought about it.

The truth was she probably didn't *want* him taking Nanny Reece, because she relished the thought of Lulu jumping all over him so that he couldn't concentrate on his bride-to-be. A signature Mariska move.

Yes. It crossed his mind for the thousandth time that divorcing Mariska had been the best thing he'd ever done.

Chapter Thirty-One

Sitting in the make-up chair on Sunday morning, Liberty decided she could easily get used to all the attention. She was getting the full-on glamour treatment, and she couldn't help liking it.

The hairdresser, a gay guy in a chartreuse tracksuit, brought in several falls to add to her hair. Beverly was busy contouring her face and applying false eyelashes one by one, while Fantasia made sure the scarlet dress fit her like a second skin.

She knew she looked damn good. She also knew it wasn't her, it wasn't Liberty – the would-be singer-waitress. They'd turned her into some kind of amazing fantasy girl. But, she had to admit, it *was* exciting.

When she hit the set, Maleek was all over her, calling her 'sugar' and showing her exactly how he wanted her to slink around Slick Jimmy.

Slick Jimmy was all over her too. 'You into anyone?' he asked, honouring her with a snaggled-tooth leer. 'You an' me should hook up 'cause *I'm* gonna be the *biggest*. Ya better catch me while ya can. All them bitches and 'ho's gonna be *creamin'* themselves over me.'

'No, thanks,' Liberty answered. 'But if you ever need a back-up singer . . .'

'I be a rap artist, baby. *Rap*,' he said, shooting her an angry glare. 'Not one a them fancy soul singers like Brian McNight or fuckin' Keith Sweat. I ain't down with *that* shit. This dude's *today*!'

'Lucky you,' she murmured.

'You *dissin'* me, girl?' he said, sweat beading his brow. ''Cause you do that an' I'm gonna have your ass thrown *off* this mothafuckin' shoot. I don't give no fast shit *how* fine it be.'

'What's the deal with the sexist lyrics?' Liberty asked, ignoring his threat. 'I'm sure you can write more original stuff.'

'Fuck *you*,' he said, glaring at her. '"Fat Girls" gonna be the number-one song of the year, off the freakin' *hook*. What you know 'bout singin' anyway?'

'It's what I do. I'm a singer, and I write my own songs.'

'You recorded anythin'?' he said, staring at her with a challenging sneer.

'No, but Damon P. Donnell wants to hear my stuff.'

'Yeah, baby,' Slick Jimmy said, with a full-on smirk. 'He wanna get *into* your stuff, *that* what the man want.'

Why was it that everybody was under the same impression? Because she looked good, was that what *everyone* thought?

The morning passed quickly. Maleek seemed happy with her interaction with Slick Jimmy. Much as she didn't like the rapper, she was getting into it, pretending it was a game. Acting, that was what it was.

At the lunch break Damon P. Donnell appeared.

She wasn't sure how to behave. Was she supposed to rush over and thank him? After all, he'd picked her out and was paying her all this money to appear in the video. According to Maleek via Beverly, he *liked* her. What exactly did that *mean*?

Then she thought, no, kissing his ass like everyone else was not her style.

He was dressed casually in a cream-coloured cashmere sweater, black pants and a New York Jets baseball cap worn backwards. Once more, everyone started fussing around him, making sure he had everything he needed. He accepted all the attention as if it was his due.

After a few minutes he and Maleek got into a conversation, and then the two of them strolled over to the video assist so that Damon could view what had already been shot.

'Go say hi,' Cindi urged, nudging her. 'Go *on*.'

'Why would I do that?'

''Cause he *likes* you, an' you *like* him,' Cindi teased.

'No, I *don't*,' she said crossly, wishing she hadn't passed on that piece of information to Cindi. 'How many times do I have to tell you? All I need from him is to listen to my demo. Besides, if he wants to speak to me, he can come over here.'

'Oooh, Miss Playin' It Cool,' Cindi taunted. 'Get *you*.'

Cindi's words didn't faze her: she'd made her decision and she was sticking to it.

The assistant director had assigned her a director's chair, and she walked over and sat in it.

Cindi trotted after her. 'I'm gonna grab me some lunch at the catering truck,' she announced, clutching a flimsy wrap around her bountiful curves. 'You comin'?'

'This dress is so tight I can't eat,' Liberty said.

'Want me to bring you somethin'?'

'I'm not hungry. Think I'll stay here.'

'Sure, *starve* yourself to death,' Cindi said, taking off.

Somebody had left a copy of *People* magazine lying around: Liberty picked it up and began leafing through it.

A few moments later he was standing next to her. She knew he was there because she could smell his very expensive, very distinctive masculine cologne. She forced herself not to look up.

'Hey,' he said, tapping her shoulder. 'Thought I'd be receiving a very big thank-you right about now.'

She glanced up. 'Mr Donnell,' she said, feigning surprise. 'Of course I thank you, only this is not what I do. It's an experience, that's all. Oh, yes – and I do appreciate the money.'

'Somethin' different about you,' he said, raising his tinted shades and squinting at her.

'Good or bad different?' she responded, putting down the magazine.

'You was a beauty before,' he observed, 'now you're really stylin'.'

'Thanks, Mr Donnell.' And she wanted to add, *How come you never noticed me when I was serving you coffee every morning? What was I – invisible?*

'Think you'd better call me Damon,' he said, giving her a long, lazy stare. 'Gotta hunch we're gonna be tight.'

Trying to ignore his incredibly sexy eyes, she stayed on the subject of her music. 'I brought my demo with me today – I'd like to play it for you.'

'You would, huh?' he said, not taking his eyes off her.

'Yes, I would,' she said, still pretending not to notice his intense scrutiny.

'So . . . Liberty,' he said, rubbing his slightly stubbled chin with his index finger, 'you're serious? You *are* a singer.'

'Did you think I was making it up?'

'Who knows today? Everyone's chasin' a piece of the action.'

'Then how come you sound surprised?'

'Y' know,' he said, suddenly serious, 'straight singers ain't my deal. I'm in the hip-hop, rap business.'

'No,' she corrected. 'You're in the *record* business, you can *deal* with who you like.'

'I can?'

'You're the boss, aren't you?'

'Yeah,' he agreed, with an amused grin. 'I'm the boss.'

'If you can't listen to my demo now, can I come to your office tomorrow and you'll listen to it then?'

'Got no reason to stop you.'

'What time?' she asked, determined to pin him down.

'You could show up around six-thirty.'

'I'll be there.'

'And, uh . . . Liberty—'

'Yes?'

'Keep it between us,' he said, then walked away.

Beverly was right, he was definitely coming onto her. Not that he'd actually *said* anything: it was all in his eyes – those smoky incredibly sexy eyes.

And yet, if he *was* on the make, how come he'd walked away? And what was with the 'keep it between us'? Like, *who* was she going to tell?

Hmm . . . He was into game-playing. Yes, that was it.

Well, she might not be in his league, but she knew how to play a game or two herself.

And the best news of all was that she had an appointment with him tomorrow, six-thirty, at his office.

And she *would* be there. Because Damon P. Donnell was her one big shot at the future.

Chapter Thirty-Two

The rehearsal dinner was being held at the Waldorf Astoria to accommodate Grandma Poppy. She was ninety years old, so having the dinner at her residence hotel made it easier for her.

Amy arrived early, and took the elevator upstairs to fetch her. 'Hi, Grams,' she said, kissing her adored grandmother on both cheeks. 'Don't *you* look lovely?'

'Thank you, dear.'

'You're *sure* you're up to this?' Amy asked, concerned that it might be too much for the old lady.

'Wouldn't miss your party,' Grandma Poppy said, fiddling in a beaded bag. 'The moment I've had enough, Hueng will bring me back upstairs.'

'Then you'd better be sure you tell him when you're ready,' Amy said sternly. 'No overdoing it.'

'Allow me to look at you, child,' Grandma Poppy said.

Amy executed a little twirl, showing off her dress.

'Delightful!' Grandma Poppy exclaimed. 'I'm *so* proud of you, dear. I do hope your young man appreciates the prize he's getting.'

'He's not so young, Grams,' Amy said, with a faint smile. 'Max is in his forties.'

'That's young, dear.'

Hmm . . . Amy thought. *Anyone under seventy is probably young to Grams.* 'Shall we go downstairs?' she asked. 'Are you ready?'

'In a minute,' Grandma Poppy replied, fishing an old

leather ring box out of her bag and handing it to her grand-daughter. 'First, I have something for you.'

Amy accepted the gift and opened the box. Inside was an antique emerald ring, with diamonds and tiny pearls. 'Grams, this is exquisite,' she gasped. 'Are you absolutely *sure* you want to give it to me?'

'It was a present from an Indian prince when I was a mere girl,' Grandma Poppy said, a faraway look in her eyes. 'He promised it would bring me long life and happiness. It seems he was right, so now I bestow those precious gifts on you.'

'Thank you *so* much,' Amy said, slipping the ring on her finger. 'I couldn't love it more.'

'I'm ready to go,' Grandma Poppy said crisply. 'I refuse to miss one moment of this extremely important occasion. Come along, dear, it's time we started celebrating.'

*　　*　　*

'How I look?' Gianna asked, knowing full well she looked incredible.

'Not bad,' Jett replied, provoking her.

'*Scusi!*' she exploded, not taking him seriously at all. '*Bastardo!*'

They both began to laugh.

He couldn't wait to see the expressions on his brothers' faces when they got an eyeful of Gianna. She was featuring her Italian supermodel look – a Roberto Cavalli outfit that was totally wild. It consisted of a long gypsy-style skirt, a suede and leather-studded vest worn over a skimpy python-print bra, multiple ivory and gold crosses strung round her swan-like neck, plus fourteen ivory and silver bangles. There was plenty of toned, taut skin on display.

So what? Jett thought. *Give the New York natives a show.*

He was wearing his new Armani suit, which fitted him perfectly, and a black silk shirt unbuttoned at the collar. They made a striking couple.

Jett wondered if there was any way he could palm off Gianna on Chris. His brother had told him he was breaking up with his current girlfriend, so why not? Gianna was the perfect girl to help a man get over a break-up. She was a fun-loving, sex-mad goddess. What more could any man ask for?

'Come on,' he said, dragging her away from the mirror and out of the apartment. As they crowded into the tiny elevator he said, 'Did I tell you about my brother, Chris? He's a major entertainment lawyer in Hollywood. Looks after all kinds of stars – Birdy Marvel, Jonathan Goode.'

'I like – how you say? Jamie Foxx,' Gianna said, licking her lips. 'Veree sexy, no?'

'Don't think he's Chris's client. But, hey, you ever thought of movin' into acting?'

'*Scusi?*'

'Maybe you should talk to Chris about it, I'm sure he could hook you up.'

'*Sì?*' Gianna said, not particularly interested.

'Yeah, really,' Jett said, pushing it. 'Y'know, a lot of actresses start out as models. Cameron Diaz is example number one.'

'Cameron *who?*'

'Diaz. She's big in America. Look, I'll make sure you get a chance to talk to Chris tonight. Could be the start of something.'

*   *   *

Lady Jane Bentley was on a mission, and that mission was to gain entry to Red Diamond's safe. All she needed was the combination and, knowing Red, he would have written it down somewhere.

As she continued her thorough search, she couldn't help recalling their first meeting. He'd lured her into his bed with lavish gifts and promises of what she would get if she left her husband and moved in with him – at the time she was married to one of his business rivals, Lord James Bentley, an English media tycoon whom Red loathed.

When it came to the pursuit of a business he wished to acquire or a woman he wanted, Red Diamond was ruthless. It had taken him many months, but eventually he'd won her over: she'd left her husband, and moved back to America to be with Red.

The headlines were lurid. There was nothing like a good juicy scandal in Billionaire Land. And Red was triumphant. As usual, he'd won.

At first Lady Jane had been fascinated by Red Diamond. His very ruthlessness was an aphrodisiac, not to mention his vast fortune, plus he was a ferocious lover. She also preferred New York to London: it was more exciting, and moving back she'd been looking forward to entertaining on a grand scale. However, after a while she realized that Red Diamond was not the man she'd left her husband for. He was a cruel tyrant, who cared about nobody but himself. He had no desire to entertain, no wish to travel, he was estranged from his three sons, and he hardly ever left his house. The lovemaking stopped as soon as she was in residence. All he required was that she service him orally twice a day, a sexual act she considered repugnant and demeaning.

Lady Jane found herself in an impossible position: she'd left her husband to be with Red in such a public fashion that it would be a major embarrassment to admit defeat. She had chosen to ignore Red's shortcomings and made a life with him – because how much longer did he have? After all, she was thirty years younger than him and could afford to wait.

When she'd first moved in he'd assured her she was well taken care of in his will. What exactly did that mean? And now that he was telling her to get out, how did that affect her position?

It was imperative that she find his will so that she could see for herself exactly what it said.

Since he had failed to return home on Saturday night she had had plenty of time to conduct an even more thorough search of his personal papers.

At six o'clock on Sunday night she had discovered the entry code to his personal safe written on a packet of book matches hidden in the inside pocket of one of his suits. It was a satisfying moment for she knew she had discovered the gateway to all his secrets.

*   *   *

Lulu was the only child at the rehearsal dinner so everyone was oohing and aahing about how adorable she was. Everyone except Nancy Scott-Simon, who was not happy that her future son-in-law already had a child with some dreadful foreign woman who was known in New York society to be a relentless social-climber. Nancy would have preferred her only daughter to be marrying a man *without* baggage. But at least Maxwell Diamond was rich, and could support Amy without expecting her to contribute. Young, pretty heiresses had to be extremely careful: fortune-hunters lurked round every corner. And Amy wasn't the most stable girl: she needed a man who would assume control.

Amy led Grandma Poppy over to Max. 'You remember Grams,' she said, holding onto her grandmother's frail arm.

Checking out his bride-to-be, Max couldn't get over what a lucky man he was. Amy was a vision of perfection in her pale lilac dress, with her natural blonde hair half up, half down, wearing exactly the right amount of jewellery. Amy Scott-Simon was a class act. A world apart from Mariska. 'Of course I do,' he said, bending down to kiss the old lady's cheek. 'How are you, Grandma?'

'I'm not *your* grandma, young man,' Grandma Poppy said, giving him a withering look. '*You* may call me Poppy.'

'I'll be happy to,' Max said, suitably deflated.

'I'd like Grams to meet Lulu,' Amy said quickly. 'Where is she?'

'Over there in the middle of an admiring crowd,' Max said, waving across the room.

'I do hope she has a nice time tonight,' Amy said, thinking it wouldn't be pleasant if Max's little girl threw one of her tantrums.

'I'm sure she'll behave,' Max assured her, 'and if she doesn't, too bad. This is *our* night, sweetheart. Nobody can spoil it.'

'It certainly is,' she answered warmly. 'Oh, there's Tina. I should run over and say hello. Grams, would you like to come with me?'

'No, thank you,' Grandma Poppy said grandly. 'Lead me to my seat and I will allow people to come to *me*. I won't trail behind you all night as if I am an ancient appendage!'

Amy glanced around, searching for her mother. As soon as she saw her, she took Grandma Poppy over and settled her at the main table, with Hueng in attendance, then made her way over to Tina and Brad's table where they were about to sit down with a group of her friends from work. Yolanda, Dana and Carolee had all brought dates, while Nigel was with his significant other, the languid Marcello, who – much to Nigel's annoyance – seemed quite taken with Yolanda's date, a barely legal toy-boy.

Amy wished she was sitting at their table: she knew they were all set to have a great time. Rehearsal dinners were far less formal than actual weddings, and now that she was over her mystery man, she was determined to enjoy herself. She wanted Max to do the same. He had to stop worrying and let himself go for once.

'You okay?' Tina asked, her stomach bulging out of a blue satin dress that appeared to be bursting at the seams.

'*You*'re the one about to give birth,' Amy replied.

'Not tonight, I hope,' Tina responded, patting her huge belly.

'Let us pray,' said Brad, Tina's stockbroker husband, rolling his eyes.

'Soon as I can, I'll be back to sit with you,' Amy promised. 'Your table is definitely the most fun.'

'That's if I don't give birth,' Tina joked.

'What, and ruin my party?' Amy quipped.

Everyone laughed.

'*Very* stylish,' Carolee said admiringly, fingering the material of Amy's dress.

'Vera Wang,' Nigel said. 'Made especially for little missy.'

'Yeah, well, *little* missy better not let *big* missy Courtenelli find out,' Yolanda said. 'Lucky she's not here tonight.'

Amy was already hurrying back across the room to Max.

'Good job I brought the nanny,' Max said. 'Otherwise I'd be stuck worrying about the kid all night. You know how she can get.'

'Not *stuck* with her, Max,' Amy corrected gently. 'She's your daughter.'

'She'll be *our* daughter soon.'

'No,' Amy said. 'I'll be her step-mom. She already *has* a mother.'

'You're sure that taking on a ready-made family is okay with you?' he asked, scratching his chin.

'One little girl is hardly a ready-made family,' Amy said, smiling softly. 'Besides, we'll have our own children one day.'

'That's right,' he said. 'I was thinking a boy and a girl.'

'You can't order what you want, Max,' she teased.

'Oh, no? 'Cause I read there are ways of deciding.'

'Where did you read *that*?'

'Apparently you stand on your head for a girl, or hang out of the window for a boy.'

Amy began to laugh. 'You're funny when you talk like that.'

'I am?'

'Yes, and you're usually so serious.'

'Guess I've been mixing with my brothers too much,' he said wryly. 'I hope you like them.'

'I can't wait to meet them. Where are they?'

'Chris is coming straight from the airport and, big surprise, Jett's late.'

'Is that his reputation?'

'Excuse me?'

'Always late.'

'Jett has a far bigger reputation than that.'

'He does?'

'I should warn you, he seems to have cleaned himself up, but a few years ago he was heavily into drugs.'

'That's a shame.'

'Yes, it is, but in a way it's understandable. Red was a hard taskmaster, and none of us had it easy, but Jett, being the youngest, got the brunt.'

'So, once again, it's all your father's fault?'

'You could say that.'

'He sounds like a dreadful man.'

'Believe me, he is.'

'What's Chris like?'

'Smart, easy-going. You'll enjoy his company.'

Impulsively Amy leaned over and kissed her future husband's cheek.

'What's *that* for?' Max asked.

'Just for nothing,' she said, once more smiling softly.

* * *

As the guests began finding their appointed tables and sitting
down for dinner, Jett arrived, Gianna at his side. They didn't
so much arrive as make an entrance. A big entrance.

Reactions were mixed.

'Who on *earth* is *that*?' Nancy Scott-Simon demanded of
Lynda Colefax, who had no idea. She turned to Amy to find
out, but Amy had gone to the ladies' room.

'What a divine creature,' Grandma Poppy murmured,
observing Gianna. 'I can see she is a free spirit – exactly like I
used to be when *I* was a young girl.'

Across the room Brad nudged Tina. 'Who's the babe?' he
asked.

'Stop looking!' Tina said crossly, slapping his wrist. 'You
have a pregnant *wife*! Keep your lecherous eyes to yourself.'

'It's the Italian supermodel, Gianna,' Nigel said, totally in
awe. 'She's in town to appear in our new ad campaign.'

'Never mind the girl,' Yolanda said, fanning herself with a
napkin. 'Feast your eyes on the hottie she's with. Now *he* can
join me in my bed *anytime*.'

'*Very* sexy,' murmured Marcello, causing Nigel to fix him
with a jealous glare.

'He looks sort of familiar,' Tina said, peering across the
room. 'Wasn't he—'

'I think *he*'s a model too,' Nigel said, always a fount of
information. 'I'm sure I've seen his picture in Italian *Vogue*.'

'I wonder what they're doing *here*?' Tina said.

'Perhaps they're friends of Max's,' Nigel suggested.

While everyone stared, Max stood up and went over to
greet his brother and girlfriend.

'Max,' Jett said, loosening his collar. 'Meet Gianna.
Gianna, this is my big brother, Max.'

Before Max could say a word, Gianna flung her arms round

him, kissing him on both cheeks. 'Soon you be married,' she gushed. '*Molto bene. Salutations.*'

'Thank you,' Max said, taking a step back, her rich, musky perfume overwhelming him.

'Where is your bride? I must say *ciao*,' Gianna said, the ivory and silver bracelets jangling half-way up her tanned bare arms.

'Here she comes now,' Max said, relieved to see Amy approaching.

Gianna turned around, so did Jett.

And there she was. Amy. Cool and pretty. Walking towards them. A smile on her face until she spotted Jett standing with the beautiful woman from outside his apartment.

Her smile froze. What was going on? Why were they here? Had Max found out and was this his revenge?

Oh, God! She wished she could close her eyes, open them, and find this was all an out-of-control nightmare.

But she couldn't. This was real, and she was totally helpless.

'Sweetheart,' Max said, seemingly unperturbed. 'This is my brother Jett, and his girlfriend Gianna. Jett, say hello to Amy, my fiancée.'

Amy felt faint. Was this some kind of sick joke? His brother. Max's *brother*.

No. It wasn't possible.

And how could he be called Jett? His name was Scott or Sonny or Simon. S. Lucas, that was who he was.

This couldn't be happening!

Before she could think straight, the woman was enveloping her in a hug, offering congratulations in a mixture of broken English and fluent Italian.

Then it was Jett's turn. She could read the shock in his eyes. Obviously this was a surprise to him also.

He proffered his hand, acting as if they'd never met – which, of course, was the only sane way to play it.

She took his hand, shook it, and a jolt of pure electricity coursed through her body.

'You Americans!' Gianna exclaimed, with a husky laugh. 'So *uptight*. Kiss the girl, *carino*. Soon she will be part of your family.'

Stunned, Jett withdrew his hand, and at that exact moment Lulu raced over, throwing herself into his arms. 'Lulu's uncle,' she chanted. 'Uncle! Uncle! *Uncle!*'

He swung the little girl round, grateful for the diversion because he, too, was in deep shock.

'So *dolce*!' Gianna said, smiling agreeably at Max. 'Is yours?'

'Yes, she's mine,' he answered proudly. 'My little Lulu.'

'You are *very* lucky man,' Gianna said, and turned to include Amy. 'You will find much *amore* and happiness together.'

What is she – a witch? Amy thought. *A witch with the best body I've ever seen.*

I hate her.

No, I don't. It's not her fault. She probably has no clue that her boyfriend is a cheat.

'Let's all sit down,' Max suggested. 'I can see your mother is getting agitated.'

Lulu was still clinging to Jett. He carried the little girl to the table. 'Me sit next to *you*,' Lulu said, fluttering her long eyelashes at him.

'Sure, honey,' he said, shooting a covert glance at Amy, who looked even more lovely than he remembered. That gorgeous face. Those wide, innocent eyes. Her silky hair and glowing skin.

I'm in love, he thought. *I'm in love with my brother's fiancée. And what the hell am I supposed to do about that?*

Chapter Thirty-Three

By the time Chris arrived at the rehearsal dinner things were in full swing. Harold was in the middle of making a heartfelt speech about his step-daughter, of whom he was very fond, while the main course of steak and lobster had just been served.

'Over here,' Max called out, waving him to the table.

Chris slid quietly into the seat between Nancy's best friend – a true Tom Wolfe type social X-ray, and Gianna, who turned to him with an animated expression and exclaimed in a loud whisper, 'I *love* your brother. You and I be *bene bene* friends, *capisce?*'

So this was the fabulous Gianna, she of the famous blow-jobs and proud Lamborghini owner. 'Sure,' Chris said, thinking that Jett was one lucky baby brother.

On the way in from the airport he'd called Jonathan and told him everything was taken care of. 'It'll cost you seventy-five grand and he'll sign a non-disclosure contract, which is being couriered to him now.'

'You're the best!' Jonathan had exclaimed, sounding suitably grateful. 'Anything I can do for you, Chris, anything at all, never hesitate to ask.'

Harold finished his speech to much applause. Max immediately leaned across the table and introduced Chris to Amy. Chris was impressed: it seemed that both of his brothers had done well for themselves in the girlfriend department.

'I gotta hit the head,' Jett said, standing up. 'Come with, Chris.'

'That's okay, I don't—'

'I *need* to talk to you,' Jett said, throwing him a meaningful look.

'Sure,' Chris said, pushing his chair away from the table. 'What's up?' he asked, as they headed for the men's room.

'What's up?' Jett repeated, groping for a cigarette in his jacket pocket. 'What's freaking *up*? That girl in there, that gorgeous incredible girl—'

'Gianna?' Chris interrupted.

'No, not freaking Gianna,' Jett snapped, confused and frustrated. 'Amy, Max's fiancée.'

'What about her?' Chris asked, wondering what he was missing.

'She's *my* girl, *the* girl,' Jett said, his hand shaking slightly as he lit his cigarette. 'The one I've been trying to find.'

'You're *not* telling me—'

'Yeah,' Jett said grimly. 'That's *exactly* what I'm telling you.'

'Jesus *Christ*!' Chris exclaimed. 'You *screwed* Max's fiancée? *She's* the one?'

'What the *fuck* am I gonna do?' Jett demanded, exhaling smoke.

Chris had no idea what Jett expected him to say. 'Are you *sure* it's her?' he asked.

'C'*mon*, Chris,' Jett said, shooting his brother a dirty look. 'I'm not crazy. *Of course* it's her.'

'Has she said anything to you?'

'How can she? She's sitting right next to Max and she's surrounded by her family.'

'Jeez – do you think she *knew* you were Max's brother when she went home with you?'

'No way. I mean, why the hell would she sleep with her fiancé's brother? What kind of a fucked-up deal is *that*?'

'Here's my question. Why would she sleep with *anyone* when she's about to get married?'

'Yeah,' Jett said, 'that's exactly what I keep asking myself.'

'There's no way you can tell him,' Chris said, imagining the consequences of Max finding out. 'Don't even consider it.'

'Like I'd do that.'

'Here's what you've got to do. Suck it up, forget it ever happened. Move on.'

'Easy for you to say,' Jett said miserably. 'Only it *did* happen, and she's not a girl I can forget.'

'Then, little bro', you'd better start trying. And my suggestion is that you do *not* mention this to anyone else. Keep it between us and we'll figure something out.'

'I need a drink,' Jett muttered.

'No,' Chris said, knowing how impossible it would be if Jett were to get drunk. 'That's exactly what you *don't* need.'

'I can handle it.'

'Getting shit-faced is a dumb move, Jett.'

'So *what*? You think I can go back in there stone-cold sober?'

'If you plan on making it through the night – yes.'

'You're a big fucking help,' Jett muttered.

'Just watching out for you, surfer kid.'

'Yeah,' Jett said wryly. 'I guess you're getting good at that.'

*　*　*

Back at the party they were showing a slide show of Amy and Max's childhood photos. There was Amy aged two, naked and curly-haired, lying on a fur rug – Max aged four, all dressed up in a grown up suit, solemnly saluting – Amy, five and adorable – Max, ten and stern – Amy at her junior prom – Max at his. And so on . . .

Amy could barely concentrate, her mind was racing in a hundred different directions. She kept glancing at Max, making sure he hadn't set this up to punish and humiliate her.

No. It was just one of those things. An error of judgement. *Her* error.

Gianna was busy charming everyone, speaking non-stop to anyone who would listen. She'd already bonded with Grandma Poppy, who pronounced her an absolute delight.

Finally Chris and Jett returned to the table.

Amy wondered if Jett had confided in his brother. Had he revealed the horrible truth? And would his next move be to tell Max?

Oh, God! Maybe *she* should get to Max before *he* did and confess everything.

For a fleeting second her eyes met Jett's. Quickly she looked away. What must he think of her?

As soon as she felt she could, she made a mad dash across the room to Tina's table, ready to divulge everything to her best friend, and beg for her counsel, because there was no way she could handle this by herself. Her stomach was churning, she felt totally shaky – what was she going to *do*?

When she reached Tina's table some sort of commotion was taking place.

'Thank *God*!' Brad exclaimed, grabbing her by the shoulders. 'For Crissakes, Tina's gone into labour!'

'*What?*' Amy cried out.

And from there it was all one big blur as Amy elected to go with Tina and Brad to the hospital.

As soon as Nancy found out, she was livid. 'You cannot leave your own rehearsal dinner,' she fumed. 'I will not allow it.'

'Sorry,' Amy yelled, as she assisted Tina past the main table. 'This is my best friend and she needs me.'

'Go!' Max said encouragingly. 'I know how important this is to you, sweetie. Take the car – my driver's downstairs.'

Oh, great! Now he was being understanding and selfless. She wished he would scream and act like a man betrayed. She deserved it. Only he couldn't do that, could he? *Because he didn't know.*

She caught another brief glimpse of Jett. He was staring at her. She pretended not to notice.

'Stop!' Tina yelled, as they reached the door. 'I think my waters are breaking.'

'Oh, my God!' exclaimed Brad, starting to panic. 'You can't give birth to our baby here!'

'I'll have our baby wherever I damn well please!' shouted Tina. 'Go find the car, you idiot. Don't you understand? WE'RE HAVING A BABY!'

* * *

So that was it. There one minute. Gone the next. And he hadn't even had a chance to say a word to her.

Amy Scott-Simon.

He knew her name.

A rich girl, so her mother's best friend – a skeleton on stick legs in an Oscar de la Renta fancy suit – had informed him. 'When Grandma goes, the will bypasses Nancy and Amy inherits everything,' the woman had confided in a stage-whisper. 'We're all so happy that Max is obviously not a fortune-hunter. They make a delightful couple, don't you agree?'

No. He didn't agree. Max was too old for her. And who gave a fast crap if she had money or not?

He'd fallen for a girl. A girl without a name or pedigree. An incredible girl with soft golden hair, an amazing body and the face of an angel. And there was nothing he could do about it except sit back and watch.

Max was beaming, even though Amy had run off with her pregnant friend – which proved she was a loyal and decent person. Birth of best friend's baby before rehearsal dinner. Good for her.

Amy Scott-Simon.

Even her name had a ring to it.

Gianna was swigging champagne like it was going out of style. She enjoyed being the centre of attention. Max was obviously enjoying her, too, as she laughed and flirted with him. Jett was well aware that it was just Gianna's affectionate Italian way – she was a very touchy-feely person, who got her kicks telling men how handsome and virile they were, making them feel good about themselves. And if they fell in love with her, all the better.

Lulu had decided he was her favourite uncle and kept crawling onto his knee and locking her arms round his neck. He didn't object – she was so cute.

'Can Lulu come live with you?' she asked, all bright eyes and puffy lips.

'No, baby, you have a daddy and a mommy,' he said, somewhat distracted. 'You're very happy at home.'

'Not happy,' she said, vigorously shaking her head.

'Huh?' he said vaguely.

'My mommy's divorcing my daddy 'cause *he* doesn't like her,' Lulu said, blinking several times. 'That makes Lulu sad.'

'Hey, sugar cake, I'm sure it's not as simple as that.'

''Tis,' Lulu said stubbornly. 'Daddy likes stupid Amy.'

'Don't say that about Amy.'

'Why?' she asked, pulling a face. 'Mommy says it.'

''Cause it's not true. Amy's a great girl.'

'No,' Lulu cried. 'Amy stupid! Stupid! *Stupid!*'

The skeleton decided to find out more about Jett. 'And what do *you* do?' she asked, tapping talon-like fingernails on the table. 'Are you in the same business as your brother?'

'No, I'm uh . . .' He knew that once he said he was a male model she would dismiss him on the spot. 'I . . . I kinda work in fashion.'

'How *divine*,' she gushed. 'Valentino is a dear friend. I adore his clothes, don't you?'

It was obvious that now she assumed he was gay.

He wondered if he could sneak a drink without Chris noticing. Then the voice of his sponsor in Italy came back to haunt him. *Remember, booze doesn't solve anything. It only makes things worse.*

'Chris,' he said, touching his brother's shoulder, 'I gotta get out of here. I can't take much more of this.'

'Don't blame you,' Chris responded.

'Uh . . . before I go, I wanted to thank you.'

'For what?'

'I talked to Edie earlier. She let it slip that it was *you* who sponsored my trip to Italy and got me out of the crap-hole I was in. I always thought it was Sam. You did me a big favour, 'cause I don't know how many more ledges I would've stood on, thinking, Hey, wouldn't it be fun to fly. You saved me finding out.'

'No need to thank me,' Chris said, slightly embarrassed. 'You're my kid brother. We share a father, bad as he might be.'

'Yeah.' Jett laughed ruefully. 'We grew up with the same beatings and the same favourite rants – "You're useless, you're ugly, you're dumb, you'll never amount to anything."'

'I remember all of them,' Chris said. 'It's amazing we survived.'

'Well, we did, so fuck him.'

'Now I'm wondering what the old bastard's going to say in the morning.'

'Who gives a shit?' Jett said. 'At least we got to hang out this weekend.'

'Makes this trip worth it for me,' Chris agreed. 'And tomorrow I'll tell you about *my* problems.'

'You got problems too?'

'Major.'

'Wanna share?'

'You sure?'

'Go ahead,' Jett said, thinking they couldn't be any worse than his.

'Well . . . I have one famous client who thinks the public is about to discover he's gay, another client who's all set to marry some low-down wife-beater – and, here's the *real* kicker, I lost my house.'

'What do you mean, you *lost* your house?'

'You were right about the storms in L.A. People are getting killed, mudslides, floods, it's a real mess.'

'You *lost* your fucking house, and you're only telling me now?'

'Nothing you could do.'

'Except be there for you.'

'And you are.'

'No, I'm not. I'm busy bitching about *my* life, while you lost your house. I'm sorry, man, I really am.'

'Yeah,' Chris said ruefully. 'I'm kinda sorry myself. But, hey, keeps you grounded.'

'You *sure* there's nothing I can do?'

'We should get together for an early breakfast before we meet Red tomorrow.'

'I'm there,' Jett said. 'Your hotel?'

Chris nodded. 'And for now, what can I say? We'll talk about everything in the morning.'

'Thanks, bro',' Jett said, leaning over to tap Gianna on her shoulder. 'We're outta here.'

'Why we leave?' she asked, turning to him with a disappointed expression. Attention was like an aphrodisiac to the Italian supermodel, and tonight she was basking in it.

''Cause it's late, an' you're on a different time zone.''

'No, *carino*, we stay,' she said firmly. 'Your brother, he need us. We cannot desert him.'

Oh, yeah – this was all he needed, the bonding of Gianna and Max. One big happy family. *Great!*

'We can't, huh?' he said wearily.

Why the fuck not?

* * *

And while the rehearsal dinner was taking place, and Red had *still* not returned home, Lady Jane opened his safe. She studied his will and several other private documents. Red's Will was dated six months previously, and witnessed by two of his top executives.

She read everything and the colour drained from her face.

Red Diamond was even more of a devious bastard than even *she*'d imagined.

The information she discovered was quite unbelievable, and yet . . . she should have known.

Damn him. Damn him to hell and back.

Chapter Thirty-Four

The girls were working hard, Cindi still shaking her ass, Liberty draping herself over Slick Jimmy for the cameras.

It wasn't as easy as it looked. Slick Jimmy was not a polished lip-syncher so they had to keep repeating take after take until he got it right. He'd also stopped talking to Liberty because, in his eyes, she wasn't being respectful to his music.

As if she cared. She had an appointment to play her demo for Damon. Nothing could be better than *that*.

'We scored an invite to the wrap party,' Cindi confided, during one of the numerous breaks.

'I thought we were dropping by your mom's.'

'Mom's first, party later,' Cindi said, with a big grin. 'It's gonna be a happenin'!'

'I'm not in the mood for a party,' Liberty said.

'Oh, *c'mon*,' Cindi scolded. 'Tomorrow it's back to *real* work, an' all this'll seem like a freakin' *dream*. So tonight we're gettin' *down*, girl, make *no* mistake.'

Liberty frowned. She had no desire to get down. Thinking about returning to her job at the coffee shop was depressing enough. How could she possibly waitress for Damon now? It didn't seem right. 'I'm not going in to work tomorrow,' she informed Cindi.

'How come?'

''Cause I'm not ready.'

'Oh, *I* get why you don't wanna come in,' Cindi taunted knowingly. ''Cause of Mr Bigshot Damon himself.'

'That's not true.'

'I'm tellin' you, girl, you'd better remember that workin' in the coffee shop is what we *do*. It's *real*. This shit *ain't*.'

'You seem to forget I was hurt on the job,' Liberty reminded her. 'That means I can take a couple of days off. They should understand.'

'Okay,' Cindi sighed, 'I'll cover for you, but only if you come to the party tonight.'

'Where is it anyway?'

'Slick Jimmy's place.'

'Oh,' Liberty drawled sarcastically. 'Now I'm *really* tempted.'

'Chill, girl,' Cindi said cheerfully. 'Take away the baggy clothes an' Slick Jimmy could be one *sexy*-lookin' dude. Believe big momma, *I* know sexy.'

'Yeah,' Liberty said drily. 'Two legs an' a dick, you'll find *anything* sexy.'

'That's *rude*, girl.'

'No, it's truthful.'

'He could turn out to be a big star, an' I could be *Mrs* Slick Jimmy,' Cindi said. Then, lowering her voice, she added, 'I didn't tell you this, but he's bin doggin' me for my number. The dude is ready t' rock, an' so am I.'

'Get real, Cindi. He's coming onto every girl on the set.'

'Maybe,' Cindi said, unfazed. 'Only those skanks ain't *me*. When it comes to guys, I got a little somethin' that gets their blood boilin' an' their engine racin'.'

'Sure you do. It's called a pussy.'

'That's *right*!' Cindi said, laughing. 'An' if I have anythin' t' do with it, tonight it's gonna be a *workin'* pussy!'

Liberty loved her cousin, but the two of them were on such different tracks. To Cindi, it was all about getting laid and partying. To Liberty, it was allowing her talent to shine and working hard on her music. The last thing she needed was to be partying at Slick Jimmy's.

Later, she cornered Beverly. 'Did you mean it when you mentioned you could get me in to see a modelling agent?'

'I certainly did,' Beverly said, packing her brushes and make-up equipment into a large Fendi carry-all bag. 'Why? You takin' me up on it?'

'I'd like to,' Liberty said hesitantly. 'I mean, if you really think I've got what it takes.'

'Don't be screwin' with me,' Beverly warned. 'If I start hookin' you up, you gotta be serious.'

'I am,' Liberty assured her.

'Then let's do it. I'll call a friend of mine an' set somethin' up.'

'Honestly?'

'Done deal, babe. They're gonna love you.'

*   *   *

Any excuse and Aretha took to her kitchen, cooking up a storm to celebrate her daughter's appearance in a video shoot. She was busy preparing fried chicken, sweet potatoes, monkey bread, hot rolls, cookies and cakes.

Earlier Cindi had called to inform her that Liberty was also in the video. Aretha had immediately invited Diahann to join them.

When the girls arrived, the table was groaning with Aretha's culinary delights.

Liberty was tired, her arm hurt and so did her ankle. All she *really* wanted to do was go home and start concentrating on her meeting with Damon. What should she wear? How should she act? And, even more important, would he like her music?

Then her mother walked out of the kitchen and she was furious. She'd *told* Cindi she didn't want to see her. The problem with Cindi was that she never *listened*. As long as the prospect of getting laid was on her mind, she was unable to concentrate.

'So, girls,' Diahann said, 'I want to hear all about this video shoot. It sounds exciting.'

Cindi started filling her in, while Liberty retreated to the kitchen and helped Aretha place crispy pieces of fried chicken on a large platter.

'Put the dish in the centre of the table,' Aretha instructed her, when they had finished. 'Then get everyone to sit down. It's time to eat.'

'Anyone else coming?' Liberty asked. 'You've made enough food for the whole neighbourhood.'

'Only us, sweet girl,' Aretha said, chuckling. 'It's family night. You an' Cindi can take food home for tomorrow. I know you girls never got nothin' to eat at your place.'

'We do,' Liberty objected.

'No, honey, you don't, but that's fine, s' long as I feed you plenty here.'

'You certainly do that.'

'I understand you an' your mama had a little talk,' Aretha said, pausing to give Liberty a long, penetrating look.

'Who told you? Cindi?'

'No, for once it wasn't my Cindi. It was your mama herself.'

'And you believe everything she said?'

'Bout what?'

'Germany, and my daddy being dead, an' there's no way I can contact his family.'

'If that's what she says, sweet thing,' Aretha answered gently. 'She'd have no reason to lie 'bout somethin' so important, now, would she?'

'I guess not.'

'Y' know, your mama feels *real* bad, so mebbe you should tell her that everythin's all right between the two of you.'

But it's not! Liberty wanted to scream. *It's not all right at all. I want a father just like everyone else.* 'Sure,' she said listlessly.

Aretha gave her a great big hug. 'That's my girl. That's my little Libby.'

Chapter Thirty-Five

As she sat in Tina's hospital room, holding her friend's hand, Amy tried to put everything in perspective. She was well aware that she'd made a mistake – a huge mistake. She'd had a one-night fling with a stranger who'd turned out to be not such a stranger after all.

Max's brother. His younger *half*-brother, who, from what she'd gleaned listening to the conversation at the table, had been living in Italy for the past three years. With Gianna, the gorgeous woman who'd had every man at the party completely entranced. And – extra bonus – he was an ex-druggie.

Yippee! How much better could it get?

'*Fuck!*' Amy muttered, under her breath. She didn't usually swear, but this seemed like the perfect occasion to do so.

'Whassamatter?' mumbled Tina, who for the past twenty minutes had seemed quite calm and peaceful. In the car on their way to the hospital she had spent twenty minutes howling frantically, and in the waiting hall she'd yelled, 'GET ME MY FUCKING EPIDURAL!' at full volume, and kicked Brad in the balls.

Well, she'd had her epidural now, and she was quite composed, lying there in a tranquil state.

A shaken Brad had gone to get coffee.

'I feel amazing!' Tina said dreamily. 'Like I'm floating in the middle of the ocean on one of those rubber thingies.'

'That's nice,' Amy said. 'Drugs'll do it every time.'

'Sorry about your party.'

'Don't be. It wasn't exactly going as I expected.'

'Hmmm . . .' Tina murmured, not at all interested. 'Baby

253

out soon. Tina thin again. New Jimmy Choos and Tiffany baubles. Tell Brad Tiffany's, *not* Fortunoff. Sometimes he doesn't quite get it.' She closed her eyes, a smile hovering round her lips. 'I feel so peaceful . . .'

Much as she wanted to, Amy realized that this was neither the time nor the place to advise her best friend of the 'situation' she was caught in. Tina would probably listen without really hearing, smile and flip her the peace sign.

Tina's obstetrician had been and gone, promising to return shortly.

'I'm having a baby,' Tina murmured, patting her over-extended stomach. 'Isn't that something?'

'It sure is,' Amy agreed, squeezing her hand.

'A little Brad.' Tina giggled.

'Not so little,' Amy corrected. 'Your OB says this baby's going to be a big one.'

'Brad'll like that,' Tina said, closing her eyes. 'Brad'll be *such* a proud papa . . .' And she drifted off into a happy half-sleep.

* * *

Two hours later Brad junior was born, all eight pounds, six ounces of him.

The birth was effortless. A few pushes and the baby's curly black head entered the world. Amy decided that whoever had invented epidurals was a major genius.

'Oh, my *God*!' Tina gasped, as a nurse wrapped the baby in a blanket and handed him to her. 'This is a miracle!'

In the room for the entire delivery, Amy and Brad had clutched each other, in awe at how smoothly everything went.

'Congratulations,' Amy whispered to Brad. 'And now it's time I left you three alone.'

'Thanks for everything,' Brad said, hugging her tightly. 'I'm sorry you had to miss your party. We all are.'

'Don't be silly. Seeing little Brad junior enter the world was better than any party.'

'Handsome little devil, isn't he?' Brad said, grinning proudly. 'And well hung too!'

'*Brad!*'

'Just telling the truth.'

'Anyway, he's fantastic!' Amy raved. 'He's got your eyes, and Tina's mouth.'

'And maybe your disposition?'

'Don't flatter me,' she said modestly.

'You're the best,' Brad said, hugging her. 'A true friend.'

She kissed Tina and the baby, then quietly made her way out. It was almost midnight and the maternity floor was deserted. She hesitated a moment, then called Max on her cell.

'Sweetheart!' he said, sounding more than pleased to hear from her. 'I just this minute got home. Where are you?'

'Leaving the hospital now.'

'Did everything go okay?'

'Yes. A healthy eight-pound six-ounce baby boy.'

'I'll come get you and drive you to your apartment.'

'I can take a cab,' she said, walking towards the elevator.

'Wouldn't hear of it. I'm on my way out of the door now.'

'You don't have to.'

'Yes. I do,' he insisted. 'You must be anxious to hear all about our party.'

'I certainly am,' she said. 'Was my mother furious?'

'*You* know Nancy. But Gianna – Jett's girlfriend – saved the day. What a charmer! She had everyone under her spell, including Grandma Poppy. And, yes, *even* your mother.'

'Great,' Amy said flatly, thinking this was *all* she needed to hear. Not only was Gianna the most beautiful girl she'd ever seen, apparently she was the most charming too.

Ha! Lucky Jett.

Lucky Jett, the *seducer*, the *cheat*, the *ex-druggie* who'd got her drunk and lured her back to his apartment.

Screw *him*!

And yet . . . she'd gone willingly. She had not put up a fight. In fact, when he'd backed off due to her virginal state, *she* was the one who'd insisted he carry on.

He was *still* a cheat.

And what did that make her?

She didn't want to think about it. She didn't want to

think about *him*. As far as she was concerned, it was one big nightmare she never planned on revisiting.

* * *

By the time Jett finally got Gianna out of the party his Italian supermodel was *still* ready to rock 'n' roll.

'We go clubbing, *carino*,' she announced, throwing her arms round his neck, and flicking her tongue across his lips. 'Gianna feel like dancing.'

Christ! She was the original Energizer Bunny. Wind her up and she'd go all night, when all he really wanted to do was clear his head and try to make sense of the night's events.

What the *fuck* was he going to do? Amy Scott-Simon, the girl of his dreams, was about to marry his freakin' bigshot brother – a man who could give her everything she wanted. Whereas he could give her – *what*? His undying love? It was wrong, all wrong, yet how could he stop it? What could *he* do?

Hang on. No need to get carried away. She was not the girl of his dreams: she was a one-night adventure, cheating on her fiancé. And yet she'd obviously never slept with Max, so what was *that* about? How come she'd never had sex with her fiancé, but she was happy to jump into bed with *him*?

They needed to sit down and talk, discover the truth of the situation. And the sooner the better.

'*Carino!*' Gianna purred, her tongue snaking its way into his ear. 'Where we go now?'

Good question. Where *was* he supposed to take her?

He pulled out his cell and called Beverly. 'I'm here with my girlfriend,' he began, 'and—'

'You found her!' Beverly exclaimed. 'Who *is* she? What's the lucky girl's name? And, even *more* important, is she as hot as you remember?'

'Uh . . . my *girlfriend*, Gianna, from Italy,' he said pointedly, glancing at Gianna to see if she'd overheard.

'Oops!' Beverly exclaimed.

'She wants to go dancing,' Jett continued. 'Any ideas?'

'I'm on my way to meet Chet at Gatsby's, then there's a party at Slick Jimmy's. You and your *girlfriend* can come with.'

'If you're sure . . .'

'Meet us at Gatsby's, babe.'

'You're the best, Bev. We'll see you there.'

*   *   *

Back at the hotel Chris called Andy for an update on his house.

'The news is not good,' Andy informed him. 'They think your house was built on the site of an ancient landslide, and that at any time it could slip on down the hill.'

'Shit!'

'I'll contact the insurance agents first thing tomorrow. You're fully covered, right?'

'Who the fuck knows? Mudslides are a force of nature, don't think that's covered.'

He hung up and couldn't sleep. Then he remembered the actress from the plane. Inez Fallon. Talkative but still attractive, and tonight he definitely needed company.

She was staying in the same hotel, so even though it was almost midnight he took a chance, picked up the phone and called her. She answered on the second ring.

'Inez,' he said.

'Who's this?'

'Chris Diamond. We sat next to each other on the plane.'

'Of *course* I remember,' she purred. 'What can I do for you, Chris?'

You can come to my room and suck my dick 'cause I'm too tense to sleep.

'I'm sitting here on L.A. time unable to crash. I thought you might be doing the same.'

'Actually,' she confessed, 'I'm watching a porno.'

'You are?'

'Yes,' she said, with a wicked laugh. 'It's what I always do when I'm trapped in a hotel room by myself. *Very* relaxing. You should try it.'

'Seems like a reasonable way to pass the time.'

'I was thinking I could talk to Dave about it tomorrow on his show. Had to come up with *something* that'll outdo Drew and her tits.'

'Sounds like a plan.'

'It does, doesn't it?'

'So . . . how about coming up to my suite and watching a porno with *me*?'

A three-second pause. 'Sure. Why not?'

Ten minutes later they were making out on the couch. She wore a skimpy purple dress, short and low-cut. It did not take him long to manoeuvre her out of it. Underwear was not her thing. Neither was pubic hair. She was shaved to within an inch of her life, and pierced right on her clit.

Naked, she straddled him, large erect nipples on small breasts. Real. Made a nice change.

She thrust them into his mouth, urging him to suck hard. He did so, and she shuddered to a climax within seconds, screaming like a wild woman. Then she bent her head to blow him, and he discovered that this was one practised actress. She had it down – the tongue-teasing and the hand-twisting. Stopping. Starting. Driving him fucking crazy.

When he came, it was an explosion big enough to make him forget about his house, Birdy and Jonathan.

He lay back on the couch and, within minutes, had fallen into a much-needed deep sleep.

Chapter Thirty-Six

Max was waiting when Amy walked out of the hospital. He jumped out of his car and grabbed her in a hug. 'You're really a remarkable girl,' he said, squeezing her tight.

'I'm not so remarkable,' she said, extracting herself.

'Yes, you are,' he insisted. 'You stood up to your mother – you actually walked out on her. I don't care about you missing our rehearsal dinner because I didn't want it in the first place, but Nancy was *not* happy.'

'I'm sure she got over it after a while.'

'She did,' he said, holding open the car door for her.

'Good,' she said, sliding into the passenger seat.

'Thank God I had Chris and Jett for support. I'm really getting to know the two of them. It's nice.'

'Did they, uh, stay for the whole party?' she asked, thinking that, as far as she was concerned, it wasn't nice at all. In her eyes, Max bonding with his brothers was a disaster.

'Let's just say they did their brotherly duty,' Max said. 'And, as I told you on the phone, Gianna was charming everyone.'

'Wonderful.'

'You met Gianna, didn't you?'

'That Italian woman?'

'Yes. She's Jett's steady girlfriend. They live together in Italy. Apparently she's a top model there.'

'Nigel told me. She's doing the ad campaign for Courtenelli.'

'What a striking girl,' Max said admiringly. 'And a lot of fun.'

'I'm sure she is,' Amy said, wishing he'd stop singing the woman's praises.

'Not as gorgeous as my Amy, though,' Max said, reaching over to pat her on the knee.

'How long are they staying in New York?' Amy asked, attempting to sound casual.

'Who?'

'Gianna and, uh . . . Jett.' It was an effort to speak his name.

'I didn't ask,' Max said. 'I'd like it if they could stay around for the wedding. Your mother would have to rearrange her seating, but I'm sure she can deal with that.'

Oh, yes, Jett at her wedding. How exciting was *that*?

She decided she had to do something special to make it up to Max. The guilt was killing her – especially now that she knew the identity of her mystery man.

'You need to get some sleep,' Max said, glancing at her. 'What with the party and the upcoming wedding, you're under a tremendous strain.'

'No, I'm not,' she objected.

'You simply don't know it, sweetie.'

'Max,' she said, putting her hand on his arm.

'Yes?'

'I'd like to go to *your* apartment.'

'*My* apartment?' he said, surprised. 'Why?'

'I was thinking that, since I ran out on our party, it might be nice if we spent some quiet time together.'

'It's late,' he said, checking his watch.

'I know.'

'And tomorrow's Monday.'

'I know that too. But I still want to come to your apartment.'

'Uh . . . Lulu and her nanny are staying the night.'

'They'll be asleep, won't they?'

'Yes.'

'Then it's okay if I come over.'

'If that's what you want,' he said reluctantly.

'Yes, Max,' she said softly. 'That's exactly what I want.'

*   *   *

'So,' Gianna said, twirling her multiple bangles up and down her arm. 'This friend of yours, what she do?'

'Beverly's a top make-up artist,' Jett said, hailing a cab. 'You're gonna love her. Everyone does.'

'You and this *friend* – you do the wild thing?'

'Babe!' he said, laughing. 'No *way*. Bev and I are purely platonic.'

'Americans are so *timido* about sex,' Gianna teased, getting in the cab. 'In Italy is *bene* to have sex with good friend. Nothing wrong, huh, *carino*?'

'You're crazy,' he said, jumping into the cab beside her.

'Where we meet your friend?'

'A drink at Gatsby's, then she's taking us to a party. That's if you're not too beat.'

'Me?' she said, laughing gaily. 'Gianna *never* get tired. Pour me champagne and I'm good as new.'

*   *   *

Rushing into his apartment ahead of Amy, Max switched on lights and activated music.

'I'm not a guest, you know,' Amy said, following him in and smiling. 'You don't have to entertain me.'

'You very rarely come here,' he said.

'That's because you never invite me.'

'We're engaged, sweetheart. You'll be moving in here soon. Surely you know you're welcome at any time. I should give you a key.'

They had decided that after the wedding, Amy would move in with him until they found a new apartment she could decorate any way she wanted. She hadn't really given it much thought – getting married was scary enough.

'Can I get you a drink?' he asked.

'Orange juice. Is there a juicer in the kitchen?'

'I have no idea *what's* in the kitchen. My housekeeper takes care of that department.'

'Let's go see.'

His kitchen looked like it was never used. She found a juicer in one of the cabinets, and some oranges in the fridge.

'Shall I squeeze you some too?' she asked, slicing the oranges in half.

'Do I look like I need a dose of vitamin C?' he said, amused.

'No, in fact I've been meaning to tell you how handsome you look tonight. I was proud to be at the party with you. Oh, yes, and I *loved* our slide show. You were such a serious little boy – do you realize you never smiled?'

'And *you* were unbearably cute.'

'Unbearably?'

'I meant that as a compliment.'

She handed him a glass of juice. 'Drink up. It's good for you.'

'*You*'re good for me,' he said, coming up behind her and nuzzling her neck. 'You really are, Amy.'

'I hope you understand why I had to leave the party tonight,' she said quietly. 'Tina needed me, and I promised her that when the time came I'd be there.'

'It's admirable that you were there for your best friend.'

They moved into the living room and sat down on the couch. Amy snuggled up close and began to kiss him.

After a few moments he pulled away. 'Amy,' he said warningly, 'don't get me all hot and bothered, then go home.'

'That wasn't my intention.'

'Okay, *what*?' he said, bemused.

'Well,' she said slowly. 'We're getting married soon, and even though I told you I wanted to wait, I was thinking that tonight we should . . . do it.'

'Now, hold on' he said, startled.

'Don't you want to?'

'Well, yes,' he responded, although he wasn't at all sure that tonight was the night to sleep with his fiancée for the first time. Mariska and her threats regarding Vladimir were on his mind. Not to mention the upcoming face-to-face with Red, followed by the crucial meeting with the Japanese bankers. And as if that wasn't enough, Lulu and Nanny Reece were sleeping in the guest room. Amy's timing was totally off.

'Then . . . can I spend the night?' Amy asked, unaware of what was going on in his mind.

'Are you *sure* about this?' he said, wondering how he could talk her out of it.

'Absolutely.'

* * *

There was the usual pushing and shoving crowd gathered outside Gatsby's. Jett felt like a regular when the doorman waved him through as if he was an old friend. Hey, nobody was about to stop the fabulous Gianna. She blew the doorman a series of kisses, making the man's night.

They found Beverly and Chet ensconced at a corner table downing apple martinis. Beverly waved them over. 'One drink, then let's go party!' she called out.

'*Ciao!*' Gianna said, dazzling everyone with her smile and flamboyant style.

'I'm a fan,' Beverly said, acknowledging the Italian supermodel. 'Seen you in all the Italian magazines.'

'*Grazie,*' Gianna said, loving any form of attention.

'An' here's the news of the day,' Beverly added. 'I'm booked to do the make-up for your Courtenelli shoot.'

'*Bene!*' Gianna laughed. 'This *piccolo* world, no?'

'Yeah,' Beverly said, grinning. '*Very* small.'

'Jett, he do photos too,' Gianna announced.

'You mean I finally get my hands on that face?' Beverly exclaimed.

'Is nice face,' Gianna said affectionately, patting his cheek. '*Bello, sì?*'

Chet was his usual non-talkative self, but Gianna quickly found out what he did and plied him with questions about his music. He soon livened up – she had that effect on men.

After twenty minutes Beverly suggested it was time to make a move.

'You *sure* you wanna go?' Jett asked Gianna, hoping she would flake out so they could go home and he could let his mind run riot about Amy, and what he was going to do regarding their totally fucked-up situation.

'We go,' she said, laughing that he should think otherwise.

She winked at Beverly. 'These boys, they have – how you say? – no *energia*. You and me, we like to party – *sì?*'

'You bet your ass,' Beverly agreed, smiling broadly.

* * *

Now that they were alone in Max's bedroom it was awkward. They stood at the end of his oversize masculine-style bed, all dark wood and chocolate brown sheets. They'd been kissing for a while, but he didn't seem in any hurry to take it further.

Amy realized she needed something to loosen up, she was treading on uncharted territory and it was making her nervous. Sleeping with Jett had been so spontaneous and unplanned – they'd fallen into bed together, filled with desire and passion. It had been a lustful, crazy and, most of all, insanely pleasurable experience.

Tonight with Max was different. First, she was stone-cold sober. Second, Max wasn't making much of a move: *she* was the one kissing him, and although he was responding, he was allowing *her* to set the pace. Also he wasn't the greatest kisser in the world.

'I think I'd like a drink,' she said, in a small voice.

'What kind of drink?' he asked, drawing away from her.

'Vodka,' she said tentatively.

'Sweetie, you *never* drink hard liquor.'

'I'll make an exception.'

'Look,' he said, 'if this is making you uncomfortable—'

'No, Max,' she said vehemently. 'I *want* us to be together.'

'So do I, sweetie, but tonight might not be the right time.'

'The thing is, I need to relax,' she said, ignoring him, 'and a drink'll do it. I missed out on the champagne at our party, so one little vodka won't hurt.'

'Amy,' he said seriously, 'you're stressed out. And, much as I'd love you to spend the night, I think we should wait.'

'You do?'

'We'll be married soon, so why rush into something you might regret?'

'But, Max—'

'No buts,' he said resolutely. 'Believe me, I *know* what's best for you.'

How humiliating was this? Her husband-to-be had no desire to sleep with her. He was turning her down flat. Oh, *God*! She felt like such a fool.

'Get your coat, sweetie,' he said, heading out of the bedroom. 'I'm taking you home.'

With that he picked up his car keys from the hall table and started for the front door.

Chapter Thirty-Seven

Party-time meant loud music, plenty of booze, writhing, sweaty bodies, and an over-abundance of weed – so strong a person could get a contact high merely breathing the air.

This was all taking place in the living room of Slick Jimmy's basement house in Harlem, which he shared with two other rappers. The place was a comfortable dump with an insanely expensive sound system that was blasting heavy-core rap.

Cindi hit the scene and was in heaven. Liberty found a corner to lurk in, wishing she had not allowed Cindi to talk her into coming. But that was their relationship, wasn't it? Cindi was forever talking her into things she didn't want to do.

'You let that 'ho walk all over you,' Kev often complained. 'Whyn't you dump her an' move in with me? You don't need her.'

'Cindi's like my *sister*, Kev, so don't be calling her a 'ho.'

'She uses you 'cause you're so fine an' she's so *not* fine.'

'That's not a very nice way to talk. Cindi would do anything for me.'

Although sometimes she wasn't so sure. Cindi *did* have a pushy way about her, and tonight was a prime example. Here she was, at a party she didn't want to be at, sitting in a corner by herself, while Cindi was out there in the midst of it, coming onto every guy she could get her hands on.

But then again, Cindi and her mom had taken her in when Diahann had pushed her out. She'd lived with them as though she *was* Cindi's sister, and when it was time to move out, she and Cindi had done it together. It was Cindi who'd found them an apartment and scored them jobs at the coffee shop. Cindi had *always* watched out for her and, yeah, maybe her cousin did use her sometimes because she was better-looking, but so what? Looks weren't everything, and Cindi had a great big heart.

Since she didn't know anyone at the party, Liberty found herself stuck in the corner sorting through the many CDs stacked next to the sound system.

'Finding anything you like?' asked a familiar voice.

She turned round. It was Maleek. 'Oh, hi,' she said, pleased to see someone she knew.

'You did great today,' Maleek said. 'You could make yourself a living appearing in videos. You got the look.'

'I have no plans to be The Girl in the video,' she said, half smiling. 'I'm a singer-songwriter – didn't I tell you?'

'Maybe you did an' maybe you didn't,' Maleek said, swigging from a bottle of beer. 'But in *my* experience you gotta use what you got. I wanted to be a dancer and look what happened to me.'

'Directing's way cool.'

'*I* enjoy it, and so does my wife. You should meet her – she's smart, like you.'

'You're married?' Liberty asked, pleased that Maleek considered her smart.

'Surprised?'

'You're young to be married.'

Maleek shrugged. 'Twenty-eight. Got married 'cause my wife was knocked up an' I didn't want to bring another child into the world who wasn't sure who her daddy was.'

'That's cool,' Liberty said. 'What does your wife do?'

'She's a dancer,' he said proudly.

'Was she at the shoot today?'

'No, honey, not *that* kinda dancer. My wife's a ballet dancer.'

'Wow! That's impressive.'

'Yeah, she's one talented white woman,' he said, taking another swig of beer. 'You're bi-racial, right?'

'I'm not sure *what* I am,' Liberty said, shrugging. 'My mom's always telling me I'm black, but I have a feeling there's some white blood running through my veins.'

'You don't know who your father is? Is that where this conversation's headin'?'

'I never got to meet him. He died before I was born.'

'Must've bin tough for you,' Maleek said sympathetically.

'My mom raised me. She *was* a singer, but she gave it up.'

'To do what?'

'It doesn't matter.'

'Something bad you can't tell me?'

'Something dumb I don't *want* to tell you.'

'Here comes my wife,' Maleek said, as a brittle-looking white woman at least ten years older than him approached. Her dark hair was scraped back into a tight bun, and she wore a long white dress. She did not seem particularly friendly as she gave Liberty a cursory nod, took Maleek's arm and said, 'You need to come with me.' She promptly dragged him away.

So much for new friendships.

Cindi was out on the dance-floor rockin' an' rollin' with Slick Jimmy. Large as she was, she had plenty of rhythm and an abundance of style – Cindi could shake it with the best of them.

Liberty wondered how long she'd have to stay at the party before she could leave, grab a cab and go home. Cindi wouldn't even notice she'd left.

So why was she waiting? Who did she think was going to appear? Damon?

Yeah, sure.

She looked around the room and thought, Why would Damon choose to hang with these people? They were just a bunch of stoners and Damon didn't fit in. Although Maleek was here, so maybe Damon *would* come.

She wished Kev was with her. There was something soul-destroying about being at a party by yourself – it looked like you were trying to hook up or get laid, and she wasn't into doing either of those things.

Very slowly she began edging towards the door.

And then it happened. Just as she was almost there, Damon appeared.

As usual he was Mr Cool. Tonight he was all in black, a giant diamond cross hanging round his neck, diamond studs in both ears, a circular watch, studded with diamonds, and a short fur coat flung casually around his shoulders.

He gave her a quick glance, not at all surprised to see her. 'Hey, Liberty,' he said, flashing a friendly smile. 'I got a new name for you.'

'You do?' she said, determined to remain calm.

'Yeah, from now on I'm callin' you LL.'

'LL?' she questioned.

'Lady Liberty,' he said, with a lazy grin. 'You dig?'

'If you say so.'

'You're not leaving?'

'Uh . . . yes,' she managed. 'I kinda am.'

'Got a ride?'

'Oh, sure,' she murmured, recovering her composure. 'I never go anywhere without my car and driver. He even drops me off at the coffee shop every morning.'

'Funny girl.'

'You think?'

They exchanged a long look.

'I gotta go say hello to Slick Jimmy, mebbe hang for ten minutes,' Damon said. 'If you wanna wait around, I'll drop you somewhere.'

'That's okay,' she said, feeling his heat.

'You don't wanna ride with me?' he said, pinning her with his sexy eyes.

'I didn't say that,' she said, trying to control the dizzying effect he had on her.

'So chill,' he said. 'I'll go say hi to Jimmy, then we'll split.'

'Okay,' she found herself saying.

'You hungry?'

'I ate at my aunt's place. She's kind of a major cook.'

'What'd she make?' he asked, moving closer, enabling her to get a whiff of his expensive cologne.

'Um, let me see. Tonight she made fried chicken, honey spare ribs and monkey bread. Lots of good things.'

'Sounds like I need an invite.'

'I don't think hanging at Aunt Aretha's is exactly your scene.'

'Why not? Restaurant food gets tired, baby. There's times I *crave* a little down-home cookin'.'

'You do?' she said, wondering if his wife ever hustled her expensive ass into the kitchen. Probably not.

'Hey,' he said, zeroing in with those eyes of his, 'I'm a normal man with normal appetites.'

'I'll see what I can arrange,' she said, thinking there was nothing normal about Damon P. Donnell. Then she started imagining Aunt Aretha's face if she ever got a close-up look at Damon's outrageous bling. She'd crap herself!

Casually he took her hand and led her over to Slick Jimmy, who was busy doing his thing with Cindi. The two of them were not so much dancing, more like a whole lot of shaking and touching. Suddenly Liberty realized she felt very comfortable with Damon, they were totally in sync.

'Hey, it's my *man*!' Slick Jimmy yelled, stopping everything. The two men banged fists, followed by a macho hug.

Cindi shot Liberty a *what-is-goin'-on-here?* look, while Liberty attempted to stay casual. Then Damon let go of her hand and went over to greet Maleek. Liberty noticed that Maleek's wife cheered up at the sight of Damon – the woman actually managed a tight-assed smile. After a few minutes of standing there, Liberty made her way back to her corner. She didn't think it was cool to be trailing around behind Damon looking like she was some girl he'd picked up and was about to take home and screw.

The music was getting louder, the air was getting smokier, and she wondered how long it would be before Damon chose to leave. She decided to give him ten minutes and then, ride or no ride, she was out of there.

Twenty minutes later Beverly burst in with a group of friends. 'This looks like a *party*!' she exclaimed, swooping down on Liberty. 'You remember Jett, an' this is *my* man, Chet.'

Gianna grabbed Jett's arm. 'Come, *carino*, we dance,' she said, dragging him off into the moving throng.

'You here with Cindi?' Beverly yelled, over the loud music.

'I was,' Liberty shouted back. 'She's over there with Slick Jimmy. They seem to have a thing going. I'm leaving soon.'

'You need a cab?'

'Damon's giving me a ride.'

Beverly raised a disapproving eyebrow. 'Damon?'

'He's just dropping me off.'

'Don't be forgettin' what I told you,' Beverly admonished. 'Believe me, I'm not interested in seein' your sorry ass when he sweet-talks you into bed, an' that's *it*. Damon's never gonna change, you'd best remember that.'

'He's not sweet-talking me into anything,' Liberty said, annoyed that Beverly considered her such an easy mark.

'Hey – you've been warned. The man is a *player*, girl, so stay smart.'

'Thanks for the advice, but I *do* know what I'm doing.'

By the time Damon was ready to leave, another half-hour had passed. Like a fool, Liberty had waited. Mad at herself, yet unable to resist, she had watched him from afar, until eventually he came over, grabbed her hand and led her outside to where his silver Cadillac Escalade with special wheel rims was parked curbside, a female uniformed driver standing to attention next to it.

'Get in the back, baby,' Damon ordered.

'Shouldn't I give the driver my address?'

'Thought we'd hit a coupla clubs,' he said, leaning against the side of the car chewing on a toothpick.

'I don't feel like doing that.'

'Then we'll stop by a bar, have ourselves a drink, get to know each other.'

'I'm really tired,' she said, trying not to sound pissed off, although she was more mad at herself for hanging around waiting for him like some dumb groupie. 'You took forever,' she couldn't help adding.

'Yeah?' he said unconcernedly.

'Yes,' she answered, realizing she probably sounded like a nagging wife. Too bad. She wasn't about to jump.

'So you're sayin' you don't wanna have a drink with me?' he asked, throwing her a quizzical look. 'I'm gettin' a no, right?'

'It was a long day,' she said, determined not to back down. 'I'm ready to go home.'

'If that's how you wanna play it.'

'I'm not *playing* anything,' she said, tossing back her long hair.

'No problem. Give my driver your address an' she'll *take* you home.'

'Aren't you coming?' she asked, surprised.

'No. The car'll come back for me. I'm gonna party some more.'

'You are?' she said, strangely disappointed.

'Got nothin' else t' do,' he said, giving her a quick kiss on the cheek. 'See you tomorrow, LL, six-thirty. Don't be late.'

'I–I won't.'

He started to walk away, then suddenly stopped and fixed her with another look. 'You *sure* you don't wanna change your mind?'

'Positive,' she said, although she wasn't positive at all. *Oh, God, if only he wasn't married . . .*

'Got it,' he said, diamonds flashing. 'See ya.'

And with that he walked back into the house, and she was left by herself with nothing to do except wonder if she'd made the right decision.

Chapter Thirty-Eight

Sonja Sivarious studied the gold Rolex she'd stolen from Chris Diamond. Usually when she acquired a new piece of jewellery she sold it to her friendly neighbourhood fence, but there was something about the gold Rolex she coveted. It was masculine and heavy, which made her wrist appear delicate and girlish.

She was standing in the bathroom of Red Diamond's apartment on 59th Street. Red Diamond, the billionaire. He was so old it was a shock that he could still get it up.

Her girlfriend and sometime partner in sex shows, Famka, had called her over on Saturday night, telling her there was money flying. Now it was late Sunday and the old man was *still* going strong. Viagra. What a drug! It made worn-out old cocks strong again.

Sonja sighed and felt sorry for all the tired old wives who were suddenly forced to deal with their husband's raging libidos.

She sucked in her cheeks as she admired herself in the bathroom mirror. Little Sonja Sivarious from Slovakia. Somebody should write a poem about her. She'd done well for herself. A tall, skinny stick at school, the boys had taunted her and the girls had avoided her because of her impoverished background. She'd compensated by giving the boys what they wanted – the kind of things they couldn't get from so-called nice girls. The result was that the boys chased after her, and the girls avoided her even more.

At sixteen she'd run away from home and taken a train to Prague with her cousin Igor, and a car salesman twenty years her senior. The car salesman had introduced her to other men, and soon she was making money. After a while, she'd hooked up with an older girl from the Ukraine, Famká, who, at nineteen, had seemed very worldly. They hit it off, and began putting on girl-on-girl shows – which were a big success until Famka took off for America with a rich businessman.

Two years later Famka sent for her. She went willingly, paying for Igor to come too.

Famka had solid connections to whom she introduced Sonja, and it wasn't long before they were known around New York as an extremely versatile and obliging team.

Now, three years later, Sonja lived in a nice apartment. She had furs and jewels, and made plenty of money. She had her own connections, and when anyone required a special girl in New York, she was top of the recommended list. Which was how she'd come to do the job for Roth Giagante. It was a simple job – all she'd had to do was fuck the man Roth told her to, and pass on a message. She'd been unable to resist adding her own PS to the message she'd left scrawled on his bathroom mirror. Actually the guy was very attractive *and* excellent in the sack. But Sonja had a rule: she never told men they were accomplished in bed, better to let them worry.

Famka started knocking on the bathroom door. 'He wants you,' Famka called out. 'Hurry!'

Of course he wants me, Sonja thought, still admiring herself in the mirror. *I am the best.*

She strolled back into the bedroom, naked except for five-inch hooker heels and a low-slung belt of rhinestones round her waist, her flame-coloured hair reaching below her waist, matching her public hair – dyed and groomed into a neat landing-strip.

Famka had tied up the old man at his request. He was naked and decrepit, yet still unbelievably horny.

It occurred to Sonja that he'd taken too many of those stupid blue pills. He could suffer a stroke or a heart-attack, and if he did, she was out of there.

The old man didn't look sick. He looked happy, with a shit-eating grin on his leathery face. 'Come on, girlies,' he said encouragingly. 'Let's see what you can do.'

'Oh, *I* can do anything you want,' Sonja boasted, standing with her legs astride, hands on her hips. '*Anything.*'

* * *

Chris was woken at three a.m. by the phone. He'd forgotten to leave a 'Do Not Disturb' on his line, which really pissed him off.

Inez was long gone. Once the sex was over, so was she. 'A girl has to get her beauty sleep,' she'd said, quite coyly for a girl who, a few minutes earlier, had been screaming like a banshee. Then she'd left his suite, which pleased him – he hated it when he had to persuade them to leave.

It was Roth on the phone.

'Been thinkin' about your idea,' Roth said, in his raspy voice. 'I talked to my PR like you suggested, and since I ain't got my fuckin' money yet, we may as well make the most of this opportunity. We're gonna throw the fuckin' wedding for Birdy Marvel.'

'You got any idea what time it is?' Chris mumbled, staring in disbelief at the illuminated clock-radio by the bed.

'Who gives a fuck? You're lucky I'm talkin' to you.'

'Yeah, lucky me,' he said, covering a yawn.

'Lucky you is right,' Roth growled. 'This don't mean you're off the hook with your debt. It buys you more time, that's the deal.'

'Okay,' Chris said, still half asleep. 'Have your PR call me tomorrow. Birdy expects it to be special, and the media has to be strictly controlled.'

'Thought I'd give you the word before you went runnin' to Peter Morton.'

'Yeah, yeah,' Chris said, and slammed down the phone.

After that, he couldn't get back to sleep.

Should he call Inez? No. Even she wouldn't come back at three a.m. Or maybe she would.

Then he started thinking. Why was sex so important in his life? Why had he always depended on it?

He knew why. Sex was his sleeping pill, his comfort zone. Jett had chosen drugs and booze, Max had thrown himself

275

into work, while *his* vice was sex, although gambling had recently come a close second.

After a while he got out of bed and began pacing around the suite, finally settling in front of one of the huge windows. He gazed out at the view, admiring the city. New York was so beautiful at night, the sparkling lights and the streams of traffic looking like toys as they negotiated their way up and down the narrow streets.

Before long his mind was buzzing. Tomorrow, breakfast with Jett, then the meeting with Red, and after that he'd get on a plane and fly home.

Yeah – fly home. To *what*? No house, that was for sure. How depressing was *that*?

He'd lost everything, and the kicker was he couldn't even afford to rebuild until Roth was paid off.

No more gambling. The call of the tables had lost its lure.

* * *

It was almost four a.m. by the time Jett finally persuaded Gianna to leave the party.

'I *love* New York,' Gianna cried, throwing herself into a cab, bracelets jangling. 'We spend more time here, *sì*?'

'Yeah, New York's great,' Jett agreed, yawning. 'Especially when a person can get some sleep. Don't you have to work tomorrow?'

'Not until the afternoon. *We* go for fittings – you come too.'

'Can't wait!' he said, yawning again.

'Is *bene*, *carino*. They insist big name, but I say no, *you*.'

'I'm big in Italy,' he pointed out.

'Italy one thing, America another,' Gianna said sagely. 'The ad campaign will be in *all* magazines. Is good for you, *sì*?'

'It can't hurt.'

'This Slick Jimmy,' Gianna mused. 'I like his music. Is heavy beat, but good, huh?'

Everything was good, as far as Gianna was concerned. She was getting on his nerves. All he wanted to do was crawl into bed and get some sleep. Then he realized he'd only manage a few hours because he'd promised Chris he would join him for breakfast.

Gianna's hand began moving up his thigh.

Christ! The woman was insatiable.

He removed her hand. His energy was spent. Mentally and physically he needed time out.

'Something the matter, *carino*?' she asked, looking hurt.

'If I told you,' he said wearily. 'You'd never understand.'

*   *   *

Lady Jane Bentley did not sleep, she was too disturbed even to contemplate closing her eyes. She stayed up, waiting for Red to come home, determined to confront him.

Sometime in the early hours she realized he was staying out all night again.

She suspected he was *still* cavorting with whores.

To think she'd wasted six years with a despicable human being, a selfish billionaire incapable of loving anyone except himself. It was a travesty.

And the truth was that he probably did *not* love himself. How could he, when his lifelong focus had always been ruining other people's lives?

Chapter Thirty-Nine

'Y ou're like a guy,' Jett complained, as Gianna straddled him before he even had a chance to open his eyes.

It was Monday morning and he'd had, like, three hours' sleep and now his so-called girlfriend was taking advantage of his piss hard-on and crawling all over him.

Gianna was perpetually horny. Sleep, no sleep, she was always in the mood.

At least he didn't have a hangover. Back in the day he would've been wrecked, incapable of speech, unable to move. His head would've been pounding, his body quivering with misuse. Now he was merely tired.

Gianna, who'd spent the night imbibing everything from margaritas to champagne, seemed to be suffering no ill-effects. She was chirpy and horny – even her breath was sweet.

'What the fuck?' Jett groaned. 'Can't you wait until I hit the john?'

'Why waste a good thing, *carino?*' Gianna replied, lowering herself onto him, so that he slid inside her with no chance of escape.

Once he was on board, nature took its course, and before long he was as into it as she was. They rode the wave for at least ten minutes, both adept at holding back. When it was time, they came together in perfect unison.

'*Fantastico!*' Gianna exclaimed. 'My Yankee boyfriend is *buono!*'

'Don't *say* that.'

'*Scusa?*'

' "Yankee boyfriend", it sounds dumb.'

Gianna shrugged and got out of bed. 'I take shower,' she announced, stretching like a cat.

'D'you mind if I take one first?' he said quickly. 'Gotta meet my brother for breakfast.'

'We shower together,' Gianna decided, striding toward the bathroom. '*Bene, carino?*'

Oh yeah, sure – *bene*. Given half a chance, this woman would be quite happy to fuck him to death.

* * *

Once more Chris was awoken by the phone. This time it was morning, and on the line was a tearful Birdy Marvel, informing him that she was finished with Rocky and he should immediately cancel their Las Vegas wedding.

This woke him up with a vengeance. Cancel the freaking wedding just when he'd got Roth Giagante all fired up about having it at his hotel? No way. 'What's the problem?' he asked.

'You were right about Rocky,' Birdy sobbed. 'He's a pig.'

'I never said he was a pig,' Chris said patiently. 'I merely said you should be sure you're making the right decision.'

'Well, I am,' Birdy said, sounding like a truculent little girl. 'I'm making the decision to, like, *never* see him again!'

'What did he do?'

'I can't tell you,' she wailed.

'You'd better,' he responded, wondering how he was going to break the news to Roth.

'Can't!'

Oh, shit. It was obviously something bad that she would expect him to take care of. 'You can tell me, Birdy,' he said, in a low, comforting voice. 'You know you can tell me anything.'

A long pause while she thought about it. 'Okay,' she said at last. 'Only it's gotta stay between us, Chris. Promise?'

'What?' he coaxed.

'He called me ugly.'

'*Ugly?*'

'Yes, ugly,' she said indignantly. 'Don't you *dare* laugh at me, Chris.'

'Who's laughing?'

'He said I was a spoiled ugly little girl, and he was leaving. So then he, like, *left*, and I *never* wanna see him *again*.'

'Hmm . . . Well, you *know* you're not ugly. *People* magazine just picked you as one of their fifty most beautiful. You're on the cover of *W* and *Rolling Stone*. The guy is delusional if he called you ugly.'

'I know. And I'm not even *pregnant* anymore.'

At least there was *some* good news. 'Ignore him,' Chris said. 'He's obviously a moron.'

'You bet he *is*,' she said fiercely. 'A big *fat* horny moron.'

'Do you want me to come over later?'

'Hang on,' Birdy whispered excitedly. 'I think he just walked in. I'll have to call you back.'

So much for never wanting to see the big fat horny moron again.

Chris got up and stretched. His body was screaming for a workout, and not the sexual kind. He decided to hit the gym and relieve some of the stress he knew was building up inside him.

* * *

Max's housekeeper, Mrs Conner, a middle-aged stout woman, originally from Scotland, set a second batch of pancakes on Lulu's plate.

'Me *like* pancakes,' Lulu said, licking maple syrup off her fingers.

'I know you do, dear,' said Mrs Conner.

'Me too,' Max agreed, glancing up from the *New York Times*. 'You make 'em good, Mrs Conner.'

'Thank you, Mr Diamond.'

'Me *like* staying with my daddy,' Lulu crooned, tilting her head on one side. 'Daddy! Daddy! *My* daddy!'

'You're a lucky girl,' Mrs Conner said, giving Lulu a pat on the head.

'Lucky! Lucky! *Lucky!*' Lulu shrieked.

'When Daddy marries Amy and we move into a new apartment,' Max said, lowering his newspaper, 'we're going to decorate your room any way you like. What do you think of *that*?'

'Lulu *likes* Hello Kitty,' Lulu crooned, clapping her hands together. 'Hello Kitty *bed*, an' *sheets*, an' *floor*, an' *ceiling*, an' all over my *face*.' She burst into a fit of giggles. 'All over Daddy's face too!'

'Thanks.'

'And Daddy's *butt*!' she said, giggling even more.

'Excuse me?'

'Butt! Butt! *Butt!*'

'That's no way for a lady to speak,' he said sternly.

'Lulu's not a *lady*, Daddy,' she said, all wide-eyed and innocent. 'Lulu's a little girl.'

'Who taught you to say "butt"?'

'Dunno,' she answered vaguely.

'Don't say it again. It's not nice.'

Nanny Reece entered the breakfast room. 'We should be on our way, Mr Diamond,' she said, stiff English accent firmly in place. 'I have to get Lulu changed for school.'

'My driver's downstairs,' Max said. 'I'll come with you. I need to speak to Mrs Diamond.'

'Very well,' Nanny Reece said. 'Come along, Lulu.'

'Come along, Lulu,' the little girl mimicked. 'Come along! Come along! *Come along!*'

She raced over to Mrs Conner and gave her a big hug. 'Lulu go school now. 'Bye.'

'Be a good girl,' Mrs Conner said. 'Don't be doing anything *I* wouldn't do.'

Lulu giggled and dashed out of the room.

Max put down his newspaper and stood up. He'd been scanning the paper, searching for any stories of unidentified murder victims. Now he thought how foolish he was to have believed Mariska and her threats against Vladimir. He told himself once again that she was lying as usual, bluffing and lying, for that was her way.

Today he planned on clearing things up. First on his agenda was setting Mariska straight.

He was going to make *sure* that Vladimir was deported. It was the only answer.

*   *   *

'Hi,' Amy said. 'How do you *feel*?'

Tina was sitting in her hospital bed, propped up by several pillows. The baby was lying in a crib next to her.

'Like a truck zipped through my snatch,' Tina said, making a face. 'Other than that, I'm perfectly fine.'

'Sounds painful.'

'*Is* painful. Only every time I take a peek at Brad Junior, it's definitely worth it.'

'He's *so* gorgeous,' Amy said, bending down and peering into the crib. 'Those eyelashes!'

'Never mind the eyelashes, how about his thingy?' Tina quipped. 'It's *all* Brad can talk about. My husband is obsessed!'

'Typical,' Amy said, smiling. 'The proud papa.'

'Oh, he's proud all right. He can't wait to tell anyone who'll listen that size runs in the family!'

'I think that's rather sweet.'

'I'll let you know,' Tina said, taking a sip of water. 'You're here early. Everything okay?'

'I wanted to see you before I went to work.'

'Because . . .?'

'Because nothing. You just had a baby, so I thought you'd appreciate an early-morning visit.'

'Sure,' Tina said disbelievingly, moving around in search of a more comfortable position. '*You*'ve got something on your mind. You *know* you can never hide anything from me.'

'Hmm . . .' Amy murmured.

'Hmm *what*?'

'You *do* know me,' Amy said, perching on the edge of the bed.

'So?'

'Mystery Man.'

'What about him?' Tina asked eagerly.

'He's not a mystery anymore.'

'Oh, no! You *didn't*,' Tina exclaimed. 'You *bad* girl, you went to his apartment.'

'Certainly not.'

'What, then?'

'At the party last night, did you happen to notice Max's brother, the young one?'

'The guy with the Italian model?'

'That's the one.'

'What about him?'

'Uh . . . did he look familiar to you?'

'Now that you mention it . . .' Then Tina got it. 'No!' she yelled, sitting up straight. 'You are *kidding* me! That's *impossible*!'

'Unfortunately it's true,' Amy said, feeling better for sharing. 'Mystery Man is a mystery no more. Mystery Man is Jett Diamond, Max's brother.'

And before Tina could react further, Brad came bounding in laden with flowers, magazines and a big box of chocolates. 'Hi, girls,' he said. 'What's going on?'

* * *

Chris left a message at the desk for Jett to meet him at the hotel gym. He should've thought about working out before, he needed a boost of energy.

The first person he ran into at the gym was Inez. She was jogging on one of the treadmills clad in shorts and a stomach-baring red tank. 'Hi,' she said, waving at him as if they were no more than casual acquaintances.

And actually, he thought, that was *all* they were – casual acquaintances who'd enjoyed a vigorous late-night fuck.

'Hey,' he responded, making his way to the racks of weights.

There were a few other people in the gym, but no one he knew. He warmed up for a few minutes, then started lifting, enjoying the pull on his muscles, feeling the burst of strength that working out always gave him.

He couldn't help wondering that if Red hadn't summoned him to New York, would he still have lost his house?

Had he stayed in L.A., was there *some* way he could've saved it?

Common sense told him no.

Fantasy told him yes.

Damn Red Diamond. Anything he touched turned to shit.

He shouldn't have come running to New York. It had been a mistake. He didn't want the old man's money, after all. It wasn't worth the price.

And there *would* be a price. Oh, yes, with Red Diamond there was *always* a price.

*   *   *

Jett did not believe in relationships. Relationships were crap. Strictly for people who wanted to spend the rest of their sorry lives tied to one person.

Then he'd met Amy.

Then he'd slept with Amy.

And suddenly he was a believer.

Only one problem. Amy, as it turned out, was his big brother's fiancée. How lucky was *that*?

So what the hell did she see in Max?

Boring Max, who put business before all else.

Dull Max, who only shone in the boardroom.

Uptight Max, who, no doubt, was a total dud in bed.

Striding down Park Avenue on his way to meet Chris, he still couldn't get Amy off his mind. The wedding was coming up, and he felt totally helpless because there was nothing he could do to stop it. Absolutely nothing.

Unless, of course . . . he told Max the truth.

That was a thought. Tell big brother the truth and watch Amy's world crumble.

No, he couldn't do that to her. She was too special. She deserved better than him opening his big mouth.

He had to see her, that was for sure. He was determined to find out what was on her mind when she'd come back to his apartment and slept with him.

But how was he going to arrange to meet her without Max finding out?

Chris would have an answer. Chris was an expert at figuring things out.

* * *

Sitting in the back of Max's car with Nanny Reece, Lulu chatted all the way to the apartment. She commented on everything as she gazed out of the window: 'Look, Daddy, see the big dog' – 'Look, Daddy, funny man lying down on the sidewalk' – 'Look, Daddy, see the horsy go poop!'

'Language!' Max said, causing Lulu to dissolve into one of her giggling fits.

'Poop! Poop! *Poop!*' Lulu screamed, her face bright red with excitement. 'Poop! Poopie! Poo*pie*!'

'That's enough,' Max said, turning round to glare at Nanny Reece, who sat there like a stoic lump. He decided it was time to have a word with Mariska about her choice of nanny – this woman had zero personality, and no control over his child.

When they arrived at the building, Lulu jumped out of the car and raced inside. Nanny Reece followed at a snail's pace.

Max glanced at his watch. It was just before eight. He had a little time before the nine o'clock meeting with Red.

'Wait here,' he instructed his driver. 'I'll be out in fifteen minutes.'

Riding up in the elevator, Lulu started a tuneless rendition of 'Itsy Bitsy Spider'. 'Do you *like* spiders, Daddy?' she inquired, stopping for a moment, all wide-eyed and cute. '*I* don't, 'cause they go all crawly up your legs and into your *butt*.' More screams of laughter. 'Butt! Butt! *Butt!*'

Nanny Reece didn't say a word. Max was developing a major headache. Spending time with his daughter could be quite exhausting.

The elevator ground to a stop, and all three of them got out.

Max realized he should probably have called first. He hated it when Mariska greeted him in one of her floating negligees, her breasts barely contained by the flimsy material. It had happened a few times, and he was certain she was hoping he'd get turned on. Actually, the opposite happened, he got completely turned off.

Nanny Reece produced her key and opened the front door to the apartment.

Determined not to get involved in a fight, Max knew exactly what he was going to say to his ex-wife, and this time she'd better start listening.

'Mommy!' Lulu yelled excitedly, racing across the marble foyer. 'Mommy! Mommy! Mommy! Lulu's *home*.'

Max headed for the living room. 'Tell Mrs Diamond I'm here,' he said to Nanny Reece. 'And make sure she knows I'm in a hurry.'

As he said 'hurry', Lulu began to scream. They were piercing screams, and they were coming from Mariska's bedroom.

'Christ!' he said irritably, as Lulu's screams attacked his almost formed headache. Turning to Nanny Reece, he said, 'Don't you have *any* control over Lulu whatsoever?'

'Excuse *me*?' Nanny Reece said, her back stiffening.

'My *child* is screaming. *Do* something about it.'

At that moment Lulu came racing back, her dress and hands covered with blood. 'Mommy's sick!' she yelled hysterically. 'My mommy's sick! Sick! *Sick!*'

Chapter Forty

'Slick Jimmy's got moves I only ever dreamed 'bout!' Cindi raved, bursting into the apartment early on Monday morning, her face flushed with excitement. 'He's hung like a freakin' stallion, an' that man knows how t' go down an' *then* some!'

'You didn't show up for work today,' Liberty said accusingly. 'You were supposed to be there at six this morning. Manny called earlier, he was *really* pissed about neither of us coming in. I told him you had flu. Y' know, Cindi, you *promised* you'd cover for me. We really let him down.'

'Who *gives* a shit?' Cindi said. 'We got loot now, we're movin' up. No more workin' our asses off slingin' hash an' pourin' coffee.'

'Wrong,' Liberty corrected, always the responsible one. 'That money is to pay off our bills, remember? We still need to keep our jobs.'

'Not *me*. Jimmy's scorin' me a gig singin' back-up on his tour.'

'Are you serious?'

'Yup, this girl is *dead-on* serious. I'm movin' out an' goin' on the road. How ace is *that*?'

'For real?' Liberty said, shocked.

'For *damn* real. The dude is apeshit 'bout me, so I'm takin' advantage of the situation.'

'Cindi, you don't know—'

'Oh, I *know*,' Cindi said confidently. 'I know that I finally found me a man who's gonna give me everythin' I want.'

'What about our apartment?' Liberty asked. 'If you're splitting, where does that leave me?'

'I know it's sudden, little cous',' Cindi said, sounding guilty, 'but I was thinkin' you might wanna move in with Kev. He's always doggin' you t' do that, an' the two of you make a hot couple.'

'You really think I'd move in with Kev 'cause that'll make it easier for you to dump on me?' Liberty said, trying to control her growing irritation.

'I *ain't* dumpin' on you. All I'm doin' is shakin' things up, lookin' to my future.'

'Great! And what am I supposed to do?'

'You're the smart one, you're gonna be fine.'

'When are you leaving?'

'Jimmy's comin' back for me in a coupla hours. I'm throwin' some stuff in a bag, then I'm outta here.'

'So that's it – you're going today?'

'Hey, the man wants to keep me close. I ain't arguin' with *that*.'

'This is crazy. You hardly know him.'

'Ooh, I know him *good*,' Cindi said, hurrying into the bedroom. 'That fool is one hot *boy*, an' I ain't lettin' him outta my sight.'

'Then I guess this means you're giving up your job at the coffee shop?' Liberty asked, following her.

'A girl's gotta do what a girl's gotta do,' Cindi said, tossing an assortment of clothes into a large duffel bag. 'An' this be my destiny.'

'After one night it's your destiny,' Liberty said, shaking her head in amazement. 'Man, that's really something. Who's telling Manny you're not coming back?'

'I was thinkin' you'd do it for me.'

'Gee, thanks.'

'Don't go gettin' down on me, Lib,' Cindi said, making a face. 'I know it's sudden an' all, but I *gotta* do this, an' *you* gotta understand.'

'You're not giving me much choice.'

'It's not *your* choice, girl, it's *mine*.'

'If it's what you want . . .'

'It's *definitely* what I want. Only don't be tellin' my mom – she'll throw a shitfit.'

Liberty nodded, trying to make sense of what was happening. Cindi was making a move, and who knew if it was the right one? Since there was no stopping her, Liberty realized she'd better start thinking about herself.

Kev was due back at any minute. Not that she planned on moving in with him – Kev was a nice enough guy, but she wasn't looking for commitment.

Her immediate problem was what to do about the apartment. She'd have to look for somewhere smaller – either that or find a roommate to share the rent, because there was no way she could afford it on her own.

Things were changing fast, but that was okay, she could handle it.

After loading two duffel bags with clothes, Cindi finally shifted the attention off herself and asked Liberty what had happened between her and Damon. 'I *saw* you sneakin' out with him last night,' Cindi said, wagging her finger. 'You *know* we got a rule 'bout married dudes.'

'Then I guess you saw him sneaking back *into* the party, 'cause all he did was tell his driver to drop me home.'

'You askin' me t' believe he didn't try t' jump you?' Cindi said, raising her eyebrows.

'He was a gentleman all the way.'

'*Sheeit!* That's borin', girl.'

'Not to me.'

'The dude was playin' it tight, all the better t' worm his way into your panties.'

Liberty shrugged, discussion over. She didn't want to share her feelings about Damon with anyone, not even Cindi. 'How about I make us some eggs?' she suggested. 'You must be hungry.'

'Don't be all pissed at me,' Cindi wailed, putting on her please-forgive-me-'cause-I'm-adorable voice. 'Y'all *know* how much I love you, little cous'.'

'I'm not mad. I understand.'

'I was thinkin' I'd give you all my money from the video shoot. Add that t' your money, an' you'll be okay till you decide what you're gonna do.'

Didn't Cindi ever listen? The money from the video shoot was earmarked to pay off all their outstanding bills. 'Stop worrying about it, Cindi,' she said. 'I'll manage.'

'Mebbe later I can get *you* a gig singin' back-up with me.'

'No, thanks,' Liberty said, thinking there was nothing she'd like less. 'Slick Jimmy's music isn't my style.'

'Oh,' Cindi said, insulted. 'I guess you'd sooner be slingin' hash an' shovellin' eggs?'

'I'm not doing *that* forever. Something will come along.'

'Sure it will,' Cindi said magnanimously. 'You gotta have faith, girl. God'll protect you. He always does.'

Later, when Cindi had finally left, the full realization of what had just taken place dawned on her. She was totally alone. No Cindi to hang with, go shopping, share the cooking, read magazines, watch TV, catch the occasional movie, although they always argued about who was sexier – Denzel Washington or Blair Underwood. Liberty opted for Blair – he was one fine-looking specimen who didn't work enough for her liking.

Of course, she'd still have Kev, but a boyfriend was a whole different ball game. Boyfriends were good for sex and cuddling, killing bugs and fun. They came up short on real camaraderie. At least, that was her experience.

Kev called as soon as he got back into town. 'How you feelin', sugar?' he asked, over the phone. ''Cause I'm feelin' *in* the mood.'

'I'm better,' she said.

'Then I'll come get you. We can grab a burger, a beer, an' go back to my place.'

Ah, yes, a burger and beer. Mr Romance is back in town.

'Can't tonight,' she said.

'How come?'

''Cause I promised Manny I'd work the late shift, seeing as how I've been off,' she lied. For some reason she didn't want to tell Kev about her upcoming meeting with Damon.

'Sugar—' he began.

'Sorry, Kev. I know it's a drag.'

'Wanna come by when you're through?'

'No.'

'*No*, my girl says. That's a stunnin' welcome back.'

'I'll be tired. Maybe tomorrow night.'

'You got it.'

'There's a new song I've been working on.'

'Don't you *ever* take a rest?'

'I want you to hear it, see what you think.'

'Tomorrow it is.'

She didn't mean to deceive Kev, but her meeting with Damon had nothing to do with him, and right now – just in case nothing came of it – she'd decided to keep it to herself.

Damon P. Donnell. Even his name sent chills down her spine.

Chapter Forty-One

'Your wife was stabbed six times,' Detective Rodriguez said. 'Six times,' he repeated.

Slumped in a chair in the living room of Mariska's apartment, Max stared at the man, his face full of disbelief.

'Do you have any idea who could've done this?' Detective Rodriguez asked, peering at him intently.

'I thought you said it was a robbery,' Max stated.

'I didn't say it *was*,' Detective Rodriguez replied. 'What I *did* say was that it *might* have been. Start listening to me, Mr Diamond, it's important.'

Max was still in shock. The events of the morning were fresh in his mind as it had only happened less than half an hour earlier. After Lulu had emerged, screaming, he'd followed Nanny Reece into the bedroom where they'd discovered Mariska sprawled across her bed in a pool of blood. The room had been ransacked.

Stoic English Nanny Reece had become hysterical. Max had been forced to shake her. 'For God's sake, you're supposed to be looking after Lulu,' he'd shouted. 'Pull yourself together and get her away from here. Take her to a neighbour, any-where.'

'But, Mr Diamond, your wife is dead. She's *dead*.'

'We don't know that,' he'd said, although he knew she was – there was so much blood that Mariska couldn't still be alive.

Christ! Where was Lulu? He'd run out of the bedroom to find her.

His little daughter was sitting on the floor in the hall, whimpering softly. 'Everything's going to be all right, sweetheart,' he'd said, sweeping her into his arms. 'Nanny's taking you to some friends, and Daddy will come get you in a little while. Mommy's not feeling very well.'

'Okay, Daddy,' Lulu said, tears rolling down her cheeks. 'I be a good girl, Daddy. I be *very* good.'

'Yes, sweetie, I know you will.' He'd turned to Nanny Reece, who looked as if she was about to lose it again. 'Are there any friends you can take her to in the building?'

Nanny Reece nodded.

'Go, and stay there until I come for her. Call down to the desk clerk and tell him what apartment you'll be in.'

'Yes, Mr Diamond.'

As soon as they were gone, he'd picked up the phone and dialled 911. 'I'm reporting a–a murder,' he'd stammered. 'Or . . . a dead person. I–I'm not sure. My–my ex-wife, she's–she's lying on her bed – covered with blood.'

He'd given them the address, then taken up a position by the door.

Within five minutes a patrol car arrived downstairs, and a few minutes later two policemen walked into the apartment.

'Is anyone else here?' one of the cops asked, looking around, his hand hovering near his gun.

'No, I–I just got here myself.'

'Where's the body?'

'My daughter was with me, and her nanny . . . We walked in and found her.'

'*Who* exactly did you find?'

'My ex-wife.'

'Where is she?'

'In the bedroom,' he said, indicating the way.

'Okay, sir. A detective will be here shortly,' the cop assured him. 'Do not touch anything. I suggest you go sit in the living room and wait.'

So that was exactly what he'd done, too shocked to do anything else.

In the back of his mind he knew he should call his lawyer. But why would he do that? He wasn't guilty of anything. Yet every time he saw a murder on TV or in a movie, the husband or ex-husband was always the main suspect.

Jesus! He wasn't thinking straight. It was ridiculous. He'd walked into the apartment with Lulu and her nanny, there was no way anybody could possibly suspect him.

Besides, he *knew* who'd done it. Vladimir. He had no doubt about *that*. Vladimir Bushkin had murdered Mariska, because who knew what the two of them had going on between them?

Max stared at the overweight Hispanic detective. The man had a small, annoying black moustache and crooked front teeth. He wore glasses and his jacket was too tight for his large frame.

'I *am* listening, Detective,' he said, attempting to pull himself together. 'This is a terrible shock.'

'I understand, Mr Diamond,' Detective Rodriguez said, producing a well-used notebook and a stubby pencil. 'But, as I'm sure you're aware, I do have to ask you some questions.'

'I'll tell you what I can,' Max said, still trying to clear his head. 'It won't be much, because Mrs Diamond and I are – *were* – divorced.'

'Amicable?'

'Excuse me?' Max said, hunching forward.

'Were the two of you fighting? Having any problems?'

'No.'

'You're *sure* about that?'

'Yes, I'm sure.'

'Hmm . . .' the detective said, scribbling something in his notebook.

'What does *that* mean?' Max said, taking offence at the detective's attitude.

'Did the ex-Mrs Diamond have any enemies?' Detective Rodriguez asked, still scribbling.

'I shouldn't think so.'

'Was she seeing anyone?'

'Why are you asking *me*?'

'I thought you might know.'

'Well, I *don't*.'

'Where were *you* last night, Mr Diamond?'

'Excuse me?'

'Where *were* you last night?' Detective Rodriguez repeated.

'I was at a party. My rehearsal dinner actually.'

'Rehearsing for *what*?'

'It was my rehearsal dinner,' Max said, speaking slowly. 'I'm getting remarried.'

'Really?' Detective Rodriguez said, scribbling furiously. 'And I guess your ex wasn't too happy about *that*.'

'What does my getting married again have to do with anything?'

'You never know,' Detective Rodriguez said mysteriously. 'Now, tell me, Mr Diamond, what time exactly did you leave this . . . rehearsal dinner?'

Max frowned. He didn't like the way things were going. 'Do I need to call my attorney, Detective?' he asked.

'I don't know,' Detective Rodriguez replied, giving him a long penetrating look. '*Do* you?'

*　　*　　*

'Come with me while I run upstairs and take a quick shower,' Chris said, as they left the hotel gym. 'Then we'd better get going. Don't want to be late for Daddy-oh.'

'Wish you'd told me you were working out,' Jett remarked, as they headed for the elevator. 'I could've joined you instead of standing around watching.'

'Why didn't you?'

'I'm not exactly in workout clothes.'

'You could've borrowed something,' Chris pointed out. 'I'm sure they have stuff here.'

'Nah, it was more fun watching you,' Jett said, not even bothering to eyeball the pretty blonde getting out of the elevator as they got in. 'You're kinda buff for a lawyer. How come?'

'I *used* to have my own gym – that was before my house got mud-slimed.'

'I meant to ask, what're you doing about that?'

'I'll figure things out when I get back to L.A. I'm not even sure what the insurance covers – if anything.'

'Man, it's a real bummer,' Jett commiserated.

'Don't worry about me, you've got enough on your mind.'

'I'd sooner you didn't remind me,' Jett said, grimacing.

'You can't hide from it,' Chris pointed out. 'You have to decide how you're going to handle the situation.'

'You're right,' Jett said glumly. 'I can't pretend it never happened, and Amy can't pretend I don't exist.'

'Have you thought about how you're going to contact her?'

'I'll come up with something.'

Easy to say, but what exactly was he going to come up with? He felt so damn helpless.

Chris's cell rang. It was Birdy, informing him in an excited whisper that all was cool and the wedding was back on.

Big surprise.

They reached his suite where a maid was already cleaning the bathroom. 'Five minutes,' Chris said, slipping her a twenty-dollar bill, 'and we'll be out of here.'

He showered quickly, dressed, and met Jett in the living room. 'I'm not sure if I can stomach seeing the old bastard today,' he said, downing a glass of orange juice from the room-service trolley. 'What's he going to tell us? That he's not leaving us one dime, that he doesn't *have* to?'

'Hey, he's gotta leave his money to *somebody*.' Jett pointed out, biting into an apple. 'He's a freakin' *billionaire*. He's too cheap to leave it to charity, and we all know he hates everyone else.'

'He hates us too,' Chris stated.

'What makes you think it's about money anyway?' Jett asked. 'It could be—'

'Could be *what*?' Chris interrupted. 'In Red's warped mind money is the only hold he still has over us. And you know what? I'd rather be broke than beg anything from him.'

*   *   *

'You're here early,' Nigel said, greeting Amy at the office. 'Your mother's been on the phone already. I should warn you – she sounds as if she's on the warpath.'

'Not again!' Amy sighed.

'Yes, again,' Nigel said crisply. 'Where were you? According to her, she called your apartment three times this morning and got no answer.'

'I stopped by the hospital to see Tina.'

'How *is* the darling girl?'

'She's doing great, the baby is beyond gorgeous, Brad is ecstatic.'

'I presume that last night you got to the hospital in time.'

'Just about.'

'Thank God! I had visions of you delivering Tina's baby in the back of Max's car!'

'It didn't happen,' she said, smiling.

'Well, all I can say is you missed *some* night,' Nigel announced.

'I heard. Max picked me up from the hospital.'

'Naturally Marcello ruined the *entire* evening for me,' Nigel complained, narrowing his eyes. 'He's *such* a slut.'

'What did he do this time?'

'Flirted with Yolanda's toy-boy all night. As you can imagine, I was *livid*!'

'I think you've got to face up to the fact that you're reaching the end of your relationship,' Amy mused. 'It's time to make a break.'

'You could be right. I refuse to be with someone who's *constantly* flirting with other men.'

'You shouldn't put yourself through that, Nigel. You're too good for him.'

'I did love him once,' Nigel sighed, in an overdramatic fashion. 'Now the bloom has faded.'

'It happens.'

'I suppose so.'

'Max told me Gianna was the hit of the party,' Amy said, attempting to get him off the subject of Marcello – she wanted to hear more about Gianna, painful as it was.

'Ah, yes,' Nigel enthused. 'Exquisitely beautiful and such *style*!'

'Seems everyone loved her.'

'What's not to love? She's divine. As for Max's brother – *oh, my God*! Quite the hunk. Did you speak to him?'

'Never got a chance,' she answered, her heart beating fast. 'Uh . . . did you?'

'I *wish*!'

'What time is Gianna coming in today?' she asked, quickly changing the subject again because she didn't want to think about Jett. Not at all.

'Sometime this morning. Apparently she and Sofia are old friends.'

'That's convenient.'

'Isn't it, though?'

'Well, I guess I'd better go call my mother back and try to do some work.'

'Stay calm now,' Nigel warned. 'No fighting. You know how Nancy *loves* to press your buttons.'

'I promise.'

She left Nigel and shut herself in her office where she sat for a while doing nothing. The nice thing about arriving at work early was the lack of activity. No noise and people rushing around. No ringing phones and non-stop action. Just peace and calm.

She turned on her computer and stared at a bunch of e-mails she didn't feel like answering. She had no intention of calling her mother back. Nancy would be full of complaints about her so-called rudeness in running out on her own rehearsal dinner, and she wasn't in the mood to listen.

Later she'd visit Tina again, and this time maybe Brad wouldn't be around.

Not being able to talk about the Jett situation was killing her. She needed advice desperately, and Tina was the only person she could truly trust.

*   *   *

As they strode down Park Avenue on their way to Red's house, Jett asked Chris what he thought of Gianna.

'She's a real charmer,' Chris replied. 'I'm surprised you're not more into her.'

'Yeah,' Jett agreed. 'But here's the thing – Gianna is the kind of girl you're crazy about for a while, then one day you wake up and go, "Hold on a minute, this woman is driving me freakin' *nuts*." Plus she's a sex maniac,' he added, groping for a cigarette.

'And that's a bad thing?' Chris asked, laughing. 'By the way, have I mentioned that you smoke too much?'

'Gimme a break,' Jett groaned, 'it's the only vice I've got left.'

'Poor you.'

'Y' know,' Jett said casually, 'I was thinking that Gianna should be in movies. If she came out to L.A., maybe you could introduce her to some producers – you've got connections, right?'

'C'*mon*,' Chris said. 'Everyone and their mother wants to get into movies. Not to mention every model who ever walked the runway. Now you want me to hook your girlfriend up?'

'She's *not* my girlfriend,' Jett said, exhaling a stream of smoke. 'She's got – whaddaya call it? Star quality, that kinda deal. She's different.'

'They're *all* different one way or another.'

'What d'you think? Should I persuade her to buy a one-way ticket to Hollywood?'

'You trying to get rid of her?' Chris asked, amused.

Jett grinned. 'That's *exactly* my plan.'

* * *

After asking Detective Rodriguez if he should call his lawyer, Max decided it would be prudent to do so because he certainly needed someone there with him. The reality of what had taken place was only just beginning to sink in.

Mariska was dead. Murdered. The mother of his child had been the victim of unspeakable and heinous violence. He shuddered to think what would happen once the press got their feral little teeth into the story. This tragedy would change everything.

Christ! It was only the beginning of the nightmare.

* * *

Lady Jane Bentley prepared for battle. She awoke early on Monday morning and dressed accordingly. Chanel – it was definitely a day for Chanel.

Red Diamond had failed to put in an appearance all week-end. She was not worried. If anything was certain in life it was that he was holed up in his 'secret' apartment, surrounded by whores.

She decided that *she* would meet with his three sons, it was about time someone enlightened them on the ways of their father. Why shouldn't it be her?

Obviously Red was not showing up, so this was the perfect opportunity to have her say. And she would.

Oh, yes, there was no doubt about *that*.

Chapter Forty-Two

Clad in a form-fitting white suit and a blouse with a plunging neckline, her long, flame-coloured hair swept up, Sonja did not look like a highly priced call-girl – more like an expensive trophy wife. Famka, a raven-haired beauty with plumped-up lips and slanted eyes, wore a similar suit in dark green, tightly belted.

Both women – already tall – wore four-inch sling-back heels, and carried large expensive handbags stuffed with sex-toys and cash.

When it came to his sexual pleasure, Red Diamond was an extremely generous man, and these two women had spent most of the weekend with him. It had cost him plenty, but he wasn't complaining. Quite the opposite. Sex for sale. It sure beat living with a woman he'd grown to hate. Lady Jane Bentley could go to hell for all he cared.

On Monday morning Red was still active. Earlier he'd had both women going down on him simultaneously. The pleasure he'd experienced was intense and, best of all, neither of them talked. All he had to do was throw money at them, and they did whatever he required – no questions asked.

Now they were dressed and ready to spend the day with him – for a price. Two tall, striking beauties with the devil in their eyes and full, succulent lips.

Wait until Lady Jane Bentley got a look at what *he* was bringing home. If these two didn't send her packing, nothing would.

*　*　*

On her way to the library, Lady Jane passed Diahann, the housekeeper she loathed.

'Excuse me, Lady Bentley,' Diahann said, straining to be polite, because the loathing went both ways. 'I'm worried about Mr Diamond. Would you happen to know where he is?'

Lady Jane gave her an imperious look. 'Worried, are you?' she said icily. 'And why would that be?'

'As I'm sure you're aware, Mr Diamond has not been home all weekend,' Diahann said. 'You must be worried too.'

'Certainly not,' Lady Jane snapped. 'I know exactly where he is. He's at his apartment, the one where he spends all his time fucking whores.'

A startled Diahann took a step backwards. '*What* did you say?'

'You heard me,' Lady Jane said, a spiteful gleam in her eyes. 'Fucking whores. That's what your lord and master does when he's not here. *That*'s what turns him on. Now, get out of my way.' And she brushed past Diahann and swept into the library.

* * *

'God, I hate this house,' Chris muttered as they stood outside.

'Me too,' Jett said. 'No fond memories here.'

'I gotta feeling this is the last time I'm coming here,' Chris mused. 'Yeah, I'm making myself that promise.'

Jett rubbed his hands together. 'You think Max is inside?'

'Dunno. He might have a hangover. He seemed to be enjoying himself last night – he certainly liked Gianna.'

'Maybe we could arrange a switch,' Jett suggested drily. 'I'll take Amy, he can have Gianna.'

'That's more like it,' Chris said, changing his cell to vibrate. 'Baby bro's got a sense of humour.'

'I'm trying,' Jett said with a rueful grin, doing the same to his phone. 'It's not easy.'

'Okay, let's do this,' Chris said, taking a deep breath and pushing the buzzer. 'Let the final circus begin.'

* * *

With his lawyer on the way over, and Detective Rodriguez still bombarding him with questions, Max called Chris at his hotel. This was a family crisis, and he needed his brother by his side.

There was no answer from Chris's room at the Four Seasons, so he tried his cell. Voicemail instructed him to leave a message. 'It's Max,' he said tersely. 'Call me immediately you get this. It's urgent.'

People were now roaming all over Mariska's apartment: a police photographer, forensics, another detective – this time a female – and several more cops who were busy dusting for fingerprints.

'How long do I have to stay?' Max asked.

Detective Rodriguez threw him a canny look. 'Nobody's keeping you here, Mr Diamond,' he said mildly. 'You're free to leave whenever you like. You told me where you were last night, we'll check it out, and that'll be that.'

'Jesus *Christ*!' Max exploded. 'You're making it sound as if *I*'m a suspect.'

'Do you *feel* like a suspect?' Detective Rodriguez asked, lowering his glasses and peering at him.

'No, I don't,' Max snapped. 'In case you're forgetting, I just lost my wife.'

'*Ex*-wife, Mr Diamond,' Detective Rodriguez corrected. 'You're about to get married again, remember?'

'You're one smart son-of-a-bitch, aren't you?' Max said, glaring at him.

'I try to be as smart as I can. That's a detective's job.'

'Screw you,' Max said, losing it. 'My lawyer's on his way over.'

'Just exactly why do you think you *need* a lawyer, Mr Diamond?' Detective Rodriguez asked, stroking his moustache.

'Because of you and your dumbass questions,' Max raged.

'I'm sorry if my questions are disturbing you. They're merely routine. I wouldn't be doing my job if I *didn't* ask them.'

'I'm sure.'

'What really surprises me is that you haven't told me you're a friend of the mayor. Usually it's the first thing you big-shots do.'

'Oh, I see,' Max said furiously. 'Now I'm a big-shot. Is that why you're taking this attitude?'

'No attitude, Mr Diamond. As I said before, this is routine, all in a day's work.'

Max couldn't wait for his lawyer to get there so that he could straighten things out and leave. His ex-wife had been murdered, she was lying on her bed stabbed to death, and this asshole was questioning *him*.

In his mind he knew who'd done it, but he wasn't about to reveal that information to the detective. It would be bad enough when the press got hold of the story. If they ever discovered his marriage to Mariska wasn't legal, that she was a bigamist and Lulu was illegitimate, they'd crucify him.

He was not about to tell his lawyer about Vladimir either. He'd confide in Chris, see what *he* had to say. Chris might be an entertainment lawyer, but he certainly had access to criminal lawyers who could advise him on what to do if he needed them.

Where the fuck was Chris anyway?

He'd completely forgotten that they were all supposed to be meeting at Red's house. Seeing his father was the last thing on his mind.

Two maids arrived at the apartment and scampered into the kitchen like frightened mice, whispering to each other.

Max walked into the kitchen. 'Make everyone coffee,' he instructed them. Irena, Mariska's personal maid, was slumped at the kitchen table, staring into space.

Max was worried about Lulu, Detective Rodriguez claimed he needed to talk to her since she was the one who'd found the body. 'She's five years old,' Max said. 'Why do you have to talk to her?'

'I need to ask a couple of questions.'

'Didn't you hear what I said? She's *five*. You've got no right to question my daughter.'

'We'll see,' Detective Rodriguez said. 'There's a female detective who'll speak to her.'

'I suppose you consider Lulu a suspect too,' Max said sarcastically.

'Anything is possible,' Detective Rodriguez replied.

'You *son-of-a-bitch*,' Max said, almost losing it.

As the confrontation was about to become heated, Elliott Minor, Max's lawyer, arrived. He was a portly man, balding and suntanned. 'I'm so sorry, Max,' Elliott said, patting his client on the shoulder. 'This is shocking, *shocking*. Was it a home invasion?'

'That's what Detective Rodriguez thinks it might be,' Max said. 'But since he's questioned me into the ground—'

'You don't have answer anything you don't want to,' Elliott advised.

'I'm sure he knows that,' Detective Rodriguez interrupted. 'Although usually nobody minds answering questions when they have nothing to hide.'

'Kindly refrain from using that tone with me,' Elliott snapped. 'You know perfectly well that my client is not required to answer *anything*.' A long beat. 'You're not arresting him, are you?'

'Why would you think *that*?' Max said furiously.

'Of course not,' Detective Rodriguez said, fiddling with his moustache.

One of the maids entered the room bearing a tray of coffee. She poured Max a cup with a shaking hand.

He took a gulp and burned his tongue. 'They want to talk to Lulu,' he informed Elliott.

'Lulu?' Elliott questioned, raising his eyebrows. 'Why?'

'Because *she* discovered the body.'

*   *   *

The butler ushered Chris and Jett into Red's house, directing them into the library, where they were surprised to find Lady Jane Bentley sitting on the couch.

'Where's Red?' Chris asked, not prepared to put up with another runaround.

'I imagine he's on his way,' she replied, sipping camomile tea from a delicately patterned china cup. 'Can I have the maid get you boys anything?'

'On his way?' Chris said, ignoring her offer of refreshments.

'Doesn't he live here?' Jett asked, wishing he could light up a cigarette, but knowing she'd object.

'Apparently not this weekend,' she said, with an icy smile. 'I fear your dear father is becoming senile.'

'Why's that?' Chris asked.

'He has an apartment, a place he thinks I have no knowledge of.' She took a long pause, then added, 'He keeps his whores there.'

'Whores?' Jett repeated, exchanging a quick look with Chris. 'Did you say whores?'

'That's right. Your father might be old, but he's still a very sexually active man.' A meaningful pause, then, 'Fortunately, not with me.'

'Excuse me,' Chris said sharply. 'Are you sure we should be having this conversation?'

'Why not?' Lady Jane replied, cool and vindictive. 'I thought before your father got here I might share a few things with you.'

'What things?' Chris asked, sensing trouble ahead.

'Well, for one, your gambling debt.'

'How the *fuck* do you know about that?'

'Didn't you ever wonder why Roth Giagante is putting so much pressure on you to pay up?'

'You know Roth?' Chris said, shocked and surprised.

'I do not. Red does.'

'Jesus!'

'Exactly *who* do you think has been insisting Roth threaten you to make sure you pay? It's all about control and teaching you a lesson.'

'You've *gotta* be fucking kidding,' Chris exploded. '*Red*'s behind this?'

'Please control your language. I hate to be reminded of your father,' Lady Jane said. 'And you,' she added, turning to Jett. 'Red had his spies in Milan trying to dig up dirt on you. He was hoping you'd fall back into the drug lifestyle, and when you didn't, he hired people to try to lure you, but you still wouldn't bite, which made him decide you weren't worth the trouble.'

'Oh, *great*!' Jett said.

'Here's a copy of one of his e-mails,' she said, handing Jett a sheet of paper.

He read it quickly.

The boy's a fuck-up. He'll crash
and burn all by himself. Stop
wasting my time and money.

Silently he handed the e-mail to Chris, who scanned it and shook his head in disbelief.

'Why are you telling us this shit?' Jett asked, remembering all the times he'd been offered drugs over the past few months, and wondering which of his so-called friends had been working for Red.

'Oh, dear me, you *do* take after him, don't you?' Lady Jane sighed. 'Both of you use foul language, exactly like your father.'

'None of us takes after him,' Chris said angrily. 'I can assure you of that.'

She glanced at her diamond Cartier watch. 'Will Max be here?' she inquired. 'I have something important to tell him too.'

'Go ahead,' Chris said coldly. 'I'll pass on the information.'

'Please do, for I'm sure Max will be interested to know that the reason the banks withdrew from his multi-million-dollar building project in Lower Manhattan is because Red *insisted* they did so. He used his own leverage with the banks to make certain they listened to him. Some people would call it blackmail.'

'This is *crazy*,' Jett said, running his hand through his hair.

'Is that why we're here?' Chris asked. 'So that *he* can keep on flexing what he considers his control over us?'

'I have no idea why he wanted you here. I was merely the messenger,' Lady Jane said, maintaining a cool attitude. 'I can only presume he wishes to torture you further, of which, I can assure you, he is quite capable.'

'How come you're telling us this stuff?' Jett asked.

'I felt it was time you knew what an evil man your father is.'

'Like we don't already know that,' Jett scoffed. 'You

wanna see the scars on my butt? You wanna talk about a bully and an abuser? You wanna meet my *mom* – a screwed up, emotionally wrecked drunk because of him. Oh, yeah, we know all about Red Diamond.'

'This is bullshit,' Chris said impatiently. 'Is Red coming here this morning or not?'

'I really don't know.'

'Then we're taking off.'

'Wait,' she said, her voice a sharp command. 'Before you go, there's something else you should know, something that affects each and every one of us.'

'Hey – why stop now?' Chris said. 'You're on quite a roll.'

'Then I suggest you prepare yourself,' Lady Jane said. 'For I do not believe you're going to like what you hear.'

Chapter Forty-Three

'Hey,' Beverly said, over the phone.

'Hey,' Liberty responded, delighted to get a call from her new friend.

'What happened last night?' Beverly asked curiously. 'You turn the big man down?'

'I listened to you.'

'Right on, sister! Mr Stud came back into the party lookin' *way* pissed. Damon's not used to gettin' turn-downs.'

'I *am* going to his office later to play him my demo.'

'Then stay cool,' Beverly warned. ''Cause now he'll try harder. No way you can weaken.'

'I don't intend to.'

'That's my girl,' Beverly said, then – 'here's the deal. I called my friend Bruce at the Madison Modelling Agency, told him all about you. He'll see you today, only you gotta be there by noon.'

'You actually did it?' Liberty said excitedly.

'When I say I'm gonna do somethin', it's done.'

'That's amazing, Bev.'

'Bruce'll be straight with you. If he thinks you got no chance, he'll tell you.'

'Wow, how can I thank you?'

'Wait till somethin' happens before you start thankin' me.' A quick pause. 'Oh, yeah, how's Cindi doin' today? That girl was feelin' *no* pain last night.'

'Want to hear the news of the morning?'

'Go ahead, hit me.'

'Cindi left. She's moving in with Slick Jimmy.'

'You *gotta* be shittin me? After *one* night?'

'That's what *I* said. But there's no talking to Cindi once she makes up her mind. Now I'm looking for a room-mate.'

'You shouldn't be in too much of a hurry, 'cause this'll end in tears. Jimmy's a POW.'

'What's a POW?'

'Pig on wheels.'

'Huh?'

'An asshole who bones anythin' that moves.'

'Shouldn't I warn her?'

'Don't sweat it. That girl's gonna find out soon enough.'

After getting the details of where to see Bruce, Liberty put down the phone. She was worried about Cindi, but she was also excited for herself. So much was happening – it was as if the fall she'd taken had opened up a Pandora's box of new things. Finding out about her father, the video shoot, Damon, Cindi moving out, now *this* – an appointment at a modelling agency. Maybe she wouldn't have to go back to work at the coffee shop either, although there was no way she'd dump on Manny and Golda the way Cindi had, she'd give them a couple of weeks' notice.

Preparing to go see the modelling agent was not so easy without Cindi around to check with. Usually they consulted on what to wear, depending on what they were doing and where they were going. She'd never been on her own – it was kind of liberating.

She rifled through her closet, hating everything. It wasn't as if she had money to burn on clothes, and she certainly didn't have anything fancy to wear. Fancy wasn't her style anyway, so she slid into a pair of skinny beige pants, boots, and a white Gap T-shirt. With her long dark hair, creamy milk-chocolate skin and mesmerizing green eyes, she was a knock-out whatever she wore.

* * *

The Madison Modelling Agency was located in a building off Lexington, and Liberty made it just in time for her appointment. The walls in the reception area were lined with framed magazine covers of different models.

As soon as she walked in she felt insecure: the girls on the covers were all so slinky and glamorous, and what was she? Pretty? Yeah, she was pretty but, as far as she was concerned, nothing special.

Don't think that way, her inner voice warned her. *You are special, you can do whatever you set your mind on. Get some confidence, girl.*

She marched up to the reception desk. 'I'm here to see, uh . . . Bruce.'

The Asian receptionist, who was more interested in talking on the phone, gave her a cursory glance. 'And you are?'

'Liberty. Beverly arranged the appointment.'

'I'll let him know you're here,' the receptionist said. 'Take a seat.'

Liberty sat down and picked up a fashion magazine with Tyra Banks on the cover. She stared at the exotic-looking model. Now *this* girl was special.

After ten minutes, the receptionist instructed her to go in.

Bruce was sitting behind a large cluttered desk. He was a chain-smoking, middle-aged white man, with fleshy features, a brown comb-over hairstyle and bushy eyebrows.

'Liberty,' he said, a cigarette stuck to his lower lip. 'Come in. Sit down. Beverly speaks well of you.'

'I didn't have much time to get ready,' she explained, feeling inadequate in her simple outfit.

'Get ready for what?' Bruce asked, shuffling a bunch of papers on his desk. 'The perfect photographic model is a blank canvas. It's up to the photographer and client to create the look. Beverly's a good judge. She seems to think you've got *it*, whatever *it* might be.'

'I'm flattered.'

'Don't be. It's not personal,' he said, taking a gulp of Diet Coke from a can balanced precariously on the arm of his chair. 'Where's your book?'

'Book?' she asked blankly.

'Photographs, dear,' he said, cigarette ash falling on his desk. 'A portfolio of photographs.'

'I don't have any,' she explained. 'Y'see, I wasn't really thinking of being a model – it was Beverly who suggested I come see you. Actually, I'm a singer.'

'How tall are you?' he asked, not at all interested in her other career goals.

'Five-eight.'

'Too short for runway work.'

'Oh,' she said, wondering if that meant this interview was over.

'Your measurements?'

'I–I have no idea,' she said, feeling like an unprepared idiot.

'I see,' he said, drumming his fingertips on his desk. 'No book, no photographs, she doesn't know her measurements, she's not that tall, but you *have* got a face that cries out for attention, so I'm sending you on a couple of go-sees today.'

'What's a go-see?'

'Exactly what it sounds like,' he said, blowing a stream of smoke in her direction. 'You go see a client or a photographer, and they make up their minds whether they want to use you.'

'Right,' she said.

'If things work out and we decide to take you on, photographs are essential. We'll put you together with a photographer who'll do your book for free in exchange for you boosting *his* book. That way everyone's happy. He gets to photograph a beautiful girl, you get the photographs you need.'

She nodded. He'd called her beautiful, surely that was a good sign?

'Okay, then,' he said, all business. 'First appointment two o'clock, second one at three. Do not be late to either of them. Oh, yes, and when you're through, don't call us, we'll call you.'

* * *

After leaving Bruce's office, Liberty grabbed a tuna sandwich at a nearby deli, then jumped a bus to Tribeca where the studio was located.

By the time she found it she was late, and her next appointment was all the way uptown on Eighty-third Street. With the heavy traffic she'd be lucky if she made it by four, let alone three. After that she had the most important meeting of the day, taking her demo to play for Damon, and there was no way she could be late for that.

The first go-see was a joke. There were at least twenty other girls sitting around in Reception, all with portfolios and cute outfits, all looking their best. It was obviously an audition, not a go-see.

Figuring it wasn't worth staying around and missing the second appointment, Liberty turned and left, stepping into the service elevator with a tall, skinny guy wearing overalls and a trucker baseball cap. He was balancing a large pizza box in one hand.

'Want a piece?' he asked, flipping open the lid.

'Aren't you supposed to be delivering that?' she asked.

'Nope. I'm supposed to be *eating* it,' he said, grinning. 'Feel free to help yourself.'

'No thanks. I just had a sandwich.'

'You here for the audition?' he asked, helping himself to a hefty slice of pizza.

'I was, but there's too many girls waiting.'

'You came all this way and you're not gonna see anyone?' he said, between chews.

'I can't stay around – I've got to be somewhere else at three. Do you work here?'

'Guess you could say I help out.'

'What's the audition for anyway?' she asked curiously.

'A swimsuit layout.'

'Like a *Sports Illustrated* kind of thing?'

'More like a *Stuff* or *Maxim*,' he said, going for a second slice of pizza. 'You know those magazines?'

'I've seen them.'

'You're probably not the right type,' he said, a dribble of tomato sauce sliding down his chin.

'You have to be a *type* to be in those kind of magazines?'

'You gotta be a little more zaftig.'

'Oh, *thanks*.'

'You got a great look, though,' he said encouragingly. 'You could do commercials.'

His compliment softened her up. 'I saw my first modelling agent today,' she said, dying to confide in someone. 'He sent me on two go-sees, this is the first, but he didn't tell me anything about either of them.'

'Gimme your name and agency, and I'll mention you were here an' couldn't stay.'

'Liberty. The Madison Modelling Agency. Won't they think it's rude that I left?'

'At least I can tell them you made the effort.'

'Thanks, and enjoy your pizza,' she said, as the creaky elevator ground to a halt.

'I will,' he said, still busily chewing. 'Good luck with the other job.'

She made the second go-see with minutes to spare. There were no other girls present, just a mannish-looking woman sitting alone in a photographer's loft.

The woman looked her over, asked a few questions, took a couple of Polaroids, then sent her on her way.

She left feeling dizzy and hopeful, thinking that maybe – just maybe – she was finally heading for the break she'd been wishing for all her life.

Chapter Forty-Four

'Where we going?' Sonja asked, sitting in the back of Red Diamond's Rolls-Royce admiring her reflection in a small gold compact – she'd stolen it from the dressing room of a woman whose husband had been using her services while his wife was out of town.

'I do not pay you to ask questions,' Red growled. 'Questions are not part of your job.'

Sonja ignored his rudeness. She didn't give a shit. As long as the money kept coming, who cared?

Famka adjusted her skirt so that the chauffeur, who could barely concentrate on his driving, got a clearer view of her snatch. Like Sonja, Famka never wore underwear unless it was at a client's request.

Both women had seen *Basic Instinct* several times. Both women fancied themselves in the Sharon Stone role. Tough, fearless, sexy, predatory, they were true admirers of American cinema.

Sonja yawned. The decrepit old billionaire was a sex-mad little bugger. He'd wanted the entire sex menu, and then he'd wanted more. 'What we do if he dies on us?' she'd asked Famka, who was more experienced when it came to dealing with very old, sex-crazed billionaires.

'Take all his cash and run like hell,' Famka had joked.

'Here's what I require you girlies to do,' Red said, breaking into Sonja's thoughts. 'When we get to my house you walk in, one on each side of me. There'll be people there who'll probably insult you. Ignore 'em. Say nothing.'

'People insulting me cost more,' Sonja stated, clicking her gold compact firmly shut.

'Me too,' agreed Famka.

'How much more?'

'Double our agreement.'

Red cackled. He admired women who knew how to make a deal.

*   *   *

'Come in, dear,' Sofia Courtenelli said, gesturing for Amy to enter her office. 'Meet my friend and our new signature model, Gianna. Gianna, say *buon giorno* to one of my best PR girls, Amy Scott-Simon.'

'*Ciao!*' Gianna exclaimed, as if they were old friends. 'It is *you.*'

'You two know each other?' Sofia asked.

'Last night I was at a party for Amy and Maxwell Diamond,' Gianna said, looking stylish and sexy in a Dolce & Gabbana charcoal wool pinstripe pant suit. 'My *ragazzo*, Jett, is Max's younger *fratello*. Jett do the photographs with me. You'll fall in love with him, Sofia. *Every* woman falls in *amore* with my Jett. He's *delizioso, sì*?' she said to Amy, who stood transfixed to the spot.

Amy nodded silently. So Jett was the male model in the photographs with Gianna. Jett was working for Courtenelli. Could *anything* be worse?

'Where *was* this party?' Sofia asked, bristling because she hadn't been invited.

'It was my rehearsal dinner,' Amy quickly explained. 'I didn't spend much time there because my friend, Tina, went into labour, and I left to go with her and her husband to the hospital.'

'Max is *molto bene*, you are *buona* girl.' Gianna sighed. 'He is *bello*, rich, and – how you say in your country? Sexy. *Is* he sexy?' she added in a teasing voice. '*Molto* sexy?'

'Excuse me?' Amy said, taken aback.

Gianna gurgled with laughter, all gleaming white teeth and lightly tanned, glowing skin. 'If he is anything like my Jett, you are one very *contento* woman.'

'When do *I* get to meet Jett?' Sofia asked, holding out her hand and admiring her blood-red manicure.

'Today,' Gianna said casually. 'He be here later.'

'Did you need me for something?' Amy asked, realizing she'd have to come up with an excuse to leave work early if she didn't want to see him again – which, of course, she *did*.

'Ah, yes,' Sofia said, tapping her tapered fingers together. 'It would be excellent for Gianna and myself to have lunch with Liz Smith.'

'Today?' Amy questioned, startled. Did Sofia honestly believe that Liz Smith would be free on a moment's notice?

'If Liz can manage it,' Sofia said airily. 'If not, maybe tomorrow. What day you do photographs, Gianna?'

Gianna shrugged. 'I'm not sure.'

'Let me ask Nigel,' Amy said, desperate to get out of Sofia's office. 'I'll call Liz and get back to you. I'm sure she'd love to meet Gianna.'

'She *should*,' Sofia said haughtily. 'Gianna is the most famous model in Italy. During fashion week who does *every* designer beg for?' A dramatic pause. 'Gianna and Naomi Campbell. No other model can touch them.'

'I'm sure,' Amy muttered, dying to leave. 'Is there anything else?' she asked, trying not to let her feelings show.

'No,' Sofia said, dismissing her with an arrogant wave.

'Wait,' Gianna said. 'If this Liz, whoever she is, cannot lunch with us today, how about *you*, Amy?'

'Oh, no,' Amy said quickly. 'I usually grab something at my desk. I couldn't possibly encroach on your time with Sofia.'

'Is okay,' Sofia said, smiling at Amy in a patronizing way. 'Is not usual I lunch with my staff, but today I make exception. You come with us, Amy.'

'I'd love that,' Amy said, thinking, *I can't imagine anything I'd like less.* 'Uh, let me go find out if Liz Smith is available and I'll get back to you.'

She fled from Sofia's office. She'd been trying to put a good face on things, but seeing Gianna in the light of day, the reality of it all sunk in. She'd *slept* with this gorgeous super-model's boyfriend, and even though he'd turned out to be

Max's brother, she couldn't stop thinking about him. Which was sick, *really* sick.

It was supposed to have been a fling, a tempestuous one-night fling to prepare her for a great marriage, a *safe* marriage, where she'd be with Max forever, and they'd have fantastic sex and live happily ever after.

Only she and Max hadn't had sex yet, and judging from last night it wasn't going to be *that* fantastic.

Max hadn't called today. Was he mad about last night? Did he think she'd come on too strong?

If he thought that, it was ridiculous – she was *marrying* the man, they had to work things out.

She decided to give him a buzz, then she thought, no, let him call her, *he* was the one who'd rushed her out of his apartment.

She hurried to find Nigel, who was working in the design room. 'When is Gianna doing the photographs?' she asked.

'The shoot is set for tomorrow,' Nigel said, studying a series of sketches.

'And your favourite Italian also wants to know who the photographer is.'

'Ah . . . the fantastic Antonio,' Nigel replied, starry-eyed at the thought of being in the presence of such a famous photographer. 'We should all be there – you, me, Yolanda and Dana. There'll be a catered lunch and scads of champagne. It will be an amazing day.'

'Exactly what I need,' Amy said irritably.

'You sound a tad snippy.'

'I am.'

'Why?'

'Sofia wants me to have lunch with her and Gianna.'

'I'd be *honoured* if Sofia asked *me* to lunch,' Nigel said, suffering a momentary twinge of jealousy. 'And you're not pleased?'

'How can I sit there with those two women all through lunch? It's not my thing.'

'*Make* it your thing, dear,' Nigel said sagely. 'If you want to move up in this company, *make* it your thing.'

*　*　*

After fetching Nanny Reece and Lulu from a downstairs apartment, Elliott Minor allowed the female detective to question Lulu for five minutes. Max didn't like it, but as Elliot explained to him, nobody had anything to hide, and it was best to co-operate.

Nobody has anything to hide, Max thought grimly. *I do. I have Vladimir Bushkin to hide. And what am I going to do about that?*

It was a problem, because telling what he knew about Vladimir Bushkin would open up an investigation that might be ruinous for not only him but Lulu, and he was more concerned about his little daughter than anything else. The scandal and publicity would turn him into a joke – but for Lulu it would be even worse: she would be branded forever as the illegitimate child of the murdered Russian bigamist.

After speaking to the detective, a frightened and subdued Lulu ran straight into his arms. 'I want my mommy,' she whimpered, cuddling up to him. 'Somebody hurt my mommy.'

'It'll be all right, sweetie,' he assured her, enveloping her in a hug. 'Daddy's taking care of everything.'

Nanny Reece was now in the other room talking to Detective Rodriguez. Max needed to speak with Elliott, so he carried Lulu into the kitchen, switched the TV to a cartoon channel, instructed the maids to watch her for a few minutes, then went to find Elliott.

'What's going on?' he demanded. 'I have to get Lulu and her nanny out of here.'

'Be patient, Max,' Elliott counselled. 'Let's not antagonize anyone.'

'Don't talk to me about antagonizing people,' he said angrily. 'That detective has been nothing but rude to me.'

'I understand, Max. Calm down, I'll settle this.'

'You don't *get* it, do you, Elliott?' he said through gritted teeth. 'They're treating me as if I'm a suspect.'

'It's routine to question the husband, especially the *ex*-husband.'

'I'm not your average ex-husband,' Max said, steaming. 'You think I look like some construction worker who stabs his wife to death in a drunken rage?'

'Stay calm, Max.'

'Quit telling me to stay calm,' he snapped. 'My daughter's in shock. Fucking Nanny is talking to a detective, and I WANT TO GET OUT OF HERE.'

'I understand,' Elliott said. 'I'll see what I can do.' He left the room and returned almost immediately. 'I've just been advised there are press downstairs.'

'Are you kidding me?' Max said, outraged. 'How did the press find out?'

'They listen in on police scanners. They have spies in the Police Department. They find out everything.'

'I am *not* talking to the press,' Max fumed.

'I know that. I'll arrange for your driver to meet us in the underground garage.'

'This is a nightmare, Elliott.'

'Life goes on,' Elliott said, spewing out a suitable cliché. 'You'll get over this.'

'Easy for you to say,' Max said, storming back into the living room.

Five minutes later Elliott came to find him. 'Detective Rodriguez informed me you're free to go.'

'He said that, did he? So he can run and check out my alibi. Christ! I need to talk to my brother.' As soon as he mentioned Chris, he remembered the early-morning meeting with Red he'd failed to attend. '*That*'s why I can't get hold of him,' he muttered.

'Who can't you get hold of?' Elliott inquired.

'My brother, Chris.'

'I'm glad you have family to turn to, this is a sad day. Mariska was a lovely woman.'

'No, she wasn't,' Max contradicted, shaking his head. 'Mariska was a money-hungry social-climber. *You* know that better than anyone. *You* were the one who went through my divorce with me.'

'I'm sure she didn't deserve to die like this,' Elliott said, uncomfortable with Max's harsh words.

'You're right,' Max replied, suddenly weary. 'Nobody deserves that.'

Chapter Forty-Five

Before Lady Jane Bentley was able to reveal anything more to Chris and Jett, Red Diamond made his entry into the library, flanked on either side by Sonja and Famka. They made a bizarre trio, the old billionaire and the two high-class call-girls, both towering over him in their tight-fitting suits and stiletto heels.

'Sorry I'm late,' Red said, not sorry at all. 'I'm sure Janey here has been keeping you entertained.'

Lady Jane remained seated on the couch, her eyes shooting daggers. 'Red,' she said, in a deceptively quiet tone, 'we're *so* glad you could make it. I was filling the boys in on a few things I thought they should know.' Her eyes swivelled to take in Sonja and Famka. '*Do* introduce us to your friends.'

She managed to make 'friends' sound like the dirtiest word in the dictionary.

'Can't remember their names.' Red cackled. 'Only the size of their tits.'

Meanwhile Sonja had spotted Chris, and he'd recognized her. Brazenly she flaunted his stolen watch on her wrist, daring him to say anything.

He didn't. He was smart enough to stay silent and watch this scenario play out.

Famka was busy checking out Jett. She had a weakness for hot young guys. She winked at him – a wink that promised, *For you I'm available and free.*

'It looks like you're busy,' Chris said, not wishing to become involved in the scene that he knew was about to take place, 'so I guess this meeting – which, by the way, never happened – is over.'

'Over?' Red roared. 'It hasn't even begun.'

'Too bad,' Chris responded. ''Cause I never *did* like the circus, even when I was a kid.'

'You always *were* the one with the mouth,' Red said, bobbing his head up and down. 'Shame you're so weak. You could've made something of yourself if you weren't such a loser.'

'Yeah,' Chris said, remaining surprisingly calm. 'I could've been like you, right? A miserable old bastard hanging out with hookers sixty years younger.'

'Let's go, Chris,' Jett said, realizing just how nasty this could get if they didn't make a fast exit.

'Oh,' Red said, turning to glare at his youngest son. 'The fuck-up has a voice.'

'*You*'re the fuck-up,' Jett retaliated, immediately losing it. 'You and your billions think you control everything. Well, here's a news flash. You can't control us.'

'I can't, huh?' Red shouted. 'Is that why you all came running to New York when I summoned you? Run, run, run. Pick up your ticket and run to Daddy. What did you think? That I was on my *death* bed? That you were about to inherit my money? Is that why you came?'

'I came 'cause I thought you might've changed,' Jett muttered. 'Crazy, huh? To think I had a father who might've cared.'

'Red will never change,' Lady Jane said, still maintaining her composure. 'I think we all know that.'

'*You*'re still here,' Red said, feigning surprise. 'Thought I told you to pack up and get out.'

'Apparently I didn't hear you,' she said. 'Perhaps I was too busy reading your will, which I was on the point of telling your sons about. I'm sure they'll be as fascinated as I was.'

'You know *nothing* about my will,' Red snarled.

'We'll see about that.'

Sonja was getting bored. Family dramas were not her thing, she'd had enough of her own back in Slovakia. Idly she wondered about the woman sitting on the couch. An angry, repressed woman wearing Chanel and a very tasty diamond watch. Was she the old man's wife? Mistress?

Whoever she was, she was one furious bitch and, quite frankly, Sonja couldn't blame her. What woman *wouldn't* be angry if their husband or lover walked in with two incredibly sexy women on each arm?

'Excuse me, Mr Diamond.' Diahann had entered the room. With all the shouting going on, nobody had heard her knock.

Sonja and Famka both turned to inspect the newcomer. She was black and quite attractive in an understated way. Late thirties, dressed in drab clothes, she could be a knock-out if she tried.

'*What?*' Red yelled, not pleased with the interruption.

'It's the phone for Chris,' Diahann said, giving Sonja and Famka a disapproving look. 'It's Max, he says it's very important.'

'I'll take it,' Chris said, glad for the diversion. Diahann handed him the phone and he walked over to the other side of the room. 'Where are you?' he asked, in a low voice. 'You won't believe what's going on here.'

'Meet me at my apartment,' Max said urgently. 'Something terrible has happened. Mariska's dead. She's been murdered.'

*　　*　　*

Naturally Liz Smith could not make lunch given such short notice, so Amy was stuck. She rode in the car with Sofia and Gianna to the Grill Room at the Four Seasons restaurant. The two Italian women jabbered away in their native tongue, while Amy sat next to Sofia's driver feeling like a hostage on her way to an execution.

She'd already decided there was nothing to dislike about Gianna: the Italian supermodel was unbearably beautiful and just as charming as everyone said. The more time Amy spent with her, the more she was unable to understand why Jett had cheated on such a gorgeous woman. Grandma Poppy was right. All men were dogs. All men cheated. Except Max. She was sure he wouldn't cheat: he had too much character, which was why she loved him.

Yes, I do love him.

Come on.

Lunch at the Grill Room was a ritual. The spacious restaurant was crowded with various power players who occupied their usual tables. See and be seen.

Gianna was certainly seen – heads turned as the stunning supermodel followed Sofia to their table.

Amy trailed behind the two flamboyant women, feeling totally miserable. She wondered what time Jett was showing up at the House of Courtenelli. If they ran into each other, would he acknowledge her? Or was he prepared to ignore their one night of incredible, mind-blowing, fantastic sex? She wondered if he was thinking about her as much as she was thinking about him.

She *had* to get over to the hospital and discuss the situation with Tina. Somehow or other she was determined to make a daring escape from this abysmal lunch.

*   *   *

Pacing round his apartment waiting for Chris to get there, Max knew he should call Amy and tell her before she heard it on the news. Not only were the press downstairs in Mariska's building, they were also gathered outside *his* apartment building, both being part of the Max Diamond empire. This would make their story even juicier.

He'd already called Clive Barnaby and apprised him of the situation. 'You'll have to deal with the Japanese,' he'd said. 'If they're not happy with that, reschedule my meeting with them for the morning.'

Clive had assured him he'd do everything he could to persuade them to come up with the money.

Max was hoping that when he contacted Amy, she would offer to collect Lulu and take her away from the explosion of publicity he knew was about to happen: Mariska Diamond was hardly a nobody – she'd been married to *him*. The woman had courted publicity, she'd made *sure* she was part of the New York social scene. This was a headline story.

'I want my mommy,' Lulu cried, coming into his bedroom, tears streaking her pretty little face. 'When can I see my mommy?'

'Soon, baby,' he said, trying to sound cheerful. 'How about you watch a DVD of *Finding Nemo* or *The Incredibles* with Nanny? Is that a plan?'

'No *Finding Nemo*! No *Incredibles*!' Lulu shouted, stamping her foot. 'I WANT MY MOMMY!'

Christ! Where was Nanny Reece when he needed her?

He found her in the kitchen on the phone. 'Who are you talking to?' he demanded, paranoid that she might be working out a deal with the *National Enquirer* to sell her story.

'I'm sorry, Mr Diamond,' Nanny Reece said, all crisp and English. 'I'm booking a ticket home to England. America is not for me. I cannot take the violence.'

'You can't do that,' he said, quite staggered that she would even contemplate deserting Lulu at a time like this.

'Oh, I think I can,' she said, tight-lipped.

'You'd leave Lulu?'

'I'm sorry, Mr Diamond, I have to go.'

'What if I double the salary you're getting now?'

'It's not a question of money.'

Damn the woman! She wasn't any good anyway – she paid absolutely no attention to Lulu. He should have noticed it before, and Mariska *certainly* should've noticed.

'When are you leaving?' he asked, resigning himself to the situation.

'This afternoon.'

What an inconsiderate incompetent *cow*. If this was her attitude, they were better off without her.

* * *

'We have to go,' Chris said to Jett, clicking off the phone. 'Max has an emergency.'

'Why isn't Max here?' Red demanded. 'More financial disasters he's not man enough to handle?'

'You'd enjoy that, wouldn't you?' Lady Jane said, joining

in. 'Perhaps you can find *another* bank to blackmail, forcing them to withdraw from Max's big building project.'

'How dare you speak about matters that don't concern you?' Red said, his face darkening with anger.

'I can speak about anything I want,' she responded, her composure intact.

Chris was already at the door. 'Put on the TV,' he suggested. 'Find out for yourselves what's going on.'

Red was furious, he had not had the opportunity to make his planned announcement to his sons. It was all Jane's fault – she'd ruined everything. 'You see these lovely young ladies?' he said, giving her a spiteful glare. 'They'll be moving in here with me.'

Sonja and Famka exchanged a startled look – this was news to them.

'How *nice* that you plan to fill your house with whores,' Lady Jane said, remaining icy and controlled. 'According to the private papers I read, along with your Will, you always *did* enjoy helping out whores. So I suggest that if you do not wish me to make my information public, you will work out a very generous settlement with my lawyer. Only *then* will I leave this house.'

She arose from the couch and, without so much as glancing at Sonja and Famka, swept out of the room.

'Moving in?' Sonja said. 'Not me.'

'What do you mean, not you?' Red growled. 'For enough money you'll get down on all fours and lick my boots if I order you to.'

'What do you think it will cost you for us to move in?' Famka questioned, always the businesswoman. 'Possibly more money than even *you*'re prepared to spend. We are *very* expensive girls.'

'How do *you* know what I'm prepared to spend?' he said, narrowing his eyes.

'Your wife seems serious about getting a big settlement,' Sonja remarked. 'The bitch means business.'

'She's *not* my wife,' he said, scowling.

'She sure acts like one,' Sonja said, smoothing down the jacket of her tightly fitted suit.

'What's with her anyway?' Famka added. 'She certainly doesn't like you.'

Red decided he didn't want to keep them around after all, they talked too much, they asked questions, they were getting on his nerves. It was one thing when they were striding around his apartment, naked, giving him intense pleasure. But somehow, in his house, they were just two over-made-up hookers. Besides, he had to clear things up with Jane. How *dare* she pretend she knew all his secrets? *Nobody* knew all of Red Diamond's secrets, that was for sure.

'The two of you can get out now,' he said, still scowling.

'We're happy to leave,' Famka responded, 'as soon as you've paid us.'

'I've paid you plenty. Now go.'

'Not enough for *this* trip.' Sonja snorted derisively.

'Jesus Christ!' he said angrily. 'You're nothing but two greedy whores.'

'And that's just the way you like us, isn't it?' Famka said.

'Yes,' Sonja agreed, fingering her stolen Rolex. 'Especially when your little cock is in our tight mouths, and you're coming all over our tits.'

'Get out!' he shouted, reaching into his pocket and tossing a handful of hundred-dollar bills at them.

'You know where to find us when you need our services again,' Famka said pleasantly, always thinking ahead.

'GET OUT OF MY HOUSE!' Red screamed.

The two women picked up their money and made their exit, leaving the room filled with the aroma of their expensive perfumes.

Muttering to himself, Red clicked on the TV.

*   *   *

'What's going on?' Jett asked, following Chris out to the street.

'You won't believe this,' Chris said, flagging down a cab.

'Fill me in, then I'll tell you whether I believe you or not.'

'It's Mariska.'

'Max's ex?'

'That's right. According to Max, she's been killed.'

'*Huh?*'

'Murdered was the word he used. *Murdered.*'

* * *

After pushing a salad around her plate while Gianna and Sofia continued to chat animatedly in Italian, Amy finally spoke up, claiming she wasn't feeling well.

'I come with you to the ladies' room,' Gianna announced, full of concern. 'You sit for a minute, we put wet cloth on your forehead. You feel better.'

'No, no, really, it's just a splitting headache,' Amy said, determined not to get caught in anymore traps. 'Miz Courtenelli,' she added, appealing to Sofia, 'do you mind if I leave?'

Sofia shrugged. She couldn't have cared less.

'Take Sofia's car back to your apartment,' Gianna offered. 'You call later to say how you feel.'

'*Scuse?*' Sofia said, irritated that Gianna felt free to offer her car to one of her minions. 'Get a cab, Amy. Put it on your expense account.'

'Thanks,' Amy said, jumping up.

Once out of the restaurant she walked a couple of blocks, waved down a cab and told the driver to take her to the hospital, where she hoped to find Brad gone.

Maybe, if she was lucky, she'd finally get to speak to Tina.

* * *

Several TV trucks, crews and on-air talent were out on the street, with a scattering of photographers, taking up key positions outside Max's apartment building

'Keep your head down and walk right in,' Chris warned. 'They don't know us. And if they ask any questions, we know nothing.'

'Got it,' Jett replied.

Chris paid the cab and they made a dash inside.

The officious desk clerk stopped them. 'Who're you here to see?' he demanded.

'Max Diamond,' Chris said. 'Tell him his brothers are downstairs.'

The desk clerk called up to Max's apartment, then motioned them to the elevator. 'The penthouse,' he said.

'What else do you think Lady Jane was about to tell us?' Jett asked as they entered the elevator.

'Who knows? She's got *something* on her mind, and it's obviously something he'd prefer we didn't hear from her.'

'How about him walking in with those two hookers from Max's bachelor party?' Jett said, lighting up a cigarette and inhaling deeply. '*That* was a scene and a half.'

'You wanna hear the kicker?' Chris said. 'One of them was the girl who stole my watch.'

'The *your-cock-needs-a-service girl*?'

'Right on.'

'*Shit!*'

Max was waiting at the door of the elevator. He hugged them both. 'Thanks for coming,' he said, looking wrecked. 'It means a lot.'

'Just take it easy,' Chris said, putting his arm round his older brother's shoulders, 'and tell us what happened.'

'Let's go in the living room,' Max said wearily. 'I think I could manage a drink.'

*   *   *

By the time Amy got back to the hospital, Tina's room was overflowing with flower arrangements, celebratory balloons and baby gifts. To Amy's relief, Brad was nowhere in sight.

Tina's face lit up when she saw Amy. 'I'm desperately trying to feed the little tyke,' she wailed, holding baby Brad close to her breast. 'Believe me, it's not as simple as they tell you.'

'It doesn't *look* simple,' Amy remarked, checking out the cards on the flower arrangements. Naturally there was a tasteful vase of mixed roses from Nancy – a woman who prided herself on always being socially correct.

'I'm glad you're back,' Tina said enthusiastically. 'I need to hear *everything*.'

'It's like I told you earlier,' Amy said, perching on the end of the bed. 'It turns out Mystery Man is Max's *brother*.'

'That's so *not* good news.'

'Exactly,' Amy said grimly. 'Now tell me, *what* am I supposed to do about *that*?'

'There's nothing you *can* do.'

'That's helpful, Tina,' she said. 'I mean, should I make out like we've never met before, that we haven't been in bed together and shared fantastic sex? Am I supposed to pretend it never happened?'

'Maybe a conversation would be in order,' Tina suggested. 'Only if he didn't say anything to you, why would *you* be the one to open it up?'

'Because I *have* to,' Amy insisted.

'When are you doing this?' Tina asked.

'I don't know,' she wailed, as her cellphone buzzed. 'Oh, God, I'm so confused,' she added, checking out caller ID. 'It's my mother,' she said, grimacing. 'I'm not taking it.'

'Why?'

'You *know* why. She'll be full of complaints about me leaving last night.'

'I'm sure she's not mad,' Tina said, gesturing to an overcrowded side table. 'Look at the beautiful roses she sent me.'

'Ha! That's *her* doing the right thing. If I know my mother, she's mad all right.'

Almost immediately the phone next to Tina's bed started ringing. Tina reached over and picked up. 'Hi, Brad,' she said, snuggling the baby even closer. 'Brad Junior is doing well. I've got a feeling he misses you. He's so *cute*, his eyelashes are getting longer, along with everything else.' She paused to listen for a moment, then, 'Amy,' she said urgently. 'Put on the TV. Go to CNN.'

'Why?'

'Just *do* it.'

And there it was, all over the news, the story covering Mariska's murder.

Chapter Forty-Six

Damon held her face and kissed her with an intensity she'd never experienced before. Some men could kiss and some men couldn't. Damon was a master.

Liberty closed her eyes, allowing herself to be swept up in the moment.

How was this happening? How had this adventure begun? And where would it end? Damon was married, taken, unavailable.

And yet . . . she couldn't stop herself getting lost in his arms. His lips were driving her crazy, his tongue exploring her mouth, his hands starting an exploration of their own.

It took all of her willpower, but somehow or other she managed to push him away.

'What?' he said impatiently.

'You're married,' she stated.

'You got somethin' against marriage?'

'No.'

'Hey, I could tell you my wife doesn't understand me,' he said, smiling lazily. 'The deal is she understands me big-time. We, uh, kinda got an arrangement.'

'It's not my—'

Before she could finish what she was about to say, he was kissing her again, his hands slowly working their way under her sweater.

Oh, God! Why was this happening? Arrangement or not, he belonged to another woman, and she wasn't prepared to share.

She'd arrived at his office promptly at six-thirty, although she almost hadn't made it. After the second go-see she'd raced home and changed clothes. She'd put on a soft white sweater, chocolate brown cargo pants, and brown furry boots, purposely not wearing anything provocative. She'd gone for serious as opposed to sexy, tying her long dark hair back in a ponytail and adding some tinted winter shades she'd picked up for ten bucks from a shopping cart. They were a copy of a Chanel pair, and they looked cool, although she realized they'd last about ten minutes before they snapped in two.

'Hello there, LL,' he'd said, greeting her with a brief hug. 'Lookin' good.'

'Hi,' she'd responded, breathing in his expensive after-shave, her eyes darting around his office checking out the gold records and plaques on the walls, the award statues including several Grammys and many other awards. On his huge Perspex desk stood a silver-framed photo of his wife, the Princess Tashmir.

'Sit,' he'd said, indicating a comfortable leather couch.

Damn! She was intimidated by all the trappings of his success. He was Damon P. Donnell, and who was she? Just another would-be singer scratching for a break.

'Gimme,' he'd said, reaching out for her demo CD.

She'd handed it over, knowing he'd hate it, shivering with the anticipation of defeat.

There were two songs on the CD, both her own compositions. They were edgy, with lyrics true to her heart, but they certainly weren't hip-hop or rap.

He'd put on her CD and sat back behind his desk listening intently, his face expressionless, leaving her no clue as to what he was thinking.

She'd sat on the couch across from him, fists clenched, sweat trickling down her back, totally freaked out with nerves.

When the two songs were finished, he'd stood up, walked over to her, and somehow or other the kissing had begun.

She knew she should've shoved him away immediately, not allowed anything to get started. But she was so damned anxious to know what he had to say about her music. It was the reason she was here. The reason she existed.

And he'd said nothing.

Now he was kissing her, groping her. It was a cruel and unusual punishment, yet she didn't want him to stop.

Finally she summoned the strength to push him away again. 'My music,' she began, trying not to sound too needy. 'That's why I'm here.'

'Is *that* why you're here?' he asked, smoky eyes all over her.

'You *know* it's why I'm here,' she said, swallowing hard.

'Nothin' else?' he questioned, giving her that look of his, that sexy, knowing look.

'Like what?' she said, pretending she didn't know what he was talking about, although the sexual tension was steaming up the room.

'Hey, surely you understand that you an' me, we got somethin' special goin' on,' he said, those eyes of his working their usual magic.

Desperately she tried to conjure up Beverly's words of warning – *He's 'bout as married as a dude can get . . . No different from all the other horn-dogs out there . . . Damon's always out to score the prize . . . He's never gonna change . . .*

'Look,' she said, making a supreme effort not to weaken, 'special or not, you're *married*, so this has to be strictly business. Either you're into my music or you're not.'

'An' how about if I *was* into it – you think that'd score me points?'

'Points?'

'A little sugar an' cream?'

'No,' she said, refusing to meet his eyes, they were too damn tempting.

'Man, you're cold,' he complained. 'Cold an' hot at the same time. Irresistible combination, baby, an' you know it.'

'I guess you're not interested in my music,' she said, sucking up her disappointment that he was – after all – just another horny guy with one thing on his mind.

'Hey, don't get all uptight on me – you *do* have somethin'. I dig your voice. It's Mary J. Blige mixed with a little bit of Alicia Keys. Husky. Sexy. You got soul, girl. I like that.'

'Really?'

'You *know* you're cool. Gotta get that confident vibe goin'. Course, it's not the kinda stuff I usually put out on my label, but I'm thinkin' I'll get you together with a producer who'll know what t' do with you.'

'You'd do that?' she asked hopefully, not sure whether to believe him or not.

'Gotta do *somethin'* t'keep you comin' back,' he said, throwing her one of his killer smiles. 'Right, babe?'

And it was then that she realized Cindi was right – she'd fallen in love with a married man. And how dumb was *that*?

Before things progressed further, she decided she'd better get the hell out of there. It was too dangerous to stay. She was too attracted to him – and, as she kept on reminding herself over and over, HE WAS MARRIED! Plus, mixing business with pleasure was never cool.

'I have to go,' she said, edging towards the door.

'Yeah?' he said, following her. 'What's the panic?'

'I'm working,' she lied – the same lie she'd used on Kev.

'Blow it off.'

'I can't.'

'Thought we might grab a bite,' he said, moving even closer.

'Just you, me and your wife?'

'What *is* it with you?' he said, giving her a quizzical look. 'All this wife shit is gettin' old.'

'Uh . . . did I mention that I have a boyfriend?' she said, backing away from him.

'Is that supposed to scare me off?' he said teasingly, his eyes all over her.

'No,' she said breathlessly. 'Your *wife* is supposed to scare you off.'

'Oh, man!' he said, laughing.

'What?' she said, thrown by his cavalier attitude.

'Seems you're more concerned about my wife than I am.'

''Cause *I'm* the one who'll get hammered if she finds out you're playing on her.'

'My wife wouldn't mess with you,' he assured her.

'Why not?' she asked boldly.

''Cause *I* wouldn't let her.'

'Word is she's a wild thing when it comes to watching out for you.'

'No, baby, *you*'re the wild thing,' he said, taking another step towards her. 'I can feel it on your lips, it's in those crazy green eyes of yours, that body . . .'

'I have to go,' she said quickly, her hand on the door.

He handed her a black card engraved with gold lettering. 'In case you get home an' change your mind, here's my *private* cell number. You never know, LL, you could get *real* hungry later . . .'

'When can I meet with the producer?' she asked, thinking that if she stuck to business somehow she'd be safe.

'Tomorrow,' he said, watching her intently. 'Same time, same place.'

'I'll be here.' And before he could get any closer, she was out of there, almost running into the elevator, trying not to think about how irresistibly attractive she found him.

Damon P. Donnell. Who would've thought a few days ago he'd be coming onto her this way? She'd served him coffee for weeks on end and he'd ignored her, acted as if she didn't exist. Now *this*. He'd even given her his private number.

It was crazy, yet exhilarating. *And* he was putting her together with a producer in spite of the fact that she wasn't falling into his bed or his car or the couch in his office.

Wow, he's something else, she thought. *I could really go for him.*

But it's not going to happen, her stern inner voice warned. *'Cause falling in lust with Damon P. Donnell would be the worst damn thing you could do.*

Back at the apartment the answering-machine she shared with Cindi was flashing five messages. They were probably all for Cindi. They usually were.

She opened a can of Campbell's tomato soup and poured it into a pan to heat it. It occurred to her that if she wasn't so full of principles she could be sitting in a fancy restaurant eating lobster and steak with Damon. Then later she could be falling into his bed, making wild passionate love.

But, hey, she *did* have principles, and nothing was going to happen sexually, just career-wise. That was all she asked for. Let him help her get some kind of singing career started.

For a moment she thought about the way he'd kissed her.

It was *so* damn *hot*. Damon P. Donnell was some fucking great kisser. The best.

The *married* best. Married, married, *married*. Had to keep reminding herself.

The soup was bubbling, so she grabbed a bowl, poured it in, and sat at the counter that separated the minuscule kitchen area from the living space.

While she was eating she leaned over and pressed the button on the answering-machine.

Message one: *Cindi, it's Moose, an' it's Monday. You was supposed to phone me, woman, an' I'm waitin'. Don't be keepin' me waitin' like this.*

Message two: *Hey, babe, Kev here, but you know that. Just got called on another outta town gig. I'm leavin' tonight, so later.*

Message three: *Liberty, it's Mom. Please call me back, it's important.*

Message four: *Hi, Liberty, Bruce here. Congratulations. You got the job. Contact the agency immediately you receive this message.*

She leaped up, pressed repeat and listened to Bruce all over again. *You got the job!* How fantastic was *that*? Oh, man, the woman who took the Polaroids must've liked her. Unfortunately she had no clue what the job was.

She wished Cindi was around to share her good news, but no, Cindi had moved out.

Grinning to herself she played message five, it was Diahann again. What did *she* want?

Before she could find out, Bruce called a second time. 'Aren't *you* the lucky girl?' he said. 'Three days in Malibu. They want you on a ten o'clock plane to L.A. tonight.'

'Excuse me?' she said, stunned.

'Look, I'm at the theatre with my wife, so I can't talk, but I hope you're about to say yes, Liberty, because I can assure you that opportunities like this do not happen every day.'

'Tonight?' she said, her head spinning. 'I have to leave *tonight*?'

'That's what I said. Thirty thousand, all expenses paid. The agency takes a thirty-five per cent commission. Are you on e-mail?'

'Uh . . . no,' she mumbled, thinking, *Did he just say thirty thousand?*

'Then I'll fax you papers to sign.'

'I–I don't have a fax machine,' she stuttered, still in shock.

'They've booked you into *Shutters* in Santa Monica, I can fax you there. There'll be a car to pick you up at LAX. And an e-ticket waiting for you at the United desk at Kennedy. This is your shot, Liberty, do *not* blow it. *Bon voyage.*'

Chapter Forty-Seven

Max's main concern was getting Lulu settled somewhere safe, far away from the prying eyes of the press. Fortunately Amy came through. As soon as she heard the news she rushed over to his apartment, full of concern and caring. 'Oh, Max,' she said, hugging him tightly. 'I'm so sorry. It's such a terrible tragedy.'

'I know,' he responded, holding onto her.

'Did they break in? Was it a robbery?' she asked, extracting herself.

'That's what the detectives seem to think.'

'I don't know what to say. It's just awful, Max. I wish there was something I could do.'

'There is. I'd like you to take Lulu for a couple of days. Her nanny's quitting on me, and Lulu shouldn't be around here with the press setting up camp outside.'

'There's no question I'll take her. It's the very least I can do.'

'Thanks, sweetheart, it means a lot to me.'

'Don't *wanna* go, Daddy,' Lulu muttered, lower lip quivering when he informed her she was going home with Amy. 'Wanna stay *here* with *you*.'

'You can't, sweetie,' he explained. 'Daddy's got things he has to take care of. Important things.'

'Then I want my mommy,' Lulu said, putting on a stubborn face. 'Where's my mommy?'

'We had to take Mommy to the hospital, but she's going to be okay, and she wants you to spend the night with Amy.'

'We go see Mommy, Daddy,' Lulu said hopefully. 'Just you an' me. We go see her *now*!'

'Soon,' he promised.

'Then Lulu stay here with Nanny.'

'Nanny Reece has to fly back to England.'

Lulu's pretty face crumpled. 'Why, Daddy? *Why?*'

'Because she does. Don't worry, sweetie, Amy will take care of you. It's only for a day or so.'

'Do I *have* to go with stupid Amy, Daddy?' Lulu said, scowling.

'Please don't call Amy names,' Max warned. 'It's not nice.'

Jett stepped forward and scooped Lulu up into his arms. 'Hey, pretty girl, how about *I* come too? Is that okay with you?'

'Yes!' Lulu squealed, her scowl turning into a coquettish little smile. 'My uncle come too.'

'Thanks,' Max said gratefully, as Lulu snuggled up to Jett. 'That'd be a big help.'

Amy was silent. She was horrified enough about Mariska's brutal murder, and now she was going to have to deal with Jett. This wasn't the right time for them to sort out what had happened between them.

'I'll call you later,' Max said, kissing Amy's cheek as he accompanied the three of them to the elevator. 'Take care of my girls,' he said to Jett. 'They're both very precious.'

'Yeah,' Jett said. 'I'll do my best.'

As the elevator doors closed, Amy turned to Lulu. 'We're going to have so much *fun*,' she said brightly.

'No, we're not,' Lulu responded. 'We're not! We're not! We're *not*!'

Amy exchanged a quick look with Jett. 'It'll be fine,' he mouthed.

Easy for *him* to say. He wasn't a quivering, nervous, guilt-ridden *wreck*.

* * *

After everyone left, Max began filling Chris in on the Vladimir story – including Mariska's threat to have the man taken care of.

Chris listened intently. 'And *you* think he took care of *her* instead?' he said thoughtfully when Max was finished.

'That's *exactly* what I think,' Max replied, his expression grim.

'But you can't be sure?'

'I'm sure all right. Vladimir is an evil son-of-a-bitch with a big agenda. He was after money and plenty of it. Somehow Mariska must've got in his way, so he decided to get rid of her.'

'Shouldn't you tell the detectives what you know?'

'Are you *shitting* me?' Max exploded. 'Have you any idea what the press would do to me if they got hold of the truth? They'd crucify me. And what do you think they'd do to Lulu? She's *illegitimate*, Chris. And God knows what Mariska did back in Russia – it's possible she was a prostitute.'

'Then you're not telling the detectives anything?' Chris said, frowning. 'You're allowing this Vladimir to walk around loose, a suspected murderer?'

'I need to see if Mariska kept any documents concerning him.'

'What about close girlfriends? Someone she might've confided in?'

'I doubt it. All Mariska cared about was running with the social set. She was relentless – only interested in who had the most money and what charity board she should get on that would elevate her social position.'

'You didn't know she was like that when you married her?'

'Unfortunately not.'

'Too bad,' Chris said. 'You could've saved yourself a lot of grief.'

'Do you think I don't know it?'

'Well, if you want my advice, you should tell the detectives everything, let *them* get into it, that's their job.'

'I appreciate your concern, but I have to wait.'

'For *what*?'

'Vladimir.'

'It's your call.'

'I know,' Max said, walking over to the window. 'Have you *seen* what's going on downstairs?' he muttered, peering out. 'The press are getting ready for a siege. You *do* realize that the entire family will be involved. Red, you, possibly even Amy. And—'

'Not me,' Chris interrupted quickly. 'I'm not part of this family.'

'You're my brother,' Max stated grimly. 'They'll find a way to drag you into it.'

'I've *never* traded on the Diamond name,' Chris pointed out.

'You think *I* have?'

'None of us did, so there's no reason why we'd get brought into it.'

'The media will start digging for anything they can.'

'I'm a lawyer,' Chris said, scratching his chin. 'They say or print anything inaccurate and I'll sue their asses.'

'Keep that thought. It's not going to stop them.'

'You don't think so, huh?'

'Not the New York press. They're relentless.'

'You missed the morning meeting with Red,' Chris said.

'Is he leaving us everything?' Max asked sarcastically.

'He walked in with two hookers on his arm.'

'Am I supposed to be surprised?'

'Lady Jane was sitting in the library pissed as a cat on a hot tin roof, and in he marches, bold as shit.'

'Friday he fails to turn up, and today you're telling me he walks in with hookers. What kind of game is he playing?'

'Who knows?'

'I'd better call Clive Barnaby,' Max said, glancing at his watch. 'He was meeting with the Japanese bankers on my behalf.'

'Before you make the call,' Chris said, 'you should know that Lady Jane let it drop it was *Red* who forced the U.S. banks to withdraw from your building project. Seems he has that kind of leverage.'

'*What?*' Max said, shocked and angry. '*Red* is responsible?'

'She showed us copies of his e-mails to the banks involved.'

'That conniving *bastard*!'

'Sorry, Max, he really screwed you.'

'Do you *realize* what that son-of-a-bitch has put me through? I could lose everything.'

'Guess what? Me too. Remember my gambling debt? Well, the pressure to pay is apparently coming from Red. It wouldn't surprise me if he's a major shareholder in the fucking casino. He's got his bony fingers in every pie.'

'Jesus *Christ!*' Max said, still steaming. 'Nothing changes, does it?'

'Hey, the bastard can't beat us with a stick, so he devises other ways to punish us. Dear old Dad, always full of any crap he can hand out.'

* * *

Standing in the elevator as it descended to the lobby, Jett glanced over at Amy. She was staring straight ahead, her perfect face quite impassive. 'You okay?' he asked, in a low voice, wondering what she was thinking.

'Thank you, yes,' she replied, trying not to look at him. She was not okay at all, her stomach was churning and she felt sick.

'Uh . . . I guess we need to talk,' he said tentatively.

'Not now,' she said, staring pointedly at Lulu. The little girl was busily sucking her thumb, her arms firmly clutched around Jett's neck.

'I didn't mean now,' he said, remembering the incredible softness of her skin and the way she smelt of soap and perfume and all things nice.

'Maybe later,' she said hesitantly, for she knew they couldn't continue to ignore what had happened between them. She didn't know about him, but for her the tension was a killer.

'Definitely later,' he agreed, thinking how vulnerable and pretty she looked in spite of everything.

Max's car was waiting downstairs in the garage. The three of them got in and the driver whisked them straight to Amy's apartment.

As soon as they walked into her place she felt awkward. Having Jett on her territory was extremely uncomfortable, they'd shared such intimacy, yet they were still virtual strangers.

'Uh . . . can I get you anything?' she asked, glad that she'd tidied up before leaving in the morning. Unlike her mother, who had maids on twenty-four-hour call, she preferred to have a cleaning lady come in only once a week – something Nancy never stopped complaining about.

'No, thanks,' he said, removing Lulu's arms from around his neck and putting the little girl down.

'Wanna see a movie,' Lulu said, immediately aware that she was not the centre of attention.

'I'm afraid I haven't got any children's DVDs,' Amy said helplessly.

'Anything in particular you'd like to see, pretty girl?' Jett asked, bending down to her.

'Wanna see *The Incredibles*,' Lulu said, in a high-pitched voice. 'Wanna see it with *you*.'

'Maybe we should take her out for something to eat,' Amy suggested. 'I've got nothing here. There's a coffee shop on the corner.'

'You hungry, Lulee?' Jett asked.

'Wanna see *The Incredibles*,' Lulu repeated.

'Okay, here's the deal,' he said. 'You, me and Amy will go downstairs to the video store and buy you the DVD of *The Incredibles*, then we'll take you for a burger. You like big fat burgers with onions and relish and all the trimmings?'

'Mommy says I mustn't eat hamburgers,' Lulu said primly.

'Special treat,' he said. 'burgers and french fries, and after that we'll come back here and watch the movie. How does *that* sound?'

'Only if you carry me,' Lulu said, quick as a flash. 'Carry me! Carry me! *Carry me!*'

'I can't carry you *everywhere* we go,' he said, laughing. 'You're too heavy. You're like a big lumpy sack of potatoes.'

'Potatoes,' Lulu repeated, almost cracking a smile. '*Big* sack of lumpy *potatoes!*'

'That's *right*, little girl.'

'I'm *not* little.'

'Fine – *big* girl. How's that?'

'Carry me! Carry me! *Carry me!*' Lulu chanted.

'Okay, okay,' he said, sweeping her up into his arms again. Then, glancing at Amy, he said, 'Y'know, Gianna and I, we're not a couple.'

'You don't have to explain anything to me,' she said, thinking how patient and understanding he was dealing with his niece.

'I thought you should know. That's all.'

'Now I do.' *And it makes no difference. I'm engaged to Max, and that's that.*

'Okay, Lulee,' Jett said. 'We're going on an adventure. Let's *blow* this pop stand.'

'Pop stand!' Lulu said, bursting into a fit of giggles. 'Pop stand! Pop stand! *Pop stand!*'

* * *

Sonja was looking forward to getting back to her apartment. Weekend jobs were not her favourite, even though they paid handsomely. She'd worked long and hard to have her own apartment, and now that she did, she enjoyed her time alone.

One of her rules was never to entertain any of her clients at home. It was either their place, a suitable venue, or a hotel. She made no exceptions.

Walking in, she was dismayed to find her cousin Igor sprawled on her pristine white couch in front of her new flat-screen TV, stuffing potato chips into his mouth.

'What the *hell* you doing here?' she demanded. 'I told you not to use my key. You're supposed to phone first.'

Igor gave her an unconcerned look. 'I'm your cousin,' he said reproachfully. 'Do not speak to me like that. What it matter to you anyway? You were away all weekend, didn't think you'd mind.'

'You *know* I mind,' she said bad-temperedly. 'I like my privacy.'

'Privacy,' he scoffed. 'How much *privacy* do the johns you spend all your time with give you?'

'My *clients* pay lot of money,' she said, stepping out of her shoes. 'And *you* never object to taking some of it.'

Igor was her favourite cousin, the only family member who'd made it to America. She had a soft spot for him, but he was always getting himself caught in 'situations', and she was always helping him out.

Sometimes she wished he'd find himself a legitimate job and stop sponging off her.

'I'm in a . . . situation,' he said. 'It's best I not go back to my place for day or so.'

'Why?' she said accusingly. 'What you done now?'

'Nothing,' he answered, yawning. 'Just bringing you gift 'cause you nice cousin.'

'What gift?' she asked suspiciously.

'Good one,' he said, scratching his belly.

'Let me see.'

Raising his body from the couch, he fumbled in his jacket pocket and produced a string of perfect white pearls.

Sonja grabbed them, held them up to the light and inspected them with a practised eye. 'Is real?' she asked, although as a canny connoisseur of jewellery she was quite sure that she already knew the correct answer.

'Of course real,' Igor replied indignantly. 'Very excellent quality. Cost me lot.'

'Liar,' Sonja said, fixing the pearls round her neck, noticing the intricate diamond clasp shaped like a flower, and wondering where he'd come across such a prize. She was no longer mad. Real pearls were real pearls, and they went nicely with her recently acquired Rolex.

All in all it had been quite a profitable weekend.

Chapter Forty-Eight

The two brothers were sitting in Max's living room, sharing a bottle of Jack Daniel's and several cartons of Chinese food Chris had sent out for. 'You gotta eat,' he'd informed Max. 'You've had nothing all day.'

It was past seven, and Max was finally starting to think sensibly. The day was a blur, although at least the news from Clive Barnaby was good. The Japanese bankers were prepared to secure the loan he needed to support his multi-million-dollar building project. That was excellent news.

Saved by the Japanese, thank God. No thanks to Red. That wily son-of-a-bitch had almost put him out of business.

'I have to get into Mariska's apartment,' he said, standing up and starting to pace restlessly round the room.

'To do what?' Chris asked, chewing on a spare rib.

'There's a box she kept hidden and locked. I should get to it before the police.'

'Her apartment will be deemed a crime scene,' Chris cautioned. 'There's an ongoing police investigation. It'll be off limits for now.'

'You're forgetting her apartment is in *my* building.' Max stated. 'I'll have no problem getting in.'

'You're planning on crossing a police line?' Chris said, shaking his head disapprovingly. 'Is *that* what you're going to do?'

'It's my property.'

There was no doubt in his mind that Mariska's murderer was Vladimir, even though the police were saying it was a robbery. He'd spoken to his lawyer earlier, and found out that the detectives had interviewed Irena, Mariska's personal maid, and she had supplied them with a list of missing jewellery and furs. So what? It didn't make any difference. Max knew in his heart it was no mere robbery. Somehow there was a story he was not privy to. Mariska and Vladimir had been up to something, and their deal had gone sour, so Vladimir had lost his temper and stabbed her to death.

To find out more, he needed access to her apartment, the sooner the better.

'I'm going over there,' he said, heading for the door.

'Should I come with?' Chris asked, wiping his hands on a napkin. He didn't approve, but in case of trouble he thought it would be easier if he was by Max's side.

'No,' Max said, shaking his head. 'I'm better off doing this alone.'

'Then I think I'll go back to my hotel,' Chris said. 'That is, unless you want me to stop by Amy's and see how Lulu's doing?'

'I'm sure they're fine.'

I hope so, Chris thought. *As long as Jett is behaving himself and not getting out of line.*

'You should check out of your hotel and stay here,' Max said. 'I could use the company.'

'I guess I could stay for a couple of days,' Chris mused, thinking of everything he had going on. He'd already postponed his flight back to L.A. and, according to his assistants, several important clients were screaming for his attention. Plus he had Birdy's wedding to oversee. 'I've got to work out my house disaster,' he said, thinking aloud. 'Then there's the gambling debt I still owe . . .'

'I understand,' Max replied. 'And now that the Japanese are coming through, maybe I can help you with that.'

'A loan would *really* help me out.'

'You might be my brother,' Max said drily, 'but I'm still a businessman, so how about we call it a non-interest loan?'

'Sounds good to me.'

'Give me the details and I'll work out how to handle it. Oh, yes, and there's one condition.'

'What's that?'

'This marks the end of your gambling career.'

'Ain't *that* the truth.'

* * *

Amy, Jett and Lulu had just returned from the corner coffee shop where Lulu had consumed two hamburgers, a strawberry milkshake and a dish of chocolate ice-cream, when Nancy appeared at the front door.

'Mother!' Amy exclaimed. 'What are *you* doing here?'

Nancy looked from Jett to Lulu, then back at her daughter. 'Perhaps if you answered your phone I wouldn't have been forced to drag myself over here,' she said, in an extremely pissed-off tone.

'Oh, God! I'm sorry,' Amy said. Then, lowering her voice, she added, 'With the tragedy and all, I've just been so busy. Max is in a state. He asked me to take Lulu, so I did, and fortunately Jett came along to help because—'

'Hey, Mrs Scott-Simon,' Jett said, coming up behind Amy.

'Good evening,' Nancy responded, with a frosty nod.

'Uh, I'm gonna put the movie on for Lulu,' he said. 'Is that okay?'

'Thanks,' Amy replied, realizing how this must look to Nancy. 'Let's go into the kitchen, Mom,' she said, leading her mother away.

Tight-lipped, Nancy followed her daughter into the kitchen.

'You *do* realize what this means?' Nancy said, fussily brushing off one of the kitchen stools with her hand before perching uncomfortably on it.

'Yes, Mom,' Amy said patiently. 'It means that Lulu has lost her mother, so I'm looking after her because her nanny quit and—'

'Amy!' Nancy interrupted sternly. 'We have to cancel the wedding.'

'Excuse me?'

'We have to cancel the wedding,' Nancy repeated, enunciating every word.

'Oh,' Amy said, sitting down. 'Are you saying we should postpone it?'

'Postponing is not an option.'

'Then maybe we should go ahead,' Amy said. 'I'll talk to Max. I'm sure he'll—'

'Amy! Be silent. We are *not* barbarians. This man's wife—'

'*Ex*-wife, Mother.'

'This man's *ex*-wife has been brutally murdered in a most appalling way, and *our* family name cannot be connected to this scandal. I will not allow it. You have to give Max back the ring, break *off* the engagement, and leave town on an extended vacation.'

'You're not serious?' Amy said, feeling dizzy and confused.

'I am extremely serious,' Nancy said. 'You must distance yourself from the Diamond family before this appalling scandal besmirches our good name.'

'Mother, Max is my *fiancé*. I *am* marrying him.'

'No, Amy, you're *not*.'

'You can't tell me who I'm going to marry,' Amy said heatedly. 'Besides, *Max* didn't kill his wife, he had nothing to do with it.'

'How do *you* know that?'

'Oh, for God's sake, Mother.'

'Have you been watching the news on TV?'

'No.'

'They're showing pictures of Max, and mentioning *you*. I shudder to imagine what the newspapers will say tomorrow.'

'Max is an innocent victim here, Mother. He has no control over the press.'

'He's not a victim, Amy,' Nancy said stiffly. 'He's an extremely affluent, well-connected man whose wife has been brutally murdered, and the suspicion lies on him.'

'That's nonsense, Mother.'

'You *have* to cancel this wedding. I've discussed everything with our family lawyer and he agrees. I'm expecting you to obey me, Amy, and for *God's sake* get that child *and* Max's brother *out* of your apartment.'

'You're crazy, Mother.'

'I'm merely telling you what has to be done for your own

349

protection. And you'd better do it, young lady. Otherwise I will be forced to speak to your grandmother about your inheritance.' And with that Nancy was on her feet. 'I expect to hear from you later,' she said, making a grand exit.

*　*　*

Max drove into the underground parking basement of Mariska's building, buzzed up to the front desk and spoke to the desk clerk. 'Mr Diamond here,' he said. 'Are the press still outside?'

'Yes, sir, they've been around all day.'

'How about the police?'

'Most of them have left. I believe there's one cop stationed outside the, uh . . . late Mrs Diamond's apartment.'

'You're sure?'

'Yes, sir. Irena – Mrs Diamond's personal maid – tried to get in earlier to fetch some of her things, but the cop wouldn't allow her access.'

'Right,' Max said slowly. 'Well, I *do* need to get in to collect my daughter's clothes. See if you can offer the cop some refreshments.'

'I shouldn't think he's allowed to leave his post, sir.'

'Offer him something. I'm sure you can convince him to take a break.'

'I'll try.'

'You do that, and I'll make it worth your while.'

'I'll see what I can do.'

Max waited five minutes before taking the elevator up to the apartment. The doorman had done his job, there was no cop present, so he ducked under the yellow police tape and let himself in with the key he'd never relinquished.

He slipped inside the marble foyer, shut the door behind him and stood there for a moment, images of Mariska's body flashing before his eyes. Then he realized he'd better move fast.

He recalled that Mariska had kept a locked box in the top of a closet in the guest room. 'It is where I keep jewellery that's not in the bank,' she'd once informed him when he'd caught her hiding the box. He'd never bothered to check. He'd believed her – why wouldn't he?

He went straight to the guest-room closet, moved a few things around and located the box. Then in case the cop was back, he hurried into Lulu's room, scooped up an armful of clothes and a few stuffed animals, and let himself out.

The policeman was still not there. Chris had said it was going to be such a problem, but he'd found it an easy task.

Now he planned on spending the rest of the evening discovering whatever information he could about his deceased ex-wife, because he was convinced she'd had secrets, and he was determined to find out what they were.

Chapter Forty-Nine

*T**his is your shot, Liberty,* do not *blow it.*

Bruce's words kept swimming around in her head as she sat on a plane making its way to L.A. She'd taken a leap of faith and decided to go for it – a difficult decision because she hadn't wanted to miss her meeting with Damon and the producer he'd promised to set her up with. She was into *that* more than anything, but how could she turn down the kind of money she'd make doing the modelling job? Not to mention a trip to L.A. – a place she'd only ever dreamed about.

This was a once-in-a-lifetime chance she couldn't refuse. A huge break that could lead to so many other opportunities.

And yet . . . she'd been torn about blowing off the meeting with Damon's producer because, above all else, singing was her passion.

She'd left a message on Damon's private cell informing him of her situation and hoping he'd understand and reschedule. In the meantime she'd barely had time to throw some things into a bag and get herself to the airport.

This was her first plane ride and she was quite apprehensive. The sour-faced woman sitting next to her in the window seat did not seem inclined to talk, so Liberty buckled her seatbelt, and sat back, prepared to enjoy the ride.

She realized she hadn't called her mom back, and then she started thinking about Cindi. How was she supposed to reach her? Cindi had promised to call her with a phone number, but she was obviously too busy settling in with Slick Jimmy. If the plane crashed the only person who would know she was on it was Bruce, a man she'd met only once. And Damon, because of the message she'd left him.

Suddenly she felt guilty. She should've called Diahann back, it was bad energy to hold grudges, and at least she now knew the truth about her father. She made up her mind that once she reached the hotel she'd call her mom, and then Manny and Golda at the coffee shop to inform them she wasn't coming back, because if she could make this kind of money it was dumb not to take advantage of it. She felt bad about her Ragtags – they must be wondering what had happened to her. The moment she got paid she promised herself she'd drop them off some cash. That way they could buy their own food.

Once again, she started wondering what the shoot was for. Something fun, she hoped. She should've asked Bruce, but everything had happened so quickly, and he'd been in a rush so she hadn't had a chance.

After a while she fell asleep, and didn't wake until the plane landed.

Outside the gate she looked around until she spotted a middle-aged black man holding up a white card with her name on it. Hurrying over to him, she said, 'Uh, I think you're here for me?' making it sound like a question.

'Liberty?'

'That's right.'

'I'm your driver, ma'am,' he said politely. 'The car's parked outside. Do you have baggage?'

'Only the bag I'm carrying.'

'I'll take that for you,' he said, relieving her of the heavy bag filled with anything she'd been able to stuff in at such short notice.

A car and a driver, this was major cool! Cindi would have a jealous fit when she told her.

She followed the man outside to a white limo parked curbside. 'Is this for *me*?' she asked, unable to hide her surprise. 'Are you *sure*?'

'Yes, ma'am,' he said, holding open the door. 'I'm driving you to *Shutters*.'

'That's a hotel, right?'

'Yes, ma'am. It's in Santa Monica by the ocean.'

This was too much. The only time she'd visited the ocean was one Sunday she'd spent at Coney Island when she was fourteen. She hadn't enjoyed the experience – the beach was packed with sweaty, half-naked people, a giant wave had nearly drowned her, and some annoying boy had got a sticky glob of cotton candy caught in her hair.

There was a phone in the car. She wondered if she was allowed to use it. No, best to wait until she got to the hotel. And how much would phone calls cost from a hotel? Probably a fortune, although Bruce had said all expenses were taken care of, so maybe they wouldn't charge her.

The hotel was all white and quite glamorous. They were very welcoming to her at Reception, and showed her to an ocean-front room with a small balcony overlooking the beach.

She looked around in amazement. The room was nicer than the apartment she shared with Cindi. There was a mini-bar filled with miniature bottles of drinks and all kinds of delicious goodies, a flat-screen TV, a soft, luxurious bed, a bathroom with a walk-in shower and a huge tub, plus another TV, and she was sure no roaches or rats!

Kicking off her shoes she opened up the sliding doors, stepped out onto a small balcony and took a deep breath. It was past midnight, but the air was balmy and the sound of the ocean soothingly loud.

I'm dreaming, she told herself. *This is all some whacked-out crazy dream. Is this really happening to me?*

A knock on the door jolted her back to reality. 'Who is it?' she called out.

'It's Chip, your friendly neighbourhood photographer,' a male voice replied.

'Hold on a minute,' she said, slipping on her shoes, then opening the door.

Standing there was the pizza boy from the elevator on her first go-see.

'What the—'

Before she could finish, Pizza Boy gave her a lopsided grin. 'Never trust a man eating pizza in an elevator,' he said, with a jaunty wink. 'Turned out you were the fresh face my camera's gonna die for. *You* are gonna be on the cover of a major new magazine, so get a good night's sleep and don't let me down tomorrow, 'cause you're *my* choice, an' the suits're all pissed they didn't get to check you out. Six a.m. Hair, Make-up and Wardrobe will be on your doorstep. Put yourself in their hands, 'cause they *really* know their shit. Oh, yeah,' he added, with another goofy grin. 'Welcome to L.A.'

And as quickly as that he was gone, leaving her in a state of total flux.

*   *   *

It turned out that Pizza Boy was one of the hottest photographers around. Only twenty-six, he'd already scored important covers on all the major magazines with his sexy original style reminiscent of the early Annie Leibovitz.

At the present time he'd been hired to launch a new magazine, *White Cool*, aimed at the twenty to forty-five year-old male reader. He could've booked any one of the top models for the cover, but he'd been looking for someone totally new – and Liberty was that someone. Disillusioned with the familiar faces crowding his studio on the day Liberty had come in for her go-see, he'd grabbed a pizza and taken off to get some air, which was how he'd come to be sharing an elevator with her. He'd viewed her as incredibly beautiful and street smart with a streak of naïveté. He'd known immediately she was the one.

Now he had her posing on a beach in L.A., wearing a thong and a skimpy bra top in some kind of jungle print, leaning against a palm tree, her body oiled and glistening, wild exotic make-up and extensions in her hair.

She'd awoken way before six, and rushed to check out the view from her room. Miles of white sand leading to the ocean, clumps of exotic palm trees, an expanse of clear blue sky, a jogging and bike path – where people were already out and about. Wow! It was Paradise. She *still* couldn't believe this was happening to her and so fast.

The 'team' stood around watching her every move as she posed for Chip's camera. The 'team' consisted of Quinn, make-up artist supreme – a sleek black guy with shoulder length white-blond hair and bleached eyebrows – Teddy, one of the best hair stylists in L.A. and Uma, a butch celebrity stylist with an impeccable eye for detail. They were a friendly trio who'd worked on her for two hours before Chip was satisfied.

Chip's 'team' consisted of two energetic young assistants and a runner. There was also a catering team setting up lunch under hooded canopies further down the beach.

Chip had thought of everything to create the right atmosphere – he'd even set up his iPod with speakers, and sexy Brazilian music filled the air.

At first she'd felt exposed and awkward, then slowly she'd begun to relax. Chip was so encouraging, and as soon as he felt she was ready he showed her a series of Polaroids he'd shot of her. She was secretly thrilled – she could hardly believe it was her.

After that everything was easy, and she fell into the rhythm of posing seductively as if she'd done it a hundred times before.

'Bring it *on*!' Chip kept yelling at her. 'You look incredible. Yeah! Bring it on, Liberty. That's it! Bring it on!'

By the time they broke for lunch she was on a major high. The 'team' swooped down on her. Uma slipped a white towelling robe round her shoulders, while Teddy informed her that for the next set-up everything would be entirely different, so she'd better eat fast as they had work to do.

Could it get any better?

She didn't think so.

Her adrenaline was pumping at an alarming rate. Last night she'd fallen asleep with all her clothes on. She'd lain on top of the bed for a second, and that was it – total wipe-out. She hadn't phoned anyone and now she felt guilty because, like Cindi, she'd let Golda and Manny down at the coffee shop. It wasn't fair to leave them two waitresses short with no explanation.

But what could she do? It was as if she was on an express train and couldn't get off. Didn't *want* to get off. It was all such a trip.

Lunch under the softly swaying palm trees was another trip. Lobster and shrimp, mixed salads, an assortment of breads, wine and music. Aunt Aretha would be in heaven.

Chip's runner brought him the L.A. edition of the *New York Post*, and he proceeded to sit back and read the sports pages. Liberty's eye caught the garish headline on the front page.

MURDER IN MANHATTAN!
SOCIETY WIFE SLAIN!
MARISKA DIAMOND STABBED TO DEATH!

Oh, wow! So *that* was why Diahann was trying to reach her.

'Can I use your phone?' she asked Teddy. 'I think I'd better speak to my mom.'

Chapter Fifty

Sitting in his kitchen scanning the newspapers, Max realized the headlines were even worse than he could have imagined. *SOCIETY WIFE SLAIN!* screamed the *New York Post*. *SOCIETY BEAUTY STABBED SIX TIMES!* was on the cover of the *Daily News*. Even the *New York Times* and the *Wall Street Journal* featured the story on their front pages. There were plenty of pictures too, mostly of Mariska at various events, and a few of her with Max. There was even one of her with Lulu at a tennis tournament in the Hamptons.

'Jesus Christ!' Max raged out loud. 'Why do they have to put my daughter in the paper?'

Then he realized he had not called Amy. The night before, he'd been so busy going through the papers he'd found in Mariska's locked box, that he'd forgotten all about Amy and Lulu.

He picked up the phone and called her. 'I'm so sorry, sweetheart,' he said apologetically. 'I was exhausted – I must've passed out. Are you okay? Is Jett still there?'

'No,' Amy said. 'He left as soon as Lulu fell asleep.'

'How is she today?'

'Unhappy. She wants to be with you, Max, and I can't blame her. Yesterday she went through a traumatic experience and she *needs* to be with her daddy.'

'Right now it's difficult,' he said, stalling, because he had no idea what he was supposed to do with Lulu.

'Max, she hardly *knows* me,' Amy persisted. 'Surely you can persuade her nanny to come back.'

'The woman flew to England,' he said helplessly.

'Well, she should be with someone she feels safe with.'

'Do you think I don't know that?'

'Did Mariska have any close girlfriends who could take her?'

'No,' he said abruptly. 'And I'd prefer not to go there.'

'Then what *do* you want to do?'

'I'll come get her.'

'I think that's the best idea.'

'Amy,' he warned, 'you cannot let her see the newspapers. It's bad.'

'I'll make sure.'

'I was thinking that maybe next weekend the three of us could go to your mother's house in the Hamptons, you know, get out of the spotlight.'

'Not a good plan,' she said, imagining Nancy's reaction to *that*.

'Why not?'

'Uh . . . we have to talk, Max. My mother's in a state.'

'What kind of state is *she* in?'

'She wants us to . . . postpone the wedding.'

'Jesus, I hadn't even thought about it, but I suppose – in view of the circumstances – we should.'

'It seems to be the right thing to do.'

'Nancy must be driving you nuts.'

'She is,' Amy said, cradling the phone under her chin. 'She, uh . . . she really wants more than that.'

'More than what?' Max asked suspiciously.

'More than a postponement. She thinks I should give you back the ring.'

'*What?*'

'I know it's ridiculous, and I wouldn't even consider it, but that's what she's saying.'

'Your mother is a bitch,' he said harshly. 'And I don't use that word lightly.'

'I know.'

'What did you tell her when she said this?'

'That there was no way I was breaking up with you.'

'Thank God! Because I couldn't go through this without you, Amy. We both know I'm not the best at expressing

359

my feelings but, believe me, you mean *everything* to me.'

'I never wanted a big wedding anyway,' she said, attempting to lighten the conversation. 'Did you?'

'We were doing it for her,' he acknowledged.

'Absolutely,' she agreed.

'Then this could work to our advantage.'

'It could?'

'Of course. Just think, we won't have to endure a huge rigamarole with all the trimmings. We can fly off to Bali or somewhere remote and have a simple ceremony.'

'I'd like that.'

'Okay, sweetie. I'll be there to fetch Lulu within the hour.'

He hung up the phone and wondered what he could do with Lulu to keep her safe and happy. He had things to take care of and, much as he wanted to be with his daughter, now was not the time.

His housekeeper, Mrs Conner, entered the kitchen. 'I'm so sorry for your loss, Mr Diamond,' she said, in a hushed tone, her Scottish burr quite soothing. 'I wasn't certain if you'd want me to come in today. If you like I can—'

'No, no,' he said quickly. 'I *do* want you here. I was hoping you could keep Lulu company. I don't think I should send her back to school yet, and I know she enjoys spending time with you. It's difficult, and what with Nanny Reece deserting me . . .'

'Of *course* I'll spend time with the wee girl, Mr Diamond. Where is the little lassie?'

'She slept over at my fiancée's. I'm on my way to get her now.'

'I'll make her those tasty buttermilk pancakes she gobbles up. Not to worry, Mr Diamond, she'll be happy and well looked after with me. I raised three wee ones of my own.'

'Thank you, Mrs Conner,' he said gratefully.

Chris wandered into the kitchen. 'What's going on?' he asked. 'I could hear you pacing around all night. Those hardwood floors are a bitch.'

'I discovered a few things,' Max said grimly.

'Anything interesting?' Chris asked, pouring himself a glass of orange juice.

'As a matter of fact, yes,' Max said. Then, glancing at Mrs Conner, he added, 'Why don't you come with me to collect Lulu, and I'll fill you in?'

* * *

Amy put down the phone and went to find Lulu. The little girl was sitting in the middle of the bed, sobbing.

'I want my mommy,' Lulu cried, in a tear-soaked voice. 'Where's my mommy?'

'Daddy's coming to get you,' Amy promised, feeling depressed and out of her depth. 'He'll be here soon, so while we're waiting, why don't you let me help you get dressed?'

'Don't *wanna* get dressed,' Lulu shouted.

With everything that was going on, Amy did not feel at all equipped to deal with a recalcitrant five-year-old, but she was doing her best. 'Why not?' she asked patiently.

'Don't have my clothes here,' Lulu muttered.

'Yes, you do, you've got the pretty dress you had on yesterday.'

'Don't wanna wear that again.'

'Why not?'

'I WANT MY MOMMY!' Lulu yelled.

'I know,' Amy said sympathetically. 'And if you get dressed, you'll be all ready for Daddy when he gets here.'

'But I want *Mommy*, not Daddy,' Lulu said, lower lip quivering.

'Mommy can't come right now, but Daddy's in his car, and he's racing to get you. I know he'll want to see you all dressed and pretty,' she said, handing Lulu her dress.

'Wore that yesterday,' Lulu said, flinging the dress back at Amy. 'Want *other* clothes.'

'You don't have any other clothes here.'

'Want my jeans,' Lulu whined.

'I just told you,' Amy said patiently. 'We don't have your clothes here. Daddy will take you to get them.'

Lulu threw her a furious glare.

'I've got an excellent idea,' Amy said brightly. 'Let's go eat breakfast.'

'Don't *want* breakfast,' Lulu said, sulking.

'Is there anything you *do* want?'

'Yes, I want my mommy,' Lulu mumbled, her eyes filling with tears. 'Where's my mommy?'

Amy leaned over and attempted to hug her, but Lulu shoved her away. 'You know, Lulu,' Amy said softly, refusing to get upset. 'Wouldn't it be nice if you and I were friends? We could do fun things together. I could buy you that Hello Kitty stuff you like, and maybe we could take a trip to Disneyland.'

'No stupid Disneyland,' Lulu said stubbornly. '*I want my mommy!*'

'Well,' Amy said. 'I'll leave your dress here, and if you put it on and come into the kitchen, I'll make us some waffles. How's that?'

'No *waffles.*'

'Okay, I'll be in the kitchen if you change your mind.'

With Jett around it hadn't been so difficult dealing with Lulu. He'd joked and laughed with the little girl, who was obviously fond of him. But as soon as Lulu had fallen asleep watching her movie, and he'd carried her into Amy's bed, Amy had asked him to leave.

'I thought we could talk now,' he'd said.

'This isn't the right time,' she'd replied.

'We have to talk sometime,' he'd said, trying to get her to look him in the eye, which she'd refused to do.

'Not now. I'm feeling very fragile. It's been an unbelievable day, and with Lulu here I can't get into what happened between us.'

'So you're saying you don't want to talk about it?' he'd said, refusing to give up.

'What is there to say?' she'd murmured, shrugging helplessly. 'Neither of us knew the consequences of what we did. You obviously didn't know who *I* was, and I certainly didn't know who *you* were. I'm embarrassed and kind of . . . confused. So please go, Jett.'

Reluctantly he'd left.

After he'd gone she'd regretted sending him away. And then she'd been overcome with guilt for feeling that way. It wasn't fair to Max, especially in view of what was going on.

It was quite a situation to find herself in, and now she had her mother on her case, telling her she had to break up with Max and go away on a trip. What did the woman think? That she would simply give up her job and take off? It was so typical of Nancy – imagining she was doing the right thing to save the precious family name.

For as long as she could remember her mother had black-mailed her with the threat of her inheritance from Grandma Poppy, but Grandma Poppy would *never* cut her off. Her grandma was a kind, generous, and very smart old lady. There was no way she'd listen to Nancy.

Besides, Amy didn't care whether she inherited the money or not. Life wasn't about how much money you had, and there was no way she was letting Max down at this time. He was hurting and so was she.

Eventually she'd taken a blanket and curled up on the couch, sleeping fitfully.

Now she was in the kitchen toasting frozen waffles for a child who couldn't stand her.

*　*　*

On Tuesday morning Gianna was intent on dragging Jett into the famous photographer Antonio's studio, when all he wanted was to go over to Max's and see if there was anything he could do to help.

Gianna was having none of it. 'They pay you *bene* money,' she announced. 'Is nice, no?'

'Yeah, sure, but—'

'You have reputation, Jett,' Gianna said sternly, all glamorous and business-like in tight-fitting Seven jeans, a Valentino masculine-style jacket, and Jimmy Choo boots. 'You cannot bail from job at last minute. You missed fittings yesterday. Fortunately I *know* your body. I found man same size, they do the fittings anyway.' Then she decided that she'd better lighten up before he got really pissed. 'You'll *love* the clothes, *carino*, so sexy,' she purred affectionately. 'You sexy boy, *sì*?'

He hated it when she called him 'boy'. She was only five years older than him, so what was with *that*?

'I shouldn't be doing this gig,' he complained, running his hand through his hair. 'It doesn't feel right with everything my brother's going through.'

'You spent yesterday with him,' Gianna pointed out. 'Today you work, is not your problem, *carino*.'

'That's cold, Gianna,' he said restlessly. 'Max's wife was *murdered*.'

'She not his wife – he was divorced.'

'It's still something he has to deal with. Mariska was Lulu's *mother*.'

'Jett,' Gianna said, a touch icy. 'I come to New York, we do photos together. Antonio shoot the photos. I insist they use *you*, you cannot disappoint.'

So there he was in a cab with Gianna, passing the newsstands where the headlines screamed about the murder. It was all one big stinking mess.

Last night he'd got nowhere with Amy. She'd behaved like a nervous racehorse, ready to back off if he so much as touched her arm. He'd finally left because he hadn't wanted to upset her. Was he *ever* going to get a chance to tell her how he felt? Although he had to agree – the timing *was* bad.

Gianna had been out when he'd got back to Sam's apartment the night before. She and Sofia Courtenelli had apparently hit the town, clubbing until two a.m. when she'd finally come home and attempted to wake him.

He'd pretended to be asleep as she'd tried to work her sexual magic. The problem was that his cock had not been in agreement with his mind. Taking advantage, Gianna had climbed aboard and ridden him for a fast five minutes before he came. Then, unfazed, she'd rolled away and finished herself off.

All the while he'd pretended to be asleep.

Apparently nothing bothered Gianna. She was a self-contained ball of fire. A girl who took what she wanted whenever it suited her.

For the first time in his life he'd felt like a piece of meat. Not a pleasant feeling, although he guessed that during his stoned-out-of-his-mind years, he'd left a lot of girls feeling the same way. At least he wasn't that person anymore. Now he was together and caring.

Yeah, *so* freaking caring that all he could think about was getting back with his brother's fiancée.

Nice. Very nice.

And, hopelessly, he realized there was nothing he could do about it.

Chapter Fifty-One

Red Diamond did not take kindly to being dragged into the headlines. Mariska's murder and the subsequent publicity were nothing but an inconvenience, he was livid that his name was being connected to the killing of the Russian floozy Max had been foolish enough to marry. He'd warned him the first time he'd met Mariska. 'She's a Russian prostitute,' he'd informed his eldest son. 'She's marrying you for your money and a green card. That's what those Russian prostitutes do.'

'How dare you speak about my future wife like that?' Max had said. 'For your information she *has* a green card, *and* she's a very intelligent and lovely woman with a job. She doesn't need my money.'

'You'll learn,' Red had muttered. 'Just like you learned about that little tramp you took to your prom. Remember her? She couldn't *wait* for a good fucking from her boyfriend's old man.'

'You *raped* her,' Max accused.

'Is that what you think?' Red had sneered, cracking a nasty smile. 'She was begging for it, son. *Begging* for some hard cock you weren't capable of giving her.'

It was the closest Max had ever come to smashing his father in the face. Instead he'd stopped speaking to him for several months, until Lady Jane Bentley had intervened. She'd needed some support for one of her charities so she'd invited Mariska and Max to dinner. Why he'd allowed Mariska to accept still puzzled him. But, like his brothers, deep down he was hoping the old man would change and they could forge some kind of relationship. How nice it would be to have a father who gave a shit.

Mariska had loved being in the company of such an important billionaire mogul and his titled girlfriend. She had been all over Red. But Red hadn't changed – he was as appalling as ever, and Max had hated every minute, refusing to socialize with them again, in spite of Mariska's pleas.

With the headlines informing New York of Mariska's brutal murder, Red stomped around his house, yelling at anyone who got in his way. He was furious with Lady Jane – the bitch had invaded his safe and read his Will. She'd also snooped through his private papers and found out things nobody knew about. Now she was threatening to make certain things public unless he paid out an exorbitant amount of money.

Her lawyer – no slouch in the working-fast department – was requesting a settlement in the neighbourhood of thirty-five million dollars. Five million a year for the six years they'd lived together. And this was only the beginning.

'Considering how much you're worth, you're getting off easy,' she'd informed him.

Bitch. Whore. They were all whores. They all had a price. And he should know, he'd married enough of them.

* * *

Max drove erratically, jamming on the brakes at every red light causing his Mercedes to jolt to an abrupt stop. He'd dismissed his driver so that he and Chris could talk privately.

'What's going on?' Chris asked, making sure his seatbelt was tightly fastened. 'Did you go over to Mariska's apartment last night?'

Max nodded.

'You got in?'

'No problem.'

'And?'

'Mariska had plenty of secrets. I found the box she kept them locked up in,' Max said, swerving to avoid a jay-walking pedestrian.

'You took the box out of the apartment?'

'I did.'

'Which means you removed property that does not belong to you from a crime scene. That's not smart, Max.'

'I did it for my daughter. I have to protect Lulu.'

'What did you find?'

'Try half a million bucks in cash.'

'*Cash*. From you?'

'Not from me. Mariska received a very large divorce settlement, plus the apartment. The only money I pay her is child support, and that goes directly into her bank account.'

'Then where's this cash from?' Chris asked.

'Who the fuck knows? And not only cash, but several loose gemstones in plastic holders. Diamonds and emeralds, large ones, probably worth a couple of mill. It doesn't make any sense.'

'Anything else?'

'This is a good one. Her original birth certificate. She was ten years older than she claimed, which would make her forty-nine instead of thirty-nine. And a copy of her marriage certificate to Vladimir,' he said, almost rear-ending a cab. 'She certainly took me for a ride. What a lying *bitch*!'

'She's dead, Max,' Chris reminded him. 'There's nothing you can do now.'

'I know,' Max said bitterly. 'But how could she do this to Lulu? *Everything* about her was fraudulent.'

'I'm sure she never imagined it would end this way.'

'There was also a phone book filled with names I never heard her mention, mostly Russian.'

'Could be from when she lived in Moscow?'

'No. These names are attached to American phone numbers. Mariska had a secret life nobody knew about. *I* certainly didn't.'

'Have you thought of handing everything over to the detectives and letting *them* get into it?'

'It's not an option,' Max said, blasting his horn at a blonde in a Volvo, who was intent on cutting him up.

'It's not, huh?' Chris said, bracing his feet against the floor in front of his seat.

'No, Chris. I'm protecting my daughter.'

'I don't know what to say, Max. Are you planning on hunting Vladimir down? 'Cause I never figured you as the vigilante Bruce Willis type.'

'I have no idea *what* I'm going to do. I'm sure if I wait, Vladimir will come back with more blackmail threats, and *that*'s the time I'll call in the police or the FBI.'

'Y' know,' Chris said thoughtfully. 'I'm kind of not getting this. Maybe you can help me out.'

'Go ahead.'

'You can't tell them what you know *now*, but if he comes back asking for more money, you can tell them then.'

'That's right.'

'What's the difference? The headlines will read the same.'

'I know. But I need a couple of days to clear my head.'

Chris shrugged. Max was playing a dangerous game, and he didn't want any part of it. 'As long as you know what you're doing,' he said, thinking how much he didn't want to be here. He'd prefer to be back in L.A. dealing with his house and all his other problems.

'I don't,' Max said, 'but I'll figure it out.'

* * *

Antonio was a legend among photographers. He was up there with Richard Avedon, David Bailey and Helmut Newton. Seventy-five years old, Italian and crotchety, he greeted Gianna like a long-lost lover, plying her with compliments, words of praise and suggestive remarks. A diminutive man, small and neat, groomed to perfection, he was very demanding of his many assistants. He only worked when the feeling took him, his early photographs were gallery treasures and sold for thousands of dollars.

Ignoring Jett, he escorted Gianna into the make-up room, raving in Italian about how her beauty blossomed more each year.

Naturally Gianna was in compliment heaven.

'Did you fuck him?' Jett asked, as they sat near each other, having their make-up applied.

Gianna gave a secret smile, which signalled a big fat yes.

'You *gotta* be shittin' me,' Jett said, throwing her a disgusted look. 'He's old enough to be your freakin' *grand-father*.'

'I was fifteen,' Gianna said coyly. 'My first cover for Italian *Vogue*. Antonio was *so* famous and *so* adorable, I couldn't resist.'

'Adorable, my ass,' Jett muttered.

'He is brilliant, *carino*. You will see.'

'Yeah, well, all *I*'m gonna see is the two of you creamin' all over each other. Great way to spend the day.'

'Jealous?' Gianna inquired, enjoying every minute.

'Are you nuts? Of *that* old creep?'

'I love it when you get possessive, *carino*,' Gianna purred, her hand reaching over to touch his thigh. 'You are *so* sexy, *sì?*'

He didn't feel sexy, he felt edgy and unsettled. All he could think about was Amy, and here he was having a conversation with Gianna about being jealous. If she only knew! What a joke.

* * *

'Daddy!' Lulu shrieked, flinging herself at Max. 'My *daddy!*'

'What about *me?*' Chris asked ruefully. 'Don't *I* get a hug too?'

The little girl squealed with laughter, delighted to be the centre of attention once more. 'Okay, Lulu give you hug,' she said, with a shy smile.

'Have you been a good girl?' Max asked.

'She's been very good,' Amy assured him.

'Wanna go home,' Lulu said, pulling on his sleeve. 'Wanna go home *now*, Daddy.'

'We're on our way,' Max said, mouthing a silent *thank you* to Amy, as she escorted them to the door.

'Did Jett behave himself?' Chris asked. As soon as the words were out of his mouth he regretted it, for Amy blushed a deep red and he was aware that she had immediately guessed he *knew*. Shit! He'd made a big mistake.

'I'll call you later,' Max said, unaware of Amy's discomfort.

Lulu skipped out of the apartment without so much as

'Thank you.' Not that Amy minded, she was happy to see them leave.

Since when had everything become so complicated?

Oh, yes, since she'd slept with Jett, and, oh, God – Chris obviously knew all about it. The way he'd looked at her after he'd said, 'Did Jett behave himself?' It was a dead give-away. How sad was *that*? Even worse – what if he told Max?

Unthinkable.

Or was it?

Now she had something else to worry about.

* * *

Lady Jane Bentley sat in her bedroom contemplating her future. Her lawyer had acted swiftly and that was good. What *wasn't* good was the information she was burdened with. She knew one too many secrets about Red Diamond, and she'd *told* him she knew, which she should never have done until she was out of the house.

But – Catch 22 situation – if she left, Red would *never* settle the money on her that she deserved. And after living with Red Diamond for six years, she'd earned every cent.

Of course, thirty-five million was a lot of money. But Red Diamond was worth *billions*. She was entitled to a worthy pay-out – she'd put in her time.

Her lawyer had told her not to worry. 'There's nothing he can do to you,' he'd said. 'He can't throw you out, so stay where you are, and do *not* leave the house.'

Her lawyer didn't have to put up with Red invading her room every so often, and screaming abuse. She'd tried locking the door, but that had only made things worse. He'd hammered on it with his steel-tipped cane, roaring obscenities.

Diahann, Mae, the cook, and a couple of the maids had come running to see what was going on. Angrily he'd waved his stick at them, and they'd fled.

Finally Lady Jane had unlocked her door and endured even more verbal abuse.

As long as it was only verbal, she could take it. If it went any further she was calling the police, and Red would not appreciate *that*. Especially with all the dreadful publicity about the murder of Max's ex-wife – a woman to whom Lady Jane had never warmed.

Mariska Diamond had been a conniving social-climber, and Russian too. She was classless and, in Lady Jane's book, there was nothing worse than a classless over-achiever.

* * *

Running into the photo session late, Amy was greeted by an ecstatic Nigel standing outside the studio puffing on a cigarette. '*Wait* until you see them together,' he raved, blowing perfect little smoke-rings. 'Our clothes have never looked so brilliant! The men's line is *divine*. Chic and simple and *very* Italian. And as for Jett – *oh, my God*!' He paused to take a breath. 'Oh dear, *sorry*, here I am carrying on about *fashion*, while *you*, poor girl—'

'I don't want to talk about it,' Amy said, holding up her hand. 'Except to say that we're postponing the wedding, so pass the word.'

'No!' Nigel exclaimed in a shocked tone. 'How can you?'

'In view of what's happened, it's necessary, Nigel. Think about it.'

'I suppose you're right,' he said, stubbing out his cigarette on the ground. 'But it's such a *shame*.'

'Is the journalist from *People* here?' she asked briskly, determined to get back to work.

'Yolanda's dealing with him. We didn't think you'd be in today, let alone come to the photo shoot.'

'There's nothing *I* can do,' Amy said. 'I looked after Lulu last night, but now she's back with Max.'

'But surely Max—'

'I told you, he's with his daughter,' she said, walking into the studio. 'He's fine, Nigel. You don't have to worry about him.'

Then she spotted Jett. He was standing in front of the camera, looking sensational in a lightweight cream-coloured sports jacket, a blue striped shirt and faded jeans. His hair was slightly messed up, his intense blue eyes mesmerizing.

Gianna was draped all over him in an almost transparent white shirt tied under her magnificent breasts, tight white pants and high-heeled, jewelled sandals. Her auburn hair, piled on top of her head, was a jumble of sexy curls.

Nigel was right, they made an amazing-looking couple.

Frank Sinatra crooning 'Come Fly With Me' was blaring over the sound system. Antonio would only work to the voices of Sinatra, Tony Bennett or Dean Martin. He was an old-time kind of guy.

'Amy!' Gianna cooed, spotting Amy and running over to her. 'I am so *sorry*! What a *tragedia*.' She enveloped Amy in a big warm hug. 'You will be *bene*, no?'

'Thanks, Gianna,' Amy said, exchanging a quick glance with Jett. Were they *ever* going to get a chance to talk things through? She doubted it.

'*Scusi*!' Antonio shouted. 'We working here! Gianna, *bella*, the camera, *immediatamente!*'

'The maestro calls,' Gianna said, licking her full lips. 'Did you see Jett? My Yankee boyfriend looks so *delizioso*. How you say in America – tasty enough to eat?'

For a moment Amy wanted to scream, just let loose and yell her lungs out. But what good would that do? Everyone would think she was crazy, and she still had a job to take care of. Fixing a smile on her face, she approached Yolanda and the journalist from *People*. It was time to stop thinking about herself and get back to work.

Chapter Fifty-Two

'I was hoping we could talk before you read about Mrs Diamond's murder in the newspapers,' Diahann said, over the phone. 'I left several messages. Why didn't you call me back before?'

'I'm sorry,' Liberty said. 'I only just saw a copy of the *New York Post*.'

'As terrible as it is, it hasn't really affected us at the house,' Diahann continued. 'Max Diamond was divorced from her, although Red Diamond is quite upset about all the publicity.'

Who cares whether Red Diamond is upset? Liberty thought. *I certainly don't.*

'I'm in L.A.,' she blurted.

'Excuse me?' Diahann responded.

'I've been booked on a modelling assignment.'

'You flew to L.A. without telling me?'

'It happened suddenly.'

'*What* happened suddenly?'

'My friend Beverly introduced me to a modelling agent,' she explained. 'He sent me out on an interview and I got the job. Exciting, isn't it?'

Obviously Diahann did not think it was exciting at all. 'You're only nineteen, inexperienced,' she said, sounding worried. 'What makes you think the people you're working for are legitimate? They could be white-slaving you. That kind of thing still goes on, you know.'

'You've been watching too much *CSI* on TV, Mama,' Liberty said. 'Anyway, in my case it would be *black*-slaving, wouldn't it?'

'It's true, Liberty,' Diahann said, ignoring her daughter's sarcasm. 'Do you know anything at all about the people who took you there?'

'Nobody *took* me here,' Liberty said. 'The modelling agency is very reputable. I'm staying in a great hotel by the beach, and they're treating me like a princess. Plus I'm working with a well-known photographer who's shooting me for the cover of a new magazine.'

'This is all moving too fast for me.' Diahann sighed. 'One day you want to be a singer, the next you're a model.'

'I *still* want to sing, Mama,' Liberty said softly. 'You *know* that's always been my ambition. But this job pays a lot of money. I couldn't turn it down, and I'm glad I didn't.'

'Everything isn't *always* about money,' Diahann said.

'Really?' Liberty responded. 'Wasn't that why you went to work for Mr Diamond, 'cause you needed the *money*?'

'That was different.'

'Okay, Mama,' Liberty said, anxious to get off the phone. 'Why don't I tell you all about it when I get home? I'll even treat you to a big fancy dinner. How's that?'

'When *will* you be back?'

'Thursday night.'

'Libby,' Diahann said hesitantly, 'the two of us . . . we need to sit down and have a conversation.'

'About what?' Liberty asked, wondering if Diahann had heard that Cindi had moved out, and now she was preparing to give her a lecture on the dangers of a young girl living alone in New York.

'The things I told you about your father, well . . . I wasn't quite truthful with you.'

'Huh?'

'There's something else you should know.'

'What?' she asked sharply.

'Not over the phone.'

'Mama,' she sighed, 'for God's sake, *why* are you playing with my emotions like this?'

'When I explain it to you, you'll understand.'

'Will I, Mama?' she said, shaking her head. '*Will* I?'

Upset and confused, she walked back to the lunch table

and handed Teddy his phone. Just when she'd thought she had answers, Diahann had to come up with this.

She wished she hadn't phoned her mom back, it had ruined her day. And where was Cindi when she needed her? They'd always talked about everything and now she had nobody to share things with – good *or* bad.

The 'team' whisked her off for more changes. A different hairstyle, make-up touch-ups, an incredibly sexy one-piece red swimsuit with strategic cut-outs.

Once they were back on the beach, Teddy, who was a real sweetheart, asked her if everything was all right.

'Why?' she asked apprehensively. 'Am I not looking Okay?'

'You're coming across in the Polaroids as a tad uptight.'

'Oh, God, I'm sorry. It's my mom,' she confessed. 'She's impossible to understand.'

'Ah,' Teddy said wisely. 'If we understood our parents, the world would be a much calmer place.'

'Right,' Liberty agreed.

Making a concentrated effort, she put the conversation with Diahann out of her head, and once more threw herself into posing.

At six o'clock Chip announced they were through for the day. 'I'm inviting everyone for dinner,' he said, crooked grin going full force. 'Ivy at the Shore. Seven-thirty in the lobby.'

'What's Ivy at the Shore?' Liberty asked Uma, the stylist, as they walked towards the hotel.

'A restaurant,' Uma replied, giving her a look as if to say, *What rock have you been hiding under?*

'Uh . . . I don't have anything to wear.' Liberty said, frowning.

'This is L.A.,' Teddy said. 'Nobody dresses up here, unless it's a big event or you're Paris Hilton.'

'Jeans'll do it,' Quinn added. 'It's casual.'

They all headed into the lobby of Shutters. As they started towards the elevator a male voice called out, 'Lib?'

'Ohmi*God*!' Quinn exclaimed, in a stage whisper. 'It's Tony A. Do you *know* him?'

Liberty stopped and stared as a handsome young man

dressed all in white rushed towards them, trailed by what appeared to be *his* 'team'.

'Tony?' she questioned excitedly. 'Is that *you*?'

'Libby? I don't *believe* it!' he yelled, hugging her, then standing back. '*Look* at you! You're a glamour queen.'

'You're the queen,' Quinn muttered, under his breath.

'Shut *up*!' Teddy hissed. 'Liberty actually *knows* him!'

'Who's Tony A?' Uma asked, as they all watched Liberty and Tony embrace.

'Only the hottest Latino singer since Ricky Martin wowed 'em at the Grammys,' Teddy said, rubbing his hands together.

'Gay playing it straight,' Quinn said, *sotto voce*. 'But, I have to admit, gorgeous all the same.'

'This is *amazing*!' Tony said, shaking his head in admiration as he checked Liberty out. 'What are you *doing* here?'

'Shooting a cover for a magazine.'

'You're a *model*?' he said, flashing whiter than white teeth in a dazzling smile.

'And you're Tony A,' she responded. 'Wow! I've listened to your song on the radio. I never put it together that it was *you*.'

Tony Artura, the Puerto Rican boy who used to live next door to her in Harlem, until Diahann had yanked her away to Manhattan and the Diamond mansion. The boy who'd taken her roller-blading in Central Park, taught her to pick at a guitar, helped her with her homework. And then, when she'd moved back to live with Aunt Aretha and Cindi, he was the boy she'd been serious with until his mom had decided they were moving to Miami.

Tony Artura, her first big crush. Now he was Tony A – the new Latino singing sensation with a big hit record. What a rush!

'Y' know,' he said, still smiling, 'I often thought about you, wondered how you were doin'.'

'Then how come you didn't phone or write?'

He shrugged. 'Things changed when we moved out of New York. I got into a performing-arts school that kept me *real* busy. It was all work, work, work. My mom had big ambitions for me.'

'You look *great*,' Liberty said, reaching out to touch his spiky blond hair, streaked by the sun.

'So do you. I always *knew* you'd turn out to be a beauty.'

'Thanks.'

'You were such a skinny little runt – with those long spider legs and wild green eyes.'

'And *you* had a mullet!' she teased. 'Guess you want to forget about *that*.'

They both started laughing. 'How about we get together later for a drink?' Tony suggested. 'Catch up on everything.'

'What time?'

'I'm performing at a charity event in Beverly Hills. I should be back around eleven.'

'Call me,' she said, hoping he would. 'If I'm still awake I'd love to.'

A dark-haired, slim-hipped Hispanic man inserted himself between them. 'Aren't you going to introduce me to your friend?' he said to Tony, arching his finely plucked eyebrows.

'Yeah, sure,' Tony replied, a touch awkwardly. 'Hector, this is Liberty.'

'Hello . . . Liberty,' Hector said, giving her a full-on dirty look.

'Libby and me were at school together,' Tony explained, '*and* we lived next door to each other.'

'Back in the day,' Liberty said, smiling.

'Cosy,' Hector said, placing a hand possessively on Tony's arm – a gesture that was not lost on Liberty. 'We have to go,' Hector continued. 'We cannot be late.'

'Well,' Liberty said wistfully, 'it was great seeing you, Tony. Your success is fantastic.'

'You too, my little Libby. *Sooo* beautiful.'

'Come *on*,' Hector said, impatiently tapping his watch. 'The limo is waiting.'

'I guess the limo is waiting,' Liberty said, still smiling.

'I guess it is,' Tony responded, smiling back. ''Bye for now. Don't forget, I'll call you later.'

Impulsively she leaned forward and kissed his cheek. 'Thanks for all the fun memories,' she whispered. 'You made growing up kind of special.'

Before she could say anything else, Hector successfully dragged him away.

Teddy was in a state of excitement. 'You *know* Tony A,' he said, his voice filled with admiration. 'You actually *know* him.'

'Obviously she does,' Uma said drily, herding them all into the elevator.

'Then if you know him so well,' Quinn said, 'you should advise him to haul his sexy little *butt* out of the closet. His gay fans are not pleased he's pretending to be straight. *Who* exactly does he think he's fooling?'

'He wasn't gay when *I* knew him,' Liberty said.

'He certainly is now,' Quinn replied crisply. 'He's the talk of the gay community.'

'He is?'

'*Everyone* knows. And *that* was the boyfriend.'

'What makes you think he's got a boyfriend?' Liberty asked, remembering the fun she and Tony had shared, fooling around without actually going all the way. She'd been a very young teenager at the time, but she recalled that Tony had been a fantastic kisser – almost on a par with Damon. And he'd never objected to the many blow-jobs she'd put his way.

Ah . . . fond memories . . .

'Because it's *obvious*,' Quinn snapped. 'That guy was in full *drool* mode over Tony, and he hated *you*.'

'He did?'

'*Hated* you. If Tony had stayed any longer, Hector would've thrown a jealous *fit*! Do *not* expect a phone call later. Hector will *not* allow it.'

The elevator ground to a halt at her floor, and she got off.

'See you in the lobby at seven-thirty,' Teddy called after her. 'Don't forget – very casual.'

Sure. Like she had anything that *wasn't* casual. She hadn't possessed a dress since she was twelve.

So, she thought, *Tony Artura is Tony A. If it can happen for him* . . .

She opened the door to her room and was amazed to find it filled with orchids. White orchids, lilac orchids, pink orchids – exotic and beautiful baskets dominated every surface space.

A white card was propped up against the biggest arrangement. She opened the card and read the message:

Orchids stun my senses.
So do you, LL.
  Damon

* * *

'LL?'

It was Damon. Nobody else called her LL.

She experienced a shiver of excitement. As if the orchids weren't enough, five minutes later he was on the phone.

'Thanks for the beautiful orchids,' she said. 'How am I supposed to get them back to New York?'

'On the plane,' he said casually.

'I won't be able to carry them – there're too many. Besides, I don't think airlines allow—'

'My plane,' he interrupted.

'*Your* plane,' she said disbelievingly.

'That's right.'

'You've got a plane?'

'The company does. I call it mine 'cause *I* own the company.'

'Damon—'

'I like it when you use my name. You got a sexy voice, LL. You know that?'

'You're crazy.'

'No, *you*'re the crazy one,' he insisted. 'Runnin' out on me when I was all set to hook you up with the right producer. Weren't *you* the girl who was raggin' on me to get her a singin' career?'

'I *still* want it,' she said, delighted to hear his voice. 'It was just that this modelling thing came along, and I really need the money, so I couldn't say no.'

'Hey, I was under the impression you were an expert at saying no.'

'Excuse me?'

'You've managed to say it to me a few times.'

'That's different.'

'It is? 'Splain to me how.'

'If I have to mention that you're married one more time—'

'Are you dressed?' he interrupted.

'What?'

'Dressed? Clothes on?'

'Why?'

''Cause there's someone at your door.'

'No, there's not.'

And, sure enough, there was a knock on the door.

'Who is it?' she called out.

'Room Service.'

'Hang on,' she said to Damon, thinking, *What now?*

She opened the door expecting more orchids, because over-the-top seemed to be Damon's style.

What she didn't expect was Damon himself. Handsome, cool, killer grin, black pants and a black shirt. Diamond studs in his ears, extravagant diamond watch, cellphone in hand.

Behind him stood another man, bigger and blacker, dressed in a casual maroon outfit.

'LL,' Damon said. 'Meet Parker J. Jones, he's gonna be your producer.'

Chapter Fifty-Three

Sometime in the middle of a break during the Courtenelli photo shoot, Jett managed to corner Amy and insist they got together later to talk things through. 'Tonight,' he said, sounding like he meant business.

'I can't,' she demurred, wishing she could stop dissolving into a shivering wreck every time he was close to her.

'Why not?' he demanded.

'Because we've, uh, had to postpone the wedding. My mother wants me over at her house to check through lists, make sure everyone is covered.'

'Hey,' he said, fixing her with his laser-like blue eyes, 'isn't you and I talking more important than that?'

'And then I might have to see Max,' she added, although she already knew she wasn't seeing him that night.

'Amy, Amy,' Jett said, shaking his head. 'Stop fighting the inevitable. I'll come to your apartment. It's the only place we can be private. Just tell me what time, and I'll be there.'

'No, not my apartment,' she said quickly.

'Why not?' he asked, glancing around to make sure Gianna wasn't nearby.

Why not? Good question. Could it be because she didn't trust herself to be alone with him?

No. Absolutely not. He was a one-night fling, her future brother-in-law, and nothing like that would *ever* happen again.

'Okay,' she said, agreeing reluctantly. 'Seven o'clock.'

'I'll be there.'

'*Where* will you be, *carino*?' Gianna asked sweetly, appearing out of nowhere, flinging an arm round Jett's shoulders.

382

He didn't take a beat. 'Amy's arranging a surprise for Max. I'm helping her out.'

'*Che cosa* surprise?' Gianna cooed, stroking his cheek.

'It wouldn't be a surprise if we told everyone, would it?' he said, edging away from her.

Amy remembered his words from the day before – *Gianna and I, we're not a couple.*

Well, they sure *looked* like a couple. *And* Gianna was living in his apartment. So what did that make them?

Oh, yes. A couple!

Not that she cared. Why should she?

And yet, somehow, she did.

As each day passed she was becoming more and more confused. If only Jett hadn't reappeared in her life she would probably have been able to forget all about him. But no, that hadn't happened, he was everywhere.

Later, as the photo shoot wound down, Nigel cornered her. 'Feel like going for a drink?' he asked. 'An apple martini would slide down *very* nicely.'

'I can't,' Amy responded. 'I'm meeting my mother – we're going over cancellation lists and stuff.'

'Poor you,' Nigel commiserated. 'Nancy must be driving you insane. I know how anal she can be.'

'Hmm . . .' Amy answered, thinking what an astute liar she was becoming.

'I stole a couple of Polaroids,' Nigel confessed, lowering his voice like a naughty schoolboy. 'Aren't *I* the bad one?'

'You did?' she murmured, her mind elsewhere.

'Antonio does *not* allow his Polaroids to leave his studio, but I fail to see why we shouldn't have some. Here,' he said, handing her a photo, 'one for you.'

She glanced at the Polaroid. Naturally it was of Jett looking unbelievably handsome, with Gianna behind him, her arms draped lovingly round his neck.

'What am I supposed to do with it?' she asked blankly.

'I thought you'd like to have it,' Nigel said. 'Stick it on your screen saver and enjoy the view.'

'I'm sure Max would be pleased about that,' she said tartly.

'Isn't it a coincidence,' Nigel mused, 'that this *hot* male model should turn out to be your fiancé's brother? He's *your* family too, or at least he soon will be. Can you imagine Christmas and Thanksgiving and all the holidays you'll spend together? He and Gianna will have *beautiful* babies. You and Max will too. You'll be *such* a gorgeous family, straight out of a Ralph Lauren ad.'

'Stop thinking ahead, Nigel,' she said, wishing he'd shut up.

'Oh, sorry,' Nigel said apologetically. 'I keep on forgetting what you're going through. Postponing the wedding must be getting you down.'

'It is.'

'I understand *perfectly*,' Nigel said, giving her a sympathetic pat on the shoulder. 'Please give Max my best regards and tell him I'm *so* sorry about everything.'

'I'll do that,' she said, heading out of the door.

She had no intention of seeing her mother *or* Max. Her plan was to rush home, take a shower, get herself together, and be ready for Jett at seven o'clock.

Suddenly she was radiating excitement.

* * *

Across the studio Jett watched as Amy left. This had been one of the most uncomfortable days he could remember. Standing in front of the camera attempting to look edgy and macho, with Amy somewhere behind the lights watching him while Gianna draped herself all over him. It was pure torture.

And, to make it even worse, he couldn't stand Antonio. The fussy little photographer was getting on his nerves the way he was constantly kissing up to Gianna.

Half-way through the afternoon, Sofia Courtenelli had appeared, dragging with her a young Italian guy who had done nothing but lounge around throwing Jett disgusted looks.

'Did I happen to take his job?' Jett asked Gianna, between set-ups.

'No, *carino*,' she purred. 'It's simply that Sofia is *so* competitive. She thinks if *you* can be a model, why can't Carlo? She doesn't understand you are a professional.'

'Great,' Jett said.

'They pay us lot of money. You no worry.'

'Who's worried?' he said irritably.

'*Bene*, because tonight we have dinner with them.'

'Can't do that, I have to see Max,' he said quickly, thinking of his meeting with Amy. Besides, there was nothing he'd like less than dinner with Sofia Courtenelli and her jealous boyfriend.

'*Prego*,' Gianna said unconcernedly. 'Then you join us later.'

'Sure,' he agreed, with no intention of doing so.

It occurred to him that it was about time he told Gianna they were over, that he wasn't coming back to Italy, that he didn't want to live with her anymore, that she wasn't his girlfriend and she should go ahead and find some other guy.

But what if Amy didn't want anything more to do with him? What if she *was* in love with Max, and he'd been no more than a casual one-nighter? Did he really want to leave himself with no options?

Man, it was some situation. He'd never felt this way about anyone before, and it wasn't because Amy belonged to someone else. It was because he genuinely cared about her.

The bitter truth was that he'd fallen in love with Amy long before he'd realized she was taken.

*　*　*

After a busy day finalizing things with the Japanese bankers, meeting with his executives, visiting the building site and making sure Lulu was happy with Mrs Conner – who had agreed to stay over for the rest of the week until he hired a new nanny – Max had an early steak dinner with Chris, then met with Detective Rodriguez who had requested another meeting.

Before he'd got together with the detective, Max had checked with his lawyer, Elliott Minor, who'd assured him it was just as well to co-operate.

'Why?' he'd asked.

'Because if you don't,' Elliott had answered patiently, 'it looks as if you've got something to hide.'

'Well, I don't.'

'*I* know that. So do they.'

'Then *why*, Elliott?'

'Because it's not *about* you, Max. It's about them finding out more about Mariska.'

'What's to find out?' he'd asked guardedly.

'How should I know? Friends, family, you might have answers they haven't come up with. Did she have a boy-friend for instance? They're investigating a *murder*, Max, and a very high-profile one at that. Look, if it makes you more comfortable, I can be there.'

'That's not necessary,' he said, thinking if he couldn't handle Detective Rodriguez, he was certainly in a sorry state. Besides, he had nothing to hide. Only the fact that he'd taken Mariska's box from her apartment, which contained more than a few things she obviously hadn't wanted anybody to know about.

Detective Rodriguez turned up on time. As far as Max was concerned, the man was as annoying as ever, with his cheap aftershave and joke of a moustache.

'Mr Diamond,' Detective Rodriguez said, proffering his clammy hand. 'I'm sorry to bother you again. Is it all right if my colleague and I come in and I ask you a few more questions?'

'Certainly,' Max said, leading them into the living room.

Detective Rodriguez's colleague was a broad-faced, overly tall woman, with stringy brown hair and an incongruous vampy red lipstick dominating her rather large mouth. She was the same detective who'd spoken to Lulu the day before.

'Good evening, Mr Diamond,' she said, in a barely-there voice. 'Excuse the way I sound, but I think I'm coming down with something.'

Nice! A detective breathing germs all over him.

'Can I fix you a drink, Detectives?' Max asked, pouring himself a brandy.

'Not allowed to drink on duty,' Detective Rodriguez said, sitting down on the couch. 'But I wouldn't say no to a Seven-Up.'

'Let me see,' Max said, checking out the small fridge behind the bar, 'how about Diet Coke?'

'Too sweet for me,' Detective Rodriguez responded. 'I'll take a bottle of water if you've got it.'

'Anything for you?' Max asked the female detective.

She shook her head.

Max handed Detective Rodriguez a bottle of Evian, and sat down on the other couch, facing them.

'I expect you're wondering what we've found out,' Detective Rodriguez said, rolling the Evian bottle between his large hands. 'I would've thought we might've heard from you.'

'Why would you hear from me?' Max asked.

'Usually when there's a murder in the family the relatives are anxious to get an update on any information they can.'

'It's been less than forty-eight hours,' Max pointed out. 'I presume that when you discover who did this, you'll let me know.'

'That's if you don't read about it first,' Detective Rodriguez said, stroking his moustache. 'I see the press are all over this. I didn't realize your family was so powerful and important.'

Was the detective being sarcastic? Max couldn't tell. He decided to give him the benefit of the doubt. 'How can I help you?' he said, hoping to make this a short meeting.

'Were you by any chance in your wife's apartment last night?' Detective Rodriguez asked, producing his weathered notebook and the usual stubby pencil.

This was a tricky one, and quite unexpected. Max couldn't decide whether to lie or tell the truth. Since lying didn't seem like such a clever idea, he answered truthfully. 'As a matter of fact I was,' he said casually. 'I stopped by to pick up some clothes and a few toys for my little girl. She was very upset, as you can imagine, a child of her age discovering her mother's body. She doesn't realize her mommy's dead. We've told her she's in the hospital. But it's still very traumatic and I felt that Lulu needed her things around her.'

'You crossed a police line,' Detective Rodriguez said, pursing his lips disapprovingly.

'I didn't think it would matter,' Max replied. 'It was my home once, you know. I lived there.'

'That was when you were married to Mrs Diamond, I presume,' Detective Rodriguez said, jotting something in his notebook. 'However, it's not your residence now, is it?'

'I own the building,' Max couldn't help saying.

'Yes, Mr Diamond, only I'm sure you understand that there are rules, strict *reasons* why we secure a crime scene. It's so that people can't go in and tamper with evidence.'

'I didn't touch anything,' Max said, trying not to stare at the detective's crooked front teeth. 'I went straight to my daughter's room, collected her things and left.'

'I see,' Detective Rodriguez said, putting down his notebook and undoing the cap on the bottle of water he'd been hanging on to. 'Well, I'm sure you'll be glad to know that your alibi checks out.'

'My *alibi*?'

'The rehearsal dinner.'

'Why wouldn't it?' Max said, his temper rising.

The female detective began to cough.

'You *were* where you said you were,' Detective Rodriguez continued, ignoring both Max's obvious irritation and his colleague's coughing fit. 'But Irena, who we just found out is Mrs Diamond's mother—'

Max almost choked on his drink. 'Excuse me?' he said. 'Irena, Mariska's personal *maid*?'

'Yes, we checked things out, and it's clear she *is* Mrs Diamond's mother, although for some obscure reason she's not exactly admitting it.'

The female detective, still coughing, stood up and requested the bathroom. 'By the front door,' Max said, more interested in finding out what else Detective Rodriguez had to say. 'What do you mean, she's not admitting it?'

'It always strikes me as strange the way people act when there's been a murder,' Detective Rodriguez mused. 'It's almost as though everyone has something to hide, and sometimes they do.'

'Surely you can't suspect *Irena* of murdering Mariska?'

'No, not at all. In fact, it was Irena who informed us that

Mrs Diamond had many friends in the Russian community. Did you know that, Mr Diamond?'

'No, I didn't,' he said, thinking of the book he'd found filled with names he'd never heard of.

'Irena seems to think there's a phone book missing,' Detective Rodriguez said.

Max stared at the man. Was he by chance a thought-reader in his spare time?

'It contains the names and numbers of Mrs Diamond's Russian acquaintances,' Detective Rodriguez continued. 'Problem is, I can't seem to find it in the apartment. You didn't happen to notice it when you broke in, did you?'

'I didn't *break* in,' Max said, resenting the detective's attitude. 'I thought I explained it to you. I *own* the building. I *lived* in the apartment. I didn't think there was anything wrong with collecting some of my child's personal possessions.'

'Right.' A long, silent beat. 'Please make sure it doesn't happen again, Mr Diamond.'

'What else can I do for you?' Max asked, standing up in the hope it would indicate their meeting was over.

'I was wondering if you've thought of anything at all that might help us.'

'Regarding what?'

'Mrs Diamond's Russian connections.'

'I just told you. I know nothing about them.'

'I have a strong hunch it's an inside job,' Detective Rodriguez said, peering intently at Max. 'No sign of forced entry, and the robbery was slap-dash, almost as though the perpetrator murdered the woman, then decided he or she better make it *look* like a robbery. This crime was committed by someone she knew.'

'Really?' Max said, refilling his brandy glass.

'Yes. I'm almost *positive* she knew her killer.'

'That's interesting,' Max said, returning to the couch.

'I'm wondering if you have any ideas?'

'No,' Max said brusquely, anxious to be rid of the man. 'We've been divorced for over a year. Mariska had her own life. I *do* know she had many acquaintances in New York society, but if she was close to anybody in particular, I didn't know about it.'

'Hmm . . .' Detective Rodriguez said, picking up his notebook again. 'Oh, yes, remind me,' he added, chewing on the pencil stub. 'Did you say you were unaware that Irena was related to your ex-wife?'

'I was completely unaware of it.'

The female detective returned to the room and sat down. She was no longer coughing. Max found it unnerving that she'd hardly said anything.

'Have you spoken to Irena since the murder?' Detective Rodriguez inquired, scribbling something else.

'No, I haven't,' Max snapped. He'd had enough and was anxious for them to leave.

'You might want to.'

'Why would I?'

'If Mrs Diamond *was* her daughter, then that makes Lulu her granddaughter, doesn't it?'

'I suppose so,' Max said, reluctant to give *that* thought any credit.

'Irena is carrying on about missing money. It seems Mrs Diamond was her sole means of support. Apparently she paid her in cash every week. Irena says there was a stash of cash in the apartment.' A short silence. 'We can't locate it,' Detective Rodriguez said, in an almost accusatory tone. 'Strange, don't you think?'

'Not at all,' Max answered smoothly. 'You said it was a robbery. Obviously if there *was* cash lying around, the burglar or burglars took it.'

'Hmm . . . maybe.' A beat. 'Irena never lived in, did she?'

'No. I think she came three times a week to take care of Mariska's clothes and personal items.'

'Did she have a key?'

'Surely you've asked *her*?'

'Just double-checking,' Detective Rodriguez said, finally standing up.

Max stood also.

'Um, by the way, was Irena working for your ex-wife when you first got married?'

'No,' Max said, tired of the questions. 'Mariska brought her in a year after that. I was under the impression that she'd hired her from an employment agency.'

'I can't think of anything else for now. Can you?' the detective said, glancing over at his colleague.

The female detective shook her head.

Detective Rodriguez moved towards the door. 'We'll be in touch,' he promised.

Max walked behind him.

'Oh,' the detective said, stopping for a moment. 'And you're *sure* you didn't happen to notice that phone book lying around?'

'I'm positive,' Max said.

'Good night, Mr Diamond.'

'Good night, Detective.'

*   *   *

While Max met with the detectives, Chris shut himself in the guest room and started making numerous phone calls, attempting to catch up.

One of the first was to Roth Giagante to check that Roth's people were handling all the proper preparations for Birdy's upcoming Vegas wedding.

'Don't worry 'bout it,' Roth said, in his raspy voice. 'Worry 'bout payin' me my fuckin' money.'

'Red sends you his best regards,' Chris said evenly. 'We both enjoyed the joke. You should've been an actor, you missed your calling.'

'*What* fuckin' joke?'

'The putting on the pressure and the hooker. By the way, I think I told you she stole my Rolex. Next time hire a better class of girl. Thieving doesn't reflect well on you.'

'Shit!' Roth growled.

'Yeah, shit,' Chris agreed. 'When I fly in for the wedding I'll have your money.'

He hung up, feeling satisfied. Screw Roth Giagante. He'd thought they were friends, but one word from Red and it was over.

At least something positive had come out of it. The experience had definitely cured him of gambling fever.

Next he called Jett. He'd spoken to him earlier and invited him for dinner with Max, but Jett had explained that he and Gianna had to get together with Sofia Courtenelli and her boyfriend. Chris hoped his baby brother wasn't bullshitting him. It wouldn't be cool if he was sniffing around after Amy although, according to Max, Amy was spending the evening with her mother.

There was no answer from Jett's cell, so Chris called Birdy, who was in a sweet-as-apple-pie mood, all giggly and girly and full of Las Vegas wedding plans.

'Rocky's flying to Vegas a few days earlier,' she revealed. 'Some of his guys are throwing him a bachelor retreat. Isn't that like the *coolest*?'

'What's a bachelor retreat?' Chris asked, inwardly groaning because he knew it would turn out to be trouble.

'Y' know, the guys sit around, play cards, run movies, hit a few balls, take a boat out on Lake Mead.'

Translation: *The guys go to Vegas, get totally blasted on tequila shooters and visit every strip club in town.*

'Are you happy about him doing that?' Chris asked.

'Course,' Birdy trilled. 'My girls are booking us a bungalow at the Beverly Hills Hotel, and we're like going to have mani-pedis, facials, mud baths, all *kinds* of girly stuff.'

Translation: *The girls sit out by the pool at the Beverly Hills Hotel downing cosmopolitans and bitching endlessly about their boyfriends.*

'Sounds great,' Chris lied.

'I know!' Birdy said enthusiastically. 'I'm flying back to L.A. tomorrow. You should come with. My record company's sending me a plane.'

'Is Rocky on it?'

'No. He's gotta see some family, then he'll go directly to Vegas.'

Why not fly with Birdy? Chris thought. He couldn't stay away forever, and Max seemed intent on doing his own thing.

He'd spoken to Andy several times. The rain had finally

stopped, and Andy informed him that he'd managed to salvage quite a lot from his house – *including* his safe. He had arranged for everything to be cleaned and put in storage, except the safe, which he'd had transported to his own apartment for safe-keeping.

Fortunately the house itself had *not* slid down the hillside. That was a major bonus.

Andy was a smart kid: he'd already hired architectural contractors to see what could be done about securing the foundations and repairing the damage. A big fat raise was definitely in his future.

Yes, Chris decided, there were many reasons he should get back. 'What time are you taking off?' he asked Birdy.

'Around noon,' she chirped. '*Please* come.'

'I'll meet you at the airport,' he said.

He'd tell Max later, he was sure his brother would understand.

Chapter Fifty-Four

The Soviet Club was a home away from home for the many Russian expatriates who had made New York their place of residence. The food was good, the vodka the finest, and the atmosphere reminiscent of a fancy European nightspot.

Sonja Sivarious always enjoyed spending time at the Soviet Club: she felt comfortable there. It was light years away from her real life of girl-on-girl shows and sleeping with rich old men for money. At the Soviet Club she was regarded as a beautiful woman who loved to enjoy herself. Most people thought she was a beauty consultant, and sometimes if she liked a man she met there, she would sleep with him for free.

Her cousin Igor, when he bothered to dress properly, was quite a handsome escort in spite of his tendency to put on weight. Vladimir, Igor's friend, always managed to look shabby, although tonight he, too, had made quite an effort. Sonja knew it was on account of Famka. The poor man lusted after Famka, who usually chose to ignore him. Tonight something was different. Tonight Vladimir had acquired a certain energy that he did not usually possess.

Famka, dazzling in a purple cocktail dress, noticed it too. Swilling back her second White Russian, she hiccuped delicately, and said to Sonja, 'What is with Vladimir? You notice change?'

'Yes,' Sonja agreed, resplendent in a clinging yellow jersey dress, her new pearls fastened proudly round her neck. 'Igor says he has something to tell us.' Lowering her voice, Sonja added, 'Igor says he is getting plenty money.'

'No!' Famka said. 'Not Vladimir.'

'Yes,' Sonja insisted. 'Igor is sure.'

There was a noisy group at the next table: three very young American girls with two older Russian men. Sonja knew one of the guys, Alex Pinchinoff, a man to steer clear of. Russian Mafia. Dangerous. She'd slept with him once, and that was enough. He'd handcuffed her to his bed and practically choked her to death with his enormous member. She felt sorry for the three young girls sitting at his table. One was going to get very unlucky indeed.

After a hearty meal of borscht and blinis, beef Stroganoff and red cabbage, Vladimir said he had an announcement to make.

Sonja downed her third shot glass of vodka and gave him a challenging look. 'Go ahead,' she said. 'Surprise us.'

'I will!' Vladimir said boldly, shooting an admiring glance at Famka. 'I surprise you good.'

Famka leaned a little closer to him, her large breasts almost popping out of her purple dress. 'Go ahead,' she murmured, wondering how he'd be in bed. Plain men were usually better at sex than handsome ones. Famka enjoyed a man who could make her come. Her clients never did, hard as some of them tried.

'My wife,' he said, slurring his words. 'She die.'

'Wife?' Famka said scornfully. 'You not *have* wife. Who would marry *you*?'

'Go on, tell them,' Igor encouraged, his eyes bulging.

'Famous *woman*, my wife,' Vladimir boasted. 'Famous and *rich*.'

'Julia Roberts,' Famka teased.

'Nicole Kidman,' Sonja said, joining in the fun.

'Or Angelina Jolie. She *veree* sexy,' Famka said, licking her lips. 'Good for *me*, not you.'

'Vladimir is *not* shitting with you,' Igor said, defending his friend. 'Vladimir was married to woman in newspapers. Murder victim. *Famous* murder victim. And rich.'

'Yes, rich,' Vladimir agreed. 'And she was *my* wife. I am legal husband, so all money is *mine*.'

'No!' Famka said, laughing derisively. 'You make up story.'

'Show them the document,' Igor urged, giving Vladimir a sharp nudge. 'Show it to them. *Then* the bitches will believe you.'

'Who you calling bitches?' Sonja objected, while Vladimir dug into his pocket and came up with a crumpled marriage certificate. He handed it to Sonja.

'Who's Paulina Kuchinova?' Sonja said, studying it. 'Never heard of her.'

'Mariska Diamond, the society woman who get herself murdered,' Vladimir said.

Now Sonja burst out laughing. 'You full of shit.'

'I can prove it.'

'How?'

'I have wedding picture that tell story. She was prostitute – like you.'

'I *not* prostitute,' Sonja said angrily. 'I am therapist to very rich men. *Prostitutes* work the street. They *dirty* girls.'

'You *not* dirty girl?' Vladimir said slyly.

'Show me picture, or you nothing but lying scum,' Sonja said, picking up the bottle of vodka from the table and pouring herself another shot.

'I get picture to show you,' Vladimir said.

'Then what?' Famka asked, curious as to why he would invent such a story. 'You go to police and tell them she your wife?'

'After they catch murderer, yes.'

'How you *know* they catch him?' Sonja asked, with a sly wink. 'Mebbe they think it *you*. Mebbe they arrest *you*.'

'Me?' Vladimir said, outraged. 'I do lot of bad things, but not murder.'

'Yeah,' Sonja said, beginning to feel horny, and not believing Vladimir's pathetic story. She glanced over at the gangster sitting at the next table.

Alex Pinchinoff caught her eye and raised his glass to her. Apparently he'd enjoyed a better time than she had during their previous encounter in bed.

Maybe she should give him a second chance, after all. There were no other likely prospects in sight.

* * *

'Hi,' Amy said, throwing open her front door.

'Hey,' Jett responded, stepping inside. 'For you,' he said, thrusting a bunch of yellow roses at her.

Why had he bought her flowers? It was a romantic gesture he should not be making. And yet – who was she kidding? It was a sweet thing for him to do.

'How are you?' she asked, in her best polite voice.

Dumb question because she'd only left the photo shoot an hour ago and he'd been fine then.

'Okay,' he said, wandering into her living room.

'Uh . . . would you like a glass of wine?' she asked, feeling awkward as she followed him, clutching the roses, which were beginning to drip.

'I don't drink,' he said, realizing how little they knew about each other. Should he confess that he was once a raging alcoholic? A stoned-out-of-his-mind, sex-crazed, drugs-and-booze junkie? Or should he wait and let her discover his nefarious past for herself?

The diplomatic move was to wait. But what the hell? He was determined to be up-front about everything. 'I'm in the programme,' he blurted.

'Oh, uh . . . sorry,' she said, taking the flowers into her small kitchen and searching for a vase.

'Sorry that I'm in the programme? Or that I don't drink?' he asked, walking in behind her.

'I'm not big on drinking,' she said, finding a vase and filling it with water.

'You could've fooled me,' he said lightly. 'The other night you were certainly feeling no pain.'

Just like that he was bringing it up. And now it was up to her to defend herself and her actions. 'Yes,' she admitted, trying not to get uptight. 'I *was* drunk, and I guess that's why I did what I did.'

'You weren't *that* wasted,' he said, leaning on the counter-top, watching her as she arranged the flowers.

'Yes, I was,' she said, trying not to look at him.

'Does this mean that every time you have too much to drink, you fall into bed with a stranger?' he asked, gently teasing her. 'Is that what I'm getting here?'

'No. But—'

'Tell me, Amy,' he said, becoming serious, 'I gotta know – what happened between us?'

'I . . . I don't know,' she managed, thinking, *I'm not ready for a confrontation*.

'It's kinda obvious you're not sleeping with Max.'

She didn't answer.

A long beat. 'Do you love him?'

'It's – it's none of your business,' she said, picking up the vase and carrying it into the living room.

'Well, *that*'s a resounding no,' he said, once more right behind her.

'Do *not* put words into my mouth.'

'I'm not.'

'Yes, you *are*,' she said crossly. 'Max and I are very happy together.'

'So *that*'s why you slept with me. *Now* I understand, it's 'cause you're so wildly happy with *him*.'

'You know what, Jett?' she said agitatedly. 'Meeting like this was a mistake. We have nothing to say to each other and I don't care to fight. What happened – well, it just happened. We should leave it at that.'

'What if I can't?' he said, moving closer to her.

'Excuse me?' she said, backing away.

'What if I *can't*, Amy?' he said insistently. 'What if I've fallen for you in a big way? What if you're the girl I've been looking for?'

'That's ridiculous,' she murmured, shaking her head as if to convince herself that what he was saying was nonsense.

'Is it?'

'You're with Gianna,' she said breathlessly. 'I'm with Max. We had a moment—'

'Hey,' he interrupted, giving her a long, intense look, 'it was a lot more than a moment *and* you know it.'

'No, I don't,' she said, totally flustered.

'Yes, you *do*,' he said, moving closer again.

And before either of them realized what was happening, he was touching her shoulder, and somehow his touch turned into an embrace, and the embrace turned into a frenzy of passionate kissing. *I'm sober*, Amy thought, *and I'm doing this. What's wrong with me?*

But she couldn't stop kissing him, didn't want to. And soon his hands were on her breasts, then they were under the silk camisole top she'd changed into as soon as she'd stepped out of the shower. She'd wanted to look pretty for him. Deep down, she'd *known* this was going to happen.

No! screamed her inner voice.

Yes! it screamed back at her.

He started kissing her neck, causing her to shudder with the anticipation of what was to come.

Half-heartedly she attempted to push him away. 'We can't do this,' she said, in a low voice. 'It's not fair to Max.'

'I know,' he said, and then he was kissing her again, and somehow or other they made it to the bedroom, magically losing their clothes along the way.

'You are so fucking *perfect*,' he muttered, rolling on the bed with her, stroking her breasts, kissing her nipples, moving his lips down to her flat stomach, then moving further down and slowly but surely spreading her legs. Within seconds his head was between her thighs, his tongue doing unbelievable things.

She grabbed a pillow, covering her face, waves of desire flooding her senses.

He was taking her on a trip, a trip so exciting and sensual that she could barely contain her groans of sheer pleasure, until finally she gave it up, moaning with delight as she reached the ultimate peak.

He emerged from between her thighs, hair rumpled, a pleased look on his face. 'Good, huh?'

'Beyond good,' she murmured, embarrassed to look at him.

'Hey,' he said, removing the pillow she was attempting to hide behind, 'There's more where that came from.'

And then he was moving on top of her, and she made no attempt to stop him. She *wanted* him inside her. She *wanted* to feel him close to her.

And once again it was everything and more, even better than the first time.

After it was over, and they were lying on her bed in the dark, the guilt began creeping back.

'Jett . . .' she said tentatively.

'What, baby?' he asked, reaching over to touch her.

'This – this isn't right,' she said, forcing herself to say the words.

'Feels like it is,' he said, stretching lazily.

'No, it isn't. We can't do this.'

'Why not?'

'You *know* why.'

'Because of Max, huh?' he said, wondering if she'd mind if he lit a cigarette, then deciding she definitely would, so he didn't bother asking.

'That's right.'

'But, Amy,' he said, propping himself up on one elbow and gazing down at her, 'you gotta realize that Max isn't right for you.'

'Please listen to me, Jett,' she said earnestly. 'I *can't* leave him, not with everything he's going through. Besides, you're with Gianna, you live in Italy.'

'How many times have I gotta tell you?' he said impatiently. 'Gianna an' me, we're *not* together.'

'You sleep together,' she said accusingly.

'Casual sex,' he responded.

'What's *casual* about sex?' she said, frowning. 'To me it's a commitment. A future together. A family. A *life*.'

'*Whoa*!' he exclaimed. 'You *are* a serious girl.'

'I never said I wasn't. And what we're doing is wrong.'

'Does it *feel* wrong?' he asked, stroking her face.

She sat up, reaching for a sheet to cover herself. 'Yes,' she muttered. 'To me it does.'

'You're lying.'

'If I am, it's to protect both of us,' she said, sighing deeply. 'This can't go any further. I mean it.'

'Look,' he said, 'I'm telling Gianna it's over. If it'll make a difference, I'll do it tonight.'

'You shouldn't on my account. There *is* no future for us. I *have* to stay with Max.'

'Even though you don't love him?' he questioned.

'I *never* said that.'

'You didn't have to.'

She started to cry, tears of pure frustration at the situation she found herself in.

Jett reached over and put his arms round her, cradling her against his chest, stroking her hair and kissing her forehead. 'We're gonna work this out,' he said quietly. 'I promise you, Amy, we're gonna work this out so that you and I can be together, because *you* know as sure as *I* do that it's where we both belong.'

* * *

Detective Rodriguez irritated the crap out of Max. He couldn't stand him with his dumb moustache and intrusive questions.

As soon as the two detectives were out of his apartment, Max poured himself another brandy – his third. Then he knocked on the guest-room door.

Chris was still on the phone talking to his office in L.A. He held up a hand indicating to Max that he would be through in a couple of minutes.

Max stayed in the room, forcing him to curtail his conversation with Andy.

'Here's the latest,' Chris said, hanging up. 'I have to get back to L.A. tomorrow, so I'm hitching a ride with Birdy Marvel.'

'You *are*?' Max said, trying to hide his disappointment, because having a brother to bond with was a whole new experience, and quite a pleasant one.

'It's necessary,' Chris explained. 'Clients are screaming for my attention, plus I need to deal with my house situation.'

'I understand,' Max said.

'You'll be okay?'

'Of course I will, and I've been thinking.'

'Yes?'

'How about I give you the cash I found in Mariska's box? That way you can pay off your gambling debt.'

'Are you fucking *nuts*?' Chris exploded, looking at his

brother as if he'd totally lost it. 'I wouldn't *touch* that money. Besides, it's not yours, Max. You have to give it up, hand everything over to the detectives or at *least* tell your lawyer about it. Jesus *Christ*! You're too smart to fuck around like this.'

'You think that's what I should do?'

'Damn *right*. Mariska was violently murdered. Vladimir is obviously a desperate man. Step away.'

'I suppose you're right. I *should* do that.'

'*When*, Max?'

'Soon.'

'I hope so, 'cause this is crazy shit.'

'I understand.'

'Did you hear from Red yet?'

'Why would I?'

'He must *know* what happened – it's all over the frigging news. You'd think he'd call.'

'Why are you surprised? *I*'m not.'

'Yeah. Typical Red behaviour,' Chris agreed. 'The bastard doesn't give a shit.'

'That's right.'

'How'd your session with the detective go?'

'He knew I went into the apartment.'

'I bet that pissed him off.'

'Nothing he can do about it now. Oh, and you won't believe this one.'

'Go ahead, surprise me.'

'Mariska's personal maid, Irena, the old Russian woman I can't stand – turns out she's probably Mariska's mother.'

'No *way*,' Chris said.

'Apparently so. I think I should talk to her.'

'Why would you want to do that?'

'She might know something she's not telling the police, something about Vladimir.'

'For Crissakes,' Chris snapped. 'Aren't you *listening* to me? You've gotta *stop* this crap. They're going to find out about Vladimir whatever you do.'

'You think so?'

'Look,' Chris said patiently, 'give the detectives the box

with everything in it, including the money. And remember, *they're* the detectives, not you. Do it soon, Max, because I do *not* want to be the one bailing you out of jail for holding back evidence.'

'That won't happen.'

'I hope you're right. I *really* hope you're right.'

* * *

The Russian gangster was strong, brawny and rough, with big meaty hands to match his big meaty cock.

Sonja would never admit it to anyone but herself, but she was quite into being dominated. It made a welcome change from all the old men she slept with for money. Old rich men with tired cocks and kinky tastes. A good old-fashioned fuck with a manly man made quite a welcome change. Until Alex Pinchinoff stuffed his enormous member into her mouth and attempted to choke her.

That was the moment she remembered why she hadn't wanted to see him again.

At least this time he hadn't insisted on handcuffing her, and he *was* attractive in a sinister kind of way. Tall, with heavy-set features, thick black hair and dominating eyebrows. For a moment she fantasized what it would be like to be married to a man like Alex. He'd want to fuck her every day, knock her up with a kid or two, expect her to cook and clean and give him regular blow-jobs. Then he'd take a mistress, a young American blonde with a tight little pussy and a big American smile.

Fantasy over.

She managed to give him head without gagging. Then he fucked her again until they both came for the second time and she lay there quite spent.

'You pleased to see me tonight?' he asked, lighting up a foul-smelling dark brown cigarette.

They were in the bedroom of his mostly red apartment. Red-painted walls, red carpet, even red sheets.

'You're not bad,' she allowed, with a faint smile.

His big hand went straight to her landing strip of dyed

pubic hair, which he proceeded to tug. 'I make you come?'

'Yes.'

'Not too big for you?'

'No.'

'You interesting woman. Who those morons you with tonight?'

'Not morons,' she said, defending Igor and Vladimir. 'One of them's my cousin. The other guy – he was husband of murdered rich woman. He'll get all her money.'

'What woman?' Alex asked, his interest piqued.

'Murdered *Russian* woman in newspapers,' Sonja replied, wondering where in hell Alex had come across red sheets.

'Paulina Kuchinova?' he questioned, blowing a stream of foul smoke in her direction.

'You know her real name?' Sonja said, surprised. Maybe Vladimir was telling the truth after all. Who would've thought it? 'How you know her real name?'

'I know more than her name?' Alex said, vigorously scratching his balls. 'That bitch owes me plenty money. Whoever killed her did fine job. That was one greedy bitch who had it coming. Ah, yes,' he added, nodding to himself. 'I knew Paulina. I knew her good. So, you tell me where I find Vladimir 'cause now *he* owes *me* plenty money.'

Chapter Fifty-Five

Liberty had a dilemma. Should she go to dinner with Chip and the gang or spend the evening with Damon and Parker J. Jones, her soon-to-be producer? She didn't want to offend Chip – he'd been so great towards her. On the other hand, Damon was in L.A. and, married or not, how could she resist spending time with him?

Away from New York, things seemed cooler. It was almost like she was on vacation where nothing mattered except having a good time. Not that she'd ever been on vacation – it was a luxury she'd missed out on.

Wow! So much going on, and all of it unbelievable. If it wasn't for her mother ruining everything, she'd be flying high.

Damon was staying in the same hotel. What a surprise! She'd told him she'd call him in five minutes.

First she buzzed Teddy's room to check if it was okay to bring Damon and Parker to dinner.

'Damon Donnell, the hip-hop king?' Teddy asked, sounding impressed. 'First Tony A, now Damon Donnell. Didn't you tell me you were a new girl on the scene?'

'I am.'

'*Someone*'s been making up stories.'

'Tony A is a friend from way back,' Liberty explained. 'And Damon's putting me together with Parker J. Jones, the record producer.'

'I'm sure Chip won't mind,' Teddy said. 'Want *me* to call him for you?'

'Would you? Then get straight back to me.'

Within seconds Teddy was on the phone again. 'Chip's down with it.'

Now she had to ask Damon if he'd mind joining *her* friends for dinner. She called him. 'A group scene?' Damon quipped. 'Naw, not for me. I'm into up close an' personal, just the two of us.'

'Be serious,' she scolded. 'Chip's the photographer I'm working with, and the others are fun. I'd love it if you and Parker could join us. Then later we can talk about my music.'

'Talk about her music, the girl says,' Damon drawled. 'Sure, babe. That's *'xactly* what I flew to L.A. for – to talk about your music.'

'You brought a producer with you, didn't you?'

'Yeah.'

'So?'

'So we'll come to dinner.'

'Seven-thirty in the lobby.'

'How many limos should I order?'

'How many *what*?'

'Limos – to get to the restaurant.'

'I'm sure we can grab a cab.'

'Nobody takes cabs in L.A.'

'Maybe you should meet us at the restaurant. It's Ivy at the Shore.'

'Hey, LL, you *do* know I got on a plane 'specially to see you, so don't go givin' me no I'll-catch-up-with-you-later shit.'

'I didn't *ask* you to come here.'

'It'll be worth it.'

'You think?'

He laughed. 'Yeah.'

'Really?' she said. 'But you still have a ring on your finger, right?'

'Man,' he complained. 'You *sure* are playing hard to get.'

'I'm being honest with you. Seems people being honest with you doesn't happen very often.'

'You noticed,' he said wryly.

'You're incredibly hot, Damon,' she said, deciding to throw him off guard, because in spite of what Beverly thought, she knew a thing or two about dealing with men. 'And if you were single,' she continued, 'there's *no way* we'd be having this conversation.'

'We wouldn't, huh?' he said, intrigued.

'No,' she said boldly. 'We'd be rolling around on a bed having insanely wild sex.'

'Now she's tryin' to excite me over the phone,' he groaned. 'An' it's workin'. You into phone sex, babe?'

'No, thanks,' she said crisply. 'And, believe me, I am *not* trying to excite you. I'm simply telling you the way it is – 'cause if you flew here to sleep with me, you can forget it.'

'Man, you're a tough one,' he grumbled.

'It's called self-preservation.'

'So *that*'s what it's called.'

'Reverse the roles, you'll get it.'

'Smart too.'

'I try.'

'Well, LL, you think you can ride with me to the restaurant?'

'I'm supposed to meet everybody in the lobby at seven-thirty.'

'I'll come get you at seven-fifteen. We'll arrive early, grab a mojito or two.'

She called Teddy back and told him they were coming and that they'd all meet up at the restaurant.

'Miss *Thing*!' Teddy exclaimed delightedly. 'You know absolutely *everybody*. I am *sooo impressed*!'

*   *   *

After an awkward start, everyone got along well. Liberty had to admit that Damon possessed charm and then some. He was warm and friendly, and in no way at all did he play the I'm-a-big-hip-hop-record-mogul role.

Parker J. Jones – a big man with a matching personality – was a riot. It turned out he'd produced records for Brandy, Birdy Marvel, Toni Braxton, and a host of other female stars.

Teddy and Quinn were all over him and even Uma was fascinated by his stories – especially the Birdy Marvel ones.

Uma was obsessed with Birdy Marvel, she listened avidly as Parker confided that Birdy was a major pop-tart diva, with outrageous demands, including serious perks for whatever hunk she was banging at the time.

Chip and Damon bonded. They were both into cars. Chip had recently purchased his first Ferrari – a 575 Maranello, and it turned out Damon owned three very special Ferraris, including the new Superamerica, *and* a Maserati.

'Man, I gotta photograph you with your cars,' Chip said enthusiastically. 'For sure it's a *Rolling Stone* cover. Or *Vanity Fair*. Graydon will *definitely* get off on the car thing.'

'Don't wanna disappoint, but I'm not into doin' much personal PR,' Damon admitted. 'I kinda leave that shit to my wife.'

Then he caught Liberty listening, and was sorry he'd mentioned the word *wife*.

Screw him, Liberty thought, freezing up. After two glasses of wine she'd started thinking about what *could* happen between them. Then, when she heard the wife comment, it was over. Determinedly she turned her attention to Parker, where it should've been in the first place. After all, *Parker* was her future, *he* was the one who was going to help make sure she sounded great.

'Did you get a chance to listen to my demo?' she asked him.

'That's why I'm here,' Parker said, enjoying a dish of crab cakes. 'Listened to it with Damon an' I liked what I heard. Wouldn't've flown to L.A. if I hadn't. Although I gotta say, any time I can hitch a ride on Damon's plane it's kinda hard t' say no. You bin on it?'

'I haven't.'

'Well, then, little lady, you got yourself one big freakin' treat waitin' for you. That dude sure knows how to treat himself like a king.'

'So you *really* liked my demo?' she asked, steering the conversation back to her music.

'With a few reservations,' Parker said. 'Nothin' we can't fix.'

'Reservations?' she asked, alarmed. 'Like *what*?'

'You gotta think about your material. Right now it's too damn dark 'n' gloomy. An' remember – you *ain't* no Alicia Keys, so stop tryin' to copy her style. She's an original, an' that's what you're gonna be.'

'I'm not copying anyone,' she objected.

'Now *don't* go gettin' defensive on me,' Parker warned, ''cause we gotta lotta work t' do together. Big lesson – learn to listen to criticism and take it in 'cause if you can't do that we ain't goin' nowhere. Are we understandin' each other?'

She nodded, suitably chastised. Parker was a professional. She wasn't. Not yet. She would do as he said, listen and learn.

Hopefully it would all work out.

*   *   *

Driving back to the hotel, Liberty found herself alone in the limo with Damon.

'Where's Parker?' she asked, a touch breathlessly. 'I thought he was coming with us.'

Damon laughed. 'Yeah, well, here's the deal. Parker's got himself a hot little honey he keeps stashed in Beverly Hills. *That*'s the real reason he flew to L.A. on such short notice.'

'I thought *I* was the reason,' she joked.

'Yeah, yeah, no offence, but he ain't gonna get no sweet juice outta *you*.'

'Is he married?'

'There she *goes* again.' Damon sighed, shaking his head. 'What *are* you? A secret rep for the moral majority?'

'Can't help it if I have principles,' she said, smiling lightly.

'Guess that means I'm not gettin' any tonight.'

'Tonight. Tomorrow night. You *know* why.'

'Yeah, yeah. I know,' he said ruefully. 'I'm *married*. An' it don't mean nothin' t' you that my wife an' me – we got ourselves an *arrangement*.'

'Not what *I* heard.'

'Yeah? What didja hear?'

'That your wife would beat any girl's head in with her eight-hundred-dollar Manolos if she caught you playing. Apparently she's *fierce*.'

Damon burst out laughing. '*My* wife wouldn't do nothin' with them Manolos if she thought it might damage 'em. She's a shoe-whore, baby. A shoe-whore all the way.'

'Whatever,' Liberty said, leaning back against the leather seat, thinking, *Who would've believed less than a week ago that I'd be sitting in a limo in L.A. with Damon P. Donnell himself. It's too much!*

'I've been meanin' to ask you, how come you don't sound like no other black chicks I know?' Damon asked, reaching over and taking her hand.

'I don't?'

'You know you don't.'

'I guess it's 'cause my mom got a job uptown, pulled me out of school in Harlem and sent me to a fancy one in Manhattan,' she explained, carefully withdrawing her hand from his. 'I *hated* the new school, and everyone hated *me*. I didn't fit in, but I suppose that's where I learned to speak properly.'

'What's your mom do?'

'She *was* a singer,' Liberty said, and hesitated. Then she continued, 'Uh . . . now she's a housekeeper to some crappy old billionaire.'

'A billionaire, huh? The kinda dude *I* might know?'

'Red Diamond. His son's ex-wife was found stabbed to death this week.'

'Jeez! That story's everywhere. There's a panic run on hirin' security guards.'

'There is?'

'What's the real scam?'

Liberty shrugged. 'Beats me.'

'You mean your mom don't got no inside?'

'I haven't asked her.'

'No, *you* wouldn't.'

'What do you mean by that?'

'Too many principles t' go diggin' for dirt, right?'

'Something *wrong* with that?'

'Don't sweat it. You're an original, babe, an' I'm into originals.'

The limo pulled into the driveway of the hotel and Damon

helped her out. 'Here's the plan,' he said. 'We're gonna take a romantic stroll along the beach.'

'First of all, you and I are *not* romantic, it's late, I have to be up early, and—'

'How many excuses you gonna come up with?' he asked, looking amused. 'Relax, LL, it's not often you get t' do this kinda thing.'

'Well . . .' she said unsurely.

'C'mon, babe,' he said, guiding her through a side gate. 'Live dangerously or you're not livin' at all.'

As they hit the vast expanse of sand that led down to the ocean, he bent down and started taking his Nikes off.

She slipped out of the silver sandals Uma had given her that morning, and rolled up her cargo pants. When she was done, Damon grabbed her hand and began running with her down the beach towards the ocean. The sand felt smooth and cool beneath her bare feet, and the sound of the waves crashing on the shore was quite hypnotizing. She felt invigorated and alive, realizing that this was a night to savour.

When they were almost at the ocean, he stopped, pulled her to him and, without saying a word, began to kiss her.

She found herself powerless to say no. What did it *really* matter that he was married? She wasn't planning a long love affair with him. Anyway, he'd told her that he and his wife had an arrangement, so why not?

No! She knew enough about men and their desires to realize that he was only offering to help her with her career because she was playing hard to get. A man like Damon could probably sleep with any woman he chose. He had it all – looks, power, money, not to mention a fleet of Ferraris, and, to top it all off, his own plane.

Damon P. Donnell had everything most women wanted. But he *didn't* have her. And that's what made her different.

She was thinking all this while they kissed, his tongue exciting her senses, but not enough that she was about to succumb to his advances.

'You're a great kisser,' she said breathlessly, breaking apart from him. 'But my call tomorrow is six a.m., so I'm heading back to the hotel.'

'You are?' he said, surprised. She was right, turn-downs were not an everyday occurrence in Damon's life.

She started walking, then turned and called out, 'Coming?'

'Yeah, in my pants,' he muttered, chasing after her, once more grabbing her hand. '*You* are somethin', LL.'

'I'll take that as a compliment.'

'You do that.'

They made it to the lobby, windswept and out of breath. And there stood Tony A, in all his white-suited and streaked-spiky-hair glory, an uptight Hector hovering by his side.

'Where have you *been*?' Tony asked, stepping forward with a proprietary air about him. 'I thought we'd arranged to get together.'

'She's *been* with me,' Damon said, jumping aggressively into the picture. 'So . . . you got somethin' to say, then say it to me, dude.'

Chapter Fifty-Six

First thing Wednesday morning Mrs Conner appeared in the kitchen. Max had already been up for a couple of hours unable to sleep. Try as he might, he couldn't forget the vivid image of Mariska sprawled on her bed in a pool of blood.

For a while he'd attempted to work on his computer, but there was too much on his mind for him to concentrate on business. So many questions, and how was he supposed to find the answers?

In a way it would be a relief if Vladimir turned up at his office, but he had a feeling the man would lie low for a while, stay out of sight.

He'd made up his mind that today he would contact Irena, go see her and listen to what she had to say. If she *was* Mariska's mother, then she might be the one with the answers to all his questions.

Finally he'd abandoned doing any work and gone into the kitchen to make coffee, which was where Mrs Conner found him.

'Good morning, Mr Diamond,' Mrs Conner said, bustling in and taking over the coffee-making duty.

'You're up early,' he remarked, glancing at his watch, noting it was a few minutes before seven.

'I've always been an early riser,' Mrs Conner said, filling the coffee-maker with water. 'In my home town of Glasgow, seven o'clock was considered far too late for a person to be getting their lazy selfs out of bed.'

'Where's Lulu?' he asked, suppressing a yawn.

'The wee girly is still asleep,' Mrs Conner responded. 'The two of us had quite an afternoon yesterday. I took her to the park, then we stopped for ice-cream, and after that she came to the market with me and picked out all her favourite cereals and cookies.'

'She enjoys spending time with you,' Max commented.

'And me with her,' Mrs Conner answered. 'She's a bonny little girl. This tragedy is such a shame—'

'Let's not discuss it, Mrs Conner,' he said, cutting her off. 'I think it's a subject we should consider closed as far as Lulu is concerned.'

'I hate to say this, Mr Diamond, but she's bound to find out as soon as she goes back to school. When we arrived home yesterday there were reporters and camera crews outside the building. I shielded the wee babe as best I could, but they were yelling things at her.'

'Jesus Christ!' he said furiously. 'Can't they leave *anyone* alone?'

'I have a suggestion, Mr Diamond. My sister works for a family in Montauk. They live in a lovely house right on the beach, and they've gone off to Europe for a month. They told my sister I could stay with her, and I thought – if you approve – I might take Lulu there for a few days. It will be quiet and it would certainly get the little one away from all this fuss and bother.'

'That sounds good, Mrs Conner. How does Lulu feel about it?'

'I waited to ask you first, but *I* think she'd have quite a time. My sister has twins, two wee ones only a few months younger than Lulu.'

'If she wants to go, then take her,' Max said, quite relieved. 'I haven't even started interviewing nannies yet. I was hoping you'd stay with her until things settle down.'

'It'll be my pleasure, Mr Diamond. Excuse me now. I must go see if our little princess is stirring.' She bustled off.

A few minutes later, Chris came into the kitchen. 'I'm packed and ready to go,' he announced.

'Back to your non-existent house?' Max asked.

'It's not as bad as I thought,' Chris said, pouring himself a mug of coffee. 'Andy tells me the rain has finally stopped and they're dredging the mud from my house, so as soon as everything's been cleaned – if it's not dangerous – I can move back in.'

'Listen,' Max said, 'that was no idle promise when I said I'd loan you the money to get you out of trouble with that guy in Vegas.'

'Really?' Chris said, taking a couple of gulps of hot coffee. 'You'd do that?'

'Wouldn't say it if I didn't mean it. How much do you need?'

'Well, Andy recovered my safe,' Chris said, 'and there's two hundred and fifty thousand in there, so another three hundred and fifty will do it.'

'Consider it taken care of.'

'Thanks, Max. I'm planning to be in Vegas at the weekend for Birdy's wedding. Man, you don't *know* what a freakin' pleasure it'll be to get Roth off my case.'

'I can imagine,' Max said.

'So,' Chris said, pouring himself more coffee, 'the Japanese are on board. Your project's going ahead, everything's cool.'

'It's all good,' Max agreed. 'Back to business as usual.'

'Don't forget what we talked about last night. Hand the box over, tell them Mariska left it with you for safe-keeping and you forgot about it. If they think you took it out of her apartment you'll be in deep shit. Trust me on this.'

Max nodded. He was aware that Chris was right, but at the same time he had to talk to Irena before he did anything.

Lulu bounded into the kitchen. 'Can I go to the beach with Mrs Conner, Daddy? Can I? Can I? *Can I?*' she asked excitedly, hopping up and down.

'Yes, sweetie, if that's what you'd like.'

'*Yes*, Daddy, that's what Lulu *wants*. No school! No! No! *No!* Mrs Conner is my *favourite*.'

'When am *I* gonna be your favourite?' Chris asked, bending down to give her a hug.

'Let me see,' Lulu said, with a cheeky smile, '*you* can be my favourite tomorrow.'

'Can't wait!' Chris replied, winking at Max. 'I always dreamed of meeting a girl like you.'

Lulu dissolved into a fit of childish giggles.

* * *

Amy stirred in her sleep and threw out her arm. She was startled to hit another body. Then it all came rushing back. She was in bed with Jett. Somehow or other he'd ended up spending the night.

Oh, God! What had she done now? Wasn't the first time bad enough?

He was still asleep, snoring lightly. She stared down at his face. He was *so* handsome, and it wasn't just his looks that got her, it was the way he was with her. Last night they'd talked for hours. Other than Tina, he was the first person she'd confided in about her kidnapping ordeal, and it had been such a relief sharing the experience that she'd ended up telling him everything.

'Didn't you ever see a shrink about it?' he'd asked.

'No, my mother told me I had to forget it ever happened.'

'The woman's freakin' *crazy*,' Jett had said. 'She should've immediately gotten you some help.'

'Unfortunately, she didn't.'

'*That's* why you've always been repressed sexually.'

'You think I'm repressed?'

'Until *we* got together you were a twenty-one-year-old virgin living in New York. You consider that normal?'

'I–I don't know.'

'Believe me, it's not. You were sexually molested at fourteen, Amy, and that made you terrified of sex.'

'Then why aren't I terrified with you?'

''Cause we have this amazing chemistry thing going.'

'We do?' she'd said shyly.

'That, or you were totally wasted,' he'd teased. 'It's certainly the reason you've held Max off.'

'You think so?'

'It's a sure thing. It fits right into his hang-up.'

'What's *his* hang-up?'

'He didn't tell you?'

'Tell me *what*?'

'I only know the story from Chris, but apparently when Max was in high school, he had a steady girlfriend. The night of the junior prom he brought her back to the house. Red walked in on them just as they were about to do it.'

'Oh, no!'

'Red started yelling and screaming, sent Max to his room, then the old pervert proceeded to rape the girl. She was sixteen.'

'*What?*' Amy had gasped. 'That's so awful.'

'And *that* is why he's so not into sex. So, you see, the two of you made the perfect pair.'

'He never told me about it.'

'Hey, if you and Max had *any* kind of connection, you'd both know everything about each other, wouldn't you?'

'I feel so bad for him now.'

'Cut it *out*, Amy. Max isn't right for you and you've got to break it off.'

'I can't tell him about us, Jett, I *can't*.'

'You'll do it – eventually. Or he'll find out by himself. We'll sneak around for a while, that's all.'

'I don't *want* to sneak around.'

'Not forever,' Jett had assured her. 'One day we'll bring it out into the open. By that time, Max will have found someone else so it won't break his heart.'

'You don't understand,' she'd said plaintively. 'Max loves me, he *really* loves me.'

'He *loves* you because you're Miss Pure. Don't you *get* it? Nobody can touch you except him. *That*'s what he loves about you, Amy.'

Eventually they'd fallen asleep on top of the tangled sheets, and now it was morning.

'Jett,' Amy murmured softly, catching a glimpse of the bedside clock, 'it's almost eight, we slept right through.'

He struggled to open his eyes. 'Oh, *shit*,' he mumbled.

'What?'

'Gianna's gonna be pissed. I should've let her know I wasn't coming home last night.'

'I thought you told me you had an open relationship.'

'We do, but ever since she's been in New York she's been kind of clingy. It's . . . difficult.'

'I have to get to work,' Amy said, climbing out of bed. 'And you should go do what you have to do.'

'I'll come over later.'

'No.'

'Why not?'

'Because this is all happening too fast,' she said, feeling confused. 'I don't want to sneak around like you said. As it is, *Chris* knows, and how do you think *that* makes me feel?'

'Chris *doesn't* know.'

'Don't lie to me, Jett.'

'Uh . . . well, maybe I mentioned that I like you.'

'I'm not an idiot. You told him, didn't you?' she said accusingly.

'It was a mistake,' he admitted. 'I was so shocked when I saw you at the rehearsal dinner. I'd been talking about you non-stop. Chris knew I was looking for a girl – and then she turned out to be *you*.'

'You were talking about me?' she asked softly. 'Looking for me?'

'From the moment you ran out of my apartment,' he said, pulling her back to bed.

'Yes?'

'You bet.'

'Oh, Jett.' She sighed. 'What are we going to do?'

'We're going to be very, very happy, and that, my sweet girl, is a promise.'

*   *   *

Max made the trek to Brighton Beach, where Irena lived in a run-down apartment building surrounded by shops, Russian restaurants and seedy-looking nightclubs.

Since he hadn't wanted his driver knowing where he was going, he'd driven himself in his usual erratic style.

He'd discovered Irena's address in Mariska's phone book and next to it a phone number. He'd tried the number several times, but nobody had answered, so he'd taken a chance and driven out to see her.

Now he stood outside the crumbling old apartment house, wishing he could've persuaded Chris to come with him. There was something surreal about being in this place, it was as though he'd stepped out of Manhattan into a completely different world – a world of grey skies, stormy ocean breezes drifting in from the nearby beach, drizzling rain, and run-down store-fronts.

Chris was right. Why hadn't he handed everything over to Detective Rodriguez and backed away? He was a businessman, not a goddamn detective.

A line of grimy mailboxes informed him that Irena's apartment was on the fifth floor. The elevator bore a NOT WORKING cardboard sign, so he took the concrete stairs. A strong stink of cat piss, stale beer and old cooking smells pervaded the air. If Irena *was* Mariska's mother, then Mariska sure as hell hadn't cared much about her living conditions.

When he reached the apartment he could hear music playing, loud, strident sounds that were unfamiliar to his ears. There was no doorbell, so he knocked. Once. Twice. Louder.

Nobody came.

An old man in grey pyjamas, with a matching beard and a workman's cap perched jauntily on his head, opened the door of the apartment across the hall, and muttered something in Russian – at least Max presumed it was Russian.

'Excuse me?' Max said.

'Not so much noise,' the old man grumbled, in thickly accented English.

'Is the woman who lives in this apartment home?' Max asked, speaking slowly in a louder-than-usual voice.

'No English,' the old man shouted, retreating back into his place as Irena opened the door to hers.

She stood for a moment, her face frozen with shock. She was a stout, homely-looking woman, with frizzed greyish hair and a florid complexion. 'Mr Diamond,' she said at last, her mouth popping open in surprise. 'What *you* do here?'

'Came to see you, Irena. Can I come in?'

Reluctantly she allowed him into her one cramped room

419

with an unmade bed in the corner, a hot-plate and an old-fashioned ice-box. An ancient black and white TV blared loudly, while a mangy cat lay sleeping contentedly on its back.

Irena switched off the TV and flapped her hands in the air. 'Mrs Diamond,' she lamented. 'Such a terrible thing. So terrible . . .'

As he stood awkwardly in the middle of the room, he noticed a sudden sparkle on Irena's pinky finger. It emanated from a very large diamond ring. The ring he had presented Mariska with on the day they got engaged.

* * *

When Jett burst into Sam's apartment, Gianna was busy packing. 'Hey!' he said.

She barely glanced in his direction.

'Uh, sorry about last night,' he began. 'It was—'

'Nothing,' she interrupted, bestowing an ice-cold look on him.

'Nothing?' he said, taking a crumpled pack of cigarettes from his pocket.

'We finished, Jett, you and I. Finished. *Sopra. Arrivederci.*'

Yeah, they were the words he wanted to hear, but *he* was the one supposed to be saying them, not Gianna.

'I gotta explain what happened,' he said, lighting up a much-needed cigarette.

'No, Jett,' Gianna said, folding an expensive embroidered skirt and placing it in one of her suitcases. 'You made me look *stupida* in front of Sofia. Gianna no like that.'

'I'm sorry,' he said, inhaling deeply.

'Too late, *babee*,' she said, tossing back her long auburn hair. '*Incredibile!*'

'I was with Max,' he lied.

'No,' she said, eyes flashing dangerously. 'I *call* Max, you no there. You possibly with some girl, and that's *non importa*. But to – how you say? – stand me up. Oh no, no, *no*! You cannot do that to Gianna.'

'So you're leaving?'

'*Sì*,' she said abruptly, slamming shut the last of her suitcases.

He didn't know what to say. Gianna was leaving, and that was exactly what he wanted. So why did he feel at a loss, empty, as if she was abandoning him?

Could it be because the only home he had was hers? The only place he'd been really settled and happy was Milan? The only career he had going was in Italy?

Right now he was living in Sam's apartment, he had no steady job, and Amy was shying away from making a commitment.

Apparently he didn't have much of anything. And Gianna was leaving. The beautiful, capricious, fun-loving, incredibly sexy Gianna.

What would he do without her? How would he survive?

Don't panic, he thought. *I'll be fine. I'll get hooked up with an agent in New York, rent an apartment, and eventually I'll be with Amy.*

The downstairs buzzer rang.

'My car,' Gianna said, still icing him out. 'Kindly tell driver to come up for my luggage.'

'Are you *sure* you want to do this?' he asked, shocked that *she* was walking out on *him*.

'*Sì*, Jett,' she answered, not even looking at him. 'Gianna is leaving. And Gianna will *not* be coming back.'

*   *   *

Chris had almost made it to the airport when he got the call on his cell. Red Diamond on the phone. His caring, loving father.

'Where are you?' Red demanded, as if they were in constant contact and he was entitled to know.

'I'm on my way back to L.A.,' Chris answered, surprised that his father had found him, although Red Diamond had always possessed a nose for tracking his prey.

'You flew to New York to meet with me,' Red pointed out, sounding calm for such a crotchety old bastard. 'Now you're leaving without doing so. Is that smart?'

'I'm leaving because I have a business to take care of,' Chris said. 'And our meeting never worked out, did it?'

'You ran out on me.'

'I left you to be with Max. I'm sure you heard that his ex-wife was murdered in her apartment, or did you miss that piece of news?'

'We have to reschedule,' Red said, ignoring the reference to Mariska's demise.

'I don't know when I'll be back in New York,' Chris said. 'So you can forget it.'

'Doesn't suit me,' Red replied. 'Tomorrow. Ten a.m. My house.'

'Didn't I just tell you that I'm on my way to L.A.?' Chris said, exasperated. 'I'm five minutes away from the airport. There's a plane waiting for me.'

'Too bad,' Red said abruptly.

'Too bad *what*?' Chris said, getting hooked in.

'Too bad you can't be there to listen to what I have to tell the three of you.'

'What do you have to tell us, *Dad*, that we don't already know?' Chris said, getting ready to spill some of the venom he'd been holding in for so many years. 'You want to tell us how *useless* we are? What a bunch of *fuck-ups* we turned out to be? How you always *knew* we'd never amount to anything? Is that what your meeting is all about?'

'If you're any kind of a businessman you'll be there,' Red said. '*Especially* if you're interested in hearing the true story behind your mother's unfortunate death.'

And, without further ado, Red Diamond hung up.

Chapter Fifty-Seven

Sonja did not leave Alex's garish red apartment until noon on Wednesday. The night before he'd asked her to stay over, so she'd done so, interested in listening to his diatribe about Mariska Diamond née Paulina Kochinova. According to Alex, he'd met Paulina at a club when she'd first arrived in New York. He'd fallen in lust – followed by love. Paulina/Mariska had claimed she felt the same about him, but he was soon to learn that a Russian Mob guy was not good enough for Mariska. No. She wanted more, and before long she had her hooks into Maxwell Diamond, a real-estate tycoon with excellent social standing. While dating Max, she'd managed to string Alex along – seeing both men, *sleeping* with both men. Then one day, to Alex's fury, *marrying* Max. After that, she would only meet with him sporadically, until the divorce, and then she'd come back into Alex's life, claiming she'd always loved him and they belonged together. But only if they kept their affair a secret until she received the full pay-out on her divorce settlement. They started seeing each other again on a semi-regular basis, but not in public, unless it was at one of the Russian clubs Alex frequented. Then Mariska would arrive wearing a black wig and revert to her real name – Paulina.

The sex between them was frantic – hot and dirty and frantic, the way they both liked it. After a while Mariska suggested she might be able to help him business-wise. She knew he dealt in stolen gemstones, and who better to broker them for him than a woman high up on the social scale?

So they went into business together, and for a while it worked perfectly, until Mariska decided to screw him out of several important and valuable stones and a shitload of cash.

'She found another rich man to take care of her. She didn't need me anymore,' Alex told Sonja, his mouth set in a grim line. 'She told me she loved me, promised we would be together. Then she stole from me, the bitch stole from *me*, Alex Pinchinoff. She deserved to die.'

Lying next to him in bed, Sonja had shivered, and wondered if it was *Alex* who'd murdered Mariska.

She'd then decided it couldn't be him, because Alex wouldn't have stabbed her, he'd have suffocated her with his giant cock.

After taking in his story, Sonja had sensed there was money to be made – *major* money. Mariska Diamond had been murdered, big society woman with many important connections – not the least being that she'd once been married to real-estate tycoon, Maxwell Diamond, whose father happened to be Red Diamond, the old billionaire whom she and Famka had spent the previous weekend fucking.

And yet, according to Igor, Vladimir, *and* Alex Pinchinoff, Mariska Diamond had originally been Paulina Kuchinova – a one-time Moscow prostitute who'd been married to *Vladimir* – and they'd never been divorced! Now there was Alex's story to add to the mix, although Sonja realized it would be fatal to name Alex.

Sonja was smart enough to realize that the money-making possibilities were endless. Mariska Diamond's murder was already headline news: what if people found out the *real* truth?

The story was explosive, and she, little Sonja Sivarious, was sitting on it. But not for long: if she didn't act fast, Vladimir, Igor or Alex might blow it.

Once she got home, she considered her alternatives. Sell the story to a tabloid newspaper. Or . . . see if Max Diamond was prepared to pay even more to keep the scandal from rocking his uptight world. She remembered Max from his bachelor party, he was no pushover like his brother, Chris, or the insatiable, Viagra-popping, foul-mouthed Red.

How much would Max Diamond be prepared to pay to keep the story out of the press? Enough for her to retire? Take the money and move somewhere far away – where the others,

Vladimir, Igor and Alex, couldn't find her? Because eventually they'd catch on that there was money to be made. And by that time it would be too late, she would've already scored.

Hmm . . . It was all about timing and speed. She had to move quickly before it was too late. Before Vladimir sprang forward as Mariska's legal husband so that he could claim her estate. Before Alex realized he was sitting on a hot story about his illicit love affair with the big society woman. Before Igor screwed everything up – as usual.

By Wednesday afternoon she'd made her decision. She would go to Red Diamond before anyone else. She'd tell him what she knew and the price for her silence. Red would *definitely* want to protect his family's name *and* his little grand-daughter, whom she'd seen pictured all over the newspapers. The advantage was that she knew how to contact Red directly – she'd jotted down his cell number when she and Famka had spent the weekend in his apartment.

And if he didn't want to pay, too bad – she'd go straight to one of the tabloid newspapers.

No problem. They would be happy to pay for a story as juicy as this.

*　*　*

'Hi,' Chris said, into his cell. 'Sorry, Birdy, I can't make it, you'd better take off without me.' He'd already instructed his driver to turn the car round and head back to the city.

'*Bummer!*' Birdy squealed. 'I get *off* bein' with you, Chris. You're like my totally *fave* older man.'

Older man? He was thirty-two, for Crissakes. Since when was thirty-two considered 'older'?

'It's business, Birdy,' he explained. 'I'll see you in Vegas. Oh, yes, and there'll be papers coming over to you for Rocky to sign. Make sure he does, or there'll be no wedding.'

'You're missing out, Chris,' Birdy cooed. 'I've got two hotties on the plane with me, and one of them *totally* gets off on—'

'What?' he interrupted. 'Old farts?'

'No, *silly*.' She giggled. '*Lawyers*.'

Yeah, that was all he needed to do, hook up with one of Birdy's manic teenage sex-crazed girlfriends.

'Guess she'll have to wait until Vegas,' he said, thinking about his manipulative father and what he'd like to do to him.

'I'll tell her,' Birdy promised. 'But she's gonna be *veree* disappointed.'

'I'm sure she'll live.'

Much as he'd felt the urge to get back to L.A., there was another, stronger urge pulling him towards Manhattan and a father he couldn't stand. A father who'd said, *Especially if you're interested in hearing the true story behind your mother's unfortunate death.*

Yes. He was desperate to hear the true story. There'd always been a lack of information about his mother's plane crash, just as there was a lack of information about the demise of Max's mother from a so-called heart-attack in her twenties.

Could it be that Red had somehow orchestrated the two women's deaths?

No. Not even Red Diamond would be capable of such evil.

Or would he?

*   *   *

'You wanted to see me?' Diahann said, standing uncomfortably in the doorway of Lady Jane Bentley's room.

'Yes, I do,' Lady Bentley said, waving an arm imperiously in the air. 'Come in. Close the door behind you.'

Diahann did as the woman requested. She had heard the arguments between Lady Bentley and Red Diamond. She had witnessed him screaming venom at the woman, telling her to get out. Everyone on the staff had hoped that this was it, the end of Lady Bentley and her unreasonable demands.

But no, days later she was still in residence, firmly ensconced in her tastefully decorated bedroom. She had not even begun to pack.

'How can I help you, Lady Bentley?' Diahann asked, determined to remain calm in the face of anything this bigoted, loathsome woman had to say.

Lady Bentley gave her a long, appraising look. 'How old are you?' she asked.

'Excuse me?'

'How *old* are you?' Lady Bentley repeated. 'It's not such a difficult question, is it?'

Diahann thought about telling the woman it was none of her damn business and fleeing the room. After all, what could Lady Bentley do to her? She certainly couldn't *fire* her: Diahann was under Red Diamond's employ, and he would never let her go.

But something made her stay and answer the question, she wasn't sure why.

'Thirty-eight,' she said at last, dying to add, 'Younger than you,' but she controlled the impulse.

'Thirty-eight,' Lady Bentley repeated. 'And *how* long have you worked here?'

'Almost ten years.'

'So you were quite a young woman when you decided to give up your singing career – such as it was – and come to work for Mr Diamond or *Red*, as I'm sure you called him in the early days when you were *sleeping* with him.'

Diahann felt a moment of sheer panic. No one knew about her dealings with Red Diamond, dealings that had started long before she became his housekeeper. It was a private matter between them, and they both had their reasons to make sure it stayed that way.

'I beg your pardon?' Diahann said, keeping her voice neutral.

'I *bet* you do – beg my pardon,' Lady Bentley sneered, a vindictive gleam in her eyes. 'All these years I imagined Red was out whoring around, but now I discover he had his own *black* whore, right here, stashed downstairs for his convenience whenever he wished to avail himself of her services.'

'I have no idea what you're talking about,' Diahann said, knowing she had to get out of this woman's room as fast as possible.

'Please, spare me the innocent act,' Lady Bentley said. 'I know everything. *Everything*.' A long, silent beat. 'Do you understand me?'

'I understand that we shouldn't be having this conversation,' Diahann muttered. 'Mr Diamond wouldn't like it.'

'Oh, wouldn't he?' Lady Bentley said bitterly. 'Too damn *bad*.'

Diahann turned to leave the room.

'I *know* your secret,' Lady Bentley taunted. 'I know your dirty little secret. So, if you're wise, I suggest you encourage Red to give me everything my lawyer has requested, and maybe – just maybe – your secret will stay safe with me.'

* * *

'Where have you *been*?'

'Huh?' Jett mumbled, cradling the phone. He was sitting in Sam's apartment trying to come to grips with the fact that Gianna had walked out on *him*. This was a first, and even though it saved him the trouble, he was not sure he liked it.

'Who's this?' he managed.

'Chris. Who did you *think* it was?'

'Uh . . .'

'What's up with you? Have you been drinking?'

'No way.'

'You sound fucked up.'

'I'm not.'

'Then where have you been?' Chris repeated. 'I've left messages. Don't you return calls?'

'My phone's on vibrate.'

'Great. Well, check your messages. There's probably one from Red.'

'How come?'

''Cause he's summoning us to another meeting. Wants us all there at ten tomorrow, his house.'

'Are we going?'

'You bet your ass we're going. I just blew out a flight back to L.A. so I can be there.'

'What makes you think *he* will?' Jett asked. 'He's freakin' *king* of the jack-offs. You *saw* him the other day walking in with those two hookers.'

'He'll be there,' Chris said. 'He's got something on his mind that he needs us to hear.'

'Who gives a shit?' Jett muttered.

'Have you called Max?'

'Max,' Jett said blankly. 'Why would I call him?'

'Jesus!' Chris exclaimed, suddenly realizing what was going on. 'You're *seeing* Amy, aren't you?'

'What makes you say that?'

''Cause *you're* the jack-off,' Chris said furiously. 'How can you do this to Max? *Especially* now.'

'It's complicated,' Jett mumbled.

'Fuck *you*, Jett. Grow up. She's taken, so stay away.'

'What if I can't?'

'Force yourself, little bro', force yourself.'

'I'm trying.'

'No. You're not.'

'You don't—'

'I'm on my way back to town,' Chris interrupted. 'Dinner tonight. My hotel at seven.'

'I'm not sure I can make it.'

'Be there,' Chris said. 'We'll get into it then.'

*   *   *

Unnerved by her meeting with Lady Bentley, Diahann hurried downstairs to her apartment and tried calling Liberty in L.A. There was no answer from her daughter's hotel room.

This was all no unsettling and unexpected. Nobody knew about her connection to Red Diamond. *Nobody.* And certainly not Liberty.

How had Lady Bentley found out? And what proof did she have – if any?

Lady Bentley was claiming she knew things that nobody except she and Red were privy to.

This wasn't possible.

And yet . . .

*   *   *

Money persuaded Irena to talk. One thing old Red Diamond had taught his eldest son was the power of money. Max had always used that lesson to great advantage.

Trying not to stare at the flashing diamond ring on the old woman's pinky, he began his line of questioning – quietly at first.

'*Was* Mariska your daughter?'

Irena vigorously shook her head.

'It's okay if she was, Irena,' he said, standing in the middle of the room, because sitting didn't seem to be an option, considering there was only the unmade bed and a rickety old chair. 'Nobody will do anything to you.'

'I must not talk,' Irena stated, mantra-style.

'Talk about *what*?' he pressed.

'Paulina say talking not good,' Irena muttered. 'Police. Immigration. She tell me stay quiet.'

'Paulina is *dead*.'

'I know, I know,' Irena wailed, her face crumpling, words tumbling from her mouth. 'My baby is dead.'

'I'm sorry,' Max said.

'America,' Irena mumbled, as if that explained everything.

'America?'

'In Russia this not happen.'

Apparently she'd never read a Russian newspaper where reports of violent crimes were rampant.

'Do you know who did this to Mariska?' he asked.

'No, no,' Irena said, shaking her head. 'I know nothing. That what I tell police. I know nothing.'

At this point Max took out money, a thick stack of hundred-dollar bills held together with a rubber band. He didn't offer it to her, simply kept it in his hands where she could see it.

'But you *do* know about Vladimir, don't you?' he said, watching for her reaction.

Alarm flashed across Irena's face. 'Vladimir? Who this Vladimir?' She was obviously lying.

'No more games, Irena,' Max said, flicking several bills from the stack and handing them to her. 'This stays between *you* and *me*. No police. No Immigration. Okay?'

'Okay,' she agreed.

'Did Vladimir kill Mariska?'

Irena collapsed in a heap on her unmade bed, sobbing uncontrollably. 'I know *nothing*,' she cried hysterically. 'Nothing!'

He peeled off a couple more bills and walked over to her. 'It's *good* you know nothing. It's *good* the detectives haven't found out about Vladimir.' He handed her the money. 'We should keep it that way.'

'Yes?' she said, her tears abruptly ceasing as she grabbed the money and peered up at him.

'It's best that the memory of Mariska is not dragged through the mud. Do you agree?'

'Oh, *yes*, Mr Diamond,' she said, cheering up considerably. 'It is best. I tell police *nothing* about men. Not their business.'

'Men?' Max questioned. 'Don't you mean *man*? One *man*? Vladimir?'

Irena's eyes, full of greed, slid towards the roll of bills still in his hands.

He understood immediately. Irena was telling him that there was more than one man, but that was *all* she was telling him. If he wanted more information he had to pay more money.

One thing he knew for sure, Irena was *definitely* Mariska's mother.

Chapter Fifty-Eight

D amon was staying around, and Chip and the gang didn't mind at all.

'The man is crazy about you,' Teddy informed her.

'The man is married,' Liberty responded.

'He's still crazy about you,' Teddy insisted.

'No, he's not,' she said, making sure she sounded casual, because she certainly didn't want anyone finding out how she really felt. 'He's just looking to get laid.'

'Surely he could accomplish that in New York?' Teddy pointed out, fiddling with her hair extensions during an afternoon break.

'I'm sure he can. But not with me.'

'He's gorgeous!' Quinn raved, joining in. 'Very urban and masculine and *street*. I *so* get off on that *tough*, manly quality.'

'Then maybe *you* should sleep with him,' Liberty said drily.

'I wish!' Quinn responded. 'Methinks he doesn't stroll the same boulevard as little old me.'

Liberty couldn't help smiling. Not only were Teddy and Quinn a trip, but Chip's photographs were turning out to be sensational, and the work was fun. There was also the added bonus of Damon's presence and, much as she fought her feelings for him, she couldn't help liking him more every time she saw him.

The night before he'd charmed everyone at the restaurant, followed by the walk on the beach – which, whether she cared to admit it or not – had been magical. And, after a shaky start, he'd even become friends with Tony A. They'd all sat in the hotel lobby swapping stories until two a.m., when she'd excused herself and gone up to bed, leaving Damon, Tony and even Hector having a fine old time.

Wednesday morning she was up at six, after a scant amount of sleep, and as her 'team' prepared her for the day's shoot, they began plying her with questions about Damon.

Do you like him? What's he doing here? How long's he staying? Do you like him? Exactly how rich is he? Did he fly to L.A. to see you? Have you been on his plane? Do you like him? Have you slept with him? DO YOU LIKE HIM?

Yes! She liked him. Only she wasn't about to admit it, so she played it cool, and when he appeared at the shoot around three p.m. she pretended she wasn't interested in what he'd been doing all day, although she couldn't help wondering if *he* had a hot little honey stashed in Beverly Hills just like Parker. And since *she* wasn't jumping into bed with him, was he casting his eyes around for other opportunities? There were certainly plenty of good-looking women in L.A. She'd noticed them driving up to the hotel in their Mercedes, Beamers and their husbands Hummers. They were all fresh and glowing, with perfectly coiffed blonde hair, immaculate manicures, toned bodies and lightly tanned skin.

Damon didn't so much as glance in their direction. He informed anyone who cared to listen that he'd slept until one, taken a steam and then gone shopping.

'Buy anything fab?' Teddy asked. 'Anything *leather*?'

'Maybe,' Damon replied, looking very L.A. in a white T-shirt and white pants, the usual Nikes, mirrored shades and plenty of bling. 'I'll let you know.'

Liberty admired the way he treated everyone the same. No star trips for Damon P. Donnell. He was a man of the people.

She wondered what his wife thought he was doing in L.A. Did they speak on the phone every day? Did they miss each other? Or wasn't it that kind of close relationship?

Damon watched her for a while, standing silently in the background on the beach while she did her thing.

Today it was bikini time – if you could call the two flimsy strips of leather a bikini. She was starting to feel pretty confident – it was difficult not to with all the encouragement she was getting. Chip kept up a constant stream of compliments, while Teddy and Quinn creamed over the Polaroids. Even the stoic Uma managed to throw a few nice remarks her way.

Everything was amazing. The hotel, the people she was working with, Damon turning up in L.A. with Parker, bumping into Tony who'd left for Chicago early that morning. It was all such an adventure.

At the next break, Damon informed her he was going back to the hotel for a massage. 'Dinner,' he said, in a low, commanding voice. 'Tonight. Just you and me.'

He wasn't asking her. He was telling her. She shivered. It was usually she who called the shots in a relationship. None of that with Damon, he was a take-charge kind of guy, and she had to admit it made a refreshing change. 'Where's Parker?' she ventured.

'He had to get back.'

'But—'

'Now, don't go frettin' it, babe. Parker's hot t'work with you. You'll meet up with him next week in New York. This trip was for him t' get a feel for you.'

'Do you think he liked me?' She asked, knowing that she sounded like an anxious little kid, but unable to help herself.

'What's not to like?' Damon answered smoothly. 'Oh, yeah – an' did I mention that today *you* are lookin' *SMOKIN?*'

'I bet you say that to all the girls you want to go to bed with,' she teased.

'Yeah, well, only the difficult ones,' he responded, adjusting his cool Versace shades. 'See ya later, babe.'

And he strolled off. No entourage. No bodyguards. Just a simple hip-hop mogul with a yen to get into her pants.

*   *   *

Later, dinner at Mr Chow's – a famous Beverly Hills restaurant peppered with stars, all of whom Damon seemed to know. Outside the restaurant several paparazzi jumped forward and took their photograph, then they clamoured for her name.

'Meet Liberty, guys,' Damon said, not at all worried about being photographed with her. 'You'll all be buyin' this young lady's new CD soon enough.'

Once they were settled at a table, Damon leaned over, took her hand and said, 'Here's what you gotta know. It's never too early to get the hype goin'. By the time your CD drops, everyone'll recognize your name.'

'Including Tashmir?' she asked, unable to prevent the words coming out of her mouth.

'Now *why* you into spoilin' a perfect night?' he said, his expression quizzical.

'Because if *I* was your wife, and I saw your photograph with another woman, I'd be pissed.'

'I'll remember that for when we're married.'

Had he just said that? Was she hearing things?

He ordered her a lychee martini and a selection of the most delicious food she'd ever tasted. Spare ribs and seaweed, chicken satay and duck pancakes. It was an incredible array of dishes.

After a while she realized she was eating too much. Damon was watching her with an indulgent smile on his handsome face.

'Guess I was hungry,' she said, trying not to stare at Catherine Zeta-Jones and Michael Douglas, who were being seated at the next table.

'That's okay,' Damon said easily. 'I like a girl with a big appetite.'

'When are you leaving?' she asked, taking a sip of her drink.

'Whenever you're ready.'

'I didn't mean tonight. I meant when are you leaving L.A.?'

'I *know* what you meant,' he said, leaning back.

'So?'

'So, like I said, whenever you're ready.'

They were interrupted by a buxom blonde with huge fake tits and an enhanced-lip smile. She pounced on Damon as if he was a particularly delicious item on the menu.

'How *are* you?' she gushed, leaning over to give him a jammy kiss and an excellent view of her fake tits hanging out of a skimpy orange dress.

'I'm good,' he said, coolly polite.

'How's Tash?' the blonde asked, shooting a meaningful look at Liberty.

'She's good too.'

An awkward silence. Fake Tits waited to be introduced to Liberty. It didn't happen.

'Who was *that*?' Liberty asked, when the blonde finally got the hint and moved on.

'Would you believe me if I told you I got no clue?'

'Yes, I'd believe you. She's hardly your type.'

'Oh,' he said, grinning. 'You think I have a type?'

'Well, *don't* you?'

'Yeah, *you*.'

After dinner, Damon was into club-hopping. 'Need to hear what the DJs are playin',' he explained. 'Gotta keep my ear current.'

They stopped by several clubs. He didn't dance, hardly drank, just sat back and watched the action, and there was plenty of that going on. Settled in a booth in one of the VIP rooms, Liberty observed a pretty teenage TV queen snorting a line of coke, a well-known male movie star necking with another well-known and very *married* male movie star, a couple of stoned, so-called It girls hoping to score a date, and a very lonely-looking big-time female star of forty-five, pretending to be twenty-five – or at least acting as if she was.

Like Damon, Liberty was more an observer than a doer. She was feeling great sitting next to him, taking it all in, trying to remember every single detail so that she could regale Cindi with her adventures.

With Damon she was the most comfortable she'd ever felt with a man. Yes, he wanted to sleep with her, but he wasn't all over her groping and pawing, going for a quick feel. He was a real man, laid-back and unbelievably hot, and the more time she spent with him, the more she was tempted.

Once again she started thinking, *So what if he's married? If it doesn't bother him, why should it bother me?*

'Guess I'd better get you t' bed – *your* bed,' Damon said, finally winding down. 'Thank for comin' with me tonight, LL. It was time for me t' check out the L.A. scene.'

'So *that's* why you came to L.A.'

'No, babe,' he said, giving her a long, lingering look. 'Y'*know* why I came to L.A.'

They made it into the limo, Damon ignoring the attention of even more paparazzi darting around them taking random shots.

Guess he's used to all this attention, Liberty thought. *Like P. Diddy he kind of goes with it.*

'So, LL,' Damon said, leaning back against the leather seat, 'what time you finish tomorrow?'

'They've got me booked on a nine o'clock night-time flight to New York.'

'Tell 'em to cancel it.'

'Excuse me?'

'I'm full of this crazy yen t' take you to Cabo,' he said, giving her the look she found so irresistible.

'Cabo?' she questioned.

'Cabo San Lucas. It's this happenin' resort in Mexico. Why we gotta rush back to New York when we can fly there in two hours, spend the weekend, then back to the city on Sunday? Sound cool?'

'Amazing,' she replied. 'Only I can't do it.'

'An' that would be 'cause . . .?'

'There's a lot of reasons.'

'Tell me the big one, an' Damon'll solve it,' he said confidently.

'Well . . .' she began.

'Yeah,' he groaned. 'I know, *I know*. I'm married, right?'

'You said it.'

'That's not such a big deal, y' know.'

'To you it's not.'

'No shit.'

'And what if I don't want to fly to Cabo with you?' she said, testing him.

'That ain't gonna happen.'

'No?'

'No.'

Damon P. Donnell was a difficult man to refuse. Just one look and she was hooked. 'We'll see,' she said, keeping it vague.

'We'll see, the girl says.' He laughed, rolling his eyes.

'Like, you think every girl says yes to you, Mr Unturn-downable?'

'Somethin' like that,' he said, grinning.

'Your ego is huge.'

'Believe me, baby, that's not all.'

'Damon!'

'Move closer, LL. One kiss ain't gonna kill ya.'

And so they'd started kissing again, and it was so damn hot that she'd almost forgotten he was married.

Not quite. When the limo pulled up to the hotel, she jumped out hurriedly. 'I can't do this,' she said, then rushed inside and made it to the safety of her room before she weakened and changed her mind.

God! She was so confused. Her resolve was crumbling. If she went to Cabo with him, she'd be just another girl he'd screwed outside his marriage, and then what?

Before she could give it anymore thought, her mom was on the phone. 'Why haven't you called me back?' Diahann demanded. 'I need to talk to you.'

'I was out, Mama.'

'I left messages.'

'I know, but I thought it was too late in New York to call you. Isn't it like four in the morning there? How come you're still up?'

'What time will you be back here tomorrow?' Diahann asked tensely.

'Uh . . .' Liberty replied, hesitating for a moment. 'I've kind of been invited to stay with some friends in Mexico.'

'No!' Diahann sounded distraught. 'You can't go.'

'I'm not actually asking permission,' Liberty retorted. 'The reason I'm telling you is so you don't start imagining I've been kidnapped into a life of slavery.'

Diahann gave a long-drawn-out sigh. 'There's something I have to tell you, Libby.'

'Then tell me, I'm listening.'

'Not over the phone.'

'Why not?'

'It's something I have to tell you to your face.'

'Oh, for *God's sake*,' Liberty exploded, full of frustration. 'I'm *sick* of this. First you tell me nothing at all, and now that I'm out on my own enjoying myself, you can't wait to make me crazy. What *is* it you have to say?'

'Get back to New York as quickly as possible, Libby, I'm *begging* you.'

'What's *so damn important*?'

'Come back and find out for yourself. I promise you, it'll change your life.'

Chapter Fifty-Nine

Irena fixed Max a mug of murky dark brown tea so strong he thought he might regurgitate the foul liquid on the spot. Then she indicated that he should sit, so he balanced gingerly on the one rickety chair.

Irena settled herself on the edge of her unmade bed, and proceeded to talk. Words came pouring out of her mouth, harsh words mixed with venom about her deceased daughter. 'Paulina – she was always user,' Irena spat. 'Always wanted best. Daddy's little favourite.'

'Where *is* your husband?' Max asked. Early on in their relationship, Mariska had informed him that both her parents had perished in a train wreck when she was an infant. Like everything else about Mariska, that had been a lie too.

'Dead,' Irena stated, clutching her own mug of tea. 'Shot in Moscow thirty years ago. Not nice man. Paulina take after him.'

'But she sent for you, brought you to America, didn't she?'

'Ha!' Irena snorted. 'To be her slave. Iron her clothes. Press them. Take them to the dry cleaner's. Polish her shoes. Wash her dirty underwear. Keep her secrets. I am *slave*. She live in palace. Look where *I* sleep.'

Max nodded. Irena wasn't wrong. 'Tell me about the men,' he said. 'Was she seeing Vladimir while she was married to me?'

'Vladimir,' Irena said scornfully. 'He nothing. He peasant. Paulina play with him like toy.'

'Go on,' Max encouraged.

'Paulina loved herself. Then Alex. But Alex only for sex.'

'Alex?' Max questioned.

'Boyfriend.'

'Boyfriend *when*?'

'When she need sex. Or money.' A crafty pause. 'Alex give her cash.'

Did that explain the cash he'd found stuffed into her box? That would be *some* generous boyfriend.

'Who *is* Alex?'

'Bad man,' Irena said, her face darkening. 'Gangster. Criminal. He carry gun.'

Jesus! Mariska certainly *had* led a double life.

'What's Alex's surname?' he asked, thinking that Alex might be listed in her phone book.

Irena shrugged. 'Russian man,' she said vaguely, as if that explained everything.

'Was she seeing him when she was married to me?'

'Maybe,' Irena answered cautiously.

Max wondered if Alex had stabbed Mariska to death, not Vladimir. Was that possible?

No. Vladimir was guilty. He was sure of it.

And then Mariska's words came back to haunt him. The night she'd called him to her apartment claiming Lulu was sick, the night he'd said, 'She's my daughter, isn't she.' He'd said it as a statement not a question. But Mariska had murmured a sly 'Maybe,' and now – in view of what Irena was telling him – there was a distinct possibility that Lulu might not be his child. She could be Vladimir's or even Alex's. He felt sick.

'I give police nothing,' Irena said, pursing her lips. 'You *tell* them what I say, *I* deny.' She stood up and snatched the mug out of his hand. 'You no like tea?' she said accusingly. 'Not strong enough?'

'It's a little too strong.'

'I *know* who murdered Paulina,' she said, just like that.

A chill pervaded his body. 'Who?'

Another crafty expression crossed her weatherbeaten face. 'You have Paulina's box? Her money?'

'I just gave you—'

'You want know who stabbed her,' Irena said flatly, 'come back, bring me box. It should be mine.'

'What makes you think *I* have it?'

'Someone took it from apartment. I think it you.'

'And if it wasn't me?'

'Then our talk is finished.'

* * *

'Hi, Grams,' Amy said, arriving unannounced at her grandmother's hotel apartment.

'What are *you* doing here?' Grandma Poppy asked, shushing her two dogs, who were running around in circles, barking.

'I came to tell you we're postponing the wedding.'

'I heard,' Grandma Poppy said, calming her yapping dogs with a commanding gesture. 'Your mother phoned me. In view of the terrible event that has taken place, a postponement is the correct thing to do.'

'Mom seems to think so,' Amy said. 'She's livid because *my* name has been dragged into the newspapers.'

'I'm sure she is.'

'She wants me to break off my engagement, give Max back his ring, quit my job and leave the country,' Amy continued, pulling up a chair.

'Ah,' Grandma Poppy sighed. 'Nancy. Overreacting as usual.' A pause. 'And how do *you* feel about breaking your engagement to Max?'

'Here's the thing, Grams, I, uh, have another problem that's even worse.'

'What could possibly be worse than your overly dramatic mother trying to tell you what to do?' Grandma Poppy inquired, tapping her elegant long fingers on the table beside her.

'You're so wise, Grams,' Amy said. 'That's why I came here.' She glanced at Hueng, hovering near the door.

Grandma Poppy followed her eyes. 'Hueng,' she said, raising her voice and waving a hand imperiously, '*out*. My granddaughter has private things to tell me. Go now.' Hueng made a rapid exit. 'What is it, dear girl? Speak up.'

'Well . . .' Amy said hesitantly. 'It's something my mother couldn't possibly understand. I'm not even sure you will.'

'Try me, dear.'

'I–I did something foolish,' Amy stammered, 'and now I don't know how to handle the situation.'

'Go ahead.'

'Remember I told you about my bachelorette night?'

'You'd better remind me. My memory's not what it used to be.'

'We had, y' know, drinks and fun and male strippers.'

'Ooh, male strippers,' Grandma Poppy said, eyes gleaming as she clapped her hands together. 'What a pity we didn't have those when *I* was young.'

'Anyway, it got kind of crazy.'

'Nothing wrong with a young girl getting crazy.'

'Only *I* got a little *too* crazy,' Amy admitted.

'What happened?'

'I *slept* with a stranger,' Amy blurted out. 'I didn't know his name or anything about him, and he didn't know who *I* was. It was just one of those unbelievable things.'

'I presume you regret it?' Grandma Poppy said, not appearing to be at all shocked.

'Yes – I mean, no,' Amy muttered, totally flustered. 'You see, it turns out he's someone I know.'

'I'm sure you *do* know him if you went to bed with him.'

'It's bad, Grams.' A long silent beat. 'He's Max's brother.'

'Excuse me?'

'Max's younger brother, Jett. You met him at the rehearsal dinner. He was at your table with the Italian model you thought was so charming. She's kind of his girlfriend.'

'I'm a tad confused,' Grandma Poppy said. 'You *slept* with a man whom you didn't know, and *he* didn't know you. Yet *you* have a fiancé, and *he* has a girlfriend. Am I correct?'

'Yes, that's exactly it.'

'Have you told Max?'

'No, I feel too guilty. I *want* to tell him, but I just can't.'

'That's good, because you have to keep this to yourself.'

'I do?'

'Yes,' Grandma Poppy said firmly, 'you most certainly do. Telling Max will only create bigger problems.'

'I *have* a bigger problem already. I want to be with Jett, and yet I know, especially in view of what's going on, that I must stay with Max.'

'And does Jett feel the same way?'

'Yes.'

'What about the Italian girl?'

'She's not his *steady* girlfriend. He's breaking up with her so that he can be with me.'

'Men *always* say that,' Grandma Poppy mused, a faraway look in her eyes. 'They're always after the nooky they can't have.'

'Grandma! Where did *you* learn words like "nooky"?'

'I'm telling you the truth, dear. It's best that you hear it from me.'

'I need your advice, Grams,' Amy said, beginning to feel slightly desperate. 'You're smart, you've been around the world *and* you've experienced a wonderful marriage, so please tell me what I should do.'

'This will sound *very* old-fashioned,' Grandma Poppy said, scooping up one of her dogs and petting the furry creature.

'I don't care.'

'Well, if Jett is the man for you, then you must follow your heart, dear, follow your heart. Otherwise you could spend the rest of your life regretting it.'

* * *

His mind churning with a hundred different thoughts, Max drove home from Brighton Beach to the sanctuary of his apartment.

Mariska's life was turning out to have been much more complicated than even *he* could have imagined. First there was Vladimir, who'd probably been splitting the blackmail money with her. Now he'd found out about Alex, and who the hell was *he*?

The thought occurred to him once more – had she been

sleeping with this Alex when they were married? Was she *fucking* another man while they were together? Was *Alex* Lulu's father?

Would Mariska have stooped that low?

Yes, Mariska had been capable of anything.

A fury began to build within him. A fury so white-hot he almost ran his car off the road.

Mariska had always been into sex, much more so than he. She'd often suggested threeways and handcuffs and leather fetishes. He'd turned down all her suggestions, put off by what he considered her kinky desires.

After the birth of Lulu, they'd very rarely had sex at all. Was it *then* that she'd turned to Alex for the sex she craved? Or had she been sleeping with him before?

Damn the woman. He couldn't even confront her. She was dead. Murdered. And, according to her loving mother, the killer was out there, and Irena knew who it was.

How should he handle this? Hand over Mariska's box to Irena – money and all? Or give it to the detectives?

He was torn. If the killer wasn't Vladimir, what did he care?

Of course he *cared*. Mariska had been brutally murdered, and however he felt about her it was a terrible act of violence.

Several messages were waiting for him at home. One was from Mrs Conner in Montauk, saying that Lulu was fine and having a lovely time – she had even put Lulu on the phone to say good night. Next there was an abrupt message from Red, requesting his presence at a ten a.m. meeting the next day – no mention of Mariska's demise. Did the old man think he could summon these meetings at random, and everyone would come running? It was *such* a joke.

The third message was from Chris, still in town at the Four Seasons, requesting that Max join him and Jett for dinner. The last thing he felt like doing was sitting down for dinner with his brothers. He didn't feel like seeing *anyone*, including Amy – he had too much on his mind.

Fifteen minutes later the desk clerk buzzed up to inform him that Detective Rodriguez was downstairs.

Jesus *Christ*! Was the annoying detective *ever* going to leave him alone? *Now* what was he supposed to do?

'Send him up,' he said, thinking he'd get rid of him fast.

A few minutes later Detective Rodriguez lumbered into the foyer of his apartment. This time he was alone.

'This is getting to be a habit,' Max said abruptly. 'And it's not a habit I care to keep cultivating.'

'Sorry to bother you, Mr Diamond,' Detective Rodriguez said. 'I have a couple of very quick questions to ask you. We're making progress, and there's a few things you might be able to help me out with.'

'Yes?' Max said, keeping the detective standing in the foyer, determined not to invite him in.

'According to the doorman at the ex-Mrs Diamond's apartment, she entertained several male visitors on a regular basis. Did you happen to know this?'

'I told you,' Max said. 'I had no idea who she was seeing after we separated.'

'I thought you might be able to give me names.'

'Now *why* would I be able to do that?'

'Just a thought, Mr Diamond.'

'Look,' Max said, attempting to keep his temper under wraps, 'in future, kindly contact me through my lawyer. You cannot keep turning up at my apartment whenever you feel like it.'

'I was under the impression you'd be anxious to get this case cleared up as quickly as possible,' Detective Rodriguez said, pushing his glasses up the bridge of his nose. 'I'm getting calls from the captain. *He*'s getting calls from downtown. It's becoming a very big deal.'

'I would imagine a woman being murdered in her *own* bed in the heart of Manhattan *is* a big deal,' Max said.

'Perhaps if I gave you some descriptions you'd be able to help me.'

'No,' Max said sharply. 'I wouldn't.'

'Were you *aware* that she had three regular male visitors?'

Max thought quickly. One must be Vladimir, obviously one was Alex, but who was the third?

He shook his head. 'Talk to her mother again – maybe she can help you. *I* certainly can't.'

'Have *you* spoken to Irena?' Detective Rodriguez asked, stroking his moustache.

Hmm . . . a direct question. Should he lie and say no? Or should he admit that he'd gone to visit Irena in Brighton Beach? 'You pointed out that if she *was* Mariska's mother, it would make her my child's grandmother. So, yes, I did go see her.'

'Really?' the detective said, still stroking his moustache. 'And what did she have to say?'

'Nothing that she hasn't already said to you.'

The detective gave him a long, brooding stare. 'You might be interested to know that we're putting together new evidence all the time.'

'What kind of evidence?'

'DNA samples are being tested, hair, skin.' Another long beat. 'You know, murderers never understand how they get caught. Truth is, they get caught because they're careless. They think a pair of gloves will do it. Not anymore.'

'Are we done, Detective?' Max asked impatiently.

'For now.'

Max flung open the front door, and Detective Rodriguez stepped outside. 'I'll keep you informed, Mr Diamond,' he said.

'Do that,' Max said, slamming the door and frowning. His main concern was Vladimir, and if Vladimir hadn't killed her, could it have been Alex? And who was the third man?

He needed to find out.

*   *   *

Jett didn't relish the thought of having dinner with Chris, he wanted to be with Amy. But when he called her and told her he was coming over, she gave him a speech about how she needed time and space to work out what she was going to do.

This alarmed him – he'd just broken up with his long-time girlfriend and now Amy was backing off. What kind of crap was *that*?

Then to disturb him further, his mother called. 'What the *hell*'s goin' on with that damn family?' Edie slurred, wasted and belligerent. 'I tole you t' stay 'way from the bastards. I *warned* you.'

'Hey – listen, Mom—'

'*No*. You damn well lissen t' *me*. They're degenerates, all of 'em. You stay the hell away, Jett. I mean it.'

He got her off the phone as quickly as possible. Then, to calm his nerves, he decided he needed a drink, one small shot of vodka.

What harm was there in one shot of vodka?

After a quick search of the apartment, he discovered a half-full bottle of Grey Goose nestled in Sam's kitchen cupboard. One drink after almost three years of sobriety. He could handle it. Right *on* he could handle it.

*   *   *

I'm in limbo, Amy thought. *I'm confused and unhappy and filled with guilt. Maybe my mother is right. Maybe I should get out of town.*

She'd made up her mind not to see Jett again until she'd come to a decision about Max. What *should* she do? Tell Max they were over, then start seeing his brother? How right was *that*?

Grandma Poppy had told her to follow her heart, and what did her heart say? She didn't know. She wasn't sure.

And while she was having these thoughts, it occurred to her that lately Max seemed to have become very distant, making no attempt to see her. She understood why, with all that *he* was going through – but surely, if they were really close, he would want her to be with him at a time like this.

On her way home she decided to visit Tina in the hospital, hoping they'd have a chance to talk.

When she walked into Tina's hospital room, Brad was already there and so were Tina's parents.

'Hi!' Tina said, delighted to see her. 'We're going home tomorrow. Isn't that *great*?'

The baby was thriving and Tina was glowing – no sign of

post-partum blues. 'I'm *itching* to get out of here,' Tina said excitedly. 'Isn't he the cutest?'

Amy agreed that, yes, indeed Brad Junior *was* the cutest, and she sat there for a while, feeling out of place and anxious to leave. Close as she was to Tina, it was a family event.

After a polite half-hour she excused herself, hurried home and continued to mull over her situation.

There didn't seem to be an answer in sight.

* * *

'*Her* fuckin' people are drivin' *my* fuckin' people fuckin' *loco*!' The unmistakable voice of Roth Giagante.

'Listen to me, Roth, I'm Birdy's lawyer,' Chris said evenly. 'I don't get into those kind of details. Tell them to contact her publicist or one of her assistants.'

'Fuckin' pink. She wants everything fuckin' *pink*,' Roth complained. 'She's a whack-job. She's even asked for the water in the pool to be tinted pink!'

'Did you *hear* me, Roth?'

'Yeah, yeah, I heard you.' A long beat and a change of tone. 'Where's my fuckin' money?'

'You'll have it this weekend' Chris assured him. 'In cash, just the way you wanted.'

'About time,' Roth grumbled.

Chris hung up. Since staying with Max was not on his agenda, he'd checked back into the Four Seasons. Comfortable as Max's apartment was, he preferred the freedom of a hotel. Besides, after the meeting with Red he planned on flying back to L.A. No more delays. He'd been away almost a week, much longer than he'd anticipated.

He couldn't reach Max anyway. His brother wasn't at his office and there was no answer on his cell, so he left a message about dinner.

He hoped that by this time Max had handed Mariska's box and everything in it over to the detectives. If he hadn't, he was a fool.

The news stations were still all over Mariska's murder – it was as if they had nothing else to cover. And yet all Chris could think about were Red's ominous words concerning his mother's death.

Tomorrow he'd get to the real truth – if Red was *capable* of telling the truth. And that was doubtful – *very* doubtful.

* * *

'Lady Bentley knows,' Diahann said, standing in the library.

Sprawled on the leather couch, newspapers scattered around him, Red gave her a canny look. 'What does the bitch know?'

'About Liberty,' Diahann said wearily. 'You promised me nobody would ever find out.'

'Promises mean nothing,' Red said roughly. 'You're smart enough to realize that.'

'What are you going to do?'

'You'll see, along with all of 'em. I want you in the meeting I'm having tomorrow morning. I want Liberty there too.'

'That's not possible. She's in Los Angeles.'

'Get her back.'

'I'll try.'

'Don't try,' he said roughly. 'Do it!'

* * *

After Detective Rodriguez left, Max wished he'd given him the box and stepped away, as Chris had suggested. But he couldn't do it. The information in the box would eventually lead them to Vladimir, and the truth that Mariska had been a bigamist would be revealed.

And where would that leave him and Lulu? The illegitimate child and the husband who never was. The fool who'd married a Russian ex-hooker who had still been married to another man.

He simply couldn't do it. Not to his Lulu. Not to the light of his life.

He made a sudden decision to take the box to Irena. She'd never give it to the police – she'd hide it away and make good use of the money.

Yes. That was the answer. He'd take it to her tonight, get it over with.

Fearing he'd change his mind, he picked up the phone and called her.

She answered with a raspy '*Da?*'

'Irena,' he said. 'It's Mr Diamond. About that matter we discussed. I'm bringing you what you requested on the condition you mention *nothing* about Vladimir or the other men to the police. Do we have an agreement?'

'When you come?' she asked. He could almost imagine her rubbing her hands together in anticipation of the riches she was about to inherit.

'I'll be there in an hour. And I expect you to tell me everything you know.'

Just as he was leaving the apartment, Chris phoned. 'Dinner with me and Jett,' Chris said. 'I left you a message.'

'Not tonight,' he replied abruptly. 'Maybe tomorrow.'

'I'll be in L.A. tomorrow.'

'Then we'll have lunch before you leave, after the meeting with Red.'

'You'll be at the meeting?' Chris asked.

'If you and Jett are going, I'll be there. What do you think the canny old bastard wants now?'

'When I spoke to him on the phone he mumbled something about my mother.'

'Your *mother?*' Max said, frowning.

'Why do you think I turned round and came back? I was almost at the airport when he called.'

'What did he say?'

'He intimated that her death was due to more than just a plane crash.'

'That's ridiculous.'

'Is it?' Chris said slowly. 'Do you ever think about *your* mother's death?'

'Well, of course I do. But you're not saying—'

'Hey, I don't know *what* I'm saying. It's Red Diamond we're dealing with, so consider the man and what he's capable of.'

Max hung up the phone and slumped into a deep

depression. All his life he'd wondered about his mother's untimely death. Rachel, an exquisite twenty-six-year-old woman who'd died in her sleep six months after giving birth to him. The official word was heart failure, and when, at the age of thirteen, Max had started asking questions, Red had told him that his mother had always suffered from a defective heart, and that he was never to mention her again.

The only way Max knew his mother was through the few photographs he had been able to find of her. Rachel. His mother. Dark hair. Huge eyes. A Madonna-like smile.

He missed knowing her with a deep wrenching hurt in his gut. And if Red was in any way responsible for her death . . .

It was a thought he almost couldn't face.

Chapter Sixty

The tabloids were due to hit the street on Thursday, so Red Diamond had copies – straight off the press – delivered to his house Wednesday night. The headlines were scandalous.

THE DIAMOND DYNASTY!

EX-MODEL STABBED TO DEATH!

BILLIONAIRE MEDIA TYCOON RED DIAMOND'S FAMILY SECRETS THAT LED TO SEX, DRUGS AND MURDER!

WILD DAYS OF THE DIAMOND BROTHERS!

MURDER IN MANHATTAN!

BEAUTIFUL SOCIETY WOMAN SLAIN!

WHO KILLED MARISKA?

Truth and Fact, the most scurrilous rag of all, had unearthed plenty. Mariska – the beautiful murder victim – was the only one spared, although they'd managed to dig up several semi-nude pin-up photos of her, taken when she'd first arrived in America and had apparently harboured hopes of being a model.

Maxwell Diamond was portrayed as a business-obsessed, real-estate tycoon, with a years younger fiancée who was due to inherit millions when her *über*-rich society grandmother passed. The implication being that Max had divorced Mariska

453

to get his hands on Amy's inheritance. There were pictures of Max and Amy taken at their rehearsal dinner, and a large photo of Max, Mariska and Lulu on a skiing vacation when Lulu was three.

Chris Diamond was written about as a playboy Hollywood lawyer with gambling connections to Vegas and the Mob. There were photos of him with Birdy Marvel, and several ex-girlfriends – including Holly Anton. The article even insinuated that the emancipation of Birdy Marvel had been brokered by Chris, so that he could get a large cut of her money and as many nights as he wanted with the teenage pop diva.

Jett came off worst of all. Along with several bare-chested modelling shots taken when he'd first arrived in Milan, there were photographs of him from his wild New York days – falling down drunk at various clubs and parties, mostly with girls in barely-there dresses who looked like under-age hookers.

Red Diamond was featured heavily. The billionaire patriarch of the family was a tempting target. Diligent journalists had no trouble digging up a wealth of information, including his many wives, their unfortunate deaths, the scandalous divorce and subsequent affair with Lady Jane Bentley, and numerous business machinations, including a slew of hostile takeovers and fraught relationships with other media moguls who considered themselves his peers.

Red Diamond was an old-fashioned, ego-driven, megalomaniac, and the rags relished the chance of putting their investigative skills to work – especially *Truth and Fact*, which happened to come under the umbrella of a host of publications owned by one of Red's arch-rivals, of which, over the years, he'd had quite a few.

When Red saw the tabloids – particularly *Truth and Fact* – he went berserk, stamping around his house in a frenzied fury, shouting and yelling obscenities. The entire household heard him, Lady Jane Bentley, sequestered in her room, Diahann, who'd been hoping for another chance to speak with him privately, the cook, the laundress, the maids.

'Fuck the dirty, lying, cocksucking bastards!' he screamed. 'Fuck Mariska, that Russian *cunt*! And fuck the stupid boys

I should never have allowed my dumb fucking wives to bring into this world!'

After venting for a while, he made a call, summoned his driver and stomped out of the house.

Nobody cared to deal with Red Diamond when he'd worked himself up into one of his turbulent frenzies.

*   *   *

Jett turned up for dinner an hour late and totally wasted. Watching him weave his way towards the table, Chris groaned inwardly. With all that was going on, Jett had to choose this moment to slide out of sobriety and turn into the drunk he used to be.

'Sorry I'm late,' Jett slurred, as he arrived at the table. 'Hadda go see my mom.'

'Edie's in town?' Chris questioned, wondering if mother and son had been out on a drinking binge together.

'Kinda. Sorta,' Jett said, attempting to pull out a chair and almost losing his balance. 'You know Edie, she had me trapped on the phone.'

Chris realized there was no sense in pretending he didn't know what was going on, that would just be a monumental waste of time. 'Okay,' he said, trying not to sound too judgemental. 'What made you do it?'

'Huh?' Jett said blankly. 'Do *what*?'

'Take a drink.'

'Are you fuckin' *shittin'* me?' Jett said, managing to look outraged. 'Y' *know* I'm in the goddamn programme.'

'Yes, I'm aware of that,' Chris answered calmly. 'And exactly *when* did you last attend a meeting?'

'A meetin',' Jett mumbled. 'Ah . . . let me see. A meetin' . . .' His eyes glazed over. 'Who'm I meetin'?'

Chris clicked his fingers for the check. 'I'm taking you upstairs.'

'Why we doin' that?' Jett grumbled. 'I gotta eat, gotta call my girl.' His voice started getting louder. 'Gotta call my *goddamn* girl.' Without warning he was on his feet, swaying and shouting. 'Amy. Where the fuck are ya? Amy baby. Amy *bitch*!'

Other patrons turned to stare.

Jumping up, Chris grabbed his brother's arm in a vice-like grip. 'We're outta here,' he said, steering him towards the entrance. 'Do *not* say another word.'

* * *

Before Sonja had a chance to contact Red Diamond, Famka phoned.

'He wants us,' Famka stated, sounding quite pleased with herself.

'Who wants us?' Sonja asked. After her long night of rough sex with Alex Pinchinoff, she wasn't in the mood for new action, even if it meant big bucks.

'The old guy, of course,' Famka said triumphantly. 'I knew he couldn't resist.'

'Red Diamond?' Sonja questioned. If it *was* Red, how convenient was *that*?

'Mr Viagra himself,' Famka said, with a brittle laugh. 'The old man sound agitated. I tell him two thousand apiece, double we stay all night.'

'He agreed?'

'Bring rubber handcuffs and special lotion – I run out. Had important client from UN, he want lotion head to toe, 'specially around his balls. No sex, just lotion.' She gave another brittle laugh. 'Asshole.'

'They're all assholes,' Sonja said.

'Where *you* been?' Famka asked.

'Alex Pinchinoff.'

'Ah, the dangerous one.'

'Dangerous *and* sexy.'

'You don't get enough at work?'

'It make change.'

'I call for cab, you want I pick you up?'

'How soon?'

'Fifteen minutes.'

'I'll be downstairs.'

This couldn't have worked out better. Now she could blackmail Red to his face. Well, maybe not blackmail – that was too harsh a word. Merely allow him an opportunity to pay to have certain information suppressed.

But what about Famka? She couldn't do it in front of her.

Damn! She'd have to figure *something* out.

*   *   *

Driving into a certain area of Brighton Beach at night was scary. The restaurants and nightclubs were lit up, while noisy, half-drunk patrons spilled out onto the sidewalk.

Searching for a parking spot, Max became very aware that he was carrying a box – which he'd put inside a canvas bag, then locked into the trunk – a box that contained half a million bucks in cash, plus a few priceless gemstones. The only items he'd removed from it were Mariska's address book, filled with the numbers of all her Russian acquaintances, along with her birth certificate and marriage certificate to Vladimir. The moment he got home he would burn them – burn away all traces of her duplicitous past.

Damnit, he was turning into a criminal, planning to destroy what could turn out to be very valuable evidence in a murder case. Shades of Red Diamond. It was the kind of thing Red would do without a second thought.

He didn't want to become like his father, but all rational thought seemed to have deserted him. He was convinced that this was something he *had* to do to protect his daughter – if indeed Lulu *was* his daughter. The thought that she might not be paralyzed him. She was all he had, her and Amy.

A green Buick conveniently slid out of a parking spot. Max backed his Mercedes into the vacant space, bumping the fender of an old Cadillac parked behind.

Almost immediately a man emerged from the Cadillac zipping up his fly. 'What's *wrong* with you?' the man yelled. He was big, bald and bad-tempered. 'You need a fuckin' compass to park your shitty German car?'

Max got out of his Mercedes. 'Sorry,' he muttered. The last thing he wanted was a scene. 'I don't think there's any damage.'

'You don't, huh?' the man sneered belligerently. 'That's

where you an' I differ, my friend. Take a look at my bumper! There's a coupla hundred *bucks'* worth of damage.'

Max attempted to peer at the supposedly damaged car. It was too dark to see anything.

A young girl emerged from the Cadillac, young enough to be the bald man's daughter – although she obviously wasn't, as her clothes were askew, and her lipstick smudged across her chin.

'Here's my witness,' the man said triumphantly.

'Where's my twenny?' the girl demanded in a tinny voice, pulling on his sleeve.

'Shut up,' the man hissed, glaring at her. 'You'll get your money. We're not finished.'

Max got the picture. 'Will two hundred cover it?' he asked.

The bald man thought about it for a nano-second. 'Make it two fifty an' I won't bother callin' the cops to report an accident,' he said, adjusting his crotch.

'Right,' Max said. He hated giving in to this oaf's black-mail, but anything to avoid more of a confrontation. Turning away from the man, he pulled out his wallet, extracted the right amount of money, then handed it over.

The bald man shoved the bills into his pocket and said, 'What you down here lookin' for? Mebbe I can help ya find it.'

'That's all right,' Max said. 'I'm visiting a relative.'

'A relative, huh?'

'Are we doin' it or not?' the young girl whined, tugging on the bald man's shirt-sleeve.

'Yeah, we're doin' it,' he said, throwing Max a lascivious wink.

The two of them got back into the Cadillac.

Max waited a few minutes before he opened the trunk of his Mercedes. Then he quickly took out the canvas bag, crossed the street and entered Irena's building.

* * *

Standing astride Red Diamond, wearing nothing but sheer black stockings, a leather garterbelt and ridiculously high stilettos, Sonja thought the old man looked unusually pale. Of course, he had just indulged in a series of sexual activities with two beautiful women, activities probably far too taxing for a seventy-nine-year-old man – she'd discovered his age by reading the newspapers – and then there was the matter of the Viagra he'd been taking on what seemed a regular basis. It couldn't be healthy for a man his age.

Sonja was worried about his well-being. What if he had a seizure or a heart-attack? Either could turn out to be deadly, and where would that leave her and the major pay-out she hoped to extract from him?

Right now he was demanding that she handcuff and punish him. It was one of his favourite scenarios – smack his wrinkled old ass until it was rosy.

Famka was in the bathroom taking a leisurely shower – or so she said. Famka worked hard with her clients, but she claimed they never made her come, so whenever there was a break, she locked herself away and pleasured herself.

This suited Sonja fine, because it gave *her* the opportunity she was looking for. 'How much you pay for Vladimir story to stay quiet?' she ventured.

'What?' Red growled, staring up at the woman who stood astride him. She wasn't supposed to talk. He didn't appreciate talkers.

'Your daughter-in-law's *real* husband.'

'My daughter-in-law's *what*?'

'Legitimate husband.'

He ran his gnarled hand up her thigh. 'Is this part of the punishment?'

'No. This real stuff,' Sonja said quickly. 'Mariska no marry Max, she already married to my friend Vladimir. That make her bigamist. Not only bigamist – in Moscow she prostitute.' Sonja paused to let her words sink in. 'How much you pay for story to stay quiet?'

'Are you trying to *blackmail* me?' Red asked incredulously, then burst into derisive laughter. 'You honestly think I didn't *know* who Mariska was? She was a cheap whore, like you. I understood *that* the moment I saw her.'

'I am not cheap,' Sonja muttered, her dreams of scoring a fortune crashing around her.

'No, you're not,' Red agreed. 'Now, put your mouth where it's supposed to be and shut the fuck up.'

*   *   *

The same smell of cat piss and stale beer assailed Max's nostrils as he entered Irena's building. The question occurred to him – why *had* Mariska allowed her mother to live in such squalor? Then again, it was unlikely that Mariska had ever visited the dank apartment in Brighton Beach, so he'd give her the benefit of the doubt and assume she hadn't realized how bad it was.

He climbed the darkened stairs, clutching the bag tightly to his chest. This was so unlike anything he'd ever done before. Was he losing his mind? It was insane behaviour. Chris was right, he could get himself arrested for concealing evidence.

At least by giving the box to Irena he was no longer responsible for it. And who could prove that he'd taken it from her apartment? No one.

Half-way up the second flight of stairs, a woman in a sloppy housecoat burst out of a door yelling in a foreign language. She was being chased by a skinny runt of a man wielding a leather belt. The two of them shoved their way past Max as if he didn't exist.

He took a deep breath and made it up the rest of the stairs fast.

If Irena was smart, she'd move out of this dump tomorrow. She'd have enough money to do whatever the hell she wanted, although he should warn her not to do anything with the gemstones for a while. Who knew where they had come from? He should also tell her to take off Mariska's diamond ring and put it away.

Then another question occurred to him – how *had* she got the ring? She must have stolen it, so did that mean she had been in Mariska's apartment *after* she was killed? Had she taken the ring off Mariska's lifeless finger? Or was she actually there when Mariska was stabbed to death?

At least it was kind of poetic justice that Mariska's money – and where it had come from he didn't even want to think about – was going to her mother, a woman for whose welfare she'd obviously cared nothing.

He made it to Irena's apartment and knocked on the door. It swung open and her cat darted out, hissing angrily.

The stench of burned milk hit him as he entered, calling her name.

She was sitting in the one rickety chair watching her black-and-white TV. Her back was to him. The sound of the TV was too loud, and sparks were coming from the hot-plate in the corner.

'Irena,' he said loudly, 'something's burning.'

She didn't move.

'Can you turn the TV down?' he shouted.

Still no answer.

He moved in front of her.

She was dead. A single neat bullet-hole right in the centre of her forehead.

Chapter Sixty-One

It took him a while, but Chris finally managed to sober Jett up. After gallons of coffee, an icy cold shower, several Tylenols and a major sweat-out in the hotel gym, Jett started groaning. How could he have done it? What was the matter with him? He was one big fucking *loser*.

'Shit happens,' Chris assured him, as they sat around in his suite. 'You made a wrong move, and now it's up to you to make sure it doesn't happen again.'

'I feel like such a dumb *jerk*.' Jett groaned, pushing his hands through his hair.

'Beating yourself up won't help,' Chris said. 'You did it, it's over, and as soon as possible you need to get to a meeting. It's imperative you attend on a regular basis. Plus you've got to find a sponsor.'

'I had one in Italy,' Jett said, downing his fifth cup of coffee. 'Any time I felt the urge I called this guy and he talked me down. It worked great.'

'Yeah, well, what obviously does *not* work great is you *not* going to meetings,' Chris pointed out.

'I get it.'

'I hope so.'

'Guess I wasn't thinking straight with all this stuff goin' on,' Jett said, trying to make excuses. 'Y' know, Gianna leaving. Amy not wanting to hurt Max.'

'Like, you *do*?' Chris questioned.

'There's no *way* I want to hurt him. What I *do* want is to be with Amy.'

'That's what you want, huh?' Chris sighed. 'You're sure?'

'Yeah, that's it.'

'You got anything to offer her, little bro'? You thought about that?'

'Huh?'

'If she leaves Max, what makes you think it'll work out between the two of you? You've no steady job, no apartment. You don't even have a car.'

'Make me feel better about myself, why doncha?' Jett said wryly.

'I'm being real. Are *you*?'

'What d'you mean by *that*?'

'Gianna seemed great. Beautiful, successful, fun. Could be you're making a big mistake.'

'You don't *get* it, Chris,' Jett said earnestly. 'I *love* Amy, and she loves me.'

'Did she tell you that?'

'No, but—'

'She didn't tell you?'

'It's early days.'

'So what's your plan?'

'We don't have one.'

'Try this.'

'What?'

'How about you leave her alone for a while, let her make her own decisions, *then* see what happens?'

'I don't think I can do that.'

'Look,' Chris said, the voice of reason, 'force her into doing something now and she's likely to resent you. When and *if* she decides to leave Max, it has to be her move, not because *you* talked her into it. Then, later, if the two of you do get together . . . it won't be so bad for Max.'

'I suppose you could be right,' Jett mumbled reluctantly.

'I know I am. In the meantime, I think you should fly to L.A. with me tomorrow. It'll give you a chance to get your head straight, put some space between you and this situation.'

'I can't—'

'Yes, you *can*,' Chris said forcefully. 'I'm booking you a ticket, so get your ass over to your apartment and pack. I'll see you at the house of horrors in the morning. We'll take off from there.'

* * *

Max stumbled from Irena's apartment, his heart beating wildly. This was the second dead woman he'd seen in less than a week. What the fuck was happening to his nice orderly *life*?

A few days ago he'd had everything under control – everything except his finances, and now that problem was taken care of. But his personal life was a fucking *nightmare*. And it was all the fault of Vladimir Bushkin, the Russian prick with his threats and blackmail.

Because of Vladimir, two women were dead. Somehow or other he must have discovered that Irena was about to reveal his identity as the man who'd killed Mariska, so he'd silenced her too. This time with a gun.

Totally panicked, Max raced down the concrete stairs. He'd taken one look at Irena and fled, desperate to get out of her room and away from the devastating stench of death.

As he made his way rapidly down the stairs, he started going over what he'd seen. He hadn't noticed any blood, just a small neat hole right in the middle of her forehead.

Maybe she *wasn't* dead. He should have felt her pulse. Although why would he touch her?

Should he call the police? That was the big question.

Yes.

No!

How was he going to explain a *second* visit to Irena? What if they thought *he* had had something to do with her murder?

He had no alibi. Christ! He needed an alibi.

Amy. He'd go straight to Amy. Tell the police – should they ask – that he'd been with *her* all night.

Yes. That was a plan. Had to have a plan, otherwise he'd look guilty as hell. He could just imagine Detective Rodriguez's smarmy face. *Tell me, Mr Diamond, why did you go back to visit Irena a second time? To kill her? Is that it? To stop her telling us that you murdered your wife? Sorry, Mr Diamond — your* ex-wife.

Yes, Detective Rodriguez would go to town on this one.

I should call my lawyer, he thought.

Why? I'm not guilty of anything. Best to keep quiet. Nobody knows I'm here. It would be foolish to open anything up.

Aren't you going to report a murder?

No. I'm not.

And as these thoughts flew around in his brain, he continued hurrying down the stairs, still clutching the canvas bag, sweating profusely, agonizing over what to do next.

* * *

'I thought we stay all night,' Famka said, making a disappointed face.

'Why would I *ever* want to spend the night with two whores like you?' Red Diamond said, getting off the bed and starting to dress.

'Because you like us,' Famka said, in her best girly voice. 'Because we're sexy and you like fucking us.'

'Ask your friend why you're not staying,' Red said, indicating Sonja. 'Your *blackmailing* friend.'

'What you say?' Famka said blankly, looking from Red to Sonja.

'Didn't she tell you?' Red sneered. 'Cut you in?'

Famka stared at Sonja. Sonja shrugged, as if she had no idea what he was talking about. Damn him. If the old fart said *anything*, she would deny it.

'Cut me in on what?' Famka asked at last, pouting just a little bit.

'*She*'ll tell you,' Red said, pulling on his pants. He was bored with both of them. They'd done their job and now he wanted them gone.

He walked over to the dresser, picked up his wallet and threw a flurry of hundred-dollar bills in their direction. 'Out,' he said. 'Now.'

* * *

Half-way down the stairs, Max tripped and, before he could save himself, he began to fall, crashing down several of the concrete stairs on his knees. The shock and pain hit him immediately, while the canvas bag shot out of his hands and plummeted over the stairwell to the ground floor.

'*Shit!*' he muttered, grabbing the side rail and staggering to his feet. Could this day get any worse? His pants were ripped, he could barely stand, and the pain in his right knee was excruciating.

Somehow or other, he made his way down the rest of the stairs, reaching the bag just in time as a lank-haired youth was about to scoop it up.

'That's mine,' Max said, breathing heavily.

'Says who?' the boy questioned. He was sixteen or seventeen, with sallow features and a sullen attitude.

'It's mine,' Max repeated sharply. 'I dropped it.'

'What's in it?' the boy asked, his hand hovering near the handle.

'None of your damn business,' Max shouted, snatching up the bag and limping towards the door.

'I should get a fuckin' reward,' the boy yelled after him.

'Bullshit,' Max muttered, crossing the street and reaching the safety of his car.

He leaned against the side of his Mercedes for a moment before he got in. Then he slid behind the wheel, placed the canvas bag on the passenger seat and stared at it.

What was he going to do with the money and gemstones now? What the *hell* was he going to do?

*   *   *

Somewhere in her sleep Amy could hear banging, a doorbell ringing. Slowly opening her eyes, she realized the noise wasn't part of her dream. Someone was hammering at her front door.

She groped for the bedside clock and noted it was almost midnight. Now, who would be pounding at her door so late?

Jett. It had to be Jett.

For a moment she lay very still, hoping he'd go away. But he didn't. The incessant ringing of the bell continued until she was forced to get out of bed before he woke the people in the next apartment.

She reached for a robe and made her way to the front door. 'Jett,' she said firmly, not opening the door. 'Go away.'

'It's *Max*. Will you please open up?'

Oh, God! Max had found out about her and Jett, and he was here to confront her.

For a moment she froze, not sure *what* to do.

'Hurry up, Amy,' he said, raising his voice.

Had Jett *told* him? Confessed? Or had Chris given him the bad news?

Okay. Don't panic, she thought. *I can handle this.*

Taking a long, deep breath, she flung open the door. Max stumbled inside. He looked dreadful, dishevelled and unkempt, totally unlike the Max she knew. It was obvious that he'd taken the news badly. She wasn't surprised.

'I . . . I don't know what to say,' she began, searching for the right words. 'It wasn't planned . . . It, uh, just happened.'

'I need to use the bathroom,' he said, pushing past her. 'I'll explain everything in a minute.'

He hurried past into her bedroom, then she heard her bathroom door slam.

She stood in the hallway for a moment, nonplussed. What had he meant by *I'll explain everything in a minute*? Wasn't *she* the one who was supposed to be doing the explaining?

And was it her imagination, or were his pants all ripped at the knees? And *why* did he look all sweaty and mussed up?

Had he and Jett had a fight? That would be so bad – she couldn't stand it.

Jett. She should call Jett and find out what had taken place. She could do it while Max was in the bathroom.

She ran into her bedroom and picked up the phone, keeping a close eye on the bathroom door.

'Hey,' Jett said, delighted to hear from her.

'What happened?' she asked, in a low voice.

Jett hesitated a moment. 'Look, I didn't *intend* to do it,' he said, trying to figure out how she'd found out about his drinking. 'It was just one of those things.'

'It's so *wrong*,' she said furiously.

'I'm sorry,' he said. 'It's not something I sat around planning to do.'

'If *anyone* was going to tell him, it should've been *me*. And did the two of you get in a fight?'

'Who? Me and Chris?'

'What does *Chris* have to do with this?'

'Well . . . uh . . . he helped me out. Y' know, sobered me up, got me together.'

'You were *drunk*?' she exclaimed, horrified.

'Isn't that what we're talking about?'

'No,' she said sharply. 'We're talking about you telling Max about us.'

'Huh?'

'He turned up at my apartment a few minutes ago, and he looks awful. You *did* get in a fight, didn't you?' she said accusingly.

'Are you kidding me? We did *not* get into a fight, and I sure as hell *didn't* tell him about us.'

'Then how does he know?'

They both said it at the same time. 'Chris!'

'That *son-of-a-bitch*,' Jett exclaimed.

'How *could* he?' Amy wailed.

'I'm coming over,' Jett said, making a quick decision. 'We gotta face this together.'

'No!' she said helplessly. 'If you come over it'll only make things worse.'

'There's no way you're handling it alone. I'll be there as soon as I can. Hang in there, Amy. I promise you – everything's gonna be okay.'

She put down the phone as Max emerged from the bathroom. Yes, he did look beat up, there were gaping rips in his pants legs, and one of his exposed knees was dripping blood.

'I – I don't know what to say, Max,' she began. 'I never meant for you to find out like this.'

'Listen to me carefully, Amy,' he said urgently, ignoring her words. 'If anyone asks, I was here all night.'

'Excuse me?' she said, frowning.

'All night,' he repeated. 'You understand?'

She was utterly confused. Did he know about her and Jett

or not? And if he did, it was obvious he had something else on his mind.

'I'm sorry to use you as my alibi,' he continued, 'but I witnessed something tonight, and if the police think I was there, I'll get dragged into it, and that won't be good.'

'Witnessed *what*?'

'Something bad.'

'How bad?'

'It's better you don't know.'

Suddenly she felt sick. Her mother's words came drifting back into her head: *Max is not a victim, Amy. His wife has been brutally murdered, and the suspicion lies on him.*

'What's going on, Max?' she asked, pulling her robe tightly round her.

'I told you,' he said, sitting on the edge of the bed. 'It's better you don't know.'

'If you want me to say you were here, I have to know what I'm shielding you from.'

'Jesus *Christ*!' he said furiously, standing up again. 'Why can't you do as I say for once?'

She'd never seen this side of him before, this angry person she barely recognized.

'Does – does this have something to do with Mariska's murder?' she asked tentatively.

'*Fuck!*' he exclaimed, walking over and banging his fist against the wall. 'Fuck! Fuck! FUCK!'

'I don't understand what's going on,' she said, moving across the room to get away from him. 'But whatever it is, I think you'd better go.'

'I come to you for help, and you're sending me away?' he said incredulously. 'This is *goddamn* serious, Amy. You'd better do as I tell you.'

He began to move towards her. She backed away.

'What's the *matter* with you?' he demanded. 'I ask you to do one simple thing, and you *can't*. I'm your future *husband*, for Crissake. We're getting *married*.'

His words filled her with dread. She'd thought she was in love with Max, but it dawned on her that she never had been. He'd represented safety, and now he didn't. Then she realized that she would *never* have slept with another man if she'd really been in love with him. Too much to drink or not, it simply wasn't possible.

All she wanted at this moment was to get him out of her apartment.

'Are you just going to stand there and say nothing?' he yelled. 'Jesus *Christ*, Amy. I thought I could depend on you.'

'If you tell me what's going on, then maybe I can help,' she said, her voice sounding higher than usual. 'However, if you don't . . .' Her words trailed off as she remembered that Jett was on his way over, and if Max *didn't* know about them, the timing of his finding out couldn't have been worse.

'Forget it,' Max snapped. 'I'm out of here. You're not the girl I thought you were, Amy. You're not someone I can trust.' With that he stormed his way to the front door.

She stayed in her bedroom, rooted to the spot, allowing him to go. Something very bad had happened for Max to be acting like this. Something very, *very* bad.

And then the thought popped into her head – was *Max* responsible for Mariska's murder? Had *he* killed her? Shuddering with a sudden icy fear, she ran into the hall and locked the front door behind him.

* * *

Muttering to himself, Max made it downstairs. He was furious with Amy. This was the first time he'd ever asked her for anything, and it floored him that she couldn't manage to come through.

The problem was she was too young to understand what was going on. She wasn't a woman, she was a girl. A very lovely and innocent girl, but maybe thinking they could make a marriage work was a mistake. She wasn't that great with Lulu, and Lulu needed a mother – now more than ever.

The image of Irena sitting in her chair with a bullet-hole through her forehead flashed through his mind. Who had killed her? And why?

Christ! What was happening? Why did everything seem to

be spiralling out of control? He had to get a grip, decide what to do.

Stepping out of the elevator, he came face to face with Jett. 'What the hell are *you* doing here?' he said, frowning.

'Okay, okay,' Jett began, speaking fast. 'I need to explain that it wasn't anyone's fault. It was one of those crazy things that just kinda happened. We didn't plan it, I can promise you that. I had no idea who she was – and she certainly had no clue I was your brother. It was kinda . . . fate.'

Max stared at his younger half-brother, the 'fuck-up' as Red always referred to him. Was he missing something? Earlier, when he'd hammered on Amy's door, she'd thought it was Jett. Now *why* would she think Jett was at her door in the middle of the night?

It didn't make sense . . . or did it?

And then her words came back to him – *I – I don't know what to say . . . it wasn't planned . . . It just happened.*

Almost the same words as Jett had used. And Amy wasn't herself, she was nervous and jumpy, almost *guilty*.

Of *what*?

'Tell me about the crazy thing that *just happened*?' Max demanded, a helpless anger coursing through him, for he knew he was not going to like what he heard.

'You can't take it out on Amy,' Jett said earnestly. 'You gotta understand that it wasn't her fault. She'd had too much to drink and, like I said, it was just one of those crazy things—'

Max got it. Without thinking, he hauled back and slammed his fist into Jett's chin. Hard. 'You son-of-a-bitch!' he screamed. 'You fucking *son-of-a-bitch*!'

Jett swayed on his feet. 'I'm telling you – you gotta understand,' he yelled. 'I love her, an' she feels the same way about me. There's *nothing* you can do.'

'Nothing, huh?' Max screamed, all the anger and frustration of the past few days reaching boiling point. 'You fucking asshole *loser*.'

'You're just like Red,' Jett managed, rubbing his chin. 'Same lousy attitude. Same freakin' words.'

'Don't *ever* compare me to him.'

'Jeez, Max, I feel sorry for you, 'cause you *are* like him. Why doncha admit it? You're two of a kind.'

Max experienced a cold knot of fear and anger in the pit of his stomach. He was losing everything – including his fucking mind. But he was not about to lose his identity. He would *never* be the man his father was. *Never*.

Without saying another word he hurried from the building, got into his car and drove home.

After a few tense minutes of deliberation and a stiff drink, he called his lawyer, then Chris, and finally Detective Rodriguez.

The truth was, he had nothing left to lose.

Chapter Sixty-Two

Early on Thursday morning, Liberty and Damon sat together at the caterer's table on the beach eating breakfast. It was the last day of her photo shoot, and even though it had only been three days, she already knew how much she was going to miss everyone. Being fussed over was quite addictive, and having Damon in L.A. was the cream in her coffee – not only was he capable of giving her a future career, but she found him to be incredibly sexy, interesting and generous.

She'd never felt this way about a man before. Just being with him was a total trip, and it had nothing to do with the way everyone treated him like a star with all the trimmings – the limos, clubs and expensive restaurants. To her he was Damon. Just a guy. And she'd fallen big-time.

'Last night I was thinking about Cabo and, yeah – I was about to say yes,' she said, sipping a glass of freshly squeezed orange juice.

'Keep talkin'.'

'Then my mom called, and here's the *real* reason I can't go.'

'Spill.'

'She needs to tell me something, and according to her it's about my dad and it's important.'

'*How* important?'

'I don't know until I get back to New York.'

'And two days is gonna make a difference?' he said, leaning in and giving her one of his intense looks.

She was silent for a moment. Then she said, 'You can't understand. It's too personal.'

'Try me.'

'Y'see, *I* only have my mom, never had a dad, and it was only a few days ago she told me who he was. Now she's ready to change her story, so *that*'s why I have to get back. I need to find out who I am.'

'You're *you*,' Damon said quietly. 'You always gotta remember that.'

'I knew you wouldn't understand.'

'You're wrong, baby,' he said, looking into her eyes. 'I understand big-time.'

'You're always—'

'Quit givin' me that *always* shit like I don't get it,' he interrupted, narrowing his eyes. 'You wanna hear 'bout me? I'll tell you. My grandma raised me an' my brother in the projects. We didn't have *nothin*' 'cept her love an' encouragement. That woman worked two jobs to keep us goin'. She was *never* too busy to teach me that if I *wanted* somethin' – really wanted it – then I'd better shift my lazy ass an' *make* it happen. An' that's exactly what I did.'

'I didn't know that,' Liberty said.

'No reason you should. That's private shit I keep to myself. Nobody's business 'cept mine.'

'Where's your grandma now?'

'Livin' in a fancy house I bought her in Brooklyn with my brother, his wife an' their three kids,' he said. 'I give that lady anythin' she damn well wants. She worked her ass off for me an' my little bro' an' she deserves the world.'

'How about your parents? Are *they* around?'

'Never met either of 'em. Don't even know if they're still alive. Don't even give a crap.'

'Why?' she asked curiously.

'Mom was a crackhead, my old man a dealer,' he said flatly. 'A coupla drugged-out freaks. They left us on our own till Grandma came an' took us in. If it wasn't for her we'd've been pushed into the welfare system.'

'I'm sorry,' she said softly. 'It must've been tough for you.'

'Hey,' he said, shrugging, 'you go with the breaks. My belief is you give props to the person who raised you, can't be worryin' 'bout no one else. My grandma is the best woman in the world.'

Before she could say anything, Quinn came over to inform her it was time to get to the make-up trailer. Reluctantly she got up to leave.

'So, don't go backin' away from Cabo,' Damon said, standing up. 'It's somethin' we'll both get off on. You can figure out your family shit when we get back.'

'You think?'

'I *know*, baby. I *know*.'

'Sure you do,' she said, smiling at his supreme confidence. 'You seem to know everything.'

'Ain't *that* the truth,' he said, grinning.

'Mr Big Ego,' she murmured.

'An' doncha forget it.'

'I'll try not to,' she teased.

'See ya later, LL,' he said, and began strolling off down the beach.

'*Shame* he's straight,' Quinn murmured. 'Such a *diabolical* waste!'

'I'm sure his wife doesn't think so,' she said tartly. 'He's married, y' know.'

'My! My!' Quinn dead-panned. 'I'd *never* have guessed.'

She watched Damon as he headed towards the hotel. He was everything she'd ever wanted in a man . . . and yet he was a *married* man, and she'd never been into sharing.

'Come along, dear,' Quinn said crisply. 'Time to stop lusting and come beautify.'

'I'm not lusting,' she objected, although she knew perfectly well that she was.

'You could've fooled me.'

Sitting in the make-up chair, she still couldn't stop thinking about him. Now that he'd revealed a small part of his personal story, she was anxious to hear more. Damon was an inspiration, he'd made it from nothing and look at him now. He was only thirty-six, a man who'd put himself out there and made a huge success doing something he loved. He wasn't just

475

some rich hip-hop mogul with his own record label, he'd worked hard to get where he was, and it must've been quite a jump from nothing to everything.

The great American dream. Damon was *it*.

It occurred to her that getting back to New York didn't seem so urgent. Whatever her mom had to say could wait. After all, she'd waited nineteen years to hear the truth – what difference would one weekend make?

Besides, Damon was right, if she was going to achieve anything it was because of *her* efforts. It didn't matter who her father was – he was long gone – she was her own person. It was time to stop feeling sorry for herself and seize everything life had to offer. Right now there was a trip to Cabo staring her in the face – and if Damon's wife didn't care, why should she?

For the morning shoot she was wearing a slinky, soft black-leather Versace gown, so glamorous she was almost scared to move. It was slashed in the front all the way to the top of her thigh, while the back dipped dangerously low. Teddy piled her hair on top of her head, and Uma had procured a million bucks' worth of diamond and emerald jewellery from Neil Lane – the king of the estate jewellery business. Neil himself came to the shoot, and couldn't stop raving about how fantastic his jewels looked on her.

When she finally hit the beach she was barefoot and flawless.

'Phew!' Chip was blown away when he saw her. '*This*'ll be the cover shot. No doubt in *my* mind.'

'Not one of the swimsuit shots?' she asked. 'Isn't showing *flesh* what this new magazine is all about?'

'Believe me, this shot's gonna beat 'em all,' Chip assured her. 'You got that Halle Berry mixed with Angelina Jolie thing going. Only younger and sexier. You're amazing!'

Amazing! Yes! *Everything* was amazing. A week ago she'd been toiling away as a waitress, and now here she was in L.A., wearing Versace and posing for the cover of a magazine. It was all too much! An adventure she'd never believed possible.

Damon came back in time for an early lunch break.

Before she was able to give him a positive response about

Cabo, the caterer appeared with a huge cake – chocolate decorated with strawberries, the image of her face re-created in the centre.

'What's this?' she exclaimed in surprise. 'It's not my birthday.'

'No, it's a big thank-you from all of us,' Chip said, crooked grin going full force as he mingled with all the people involved in the photo shoot. 'We wanted your first modelling experience to be memorable. Everyone, gather round, we're taking a photo for posterity.'

Damon started to move away, while Chip began to set up the shot with one of his assistants.

'Damon,' she said, calling him back boldly. 'I want you in it too.'

'This is *your* deal, LL,' he said, uncharacteristically low-key. 'Go ahead an' shine. I'm not a part of it.'

'Yes, you are,' she insisted. 'A very special part.'

'Don't tell me my charm's finally meltin' that stony heart of yours?' he said, a slight smile hovering on his lips.

'Shut up and get over here,' she said, grinning. 'I *want* you in this picture.'

'Yes, *ma'am*,' he said, mock-saluting.

'Oh, and by the way,' she added.

'What you got for me now?'

'I'm on for Cabo.'

'Yeah?'

'Separate rooms.'

'The lady builds me up just so she can let me down,' he said wryly. 'She gives with one hand, takes away with the other.'

'That's the deal. Are we going?'

'Damn straight we're goin'. Gotta hunch you an' I are gonna make sweet, *sweet* soul music.'

Chapter Sixty-Three

On Thursday morning Diahann got out of bed at the usual time, but instead of dressing quickly and heading straight to the kitchen in the main house, she took time for herself and applied a careful make-up, then styled her hair. After that was done, she chose a simple but stylish blue dress, then added a couple of pieces of gold jewellery left over from her days as a singer. If Red insisted that she be at his meeting, she certainly wasn't about to walk in looking like the dowdy housekeeper.

She stood back and appraised her appearance in the mirror. The transformation was quite startling. Like her daughter, Diahann was a beauty, a darker beauty than Liberty, but stunning with her green eyes, full lips and clouds of jet-black hair.

It was strange seeing herself all done up. It had been so long since she'd got herself together. Why now?

She knew why.

Something *big* was about to take place. Something that would startle everyone. Although perhaps not Lady Bentley – for she'd obviously, somehow or other, found out her and Red's secret. However, Red's three sons would be shocked, and so would Liberty, if only she was here. Diahann had begged her to hurry back to New York but, as usual, Liberty was stubborn – she did things her way.

Diahann thought about her daughter for a moment. When she'd been forced to send Liberty away to live with Aretha, she'd lost all control over her. Always a wild child, Liberty had grown up fast and furious. Diahann often thanked God for Cindi, at least Liberty wasn't out on her own – she had her cousin to protect her.

Diahann sighed. There'd been no one to protect *her* when she'd left home at sixteen, and arrived in New York. No one at all.

*   *   *

Diahann Dozier got off the bus from Atlanta full of excitement and big dreams. She was in New York. New York City! And even though she had only a small amount of money, her desire to succeed as perhaps the new Anita Baker or Diana Ross outweighed all the disadvantages she might face. She could sing, she was good-looking – she'd imagined it was all going to be so damn easy.

But no. Nothing was easy for a pretty black girl alone and broke in New York.

For two years she persevered, scoring a few gigs here and there. Along the way she'd hooked up with a series of jazz musicians – not a good idea, for they all treated her in a cavalier way, passing her from one to the other.

One day, at a recording session, she ran into Zippy Ventura, a two-bit manager who talked a big game and liked what he saw. 'You do for me, kiddo, an' I'll do for you,' he told her.

Zippy was a short, skinny white man in his forties. He was married to Kandie – a tough-looking black woman with bleached, white-blonde hair and enormous fake breasts.

Marriage didn't seem to hinder Zippy, who was after any outside-his-marriage action he could get. In exchange for the occasional grope in his seedy office, he began to score Diahann quite a few decent gigs singing background at sessions and, even better, solo spots at a late-night club, Gloria's in Harlem.

Gloria, a large gay woman, took an immediate shine to Diahann, nicknaming her Dini, and constantly lecturing her on the joys of being with a woman as opposed to a man.

Diahann was not convinced, although she could certainly have done without Zippy and his lascivious moves.

Diahann sang at the club twice a week. Standing on the small smoky stage, belting out jazz versions of standards like

'You Go To My Head' and 'But Not For Me', she felt very much like she was heading for the big-time.

Men chased her, especially the regular customers, but after her bad experiences with musicians, she'd kind of given up on men.

One night Red Diamond showed up. Diahann had no idea who he was, but a very impressed Zippy and Gloria soon filled her in: Red Diamond was a much-married billionaire media tycoon with a fierce reputation. Zippy and Gloria were over the moon that he'd chosen to spend time at Gloria's.

After his first visit, Red Diamond returned several times, sometimes with a woman, sometimes alone. He sat at a front table and never took his eyes off her as she went through her repertoire of old standards.

'He likes you,' Zippy informed her.

'So what?' was her reply.

'He wants you to have a drink with him,' Gloria informed her.

'Not me,' was her reply.

This went on for several weeks, until one night Zippy cornered her, and said, 'You're gonna sit down an' have a drink with him or you're outta a job.'

Red Diamond was sixty. Diahann was eighteen. This didn't seem to bother either Zippy or Gloria, so she sat down and had a drink with him.

Red insisted she drink champagne – even though she was under-age.

She obliged.

He plied her with compliments, telling her he thought she was beautiful and sexy and ripe.

Ripe? she thought. What does he mean by ripe?

'I want to fuck you,' he said.

'No way,' she said.

A week later Zippy told her that if she didn't sleep with Red Diamond she was out of a job.

Nice. But she had nothing to lose except her job, so she did it.

The experience wasn't bad and it wasn't good. It was just . . . nothing. Diahann was ashamed of herself for sleeping with a rich old man just to keep working. It wasn't right, and she knew it. However, she reconciled herself to it: he wasn't the *first man she'd slept with and he certainly wouldn't be the last.*

After that night Red Diamond stopped coming to the club.

'What didja do to turn him off?' Zippy demanded, left eye twitching as he stared at her accusingly.

'Nothing,' she answered blankly.

'You happy now?' Gloria complained to Zippy. 'You made her sleep with him and now we lost us a big-time customer.'

Diahann couldn't care less. All she wanted to do was sing. It didn't bother her that Red never came back.

Six weeks later she realized she was pregnant. She kept the news to herself until it was too late to have an abortion, whereupon she informed Zippy and Gloria that she had to go home to Atlanta and visit her family for a while. Then she took a job as a receptionist in a beauty salon on Lexington, working up until three weeks before her baby was born.

Diahann named her baby Liberty – for freedom. And when Liberty was six weeks old, she contacted Zippy, told him she was back in the city and needed work.

He grumbled that she'd been away too long, the small following she'd started to acquire had moved on.

'Don't you want to be my manager?' she asked him.

'You do for me, an'—'

'No!' she said, backing away from his hands-on approach. 'It's business or nothing.'

'Go find yourself a new manager,' he muttered, quite insulted that she would turn him down.

So she did. She found Fred Marks, an energetic go-getter who immediately booked her into a series of clubs – some as far away as Atlantic City. It didn't matter, at least she was making enough money to pay her rent and hire a woman to take care of Liberty when she was working.

Diahann adored her baby. She thought Liberty was the most beautiful little creature she'd ever seen. Sometimes, when people found out she had a child, they wanted to know who Liberty's daddy was. Diahann came up with a variety of stories, none of them true. She had no desire for Red Diamond to find out that he'd fathered her child. She could manage very nicely without him, although sometimes – when things were slow – it was quite a struggle.

Right after Liberty's fifth birthday she met a man she liked. His name was Leon, and they were both singing back-up for some female one-hit wonder. They bonded over coffee and complaints about how bad the singer was. Two weeks later Leon moved in with her, which was a big help because he immediately took over half of the expenses. The other good news was that he fell in love with Liberty, and she with him. The two were sweet together, and Diahann knew that if Leon asked her to marry him, she would do so without a moment's hesitation.

But Leon didn't ask, and one year together turned into two, and Diahann realized she wasn't getting any younger and no big breaks were staring either of them in the face, so she broke up with him.

Liberty was devastated. To her, Leon was Mr Daddy, and for him to abandon her was extremely painful. She was only seven, but it was the start of the trouble between her and Diahann.

Fred did his best, but as time passed, the gigs became fewer and fewer – girl jazz singers were out of style. So one night Diahann decided to revisit Gloria's.

The club was still open, and there – mingling with her customers – was Gloria herself, big and warm and welcoming. Unfortunately, Zippy was still around too, pushing a young singer he insisted was the new Whitney Houston. Divorced and bitter, he was not pleased to see Diahann, but Gloria was. She invited her back to sing at the club three nights a week.

Diahann gladly accepted, which pissed Zippy off, causing an angry rift between him and Gloria. This was a relief to Diahann, because now she didn't have to deal with Zippy and his wandering hands.

'Zippy's got himself a little problem,' Gloria confided, pantomiming someone sniffing a line of coke.

It wasn't long before Gloria found out about Liberty, who was now nine, and quite a budding beauty.

'When did she happen?' Gloria exclaimed.

Diahann made up an old boyfriend back in Atlanta. Gloria seemed to accept her story, and as a special treat Diahann sometimes brought Liberty to the club to listen to her sing.

One night Zippy turned up. He was an unexpected and unwelcome visitor. Unfortunately it was a night when Liberty was there, standing at the side of the stage watching her mother perform.

Zippy slobbered all over the child while Diahann was singing, telling her how pretty she was and how he was her mom's best friend so they should all get together more often.

'Where's your daddy?' he asked.

'Don't have a daddy,' Liberty replied, thinking what a funny-looking man Zippy was.

'How old are you?'

'Nine.'

'Nine, huh? When you gonna be ten?'

'May the first,' she said proudly.

'I'll buy you a present,' Zippy promised, his almost coke-addled brain figuring out a thing or two.

When Diahann got off stage, she was furious. She and Zippy became involved in a loud argument, which finished when Gloria intervened and threw him out.

Diahann had a hunch that she had not seen the last of Zippy, and she was right. A week later he turned up at her apartment. 'I know whose kid she is,' he said, taunting her. 'The dates fit, so don't go thinkin' y' can fool me.'

She blanked him.

He was insistent.

'Does Red got any idea he has a kid with you?' Zippy asked, trying to force his way past her into her apartment.

She was sure he must be bluffing, how could he possibly know? And why would he even care?

She told him that he was crazy, that he should go away and leave her alone or she'd call the police.

Zippy laughed in her face. 'Ya dumb bitch. Doncha know this means big fuckin' bucks? We gotta partner up an' take the old guy for a bundle.'

Diahann called the police to get him to stop bothering her.

She was a black woman, Zippy was a white man. The police did nothing.

A few days later Zippy accosted Liberty outside her school. He reminded her that he was a good friend of her mom's and that he had the present he'd promised her. He took her to a nearby coffee shop.

Liberty went with him willingly. Since she'd met him at the club, she figured he was her mom's friend. Besides, he had a present for her.

Zippy ordered her a strawberry smoothie, then presented her with a cheap plastic manicure set. He extracted the nail clippers from the manicure set. 'Gimme your hand,' he said, 'an' Uncle Zippy'll show you how t' use it.'

She did as he asked, and he clipped a couple of her nails. Then, as if by accident, he jammed the sharp part of the clippers into her wrist, drawing blood.

'Ouch!' she squealed.

Quick as a flash he produced a cotton swab, soaked up the blood and popped the swab into a small plastic bag.

'You hurt me,' she complained. 'I'm going home.'

'Wait a minute,' he said. 'You got somethin' caught in your hair.' And he pulled out a couple of hairs.

'Ouch!' she squealed again.

'Don't worry 'bout it,' he said, adding the hairs to his plastic bag. 'You want another smoothie?'

When Liberty got home and told her mom where she'd been, Diahann went berserk. She accepted most things, but not a roach like Zippy messing with her daughter. How dare *he?*

She had no way of contacting him, but she was certain he'd come back, and when he did, she made sure she was ready. She purchased a hand-gun, and learned how to use it. Next time Zippy came sniffing around, she planned on sticking it in his stomach and telling him that if he ever *went near her daughter again she'd blow his brains out.*

Two weeks later he turned up at her apartment on a Saturday night. He was not alone. He was accompanied by Red Diamond.

The two men marched into her small apartment as if they owned it.

She was too startled to stop them. Fortunately Liberty was away, spending the weekend with a schoolfriend.

'Where's the kid?' Zippy demanded, as if he had a right to know.

Red Diamond glared at her with cold, hard eyes. 'You had the nerve *to give birth to* my *child,' he thundered. 'How* dare *you? Who do you think you are?'*

He had aged since she'd last seen him. He seemed smaller and more wrinkled. It crossed her mind that she should never have slept with him. But if she hadn't done so, she wouldn't have Liberty, and Liberty made every day worthwhile.

'What do you want?' she said flatly.

'No. The point is what do you *want?' Red asked coldly. 'What blackmailing scheme have you and your cohort come up with?'*

She didn't know what cohort meant, but she did understand that he was referring to Zippy – who was standing there with a big shit-eating grin on his stupid face as if he'd just discovered America.

'A million bucks should do it,' Zippy said, winking at her as if they were co-conspirators. 'A million bucks, an' then we'll go away an' you'll never hear from us again.'

'Is that all?' Red drawled sarcastically. 'Surely you should demand more than that?'

'Huh?' Zippy blurted, left eye twitching out of control. 'You want the kid? She's a pretty little thing – for another two mill you can have her.'

Diahann stared at Zippy in horror. Who did he think he was? He had no rights over her child. This was insane.

'My lawyers can make you very sorry you ever thought up this scheme to get money out of me,' Red said, fairly calmly. 'I came here tonight to see if I remembered the black bitch I slept with. Yes, I do remember her. She was no good then, and she's no good now.' A long pause. 'Tell me, did you two morons honestly believe you could get away with blackmailing Red Diamond? You can't be that *stupid?'*

Suddenly Diahann found her voice. 'Get out of my apartment,' she said, in a low, angry voice. 'Both of you. Right now!'

Zippy threw her a furious look. He'd thought when she heard the amount of money involved, she'd acquiesce and shut the fuck up. But, no, she was too dumb to do that.

'Oh,' Red said. 'So now you're going to play good cop, bad cop. A little late in the day for that *game, don't you think?'*

Diahann turned to him. 'I'm not after your money. I want nothing from you.' She indicated Zippy. 'This piece of garbage here is speaking on my behalf and he has no right. He's nothing to do with me. Nothing.' *Tears filled her eyes at the injustice of it all.*

'*'Scuse* me, *chickie*,' *Zippy said quickly, trying to save a situation that could turn on him.* '*I* discovered *you. You owe everything to me. So, stop acting like an ungrateful bitch, an' accept the money Mr Diamond's gonna give us for keepin' our mouths shut tight 'bout his little black bastard.*'

Diahann began to lose it. 'Our *mouths?*' *she shouted.* '*Liberty's* mine, and she's not for sale. Both of you – get out now.'

Zippy moved toward her. 'Wimmin!' *he said, rolling his eyes at Red.* 'They're always changin' their damn minds. We had an agreement, y' know.' *He grabbed her wrist in a steel-like grip.* 'Shut up,' *he muttered, so that only she could hear him.* 'You're gonna blow this sweet deal if you don't shut yer fuckin' mouth.'

Diahann was in shock. How could this be happening? What had she done to deserve such treatment?

'A million bucks,' *Zippy whispered.* 'He'll pay, an' we'll split it right down the middle,* an' *you get to keep ya kid.*'

Something came over her, a rage so deep that she was rendered almost speechless. Zippy was the lowest of the low, and he was trying to make her *his partner. He was dragging Red Diamond into her life, upsetting everything.*

'Get out,' *she hissed.*

'*I ain't goin' nowhere, honey, not until you see your way to agree t' this. An' if ya* don't, *I'll make sure your little girl's life ain't gonna be worth livin'.*'

Very calmly she snatched her wrist out of Zippy's grasp. Then she walked over to the shelf where she kept her handgun hidden behind a pile of magazines.

'*I think we got us a deal at one million big ones,*' *Zippy said confidently, turning to Red.*

'*You are a very ignorant man,*' *Red began to say, 'and I do not do business with—*'

Before Red could finish his sentence, Diahann pulled out her gun and, hands shaking, pointed it at Zippy. 'Get . . . out,' *she repeated.*

He blanched visibly at the sight of her pointing a gun at him. 'Now hold on a minute, ch-chickie,' *he stammered.* 'Ya gotta put that thing down.'

'What kind of a scam do the two of you think you're pulling?' Red roared, stepping between them. 'I'm not some out-of-town mark who'll fall for this phoney show you're putting on.'

'The broad's crazy,' Zippy said, left eye twitching out of control as he sensed the money slipping away. 'A crazy bitch with your kid. You should take the damn kid away from her. She ain't nothin' but a two-bit slut, an' if the kid stays with her, she'll turn out the same freakin' way. Give us two mill for the girl, an' you'll be gettin' yourself a real fine bargain. I can personally—'

With all the strength she could muster, Diahann shoved Red aside and went for Zippy – forgetting she held the gun.

Red moved in to stop the fight. The three of them struggled, locked together for a few moments, and then – bang – the gun went off, and Zippy slid to the ground.

* * *

Diahann took one final look in the mirror. She was still attractive, she thought, still able to command the attention of men, if she so desired.

She did not so desire.

She was thirty-eight years old and she'd shut herself off from the world for nine long years. Nine years of looking after Red Diamond, seeing he had everything he needed, never straying far from the house on 68th Street.

It was safer that way.

Now Red Diamond was prepared to reveal a part of their secret. But not the secret about Zippy. Oh, no, that was something nobody would ever find out, something only *they* shared.

Diahann held her head high, and made her way upstairs. Whatever happened next, she was determined to face it with dignity.

Chapter Sixty-Four

At first they'd fought, then they'd made up, and making up was so delightful that when Amy stirred to the sound of her phone ringing she was in a light-hearted, happy mood. It was Thursday morning, the sun was shining, Max knew the truth about her and Jett, so no more guilt.

Well . . . a little bit of guilt, because last night had not been pretty. Max had shown a side of himself she'd never seen before – a frightening side.

Jett lay beside her, still asleep, snoring lightly. She picked up the phone, a smile on her lips, and was hit with a tirade from her usually controlled mother.

'Have you *seen* the filthy rags?' Nancy seethed. 'Do you *know* what they're saying? Our family name is being dragged through the mud. This is a *disgrace! I will sue every one of these disgusting so-called journalists.*'

'Calm down, Mother.'

'No! *You* calm down.'

'*I'm* not the one yelling.'

'You *will* be when you read this garbage,' Nancy said ominously.

'Why are you reading it anyway?'

'How can I *not*, when the staff are all gathered in the kitchen laughing at us.'

'I'm sure they aren't.'

'Our connection with the Diamond family is finished. *Finished*,' Nancy repeated sternly. 'Do you understand me, Amy?'

'Yes, Mother,' Amy said patiently. 'I'll call you later.'

She put the phone down and took another look at Jett. He

was still sleeping, one arm thrown casually across his eyes, stomach exposed – rippling abs and a very fine spattering of body hair. *This* was love, the feeling she had when she watched him sleep.

She wondered what the tabloids had written that had her mother so riled up. Nobody believed what they printed anyway, so why did it matter?

Last night, after she and Jett had made love, they'd lain in bed and talked for hours until they'd fallen asleep in each other's arms. This morning she felt as if a huge weight had been lifted from her. It was the biggest relief in the world to know she was free.

The more she thought about it, the more she realized just how wrong she and Max had been together. Surely he would realize it too? They simply hadn't fitted. Movies. Music. Books. Their tastes were polar opposites. With Jett everything was in sync. They both enjoyed adventure movies, listening to Coldplay and the Black Eyed Peas, and when it came to books there was nothing like a good old John Grisham or James Siegel thriller. Even their TV preferences matched – *Alias* and *Seinfeld*. Jett had told her that in Milan he'd caught the first two seasons of both shows on DVD.

How great was that? A man she could watch TV with. Max had considered TV a total waste of time.

Momentous decision – should she fix Jett breakfast? What would he like? Tea? Coffee? Did he take sugar and cream? Cereal or eggs?

She knew so little about him, yet she felt she knew everything. He'd told her about his drinking and drug days, the lost years wandering around New York like a zombie, sleeping with anyone and everyone, shit-faced and out of his mind most of the time.

He'd got into a few family horror stories. His abusive father. His alcoholic mother. The beatings he'd received, and his fractured childhood being shuttled back and forth between the two of them.

Then Italy and his recovery. And Gianna, whom he swore he didn't love. 'I love *you*, Amy,' he'd said. 'You're *it* for me. I'm through with other women. Over. *Done.*'

'Really?' she'd asked, tilting her head on one side.

'Yeah, really,' he'd replied, a huge grin on his face.

She smiled as she thought about his words. *I'm through with other women. Over. Done.*

How high-school. How very sweet. How *much* she loved him.

* * *

Chris awoke to a cup of strong black coffee and a nagging ache in his gut. He hadn't had much sleep, a couple of hours at most. In the early hours of the morning he'd received an urgent call from Max so he'd hauled himself out of bed and hurried over to his brother's apartment, where he'd found Elliott Minor and Detective Rodriguez.

It seemed that Max had been at a murder scene and had not immediately reported it to the police. And there was also the matter of Mariska's box – evidence Max had taken from her apartment and kept to himself, only handing it over now.

Some mess, but Elliott was definitely a lawyer with well-placed connections, and after a few phone calls to the right people Max was exonerated of any guilt and left with a stern warning about not withholding anymore crucial information concerning Mariska.

'You got off easy,' Chris told him, after everyone had taken off. But before he could make a quick exit, Max had launched into a long diatribe about Amy and Jett. Somehow or other he'd found out about them, which meant that Chris had been obliged to spend the next two hours smoothing out Max's bruised feelings, and persuading him not to have Jett beaten up and tossed in the East River.

What a night! No rest for the weary. And in between he'd fielded calls from Birdy Marvel, Lola Sanchez, Gregory Dark and Jonathan Goode, four of his most important clients. Birdy was carrying on about her upcoming wedding, Lola wanted to sue a chasing paparazzo who'd slammed into the back of her new Ferrari on purpose, Gregory was demanding more of the back-end from his upcoming studio deal, and Jonathan was claiming he'd met a girl, fallen in love, and would marry her within days.

Nuts. They were all totally nuts.

Now he had the meeting with Red to look forward to. It should be a laugh a minute with both his brothers there. He couldn't wait.

In the meantime, he was desperate to get back to the comparative sanity of L.A. He was even considering *not* breaking up with Verona, his current girlfriend in L.A. Verona could – when she wanted – be quite a calming influence, which was exactly what he needed right now, a little peace and calm. Besides, his house would need redecorating, so who better than Verona to take care of it?

The downside was that she would expect to move in. *Why not?* he thought. *But only for a few months while she gets everything organized.*

He could handle it. After the past week he could handle just about anything.

*   *   *

Elliott Minor was worth every penny of his quite exorbitant fees. Having come clean on everything to Detective Rodriguez, Max had expected to spend at least a few hours down at the precinct answering questions, but Elliott had made sure that didn't happen, although Max could tell that the detective was royally pissed after receiving a call from his captain.

By that time Max hadn't given a shit. He'd had a tough night and all he wanted was to swallow a couple of Ambien and sleep it off.

In the morning he lay in bed experiencing an overall bad feeling. His first thoughts were of Amy, his once perfect Amy. It was over, she'd betrayed him. He'd never expected it of her, for not only had she betrayed him, she'd done so with his own brother. This left a sour taste in his mouth. Jett he could understand. But Amy? Oh, no, not Amy, his innocent bride-to-be.

Bride-to-be no more. He was finished with her. She'd slept with his brother. There was no going back.

He reached for the phone, called Mrs Conner and checked on Lulu. Mrs Conner informed him that everything was fine, and that Lulu was having a lovely time.

Just thinking about his little girl made him break out in a sweat. What if she *wasn't* his? What if Vladimir or Alex or who the fuck else Mariska had slept with was Lulu's real father?

Christ! He couldn't bear it. It simply wasn't possible.

And yet . . . it was.

So what was he supposed to do? Arrange a DNA test?

No! He wasn't about to do that. Lulu was *his*. There was no doubt in his mind.

Or was there?

*　　*　　*

Because Red was so rich, people always got it into their stupid heads that he was the perfect person to blackmail. Surely they understood that to become the man he was today, he had not suffered fools easily? He was a destroyer, and those who were foolish enough to get in his way were duly destroyed.

Yesterday some low-down Russian hooker had made her move. It infuriated him when people made the mistake of treating him as if he was an easy mark. Especially women. Especially whores.

The truth according to Red Diamond was that, at some-time or another, all women behaved like whores. They all had a price. It was a question of finding out how much. And he should know – he'd married four.

Four wives, and not a winner among them.

As for Lady Jane Bentley . . . she'd turned out to be the most expensive whore of all. And she couldn't even suck a cock properly, so what good was she?

He would pay her off and good riddance. But she would not get as much as she was asking for, no damn way.

He was Red Diamond. A self-made man to be reckoned with. Nobody *ever* got the better of him, although many had tried. In business he was a killer. He conducted his personal life the same way. Only the strongest survived in Red Diamond's world.

He thought about the red-headed call-girl for a moment. Spectacular-looking. Zaftig and Russian – the kind of woman he got off on. Spewing crap about Mariska. What did he care? Mariska was dead, and *he* wasn't the fool who'd married her. Max was. His eldest son. His eldest idiot.

Why couldn't his sons have been more like him? They all took after their useless mothers, and that was a real shame. None of them had the kind of balls he possessed. Brass balls. Solid brass.

Red looked forward to the meeting that lay ahead, it should be quite an event. His three sons, Lady Jane and Diahann. Some combination.

They were probably all stressing over why he'd called the meeting.

Well . . . soon they would find out.

It was time.

Chapter Sixty-Five

Lady Jane Bentley was the first to arrive in the library. It was a magnificent room with its dark wood floor-to-ceiling bookcases, stiff leather couches and rare Persian rugs.

She ran her fingers across the mantel, picking up a residue of dust. Damned maids, they did nothing. During her time with Red he'd never allowed her to fire any of them, claiming that terminating staff was *his* privilege. He hired and fired on a whim, savouring every moment.

Now she knew why he'd kept that insolent housekeeper around. Diahann. Mother of his illegitimate child – a child she'd never even heard of until she'd discovered the revealing letter tucked into his safe.

It was a lawyer's letter, very clear and to the point. It stated that although Red Diamond had fathered Diahann's daughter, Diahann would never reveal this publicly or tell her daughter, Liberty, who her father was. Diahann also relinquished any claims on his estate, and in return she would receive a one-time payment of five hundred and fifty thousand dollars – paid out *after* he died – plus a lifetime job in his employ with her own apartment in the basement of his house. The letter was signed by Diahann and two independent witnesses.

Now why, Lady Jane thought, *would anyone sign a letter like that?* The woman had given birth to Red Diamond's baby – with a good lawyer she could probably have had anything she wanted. It was inexplicable. Was Diahann *that* dense?

Probably. Dense and uneducated with no self-respect, otherwise she would *never* have signed such a letter. Anyway, it was about time the boys knew the truth, and today Lady Jane decided she would take great pleasure in telling them that they had a sister.

Red would be livid. She didn't care. As soon as her attorney informed her that her settlement was agreed, she was out of there. Only why not cause a little trouble first? Since Red had invited her to attend this meeting, she may as well make the most of it.

Her attorney had warned her not to go. 'The less you have to do with him, the stronger our position,' he'd said. 'You have nothing to gain.'

But how could she resist seeing Red's crusty old face when she told his sons something she knew he never wanted them to find out?

She had dressed appropriately for the occasion. Hair swept up. Chanel suit. Gucci shoes. Two rows of perfect pearls. Discreet diamond and pearl earrings. Cartier diamond watch.

She'd spent the early part of the morning thumbing through some brochures of available properties. There was a Park Avenue penthouse that sounded perfect for entertaining – she'd made up her mind that, once she'd got out of this mausoleum, she was giving plenty of chic, exclusive dinner parties. Then again, there was a pre-war masterpiece on Sutton Place that reeked of elegant charm.

She had plenty of time to decide, and in the meantime she'd take a suite at the St Regis until she made up her mind. After all, she was destined to be a rich woman. Very rich indeed.

* * *

'Why are you going to a meeting with your father – a man who has never done anything for you?' Amy had asked Jett early in the morning. 'Isn't it time you gave up hoping for any kind of relationship?'

He'd shrugged. She couldn't possibly understand. Nobody could. It was complicated.

'I'm going 'cause my brothers want me to,' he'd replied, sitting at the breakfast counter, staring at Amy, who was probably the prettiest girl he'd ever seen. And it wasn't just her physical attributes, there was something else about her, a sweetness, a sense of goodness. He was crazy in love – and this was a first.

'I doubt that Max does,' she'd said.

'This'll be the last time I go there.'

She'd nodded. He'd known she'd want to talk about it later, that was Amy's way.

In the meantime he'd showered, dressed, and set off for the meeting that should've taken place the previous week.

Why *was* he going? That was a good question. Max probably wasn't speaking to him – and he couldn't blame his brother for that. Chris, a true Libra, would refuse to take sides.

Still . . . it was a family meeting, and Jett knew he was entitled to be there.

Later he'd made up his mind to call Beverly and ask her to set him up with a New York modelling agency. Even though he was a star in Italy, he didn't care to walk in anywhere cold. And since Beverly knew everyone, she could easily arrange an introduction and steer him to the best.

He considered this to be of the utmost importance. There was no way he was living off Amy so it was essential that he got his career off the ground in America. The Courtenelli campaign was a brilliant start. Once the ads started appearing in all the American magazines, everything should fall into place.

And when he started making money, he was already thinking of asking Amy to marry him.

Kind of a scary thought, but at the same time he knew it was what he wanted. Finally. A settled life.

*   *   *

After Jett had left her apartment, Amy ran around cleaning up. She was singing, unable to wipe the smile off her face as she tackled her bed, shaking out the duvet and plumping up the pillows. Jett was it for her. Somehow or other they just clicked. In bed. Out of bed. She was in love, no doubt about it.

Then she remembered her mother's phone call, and

figured she'd better take a look at the tabloids that had so upset Nancy. Best to get that little task dealt with before she went to work.

She slipped on jeans and a T-shirt, then ran downstairs to the news vendor on the corner, where she picked up all the offending magazines.

Once home, she set them out on the kitchen counter and studied the coverage. Her mother was right: it was awful – scurrilous gossip of the worst kind. And the photos were horrendous – especially the ones of Jett stoned out of his head with various girls in major states of undress.

She found it hard to understand why they were dragging Jett into this. He had had nothing to do with his brother's murdered wife. It simply wasn't fair.

Oh, God! Wait until Nancy found out that she'd switched brothers and was now with Jett. Oh, Lordy, there'd be raised voices in the Scott-Simon household.

Too bad. It was about time she stood up to her mother, and in the future that was exactly what she intended to do.

* * *

The traffic was backed up, so Chris decided to walk to Red's house from the hotel. He'd thought about calling Jett on his cell, then reconsidered. *Do I really want to get in the middle of my two brothers?* he'd thought. *It's their fight. Let them work it out.*

On the way he made a few calls. First, Lola Sanchez, his Latina diva – whom he talked out of suing, explaining that going after a cheap-shot paparazzo was a big waste of time and money. Next he called Gregory Dark and assured him he would do his best to secure him another couple of points on his studio deal. He didn't call Birdy Marvel because it was too early in L.A. But he did call Jonathan Goode, who was in Paris with his new girlfriend/fiancée – an *ingénue* actress of eighteen.

'This is crazy,' Chris informed him. 'Too fast.'

'I'm in love, man,' Jonathan enthused. 'This girl is amazing!'

'Does this mean I'm to get to work on the pre-nup?'

'I don't want to insult her.'

Sure, Chris thought. *When she discovers you're gay, she won't be at all insulted*. 'Hold off until she signs,' he advised. 'I'll have the papers to you first thing tomorrow.'

Verona was next on his list. She was cool and crisp as he explained why he hadn't called, blaming it on family problems, which was basically true. 'How about meeting me at the airport? Then we'll stop by Koi's and grab a bite,' he suggested, the old Chris Diamond charm going full force.

'I met a friend of yours,' Verona said, her tone quite icy.

'You did? Who was it?'

'Inez Fallon.'

Oh, *shit*! Inez. The actress from the plane with whom he'd shared one night of energetic sex. 'Ah, yes, Inez,' he said, hoping Inez hadn't shot her mouth off. 'Nice girl.'

'She liked you too,' Verona said, her tone getting even colder. 'Informed me you were a stud in bed, and she's expecting you to call her soon.'

Busted! What kind of luck was *that*? 'Look,' he explained. 'You and I, we were kind of on the outs, right?'

'Wrong.' A long meaningful beat. 'So, Chris, here's what I suggest. Go fuck yourself.' And Verona clicked off, leaving him without a girlfriend.

Damn. He'd been quite looking forward to Verona's professional back-rubs and somewhat Zen blow-jobs. Plus he'd had her pegged to organize the redecorating of his house. Too bad.

Finally, standing outside Red's house, he called his assistant, Andy, at home.

'Should I give you yesterday's phone list?' Andy asked. 'It's long.'

'E-mail me. I'll go over it on the plane.'

'A woman called Gianna phoned from Italy. She said she's coming to L.A. and wants to get together.'

'Gianna, huh?' Chris said, flashing onto the extremely beautiful Gianna. Hmm . . . Things were looking up. He wasn't usually into sloppy seconds, but since Jett had definitely moved on . . . 'Did she leave a number?' he asked.

'She did.'

'E-mail it to me first.'

'Right away.'

'How's my house?'

'They've started work on it.'

'Thanks, Andy.' He glanced up. Jett was approaching. 'Gotta go. See you later.'

* * *

Sonja was lurking in the underground parking garage of Max's apartment building when he emerged from the basement elevator on his way to Red's house.

Earlier she'd observed all the press and camera crews outside the front, and she'd figured that when he left his apartment it would be via the garage. So she'd made her way down there, charming her way past the security guard with a smile. Sonja had learned at a very early age that a seductive smile could get her anywhere she wanted.

She hung around somewhere between Max's car and the elevator, waiting patiently. If Red Diamond didn't want to pay, she was sure Max Diamond would. He had a child to protect. He would not relish the information she had about Mariska being made public.

When he emerged, she was ready. 'Mr Diamond,' she said, boldly approaching him.

'Who are you?' he said shortly. He'd just come off the phone with Elliott Minor, who'd informed him that Detective Rodriguez had new evidence concerning Mariska's murder and was close to making an arrest. This was surprising and startling news. Although not *that* startling, because once he'd told the detective about Vladimir, he'd known *something* would happen.

'He'd like to contact you when an arrest takes place,' Elliott said. 'Where will you be?'

'I'm on my way to my father's house.'

'We'll stay in touch,' Elliott said.

'That's fine,' Max said.

'I'm sorry about the tabloids,' Elliott added. 'We can sue the bastards if you give me the word.'

Max had no idea what Elliott was talking about. He hadn't seen the tabloids and he didn't intend to.

'I am an acquaintance of your father's,' Sonja said. 'He suggested you might have interest in certain . . . information.'

Now why would Red be sending this woman to see *him*? 'About what?' Max said, frowning.

'About your wife.'

'My wife?' he said, thinking how like Mariska this woman sounded.

'Your wife that is deceased.'

'Who *are* you?'

'I am Sonja. I know your brother also.'

She looked vaguely familiar. Long, flaming-red hair, statuesque body. He'd seen her *somewhere* before. Then it came to him. The girl-on-girl show at his bachelor party. Jesus *Christ*! What the hell did *she* want?

'We must talk,' Sonja said.

'Not now,' he said brusquely. 'I'm on my way to a meeting.'

'It is urgent,' Sonja said, licking her lips.

'It'll have to wait.'

'Until when?'

Max's patience was wearing thin. 'Look, Miss,' he said sharply, 'what is it that you want?'

'Five hundred thousand dollars for my silence regarding Mariska's marriage to a Russian man. They were never divorced. I have proof of their marriage. Money for silence. Is good American business, yes?'

First Vladimir, now *this* woman. Well, she was too late because he didn't care anymore. Soon Vladimir would be arrested, and the world would know how he'd been duped by Mariska. So be it. He'd protect Lulu as best he could. That was all he could do.

He headed for his car. She followed close behind.

He stopped for a moment, swung his head round. 'Did Vladimir send you?'

She was startled that he knew Vladimir's name.

'Well,' Max demanded, '*did* he?'

'You – you know about Vladimir?'

'Get out of here before I report you to the police,' he said sharply. 'Blackmail is a Federal offence. You could go to jail. So get the hell out of my way.'

Sonja was stunned. What was *wrong* with the Diamond family? They had plenty of money, why didn't they pay?

Now it was her turn to frown. She would go to the newspapers, that was what she'd do. She would sell their dirty secrets for a lot more than five hundred thousand. And not only would she sell their secrets, but she'd embellish – add plenty of sex. After all, she'd fucked the father *and* the son. That should be worth plenty.

Red Diamond – billionaire sex pervert. Chris Diamond . . . Hmm, he'd not been into any freak scenes. She'd have to make something up.

Perhaps like father like son . . .

Yes, that was it. Who was there to refute her story?

Famka.

Ah, Famka. Perhaps it would be wise to bring Famka in on it. Not as a full partner – after all, it had not been Famka's idea, it was hers. However, with Famka involved, her story would have back-up, making it worth all the more.

Big bucks, Sonja thought. *That's what America is all about – big bucks.*

* * *

Detective Rodriguez had experienced a busy night. A high-profile murder always increased the pressure to get the case solved as fast as possible. As if it was easy. The way the jerks in the mayor's office were screaming for action was no big help.

Solving a murder case was like assembling an intricate jigsaw puzzle. You put it together, piece by piece, until suddenly the picture is clear and everything else falls into place.

Max Diamond producing Mariska's box at one a.m. was a big help – although Detective Rodriguez would have preferred to receive it at a more civilized hour, and certainly earlier in his investigation. Over the last several days he'd had very little sleep, so after hitting the sack at midnight, he had not appreciated being awoken at one a.m. on Thursday and summoned

501

to Max Diamond's apartment. Then there was the murder of Irena to consider. After listening to Max's story, he'd dispatched a crime-squad team to Brighton Beach, then got himself there somewhere around three a.m.

Now it was nine in the morning and, after being up all night, he had Mariska Diamond's killer in his sights.

Soon . . . very soon . . . he'd be the department's hero.

And why not? He'd worked damn hard on this one.

* * *

'Hey,' Chris said.

'Hey,' Jett responded, as they exchanged an awkward hug. 'Uh . . . thanks for last night,' Jett continued. 'Guess you kinda saved me from myself. Sorry I was such an asshole. Dunno what I was thinking. It was a big mistake – it won't happen again.'

They were standing on the sidewalk outside Red's house, neither of them looking forward to going in.

'I don't see you carrying a bag,' Chris remarked.

Jett pushed his hair out of his eyes. 'A bag?'

'L.A.,' Chris reminded him. 'Remember? I booked you a ticket to come with me.'

'Oh, yeah.' A beat. 'Uh . . . listen, Chris, thanks for the offer, but I can't go. Y' see, last night—'

'I know all about last night,' Chris interrupted. 'Max called me. I went over to his place and heard the whole sorry story.'

'Is he destroyed?'

'Do you *want* him to be?'

'No way. I got nothing against Max. I wish I knew him better.'

'That ain't gonna happen, little bro'. Not when you tell him he's exactly like Red.'

'Oh, *shit*,' Jett said, shaking his head. 'I didn't mean to say that.'

'Then why did you?'

''Cause he punched me out, called me a loser,' Jett explained. 'I couldn't hit him back – I would've floored him. Guess I tried to hurt him with words.'

'Right,' Chris said. 'So you steal his fiancée, then tell him he's exactly like the father we all hate. Right on, little bro'. That'll really make him like you.'

'*Fuck!*'

'Yeah, fuck. Let's go in.'

*   *   *

Red watched from an upstairs window as his two younger sons entered the house. Lady Jane was already in the library. He'd told Diahann not to come up until he buzzed her to do so.

Now he was waiting for Max to arrive, and the moment he did – let the party begin.

Chapter Sixty-Six

Max got to the house on 68th Street ten minutes after his brothers, thanks to the woman in the parking garage who'd attempted to detain him.

He didn't care that he was late, he didn't care about anything much any more. Except Lulu – and who knew if she was even his?

Irena could've told him, but Irena was no longer around to answer his questions.

Who would have thought that one week could totally change a person's life? His business was back on track. His personal life was pure shit.

The butler opened the front door and he walked straight through to the library.

Lady Jane Bentley was sitting stiffly on one of the leather couches, while Jett and Chris stood by the window. Chris immediately came over to greet him. 'Tough night, huh?' Chris said, in a low voice. 'Did you get *any* sleep?'

'Not much,' he replied, noticing Jett over by the window and wondering if his younger brother would have the balls to speak to him. 'Where's Red?' He turned to Lady Jane and repeated the question.

She shrugged in a noncommittal way. 'I'm sure he'll be here.' Then she added, 'In the future your father and I will be going our separate ways. I thought I'd tell you before you read it in one of the columns.'

Chris raised his eyebrows. 'When did *this* happen?'

'You know what Red's like. He was always a selfish man,

504

never cared about anyone except himself. I can't change him, no one can.'

This did not exactly answer Chris's question, but he figured he'd let it go. Lady Jane was no prize, she walked around as if she had a poker shoved up her Chanel-clad ass.

'Where is he?' Max asked impatiently. 'If this is a repeat performance of the other day, I'm leaving, and this time I will *not* be coming back.'

'Ha!' Red boomed, appearing in the doorway. 'Didn't expect me to make it, huh? Well, here I am. Good morning to all of you.'

The old man seemed particularly cheerful, as if he'd recently been privy to some excellent news. He was dressed for the occasion in a blue pin-striped suit, crisp white shirt and bright red tie. At seventy-nine he still had a full head of iron-grey hair and today it was plastered back in what he obviously considered a fetching style. His faded blue eyes were alert and crafty, while a very pleased-with-himself smile hovered on his thin lips.

Red Diamond was obviously in a very good mood indeed.

Max Diamond was not. 'Why are we here?' Max demanded, surreptitiously cracking his knuckles.

'Patience,' Red replied. 'That's a quality you've never possessed.' He cleared his throat, then turned his attention to Lady Jane. 'Where are the refreshments, woman? Call the maid, for God's sake.'

Lady Jane threw him a cool look. 'I am no longer running this house,' she said frostily. 'Or perhaps you chose to forget that.'

Ignoring her, Red picked up the phone and buzzed the kitchen, ordering coffee, tea, soft drinks and cookies to be sent up immediately. 'I enjoy a cookie in the morning,' he announced, as if anyone cared.

Chris stepped forward. 'While you're enjoying your cookie, I have a flight to catch,' he said. 'You mentioned over the phone something about the true story behind my mother's plane crash. What did you mean by that?'

'Christ!' Red grumbled. 'Don't any of you have any

goddamn manners? *I* called this meeting in *my* house, and *I* will conduct the order in which it takes place.'

'Order?' Max questioned. 'I didn't realize we were in a boardroom.'

'There will be things I say today that concern all of you,' Red said. 'If you want to hear them, sit down and shut up.' He picked up the phone again and buzzed somewhere in the house. 'Get up here, *now*!' he commanded.

'I thought I should inform you that I'm arranging Mariska's funeral for early next week,' Max said. 'For Lulu's sake I'd appreciate it if you could show some respect and be there. I presume you do *know* that four days ago Mariska was brutally murdered?'

'How could I *not* know?' Red rasped. 'It's all over the goddamn newspapers. Including my photo, and a bad one at that.'

Standing by the window, Jett didn't move. He regretted comparing Max to this despicable human being, this psychologically flawed excuse for a father. It was no surprise Red had managed to turn Edie into a pathetic drunk, she was the only one to have survived the horror of being married to such an abusive bully.

He had a strong urge to leave while he could. But something kept him there, a need to hear exactly what the old man had to say.

'I'm going to be eighty in two weeks,' Red announced. 'Eighty years young.' He chuckled at his lame attempt at humour. 'Never thought of myself as old, and I'm sure you'll all be delighted to hear that I'm healthy as a goddamn thirty-year-old. Took a physical, and I might not look it, but my body is stronger than it's ever been. Good peasant genes, inherited from my dumbass father, the loser granddaddy you were lucky enough never to know.' He paused to light up a dark-coloured cigarette, indulged in a short coughing fit, then continued: 'I'll start with you, Max, my eldest son. My eldest moron. You're not that smart, you just think you are. However, you managed to build yourself a mini-empire – an empire I almost took away from you with a couple of well-placed phone calls.' Once again he chuckled. 'You must've learned *something* from me, 'cause you managed to save your ass by calling in the goddamn Japs.'

'No thanks to you,' Max said, thinking how much he'd like to smash his bigoted and egocentric father in the face.

'You got enough money,' Red continued. 'You don't need any from me.'

'Is that what you called me here to tell me?'

'No,' Red said. 'Stick around, it gets a lot better than this. But first I'll move onto Chris, who thinks he's Mr Hollywood instead of some paid shyster with a big gambling problem.'

'I'm not interested in your opinion of me,' Chris said, choking back his anger and frustration. 'Try telling me about my mother.'

'Ah . . .' Red sighed. 'The lovely Olivia. Such a beauty. Such a *sad* story. Foolish of her to divorce me. If she'd stayed around she'd still be with us today.'

'What do you mean?' Chris asked, his heart pounding.

'You should've asked your step-father when he was alive,' Red answered, plucking a Kleenex from a box and noisily blowing his nose. 'Your mother's plane crash was no damn accident. Peter Linden – her lousy choice of a second husband – handled certain clients who could take care of anything he wanted done. And since Mr Linden had the hots for some movie-star tramp, it seems your mother had become an inconvenience. So he arranged to get rid of her, freeing himself to marry the movie star, which of course he did.'

'*What?*' Chris said, dumbstruck. 'How do you know this?'

'Tough shit for Peter, though,' Red continued, exhaling a stream of dark smoke into the room. 'Six weeks after he married the movie star, the two of them got into a fatal car accident on their way to Palm Springs. I'm sure you heard about it.' A long ominous silence. Then: 'Funny how shit turns around and hits you in the face, isn't it?'

The door opened and two maids wheeled in a trolley of refreshments. They were followed by Diahann, who stood hesitantly in the doorway.

All eyes turned to stare at the transformation of Red's dowdy housekeeper. She was quite beautiful, in an understated way.

'You all know Diahann,' Red said, beckoning her to come into the room. 'Housekeeper Diahann.'

She entered the library reluctantly, not sure *what* to expect, although it was patently obvious that Red had *something* in mind.

Lady Jane Bentley glared at her, while the two maids left quickly, eager to get back to the kitchen and report what was going on. Diahann sat down on the edge of the couch, as far away from Lady Jane as possible.

'Now let me see,' Red said, enjoying every moment he spent with his captive audience. 'We've established I'm in perfect health, and that's the good news – not for you, I'm sure – but good news for me. However, I'm certain you'll all be glad to know that I *am* getting older, and one day I will not be around to keep a watchful eye on you.' A beat. 'That's a joke.' Another beat. 'Nobody's laughing. Too bad.' He swivelled his head towards his former paramour. 'Jane,' he said, 'I have considered your request for the exorbitant and quite ludicrous sum of thirty-five million dollars, and after no thought at all, I have deemed it unacceptable. Therefore, on the condition that you and all your possessions are out of my house by six p.m. tonight, I am prepared to generously offer you one million dollars for the time you spent boring me to death. This is a one-time offer, and I suggest you accept it. Because if you refuse it, I can assure you that I will have you forcibly removed from the premises. Then you can try *suing* me for the settlement you're after. I'll have you tied up in court for the rest of your dull life. I can promise you that you'll never see a penny, so once again, I suggest you say yes to my offer.'

'You *bastard*!' Lady Jane hissed.

'Not the first time I've been called that,' Red said with a nasty chuckle. 'And *speaking* of bastards—'

Diahann's head snapped up. 'Stop!' she said.

'Excuse me?' Red retorted.

The two of them had everyone's attention.

'No. Go ahead,' Lady Jane sneered. 'It's time they heard about—'

'Shut the fuck *up*!' Red said menacingly, angry eyes glaring at her. 'This is none of your goddamn business. You snooped into my private papers and that cost you a lot of money, so be smart for once and stay quiet.'

'Well, I—'

'Did . . . you . . . hear . . . me?' he said, in ominously measured tones.

Lady Jane closed her mouth.

'Jett,' Red said, turning to look at his youngest son. 'How's *your* mother? Still drinking herself into a stupor every night?'

'You gotta figure somebody made her that way,' Jett muttered, determined not to be intimidated by his bullying father.

'I suppose you're intimating that it was *me*,' Red rasped. 'News flash – it wasn't. Edie was a nympho, fucked anything that had a dick. The gardener in Tuscany, the chauffeur in the South of France, two of my business acquaintances—'

'Why are you doing this?' Chris interrupted. 'Does it make you feel like a big man? Because in our eyes, believe me, you're *not*.'

'Thank you, Chris, for reminding me that I digress. I must get to the *real* reason we're all here.' A long meaningful pause. 'Money. Inheritance. Moola. *Cash*. Right, my happy little family?'

The room was silent.

Jett thought about his mother and felt tears prick the back of his eyelids. Shit! Mustn't cry. No way. It wasn't manly. Red had told him that when he was three, shortly after paddling his ass with a leather belt, the sharp-edged buckle drawing blood.

'Jett,' Red said. 'I'm opening you a bank account. In it I will deposit five million dollars. Can't have your brothers being so far ahead of you. Competitive spirit, that's what you need. Double the five mill in five years, and there'll be more where that came from. And if *one* cent is spent on drugs, you'll find the money will mysteriously vanish.'

Jett found his voice. 'I don't want it,' he said. 'You can keep your money.'

'I called you a fuck-up not a fool,' Red said crisply. 'You have twenty-four hours to reconsider. Talk to your brothers. They'll advise you.'

Lady Jane stood up. 'You make me sick,' she said, trembling with fury.

'Everything makes *you* sick,' Red said. 'Especially sex.'

'I'm leaving,' she said grandly.

'I suggest you stay,' Red said, holding up an authoritative hand. 'I'm about to reveal exactly why I summoned you all here. Surely you don't want to miss that? You could call it a surprise ending.'

'While we're playing truth games, how did *my* mother die?' Max asked, determined to get to the real story. 'Did somebody arrange *her* death too?'

'Sorry to disappoint you,' Red replied calmly. 'Rachel had a congenital heart problem. Died of natural causes in her sleep – leaving *me* to take care of you. Rather inconsiderate of her, don't you think? I sure know how to pick 'em, don't I?'

'*You* didn't take care of me,' Max said heatedly. 'I had a different nanny for every day of the week. I never *saw* you, unless it was with a leather strap in your hand. Or unless you were *raping* one of my girlfriends.'

'Boo-hoo,' Red jeered. 'Poor little rich boy. If *you* couldn't satisfy your girlfriends, *somebody* had to.'

Max made a move toward Red. Chris quickly restrained him.

'*Someone* left their balls at home,' Red taunted. 'You wanna punch me out, go ahead.'

'Whatever you have to say, say it *now*,' Chris said. 'Otherwise we're leaving.'

Red nodded. 'You're right. Why prolong this meeting of no great minds? And, Chris, I might say, if you can conquer your gambling addiction, there's a strong possibility you could amount to something after all. I like the way you're trying to take charge here, protecting your brothers. It's quite touching.'

Watching the interaction between Red and his sons, Diahann felt sick. How could there be so much tension in one room – and why did Red Diamond hate his sons with such a passion?

Thank God she'd kept Liberty away from him. Not that she'd had any choice, Red had never expressed any desire to meet his daughter. He'd seen Liberty once when she was twelve – the fateful day he'd caught her napping on his bed. After that unfortunate incident, he'd insisted she was sent away.

Diahann wondered why Red wanted her and Liberty at this meeting. When Liberty found out that Red Diamond was her father, she'd go crazy. She had always expressed her loathing of him. Diahann knew that when she discovered the truth there would be an explosion.

'Let me get down to it,' Red said, clearing his throat. 'Unfortunately, in spite of my excellent physical condition, I will not be around forever. This means that I will be obliged to leave my estate to someone.'

'Find a charity, we're not interested,' Max muttered.

'When I'm dead and gone you'll change your minds,' Red said. 'Money has a way of making people change their minds. So . . . to prevent any untoward *claims* on my estate, I have recently made an iron-clad Will that leaves everything – and I mean *everything* – to your two sisters.'

'Sisters?' Chris said. 'We don't *have* sisters.'

'I knew there was *something* I forgot to mention,' Red said, enjoying every moment of his revelation. 'Diahann,' he ordered, 'stand up and tell them about our daughter. Sorry, Jane, I know *you* wanted to be the one to spit it out, but we can't always get what we want, can we?'

Lady Jane shot him a venomous look. She wanted to leave and call her lawyer. On the other hand she was frightened she might miss something that she could use later.

Diahann felt exposed and vulnerable. Why was he doing this to her? After Zippy's demise she'd kept her silence. She'd done everything Red had asked her to. To this day she was not sure if she or Red had shot Zippy. They'd been locked in a tangle and somehow or other the gun had gone off. Had *she* pulled the trigger or had Red? Because when Zippy slumped to the floor, the gun had thudded to the ground and she'd never been sure who'd actually shot him.

Red had been determined to avoid any scandal. He'd immediately taken over, arranging for Zippy's body to be removed, offering Diahann a job as his housekeeper. He'd

promised her room and board and a lump sum of money sometime in the future. In a veiled way he'd threatened her that if
she didn't do exactly as he suggested, Zippy's body would
be found and she'd be arrested for his murder. 'Who will the
cops believe?' he'd said. 'A black woman or a white man? Your
kid will go into the welfare system and you'll be fucked.'

Tired and scared, she'd agreed to everything. At the time
it hadn't seemed so bad, a safe haven, no more singing
for money to keep the bills paid. Red switched Liberty to an
expensive private school in Manhattan, and paid for any
incidentals. Diahann had comforted herself with the thought
that Liberty was getting a far better education than she
could've afforded to give her.

And now, almost ten years later, here she was sitting in
Red Diamond's library while he prepared to reveal that he was
Liberty's father – because *he* felt like it. *Yes*, she thought.
*Red Diamond is as bad as everyone says he is. Cruel, arrogant,
a manipulative bully.* How much longer could she put up with
him?

She was damned if she was going to tell them about
Liberty. Let *him* be the one to do so if he was so anxious for
them to know.

'Seems Diahann has lost her voice,' Red said. 'She looks
pretty today, doesn't she? Cleans up nicely. You should've
seen her when she was singing all my favourite songs – she was
quite a beauty then. A *black* beauty.' Another chuckle. 'Can't
blame a man for dipping into a chocolate sundae for a change.
But, disappointingly, Brown Sugar tricked me, got herself
pregnant. So, being the man I am, I took her and the baby in.
And in case your fertile minds are wondering, tests were done
and the child *is* mine. A man can never be too sure.'

Diahann felt like laughing in his face. Took her and the
baby in. *Really?* Liberty was almost ten years old when they
came to live with him, and the *only* reason that happened was
because of Zippy's demise and the confusion over who might
have shot him.

'Speak up, Diahann,' Red ordered. 'We're all waiting.
What's the girl's name?'

'I can tell you're as close to her as you were to us,' Chris

said, vaguely remembering that when Diahann had first come
to work for Red, he'd seen a scrawny little kid running around
a couple of times. 'You don't even know her name.'

'If I've got a sister, I want to meet her,' Jett said.

'Why?' Red questioned, adding a succinct, 'Oh, *I* get it. I
told you she's getting all my money, so why *not* make friends?'

'You said *sisters*,' Max interrupted. 'What other surprise do
you have for us?'

'One that *you*'re not going to like,' Red said, rubbing his
hands together. 'It's about Lulu.'

'What about her?'

'Mariska and I were very close, you know.'

'No, you weren't.'

'Yes. We *were*.'

'*What about Lulu?*'

'Sorry, Max, to be the one to tell you, but Mariska and I
were closer than you thought. Lulu is *my* daughter.'

Max shook his head, convinced he was in the middle of
some hideous nightmare.

'What did you say?' he managed.

'Lie down with dogs and you get fleas. Marry *whores* an'
you get what you deserve. Didn't I teach you *anything*?'

Before anyone could say a word, there was a noisy commotion outside the library, and the door burst open.

Into the room came Detective Rodriguez, his female
partner and two uniformed cops. They were followed by an
outraged butler.

'What the *hell* is going on?' Red bellowed. 'Who are you
people? And what the *hell* are you doing, bursting into my
house like this?'

'We have an arrest warrant, Mr Diamond,' Detective
Rodriguez said, waving the warrant in front of him.

'A warrant?' Red shouted, his craggy face darkening. 'For
which one of my useless sons?'

'For you, Mr Diamond,' Detective Rodriguez said, his
words slow and forceful. 'I am placing you under arrest for the
murder of Mariska Diamond.'

Chapter Sixty-Seven

After Red's revelations and subsequent arrest, somehow
or other Chris found himself in charge. Max was a
mess. Jett was in shock. And Diahann was hysterical.
She appealed to Chris to find Liberty before the press discovered that Red Diamond had an illegitimate daughter.

'Tell me where she is and I'll get her back here,' Chris
promised.

Diahann was vague – all she knew was the name of the
hotel Liberty was staying at in L.A.

With the small amount of information he had, and a
photo of Liberty supplied by Diahann, Chris called Andy in
L.A., e-mailed him the photo, and dispatched his assistant to
Shutters to find her.

Andy, being the diligent person he was, got to Shutters
just as Liberty and Damon were about to step into a limo on
their way to Damon's plane.

Andy was able to convince Liberty that her mother needed
to see her urgently. Damon reluctantly understood, and
instead of flying to Cabo, they flew directly to New York.

'I got no clue what's goin' down,' Damon said to Liberty,
when his plane landed in New York, 'but whatever it is, LL,
y' know I got your back.'

When Diahann told Liberty the truth, her world shattered.
Red Diamond was her *father*. Red Diamond, a man she
loathed. Red Diamond, the man who'd banished her from his
house and forced her mother to work as a maid.

'He didn't force me,' Diahann sighed, leaving out the part
about Zippy. 'I *chose* to work for him.'

'And now he's been arrested for *murder*?' Liberty said, horrified.

'I'm sorry, Libby. I know I should've told you about Red before. I . . . I don't know why I didn't.'

Liberty ran straight to Damon. He was the only person she felt she could trust.

'You're gettin' away,' he told her. 'Out of New York. Out of this whole scene. I got a house on Paradise Island in the Bahamas. A house, recordin' studio, the works. I already talked to Parker and he's gonna fly down there with you. The two of you are gonna work on your music.'

'Why are you doing this for me?' she asked. 'You're not getting anything out of it.'

'Oh, yes, I am, babe,' he said, giving her the look. 'I'm gettin' me a future star, so don't you be lettin' me down.'

*　*　*

Jett immediately called Amy, and asked her to meet him at Sam's place. She did so, and he told her everything before she heard it on the news.

She was there for him, in spite of the fit she knew her mother would throw.

'What about Max?' she asked. 'Shouldn't we be with him?'

'Yeah, if he wants us,' Jett agreed.

But they couldn't reach Max. He was already in his car on his way to Montauk.

When he arrived, he hugged Lulu for a long time, then sat in the garden, with her playing games. She'd already lost her mother: he was determined she wouldn't lose him too.

*　*　*

Chris waited until Red was released on ten million dollars' bail, then flew back to L.A. and onto Vegas. Birdy Marvel was on the outs with her fiancé, so he had a wedding to cancel and a debt to pay. He took care of both.

In a few days he decided he'd fly back to New York –

mainly to check on his brothers. It was a tough time for all of them, and he wanted to make sure everyone was okay.

Since when had *he* become the responsible one in the family?

He was a lawyer. Looking after people went with the territory.

*   *   *

The trial of Red Diamond for the murder of Mariska Diamond would've been huge. A mega billionaire stabbing his son's wife to death in a jealous frenzy when he'd discovered she entertained other lovers, was a story made in heaven.

However, it did not come to pass. Arrested and released on ten million dollars' bail, Red Diamond suffered a massive heart-attack and expired two weeks after his initial arrest.

Detective Rodriguez was unhappy not to get his day in court. After all, *he* was the one who had painstakingly put it together. Who else would've suspected a powerful man such as Red Diamond?

He'd started to wonder about Red when, right at the beginning of his investigation, the billionaire had refused to see him.

Flag number one: his daughter-in-law had been murdered, yet Red Diamond did not want to answer any questions about his son's wife. Why?

Flag number two: he'd looked Red Diamond up on the Internet and found a wealth of material, including his interest in swords and daggers – apparently he had quite a collection. The coroner had stated that Mariska had been stabbed with some kind of old-fashioned dagger.

Flag number three: according to the desk clerk in her building, and two parking attendants in the underground garage, Mariska had entertained three men on a regular basis. One was a reclusive elderly man, who always arrived bundled up in a scarf, a hat pulled low over his forehead and, come rain or shine, black-out sunglasses. The desk clerk recalled seeing him late Sunday night, around the time Mariska was probably killed. The man usually arrived in a town car, always with a different driver.

Detective Rodriguez had built his entire career on gut feelings. He was good, very good. And he'd had a gut feeling about Red Diamond right from the start. He didn't know why, it was just one of those things. Because of those feelings he'd followed every lead. There were fingerprints on Mariska's body, and while he was researching Red Diamond, he'd discovered there was a time when Red had decided to buy a casino in Vegas. He'd needed a gaming licence. The gaming board had needed his fingerprints.

It was a match. And Detective Rodriguez had no doubt the other DNA samples would be a match too. Sperm, hair, skin. It was all there, and one of the parking attendants was able to identify Red.

Regarding Mariska's mother, Irena, Detective Rodriguez had no gut feeling. But once Red was under arrest, he turned his attention to solving Irena's murder: it shouldn't be *that* difficult.

He started with Mariska's Russian phone book.

Epilogue: One Year Later

S ometimes careers take a long time to take off, other times it's instant stardom. Like an incandescent shooting star, the combination of Liberty's looks and her untapped talent catapulted her into the second category.

Her first CD made it to the top of the charts within weeks of hitting the stores. From unknown cover girl on *White Cool* magazine, she was suddenly Liberty, the latest female singing sensation. The critics loved her.

> *Entertainment Weekly* wrote: *Exotically beautiful with a voice to match – Liberty is the new Alicia Keys/Norah Jones/female Usher combination. Her sultry, soulful style will stop you dead. Her CD,* Revelations, *is just that. A true revelation of the highest order. Download 'Married Man', a sassy, poignant commentary on not making out with married men. Liberty is destined to go far.*

Cindi read her the review over the phone from Cleveland where she was on tour with Slick Jimmy. Surprisingly Cindi's relationship with Slick Jimmy had endured – and although Cindi was not yet *Mrs* Slick Jimmy, she *had* given birth to a gorgeous baby boy they'd named, much to Aretha's horror, Baby Rap. Cindi was happy, that was the main thing.

'Unbelievable, girl!' Cindi enthused. 'What does Damon havta say?'

'I'm not sure he's seen it yet,' Liberty answered vaguely.

She didn't want to mention that she hardly ever saw Damon anymore. After their aborted trip to Cabo, and the following dramas, he'd sent her off to the Bahamas with Parker, and totally backed away from anything personal between them.

At first she'd thought his absence was just temporary, but after a while she realized he was all-business towards her. Friendly, encouraging, but all business. She couldn't figure it out.

'Call him up,' Cindi insisted. 'Tell him to send someone out to buy the magazine. You *know* how many extra copies of your CD this is gonna sell?'

'I'm on my way to the airport.'

'Goin' where?'

'L.A. I'm appearing on *The Tonight Show*.'

'Bring it, girl!' Cindi said, impressed. 'You're a star!'

Liberty hung up the phone. She didn't feel like a star, she felt very alone. Suddenly becoming the centre of attention was a scary place to be.

Oh, yes, she was surrounded by minders – thanks to Damon – but she was still alone. All the managers, producers and publicists in the world didn't make up for not having that one special person by her side.

When she'd first arrived at Damon's house in the Bahamas she'd been so sure that, within weeks, he'd be there with her. After L.A. she'd felt as if they were just about to embark on an adventure. But no, he had never come. He called occasionally, and Parker assured her he was happy with the demo tapes of her new songs and the arrangements they were working on.

After a couple of months she decided to call Damon and ask him if it was okay if her boyfriend came to visit. 'If that's what you want,' Damon said over the phone.

She hung up, furious. That was *it* – no more thinking about Damon. It was quite clear that *he* wasn't thinking about her. He was busy doing other things, other girls. Screw *him*. She convinced herself that she didn't care anymore.

Kev arrived for a week and left after three days. She tried to let him down easy, but as far as she was concerned the thrill was definitely gone.

The night he left she sat down and wrote '*Married Man*' – a farewell ode to Damon.

Lately she'd been thinking a lot about calling her mother and reconnecting. After finding out that Red Diamond was her father, she hadn't wanted anything to do with Diahann. She hadn't wanted anything to do with any of the Diamond family either, although deep down she knew she was being unreasonable: it wasn't *their* fault that Red had turned out to be her father.

Still . . . she was sure they must hate her – the illegitimate half-black sister who was due to inherit half of Red's fortune when she hit twenty-five.

Not that she had any intention of taking his money. She didn't *want* it, it wasn't hers, and she refused to give it any serious thought.

* * *

There were three murders in Manhattan over a long hot weekend. One was a mugging that went too far. The second was a shooting. And the third was a statuesque Russian call-girl.

Detective Rodriguez stood in the hotel room where she had been discovered by a now hysterical maid. He stared down at the woman's naked body sprawled half-off, half-on the bed. She was a beauty all right, with flaming-red hair and whiter than white skin.

Someone had strangled her with their bare hands, and the bruises on her neck were already a deep purple.

Detective Rodriguez remembered the woman from his investigation of Mariska Diamond's mother's murder – Irena – shot in her tiny apartment in Brighton Beach.

After some fine detective work, he'd unearthed a ring of jewellery thieves connected to the Russian mob. Mariska Diamond had been involved somehow, along with her some-time lover, Alex Pinchinoff, a very nasty piece of work.

Several months previously, when Detective Rodriguez had arrived at Alex Pinchinoff's apartment to question the man, the red-haired woman had answered the door. She'd been quite obliging, told him she was Alex's girlfriend, and that Alex was in Europe on business. It hadn't taken him long to find out exactly who she was. Sonja Sivarious: a working call-girl.

Detective Rodriguez had been unable to prove that Alex Pinchinoff had had anything to do with Irena's murder and one of Alex's henchmen had taken the fall – Igor, a weasel of a man, who confessed to shooting Irena on nobody's orders.

Right. Nobody's orders. Sure.

Detective Rodriguez had it figured out that Alex Pinchinoff had sent the man to recover Mariska's box of cash and loose stones, which he thought Irena had. After recovering the box, he was to kill her so she couldn't talk. The man had killed her all right, without recovering a thing.

Ever since then, Detective Rodriguez had kept a watchful eye on Alex Pinchinoff. He'd nail him for something. Eventually.

Detective Rodriguez stared at the red-head's neck.

Perhaps she'd known too much.

Perhaps Alex had dispatched her himself.

There were bruises on her neck *and* fingerprints . . .

Detective Rodriguez felt the hairs on the back of his neck stand up.

He had a gut feeling . . .

* * *

Eventually Chris had talked Jett into accepting the money Red had left him. 'Why not?' Chris had said. 'You're with a girl who will inherit a fortune one day, so take advantage of five mill in the bank. After the way *we* were raised, you kinda deserve it, little bro'.'

After thinking it through and discussing it with Amy, Jett agreed. It seemed foolish *not* to accept it.

So he took the money and purchased a loft in Tribeca. He also hooked up with a top modelling agency, and after the Courtenelli ads appeared, he began getting excellent bookings, plus a couple of major endorsement deals – one to be the face of Dolce and Gabbana cologne. Quite a coup.

Amy kept her job at Courtenelli, and after a while she sold her apartment and moved in with Jett.

Her mother was beyond furious. Nancy rushed over to Grandma Poppy's and informed the old lady that under *no* account was she to leave Amy any money.

Grandma Poppy was quite amused. She told Nancy to calm down and go away. 'My money goes wherever *I* want it to go, and it's certainly not going to *you*, Nancy, dear. You have more than enough as it is.'

Grandma Poppy couldn't wait to tell Amy all about her meeting with Nancy. They both had a good laugh, and later that night Amy brought Jett over for dinner.

Grandma Poppy was quite entranced. 'This one's a keeper, dear,' she informed her granddaughter.

Amy smiled. '*I* think so.'

'Don't let him get away.'

'Got a feeling he doesn't want to, Grams.'

After several months of happy togetherness, Jett suggested that it might be a great idea if they got married.

Amy demurred. Much as she loved him, she wasn't quite sure she was ready. But after several weeks of discussing it, they decided to take out a wedding licence just in case, and a week later they got married in City Hall.

As far as Amy was concerned, it was the perfect way to do it.

* * *

Max kept Lulu. Both Jett and Chris agreed it was for the best not to tell the little girl anything until she was older and could understand.

Red Diamond was headline news for many months. Then, gradually, people moved on. The information about Red's two illegitimate daughters fortunately never made it to the newspapers or rags. It was a family secret, and it would stay that way.

The brothers agreed to sell the house on 68th Street. It was owned by a trust in their names – an asset Red had managed to overlook. Or maybe he had meant them to have *something*.

Once they'd sold the house, they made a substantial

payment to Lady Jane Bentley to secure her silence. Diahann had already sworn she would never say a word, but since Red had only left her what they considered a small amount in his Will, they compensated her too.

Max threw himself back into his business, ignoring the scandal that swirled around him. His multi-million-dollar commercial building project was almost completed. The Japanese bankers were so delighted that they wished to invest in any other projects he might bring them. Max had plans for several new towering apartment buildings to be built near the river. The Japanese assured him that money was no problem.

Socially he was invited everywhere. He was rich, successful and single, so every New York hostess had him on their A-list.

So far he had not met anyone he cared to spend time with. But it would happen. He was confident that there was *someone* out there who'd be right for him.

* * *

Free at last, Diahann left the house on 68th Street and moved in with her sister for a while. Liberty wasn't speaking to her, but Liberty *was* still in touch with Aretha, so Diahann felt that at least she had *some* connection to her daughter.

One afternoon, out shopping for groceries, she stopped off at a used record store she'd been meaning to visit. The place was full of old-time LPs with glamorous shots of stars like Aretha Franklin and Diana Ross on the sleeves. Flipping through the albums, Diahann recalled her days' singing at Gloria's, and how much she'd loved it. She wondered if the club was still there, and if Gloria was looking for a somewhat rusty jazz singer.

Why not? she thought. She could still sing, she looked okay, and she wasn't even forty, so why not? Shivering with excitement just *thinking* about it, she chose a Billie Holiday album, and took it up to the counter.

'This is out on CD,' the young girl behind the counter informed her.

'That's *not* what you're supposed to say in a store that sells old records,' the owner of the store said, emerging from an office in the back. He was tall and nice-looking – very black and very familiar.

'Leon?' Diahann questioned, recognizing him immediately.

'Diahann?' he said, his face lighting up.

She nodded.

He beamed.

It had been twelve years, but within two weeks they were living together again.

* * *

It took several arduous months for Chris to painstakingly restore his house to its pristine state, but once it was done, it was worth it. Then, a few weeks later, he received a call from Gianna.

'I am in 'Ollywood,' she announced, in her charming accent. 'I am doing beeg movie. I play the Italian girl.'

Surprise. Surprise.

'You called me once, a while ago,' he said. 'Then I never heard from you again.'

'I didn't want to bother you, Chris, with your family – how you say? – difficulties. My English *bene* now, *sì*?'

'*Sì*,' he answered, smiling, because he was genuinely pleased to hear from her.

A few days previously, sitting in his office with Birdy Marvel – currently engaged to a raunchy rock 'n' roller – the sexy young singer had leaned across his desk and said, 'Like, what you need, dude, is some *fun*. You're getting *so* freakin' *serious* in your old age.'

Old age indeed! He was only thirty-three.

Now here she was. Gianna. On the phone. And she represented fun with a capital F.

'How about dinner tonight?' he suggested.

'Is good,' she said.

'Is *very* good,' he agreed. 'Where are you staying?'

'L'Hermitage.'

'I'll pick you up. Eight o'clock suit you?'

'*Bene*, Chris. *Molto bene*.'

That was a few months ago, and they'd been together ever since. Nothing serious. Just fun.

* * *

Sitting in her dressing room, waiting to appear on *The Tonight Show*, Liberty picked up the phone and called her mother. She'd heard all about Diahann reconnecting with Leon, and she was pleased for her. She hadn't seen Leon since she was seven, but she remembered him as a great guy – always looking out for her.

A man answered the phone.

'Leon?' she said tentatively.

'Is *that* my baby girl?' he responded warmly. 'My partner in long walks through the park an' all those visits to the zoo?'

'Yes, it is,' she said, smiling. 'And guess what? I'm all grown-up.'

'So I notice. Your mama's got that photo of you from the front of your CD all around our apartment.'

'I'm really glad you and Mama are back together,' she said, genuinely meaning it.

'*You*'re glad,' he said fervently. 'How you think *I* feel after all those years without her?'

'Well, *you* left.'

'She threw me out, baby girl, 'cause I wasn't in a marryin' mood.'

'Are you in a marrying mood now?' Liberty asked, still smiling.

'You *bet* I am. Only your mama ain't.'

'Is she around?'

'Hold on. She's sure gonna be happy t' hear from *you*.'

Penny, one of the record company's publicists assigned to look after her, came into the dressing room.

'Give me a minute,' Liberty said, waving her away.

'Sure,' Penny said. 'I'll go check out the Green Room, see who the other guests are.'

Liberty waited patiently for her mother to pick up. Speaking to Leon had summoned up a lot of memories. She remembered the three of them sitting around listening to

Leon's record collection. They'd made sure she was exposed to the best – Marvin Gaye, Aretha Franklin, Al Green. Great early influences. Then there were the special nights when Leon and Mama had sung their duets for her. They'd seemed so happy together.

'Libby? Is that really you?'

Her mama's sweet voice, and she wanted to hug her, because it can't have been easy, and now it was definitely time to put the past to rest.

'Yes, Mama,' she said softly, 'it's me.'

* * *

Amy and Jett were sitting in the back of a limo on their way to *The Tonight Show*. Chris had invited them as they were visiting L.A. and Gianna was appearing on the show.

'I am so *not* jealous,' Amy said.

'You're *sure*?' Jett asked.

'Why would I be? I *like* her.'

'You do?'

'Well, I *did* when I met her. Granted that was over a year ago, but I'm sure she can't have changed.'

'I liked her too.'

'Now, *wait* a minute.'

'Hey,' he said innocently, 'nothing wrong with *liking* someone. An' now she's with Chris, so everything's cool. Right?'

'You *bet* right,' Amy said sternly. 'Let us not forget you are a *married* man, Mr Diamond.'

'Yes, Mrs Diamond.'

'You have responsibilities.'

'I certainly do.'

They both grinned and exchanged a hug.

'I suppose she's considered a movie star now,' Amy remarked.

'Not after one movie, which hasn't even opened yet.'

'She's beautiful enough to be one,' Amy said wistfully.

'You're *more* beautiful,' Jett insisted.

'Liar!' Amy said, blushing.

'I *mean* it.'

She glanced at their driver, sitting ramrod straight behind the wheel. 'How do you close the privacy panel in this car?' she asked Jett, lowering her voice.

'Huh?'

'Can you close it?'

'Oh, *I* get it,' he said, leaning forward to press the button. 'We're gonna make out in the back of a limo. It's our Hollywood thing – kinda rite of passage.'

'Honestly, Jett!'

'What?' he said, reaching for her as the dark glass slid into place, cutting them off from the driver. 'Don't you *wanna* make out?'

'Yes.'

'So?'

'First I have something to tell you.'

'Go ahead.'

'We're pregnant,' she whispered.

'Come again?'

'Pregnant. *You*, Mr Diamond, are about to become a daddy.'

'Holy shit!' he said, breaking out an enormous grin. 'Daddy Jett.'

'Yes,' she said softly, kissing him. 'Daddy Jett.'

* * *

Penny, the publicist, returned to the dressing room exactly five minutes later.

'Gotta go, Mama,' Liberty said, into the phone. 'Don't forget to watch.' She clicked off.

'Nervous?' Penny asked.

'I'm trying not to be.'

'The rehearsals went well,' Penny said briskly. 'Kevin Eubanks seems charming.'

'Hmm . . .' Liberty murmured, happy that she'd had a really nice conversation with her mother. They'd arranged to get together as soon as she got back to New York. She couldn't wait. *And* she'd see Leon – how great was *that*?

'There's a guy in the Green Room who wants to stop by and say hello,' Penny said, helping herself to a Diet Coke.

'Who?' Liberty asked, adjusting her leather gown.

'He's here with his girlfriend, Gianna – she's a guest on the show.'

'*Who* is he, Penny?'

'Uh, Chris Diamond. Says you know him.'

Chris Diamond. This was a surprise.

She was silent for a moment, trying to decide what to do.

Well . . . since she was mending bridges, why *not* see him?

'Okay.' She sighed. 'Where is he?'

'I'll go get him,' Penny said. 'Unless *you* want to make the trek to the Green Room and meet him there.'

'No. Bring him here.'

'Sure,' Penny said.

This was turning out to be some night – first her mom, now Chris Diamond. Over the past year she'd often thought about her three half-brothers and the little sister she'd never met. Somehow or other she'd locked herself into a mindset that they wanted nothing to do with her.

Now Chris Diamond was here at *The Tonight Show*, and he was asking to see her.

She attempted to compose herself while Penny went to fetch him. What was she supposed to say to him? It was such an insane situation.

Chris burst into her dressing room, not giving her a chance to say anything. 'Y' know, this is ridiculous,' he said. 'And I want to start *right* here – *right* now – to get to know you.'

Penny, immediately behind him, rolled her eyes and mouthed, *Who-is-this-guy? Shall-I-get-rid-of-him?*

'That's okay, Penny,' Liberty said quickly. 'Give us some privacy.'

Penny frowned, backed out and shut the door.

'So,' Chris said, 'we're blood. Unfortunately it's Red's blood, but we can get over that.'

'We can?' she said unsurely.

'Yes,' he said firmly. 'And you should know, up-front, that this is *not* about the money.'

'I don't *want* the money,' she said. 'I never did.'

'Well, it's yours and Lulu's to do whatever you like with.'

'I'd like to give it away to different charities who need it more than I do. I can make my *own* money – I don't want his.'

'Fine with me.'

'Yes?' she said tentatively.

'It would drive Red crazy, so I'm all for it.'

'Good.'

'Then that's taken care of. And now, in the future, *I'd* like to get to know the sister I never had. Can we do that?'

She smiled, a small smile, but it was a start. 'I think I can definitely say I'd love it.'

As soon as Chris left, Penny put her head round the door. 'Okay to come back?'

'Sure,' Liberty said.

Penny was dying to find out who Chris was, but she managed to restrain herself, as Liberty didn't seem in a talkative mood. However, she couldn't stop herself saying, 'Handsome guy.'

Liberty nodded.

'I just found out that Jay Leno might stop by the dressing room,' Penny said. 'He usually tries to greet his guests personally before they go on.'

Oh, great! Something else to make her feel nervous.

'Do you mind if I take a little alone time?' Liberty murmured.

'Absolutely,' Penny said. 'Get your head together. You've got at least an hour before you go on. I'm on my cell – call when you need me.'

Liberty nodded again, and once more Penny took off.

As soon as she was alone, Liberty checked out her reflection in the full-length mirror. Various stylists had attempted to change her look, but she'd insisted on keeping it simple. Her hair, long and dark, fell past her shoulders. Her make-up was sexy and seductive, and she'd elected to wear the Versace leather dress from her L.A. photo shoot with Chip. The moment she'd started making money, she'd tracked it down and bought it. She referred to it as her lucky dress.

Five minutes later there was a knock on the dressing-room door. She prepared herself to meet Mr Leno. Jay Leno. *The* Jay

Leno – a man she and Cindi had grown up watching on TV.

'Come in,' she called.

And he did. Only it wasn't Jay Leno. It was Damon. And he was carrying a huge bowl of purple and white orchids. 'Delivery,' he said, cool and casual. 'Where do you want 'em?'

'Damon!' she gasped, totally surprised. 'What are *you* doing here?'

He placed the orchids on a table. 'You're my artist. You record for my label. So I kinda figured that *I* should be the one to tell you that your CD hits number one next week. You're knocking off Eminem *and* Mariah Carey – so I guess we can safely say you've made it. Here,' he said, thrusting a large manilla envelope at her. 'Read this.'

'Another contract?' she asked, struggling to remain in control of her emotions.

'Kinda. Sorta,' he said casually. 'Read it.'

'Not now,' she said, because she didn't need this – she was nervous enough about appearing on Leno.

'Now.' A long beat. A long look. 'I'm askin' nicely.'

She stared at him for a moment. He was still as handsome as ever, with his close-cropped hair and diamond stud earring. Tonight he had on white – white suit, white silk T, thin black leather belt with a diamond buckle and the usual Nikes. Damon had a style that was all his own.

'If you insist,' she said, tearing open the envelope.

'Thanks,' he said.

'What *is* this?' she asked, after a few moments of reading.

'You don't get it?'

'No.'

'A signed, sealed and witnessed agreement between me and Tash.'

'Your wife?'

'*Now* you're gettin' there,' he said, giving her a long intimate look.

'How come you're showing it to *me?*' she asked, quite puzzled.

'It's a property agreement dividing up our assets.'

'Yes?'

'Y' see, when I married Tash, I didn't think it was *cool* to start askin' her to sign a pre-nup an' all that shit. So now that I'm gettin' a divorce, I wanted it all worked out up-front. I'm givin' her half of everythin'. That way she'll let me walk away clean.'

'She will?'

'Oh, yeah. No hassle. No bad vibes.'

'Can I ask why you're doing this?'

'You really mean to tell me you don't know?' he said quizzically.

'No. I don't know,' she said, thinking, *Damon is getting a divorce!*

'It's all 'cause of you, baby.'

'It is?' she asked, feeling light-headed and slightly breathless.

'Yeah. I kinda *got* your message.'

'Um . . . what message would that be?'

'That I couldn't play hit it an' run with you. That *you*, LL, are a total commitment. So . . . if you're still interested, I'm makin' myself available. An' these papers prove I ain't talkin' whack. We together on this?'

'Yes, we're together,' she whispered, trying to stop the shaking in her heart.

'Then it's all good. An' I was thinkin' that after you're through with the show tonight, my plane is waitin' an' so is Cabo. Seems like a plan to take up where we left off.' A long beat. 'Y' know what I'm sayin'? You an' me – Cabo?'

'Separate rooms?' she teased.

'No freakin' *way*.'

'Then, Damon,' she said, her spirits soaring, 'I'm *on*.'